White lights streamed into the dark, musty building, illuminating Lilly as she knelt over an open crate...

She'd pried the lids off all of them, and from every crate pairs of identical bronze faces shone like pure gold. For the first time, Mike noticed the dead, rank odor in the air. The hair on the back of his neck spiked. He'd created these to exorcise the twins, not to bring them back. He felt as claustrophobic as he had in that kiva when he'd held Emma in his arms.

"They're of Kara and Emma, aren't they?" Lilly careened recklessly, tossing lids askew. "They're so beautiful." Her face was rapturous, her voice breathy.

Some indefinable stench was suffocating him. What was it—the evil souls of the dead?

"You shouldn't have come in here."

Lilly shifted the top off another crate. A whorl of dust danced above the provocative nude he'd created of Kara. The statue splashed light back at him as if she glowed from within. Captured forever in bronze, that private little half smile of Kara's that enticed men to their doom both taunted and shocked him.

"No!" he exploded, slamming the lid down. He hurled the next lid, then the next.

"You came back here because of them. Which one did you really love, Daddy? Which one is my mother?"

INSEPARABLE

ANN MAJOR

MIRA

ISBN 1-55166-548-4

INSEPARABLE

Copyright © 1999 by Ann Major.

All rights reserved. Except for use in any review, the reproduction or
utilization of this work in whole or in part in any form by any electronic,
mechanical or other means, now known or hereafter invented, including
xerography, photocopying and recording, or in any information storage or
retrieval system, is forbidden without the written permission of the publisher,
MIRA Books, 225 Duncan Mill Road, Don Mills, Ontario, Canada M3B 3K9.

All characters in this book have no existence outside the imagination of the
author and have no relation whatsoever to anyone bearing the same name
or names. They are not even distantly inspired by any individual known or
unknown to the author, and all incidents are pure invention.

MIRA and the Star Colophon are trademarks used under license and registered
in Australia, New Zealand, Philippines, United States Patent and Trademark
Office and in other countries.

Visit us at www.mirabooks.com

Printed in U.S.A.

I would like to thank Tara Gavin for giving me the chance to write this novel. It took great faith on her part. At every step she encouraged me. I would also like to thank Dianne Moggy and the entire MIRA staff for all their hard work. I cannot leave out my husband, Ted, who was constantly supportive. I also must thank Ann and Dick Jones, who had me to their south Texas ranch for a weekend to watch them work cattle.

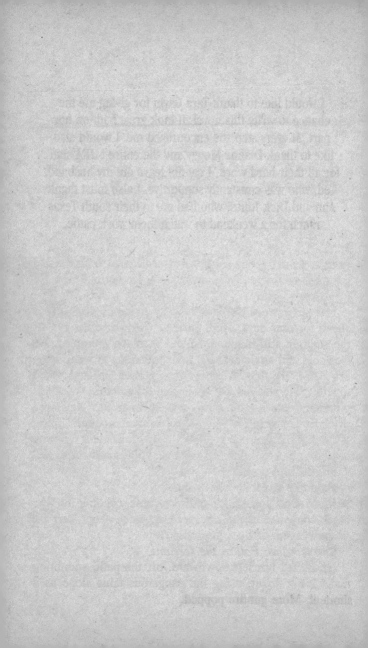

Prologue

The red sun beyond the distant purple mountains stained the mesa bloodred. Thunder rolled in the north. The night was already chilly.

Mike Greywolf had been away from the hogan with his sheep for four days. High on the mesa where the last of the sunlight still lingered, Mike's stomach grumbled. He was cold and anxious to get home, anxious to warm himself before the fire while his family teased him and talked together. He was hungry enough to eat a whole pot of his grandmother's mutton stew, and so homesick he might even let his grandfather tell his stories about the Long Walk, till the fire burned down to red coals and his gray head drooped over his thin chest and he snored sitting up.

Two abrupt cracks.

From the shadowy valley below.

More shots snapping like firecrackers, echoing into the black canyon. But the screams were what penetrated the deepest layers of his consciousness.

The screams. Follow the screams.

He hurled himself downward, off the path, stumbling and sliding down, using the dangerous talus slope as a shortcut. More gunfire popped.

Then more screams, which seemed bloodcurdling because they came from his father's hogan that lay nestled in the depths.

The gunfire stopped, and the canyon was quiet.

A chill stole through his veins. His sheep forgotten, he fell, and whole chunks of the cliff, rocks and all, tumbled with him.

He knew he had to get down, fast.

But it was a long way down from the high pastures. It took him nearly an hour. And when he got there, he was in a mad, strange world where nothing was right and everything was wrong. His feet floated beyond gravity; he felt as heavy as stone, as if he might sink through the rock earth to the hot depths of hell. For an eternity that lasted only seconds, Mike hung suspended in this no-man's-land, floating in a hellish formlessness. Then he fell back to earth.

A buzzard swirled over the hogan, landed, folded cloak-like wings and hopped toward the doorway.

Dogs whined. Coyotes howled. The buzzard's claws skittered on the rocks. The wind droned through the lonely canyon.

The sounds of death.

Stars spun in a mad, wild sky. A four-legged shadow moved toward him, and he screamed. It was only a dog slathering his warm tongue over Mike's hand.

Mike inched forward, slipping, nearly falling over the threshold into a sticky river of blood. A strange coppery smell pervaded the cool night air.

All was shadow in the silent hogan, save for red coals dying in the grate. Even before he saw the three bodies on the floor, tears streamed from his eyes.

As always his old grandfather wore his red headband. He'd been about to put another piñon log into the potbellied stove when he'd been shot point-blank in the fore-head. His sightless eyes had rolled back in his head. They looked like white marbles.

"Oh...my God!" Mike's voice was quavery. He cupped his hand over his mouth and retched.

When he sank to his knees, he nearly fell on top of his grandmother, thus disturbing a lazy cloud of flies that rose around him, buzzing.

Flies. In his ears and eyes, crawling on his skin. A dozen floated in the stagnant purple pools of blood. Weeping, screaming, he swatted the air and slapped at his face, and all the time he wept.

Then his mind floated free. He was with the sheep, descending the cliffs, hurling his long legs over the sharp rocks, happy to be on his way home, anxious to show them all the things he'd carved. Again, he was enjoying the exquisite beauty of that bloodred sunset that had stained every rock in the canyon with its magic glow.

Blood was everywhere. Black, fetid pools.

He stood up wearily, his black head grazing a beam in the ceiling. He was tall for his age, tall for a Navajo. He had a chiseled nose, a strong face, and blue-black hair.

Everybody teased him because he was too handsome and his skin too light. And his eyes...

They were hers.

Especially his grandmother teased him. A sob caught in his throat as he remembered her gentle laughter. She'd had to be both mother and grandmother to him. He looked down at her crumpled body on the slashed rugs. His harsh-featured face went cold and dark. Only his green eyes seemed alive. They were murderously alive, aglow with the hate that consumed his soul.

Whites had done this.

He wished he'd been here. He wished they'd killed him, too.

Hot bile rushed up his throat. He clutched his mouth. Staggering, he barely made it out of the hogan before he bent double and vomited.

Hours later, after he'd buried his family, the coyotes began to howl from the cliffs again.

He sank to the ground, wrapped his hands around his knees and rocked back and forth, listening for the spirits of the dead. Out of the dark, his grandfather spoke.

"Leave Dinehtah *or die."*

Lightning arced across the canyon. A cool wind gusted down from the mesa. Constellations whirled. The entire cosmos seemed to vibrate inside him with those words.

He saw an incandescent figure running toward him in a golden light. She had red hair and soft brown eyes. She was white.

His grandfather spoke.

"Leave Dinehtah *and live."*

Mike started running. Toward that light and that girl who flickered just out of reach.

He never looked back.

Not even to tell his grandfather goodbye.

The hogan was a place of death.

He could never go home again.

Part I

THE PAST

"But jealous souls will not be answer'd so;
They are not ever jealous for the cause,
But jealous for they are jealous; 'tis a monster
Begot upon itself, born on itself."
——William Shakespeare
Othello, III, iv, 158

1

If only Frances Shayne could have smelled, sensed or tasted disaster before it struck. But she had no clue that the monster was so near when she stepped out of her bathroom to the blare of her television. Not that the rebellious, young, Navajo face filling her screen didn't make her jittery. Rampantly male, his green eyes stared through her coldly.

Maybe it was for the best that the tribal police hadn't found him. She knew the type well. He was too dangerously gorgeous for his own good. He'd spell heartbreak to many a fool girl if he lived.

Murders on the rez.

Killers on the rampage.

Possible kidnapping.

Frowning, Frances scanned her bedroom for the remote. The teenager and his tragic story was just the sort of trash she most detested. Especially when she needed a few precious minutes of silence to compose herself for tonight. She picked up throw pillows, magazines, lifted dangling ivy leaves—but no remote.

Vivid shots of a squalid hogan replaced the young savage's charismatic visage. Sheep scrambled about, their bells jingling while hordes of brown boys and black dogs herded them into makeshift pens. An older man with a gummy grin, whose weather-beaten face looked more like a leather rag hung out in the sun too long, began speaking in Navajo.

Frances didn't bother with the subtitles. Besides, like everybody else in northern New Mexico, she already knew the awful story.

A famous silversmith and both his parents—gunned down. Their teenage boy missing. Their killers on the loose. Killing had gotten too easy in the good old U.S.A.

She read the word *chindi* and then the phrase, *their ghosts crying for vengeance.*

Relief flooded her when she saw the black edge of her remote under a stack of books in a bookshelf. She slid it out and punched it.

What did the murders of Navajos living like stone-age savages in a one-room hogan with a smoke hole punched in the ceiling have to do with her? Not that she hadn't posted guards, just in case.

Frances preferred beauty to ugliness. She collected beautiful things and important people. Her elegant bedroom was *so* Santa Fe, *so* Frances Shayne. Stylish high ceilings lent grandeur. Wooden vigas, the corner fireplace, the earth-tone walls, and her priceless Navajo tapestries carefully flung in artful disorder on polished tile floors had been combined with her usual flare.

Navajo, Frances mused, eyeing the tasteful grays, blacks, browns, beiges and whites at her feet. This rug, by the famous Bessie Greywolf, was one of her most prized pieces.

That woman who'd been shot…had been Navajo, too. A well-known weaver, the news commentators had said, although her name had not yet been released. Wondering who the woman was, Frances fingered her makeup jars.

With a steady hand she outlined her thin, perfect mouth in scarlet. Then she combed out her shiny red hair and coiled it at the nape of her neck, deftly shaping the lustrous mane until not a single hair escaped her snug chignon.

She stood, absently delighting in the fragrance of piñon smoke mingling with that of lilacs and roses. In an uncustomary burst of thoughtfulness, Czarina had grown the flowers in her messy greenhouse and placed them in Waterford vases in readiness for the grand party tonight.

Clad only in her black satin slip, Frances arched her brows, eyeing first her slender face with its high cheekbones and straight nose.

"Mirror, mirror," she breathed, while her critical gaze roamed her tall, regal figure. Tightening her stomach, squaring her shoulders, she whirled.

She was a vision of icy glamor. Not a single ounce of extra flesh marred her fine bone structure. If no sparkle lit her eyes, nor blush her cheeks, she was still exquisite, as a statue of cool marble, as the dolls she collected and kept locked out of the twins' reach in glass cases, were exquisite.

Z said she was too pale, too thin. What did Z know?— she was running to fat; she, who shopped in Navajo flea markets for those rags she wore.

Odd, though, how her outrageous, impossible sister's barbs stung.

The soft glow of Frances's new rose-shaded lamps and earth-tone adobe walls flattered her. She was thirty-six, the perfect age for a woman—young enough to be beautiful, desirable, but old enough to know better.

She had to finish dressing. There was still much to see

about downstairs. The doorbell had rung, which meant early birds were arriving. Probably unimportant people, those anxious to see and be seen. Maybe ambitious people, clever people on the rise.

Purposefully, she glided toward her bed. Her turquoise evening gown lay beside a rope of black pearls, her shoes and hose.

Tonight would be a triumph. Steven—he'd actually asked her to call him ''Steven''—the governor, had said he'd bring his pretty, little fool of a wife, Carey.

Frances almost wished her party was in honor of them instead of Indiana, the greatest living artist in New Mexico. The most scandalous, too.

Thoughts of Indiana brought a frown. Her artistic temperament made her unreliable. She could and would do anything to others. Indiana had stood her up more than once. Who knew her reasons? Still, she had sworn to Czarina—whom she called a kindred spirit, a spiritual sister, and her very own herbal guru—that she would come.

Herbal guru? Lazy to a fault, Z could be energetic about the most curious things. She got up at dawn and scribbled every morning in the attic. Laughingly she called her work-in-progress *The Third Testament of the Herbal Bible.*

Czarina.

Frances shook her head. The best times in her life occurred when some quarrel made Z decide to quit speaking to her.

Frances was about to put on her gown, when a bloodcurdling yell came from her lawn.

She froze.

Killers on the rampage.

Her twins!

She rushed to the window, expecting the worst.

Their dirty blue skirts hiked, their knees astride brooms, two small hideously masked figures loped about the green lawn like Apaches.

The water sprinkler was on. Their new silk dresses were damp and dirt-streaked. Their darling curls she'd so carefully tied in blue ribbons were tangled.

When Frances touched the cold windowpane, a shiver passed through her. Always, they played together. Kara was invariably putting Emma up to mischief. Frances worried about their future.

Her anxious mind grew increasingly fearful as she watched her darling, her precious—*Emma.*

Frances expected a great deal from her children. Sometimes she almost wished she belonged to some other family. To some easy family with more predictable genes.

Maybe all families had their troubles, their weaknesses. Frances didn't like thinking about the Shaynes' shameful wildness, nor her own.

Who would guess that she, the regal society matron, the heiress to a vast fortune in land, oil and real estate, had ever—

The past was dead. Frances was the perfect mother, the perfect businesswoman, the perfect hostess. Central in the artificial kingdom she had created was her great mud palace north of Santa Fe. Casa New Mexico was surrounded by emerald lawns, poplars and gnarled cottonwood trees, sparkling fountains, reflecting pools, and colorful flower beds.

With its many balconies, walled patios, and terraces, her impressive mansion resembled nothing so much as a small *pueblo*. Behind tall adobe walls, what she most wanted to protect were her three children. But the more she confined them, the more they seethed to explore. Battles with Stuart had flared into quite a little rebellion. What if the twins...Kara—

Just the thought of Kara endangering Emma sent her to that drawer where she kept her silver flask. Quickly she bolted a shot of vodka. As she swallowed her second, a heavy glass object exploded downstairs. Discordant piano notes crashed. Kara shrieked. Emma sobbed. Z shouted up the stairs.

Frances reburied the flask just as Z's plump form rolled into the bedroom like a fleshy barrel in flowered skirts, her turquoise necklaces tangled, her hideous, battered fedora askew.

With a curt nod, Frances pulled on her gown and high heels, grabbed her string of pearls. She raced out of the room and down the stairs. Z followed.

When they entered the music room, pieces of Frances's favorite Waterford vase glittered from her best Navajo eye-dazzler. On the verge of hysteria, Gloria Dobson's hands fluttered uselessly. One of the poor woman's fingertips was slightly bloody, and her black silk gown dripped water onto the priceless tapestry.

On the other side of the room, the twins cringed in a corner. Kara's face was a model of false innocence; Emma's bright, tear-streaked face held guilt and terror. Her panther mask dangled from her wrist, damningly.

When Frances knelt before her darling Emma, the cat mask tumbled to the floor. The little girl flung herself into her mother's arms.

"S-sorry," she sobbed.

"There, there. What happened, my precious darling?"

"A-all I can remember is Kara and me playing outside..." The child's hot, desperate breaths fanned Frances's cool cheek. "And...that's all...."

"How did you get in here?" Frances's voice was inexplicably tender.

"Ask K-Kara."

"Kara?" Her tone sharpened.

Kara pushed her gorilla mask tight against her face. "*She* stole my mask and ran inside," came a deliberate, muffled reply.

Frances caught the bottom edge of the gorilla mask and pulled it off. Golden eyes glared.

"What really happened?"

Kara's brows knitted. "You don't ever believe me! You love her! Her! Everybody loves her!" Then she ran from the room.

Emma tried to run after her, but Frances caught her close.

"It was my fault," Emma said. "Please don't be mad at her."

For another long moment Frances held Emma, but it was like holding a cat scrambling to be elsewhere. Her heart had fled with her wounded sister.

Frances sighed. Kara, Gloria, that marvelous vase that had been a gift from an English duke, even her party tonight were forgotten—everything but Emma and her sparkling tears were put aside. Frances smoothed the damp red curls back from the sticky brow.

Emma.

Only when Emma quieted did Frances rise and let her dash after her twin.

Inseparable. Why did they have to be so tightly bound? The skin across Frances's cheekbones felt as tight as parchment when she turned quietly to Z.

"Z. Find Stuart. He'll have to watch the girls."

"But he just got into a terrible fight with Kara. Accused her of stealing his flashlights."

Z's cheeks were suspiciously flushed. Frances lifted her chin, her cool gaze zeroing in on her martini.

She didn't have to ask how many. She let a moment pass. When Z saw the direction of her stare, her short fingers tightened on the stem, her plump cheeks brightening tellingly. "What?"

Frances stared at that martini glass till Z reddened. Tension built. In a rage Z whirled the glass and its contents into the mess on the carpet and stomped out.

No sooner was Z upstairs than Frances heard Stuart's math books banging against walls.

The doorbell rang. The governor stepped inside just as Stuart slammed downstairs.

With a glare, Frances stopped her tall, skinny son cold. He was so unpleasant looking—all that lank blond hair falling greasily across his brow, those awful Coke-bottle-thick glasses.

Her son.

She had no time for Stuart now. With a nod that said *Stay,* she swept past him to greet the governor, and his dear little Carey.

Gushingly, Frances led the glittering couple inside. "Darling, you look adorable in that red." Frances laughed and chatted, heading them toward champagne and grilled shrimp, while Stuart sulked on the bottom stair. She thought of the murders that had New Mexico in an uproar. Teenagers, they said, were the killers. Teenagers. Not much older than her Stuart.

As if little Carey read her mind, she brought up the murders and began to describe them in grisly detail—the flies, the half-buried bodies, their state of decay.

Frances laughed dismissively, saying she wouldn't allow her guests to dwell on those horrors. After all, the reservation and that awful little hogan where the *unspeak-*

able (she emphasized that word) atrocities had occurred was miles away.

The governor bit into a shrimp. "Frances is right. Surely murder and mayhem can wait. At least till I finish my shrimp." He crunched into the tail, too, swallowing it.

"Or at least," said Frances, "till my party's over."

Everybody except Stuart laughed. Soon everybody was vying to talk to her or to the governor—to Steven.... Now in her element, Frances was so happy, she almost sparkled. Everything was absolutely perfect, till Steven asked where Indiana was.

Panic. A rush of fear cut off her breath.

Where *was* she?

As she searched the room, Frances met Stuart's gaze. He looked so lost and needy. Not that she could worry about him. All that mattered was the total humiliation she faced if her guest-of-honor failed to show.

She ignored his timid smile.

She would deal with Stuart later.

2

Kara and Emma bounced up and down, their blue silk skirts ballooning open and closed like identical umbrellas.

"Take us to the ruins!"

They shouted so loudly that Stuart clamped his hands over his ears.

"Take us, please, please!"

With the toe of his black boot, Stuart spelled out two large letters in the red dirt.

"*N-O*," the twins read, and then giggled defiantly.

Stuart wished he were miles away from *this* house, *these* walls, *their* mother. Miles from *them,* too. After all, it was their fault he was in this sour mood.

They stomped on the letters. "Why not?"

"Why? Why?" he mimicked.

"What's wrong with why?"

"Why? Why don't you ever wind down? From the time you get up till you're dragged screaming to bed, you make my life hell." They were always sneaking into his room, swiping his stuff or punching buttons on his computer that made his programs go haywire.

"Go swing," he roared.

Kara stuck out her tongue.

"You little monster! Why do I always get stuck with you?"

"'Cause you're our brother," Emma said.

"I wish you'd never been born."

"'Cause we're twins, and you're not," said Kara.

It was galling how everybody thought they were such a marvel. Even his friends said how pretty they were, how perfectly alike. No wonder. Their mother never stopped bragging about them. Did she ever say anything nice about *him?* Did her friends ever pay attention to *him?*

He was first in his class. Nobody cared.

With their copper hair glinting and their oval faces aglow in the late-afternoon light, with the toes of their sneakers pawing red dirt, they seemed like a matched pair of highly energized fiends sent by the devil to persecute him.

Both of them spoke at once, as if they'd rehearsed it. Only they hadn't. They could read each other's minds. *Or they had the same mind.* When they wanted to, they split in two, Emma playing the good twin, Kara playing the bad one.

"Please take us into the woods or to the desert!" Their eager expressions were as identical as two bright poppies.

No! Red monsters. Remembering the Halloween masks that had blinded them and made them overturn that vase, he gritted his teeth.

While he seethed, piñon smoke curled lazily from the many chimneys of their adobe mansion, the dark wisps scenting the crisp, wine-clear air. New spring green was translucent against the deepening blue of the sky.

The sunset would be spectacular, Auntie Z had said.

Crazy old ding! Who cared?

"Take us, please, please, Stuart," Emma began again.

"I'm gonna kick you in your lace-pantied asses if you don't stop."

"*Asses.* You said *asses.* I'm gonna tell," Kara said.

Emma, who had a penchant for drama, got down on her knees. Her hushed whisper was so sappy he wanted to slap her. "She won't tell…if you take us."

This from the good twin, the wimpy twin. Emma was as sweet-natured as a puppy. He could kick her around anytime. Kara would rat, though.

He glared at Emma. "How many times do I have to say it before you get it, you stupid little shit? *No!*"

Tears brimmed in her dark eyes. "Please don't get mad at me, Stuart."

"Then quit pestering me."

Kara's eyes had gone gold. "You said *shit!*"

He kicked the wall. Kara placed tight little fists on her hips and swished in front of Emma. "What're you gonna do up there, anyway? The big people don't want you."

He bit his lip to keep from saying another bad word.

"Rodent Nose!" Kara spat nastily.

Stuart's eyes bulged. Red curls, upturned faces, blue silk. The twins blurred into one monstrous two-headed enemy.

Kill.

Stuart wasn't agile. He had developed no muscles, because he was either doing math or slumped over his computer.

"Beanpole," the dumb kids at school called him. They teased him about being smart, too. But it was his overlarge nose that he anguished over ceaselessly. Sometimes he stared at it in his bathroom mirror, wishing he had a knife to cut it off.

Kara stared at the bulbous thing in openmouthed horror. "Yuck."

Stuart lunged at her.

She danced away on swift, sturdy legs. "Rodent Nose! Rodent Nose!" Then, "Mother! Mother!"

He tore off the porch. Dust swirled as he yanked her, kicking and screaming, off her feet. When she jammed a toe into his groin, he sank to his knees. With a growl he grabbed her hair and pulled hard. Her teeth sank into the heel of his hand. Blood spurted.

Kill.

"Children—"

Mother.

Mother was watching. Mother's small chest rose and fell.

Three young hearts ceased to beat.

For another long moment, only Mother breathed.

Stuart could feel each individual hair on his neck stand up. His blood ran cold.

He dropped the sharp-toothed little monster so fast that Kara plunked to the ground.

"Stuart, dear, is everything all right?"

Bad timing was one of *her* special gifts; nosiness, tyranny, snobbishness were others. She looked past him, worriedly scanning the parking lot.

"He hurt me!" Kara accused.

"Hush." Frances's tone was sharp. "Stuart, come inside and tell me the minute you see Indiana."

Aye, Aye, Napoleon.

Dusting herself off, retying a blue ribbon, Kara looked the picture of injured innocence. Beside her, Stuart scowled. Not that Frances paid much attention to either of them.

Thus ignored, the tension between the warring twosome expanded like an explosive gas in a glass bottle. Kara was about to pop from holding back the insult that fairly quivered on the tip of her tongue.

She eyed Stuart and soundlessly mouthed two syllables. *Bean-pole.*

The insult bit like a viper, and he began to shake with helpless hate and fury.

"What did you say, dear?" Frances asked.

Kara smiled beguilingly. *Emma's* smile.

Their mother's face softened. Stuart wanted to tear Kara limb from limb.

"Nothing, Mother." Again she used that saccharine tone, while her wicked gold eyes zinged Stuart like a poison dart.

Emma tugged at her twin. "Let's go swing."

Then Auntie Z was there, silver bracelets jingling.

"The caterer had a wreck."

The children's mood lightened considerably when both women rushed inside. And before Stuart could grab her, Kara yelled exuberantly to Emma, "Race you!"

Emma leapt toward the swings. Kara stuck out a foot that sent her sprawling. When she began to cry, Kara took off running.

"Beat you!" Kara climbed into a swing. She threw her head back and began swinging higher and higher, her long, slim feet extended, her red curls sweeping the dirt. *Kill.*

Emma sat in the dirt rubbing her eyes, her gritty fists making mud of her tears.

"Sissy," he muttered, despising her.

When she blubbered harder, he felt a little better. He kicked a post and strode back to the porch, where he sagged miserably against a shaded adobe wall.

When Emma quit her sniffling, got up and limped toward the swing set, Stuart balled his fist against his knee.

He opened his hand, the black moons of his dirty finger-nails clawing denim.

It had happened without warning, the way bad things always do.

Baby-sitter.

He ripped off his thick glasses and wiped them on his shirt, a lump of pain quivering like raw liver in his throat.

Banished. Like he was nobody. Which he was—in his mother's house. He'd been demoted when the twin prin-cesses had been born. He'd been seven. The only boy. Adored by his hard-drinking, cowboy daddy. Barely tol-erated by his uptight mother.

Because of the twins, Daddy was gone. Stuart didn't know why. All he could remember was that Mother and Kara had stayed at the hospital a long time.

The morning before they came home, Daddy had gone upstairs, packed a bag and left. No goodbye. No hug. Nothing. Nothing except clouds of dust in the drive when Stuart had run after him. Their mother's first project had been to order the maids into the portrait gallery to take down his painting.

Sometimes Stuart sat in the portrait room, staring at the little brass plaque with his father's name and the date of his birth on it, the plaque being all that was left of his father. Mother wouldn't answer any questions about him. Neither would Auntie Z. Stuart had always blamed the twins.

The twins' voices floated across the sun-dappled lawns.

"Higher, Emma! Go higher!"

"I'm scared! The chain might break!"

He wished it would. Better, he wished those boys, those killers, would get them. Maybe shoot them. Maybe Stuart could look sad on TV.

Replacing his heavy glasses on his nose, Stuart stared

bitterly past the swing set to the pink hills that undulated for miles till they ran smack into the distant purple of the Jemez Mountains. The desert was a pitiless no-man's-land, a perfect hiding place for killers. Tonight those wild, forbidding lands matched his dark, hopeless mood.

He hated being trapped behind these walls.

Violins whined from one of the long, tall rooms with high ceilings and wooden vigas. Piano notes tinkled. His mother was having the party of the decade. And she'd stuck him out here like a watchdog.

Stay, Stuart. Bark if there's trouble. Would he get a doggie biscuit for a reward?

The twins were swinging in tandem, their little bodies stretched straight as boards, like always. Their ridiculous blue dresses hiked so high he could see their panties. They were supposed to wear shorts underneath skirts. They weren't supposed to lean their heads back like that, either, so that their long red hair dragged the dirt like brooms.

They were disgustingly pretty with the slanting light shimmering in their burnished hair as they swung back and forth beyond the emerald grass. The sprinkler's lazy spray was as dazzling as diamond droplets.

Angrily, Stuart unfurled his long skinny legs and sprawled them over his mother's carved wooden table.

Feet on the floor, young man.

Spine against the back of your chair.

Fuck you, Mother.

He was only a few feet from the party, but the rambling porch might as well have been eastern Siberia.

The sound of laughter, the clinking of glasses, and all the phony oohing and aahing over Indiana Parsons's paintings made Stuart's lonely heart ache. His sculptured mouth curled into something almost ugly while he watched the twins.

He wanted to stomp across the lawn, grab the chains of their swings, yank them to a sudden standstill.

What made the twins God's gift to his mother's universe?

With a sneer he studied the huge gravel parking areas that were jammed with the finest cars—Mercedes, Lamborghinis...limos. His face softened.

Im-*fuck-ing*-press-ive. Someday he'd have a car. And a driver like that potbellied, tough-guy in the black suit with boots and wraparound glasses. He'd be important. Someday snoots like Mother would invite *him* to their parties—and he'd be like Indiana and not show if he didn't feel like it.

Mother didn't just invite *anybody*. She was a snob about everything, especially her friends. Leaning back in the carved chair, so he could stare in the window, Stuart caught a glimpse of her. She moved soundlessly, but she made heads turn, conversation cease. Somehow her presence lent tension.

She entertained on the finest china. Her cocktails were served in delicate crystal. But she allowed only two drinks. Not that she said so. Her rules were unwritten. Sometimes even Auntie Z obeyed them.

When Stuart got up and moved stealthily toward the huge, carved front doors, the nasty little *santos* he hated seemed to mock him from the safety of his corner niche.

Lost in his own misery, he didn't pay much attention to the snatches of conversation drifting through the open doors.

"Indiana catches the universal movement—"

"I thought Parsons painted about sex—"

"—brilliance of color, violent brush strokes—"

"—sexy—"

"—tree trunks ready to explode—"

"—you're turning me on—"

"—studied with master painters—"

"She slept with them, too."

"She slept with that Navajo gardener—"

Smothered laughter.

"—lived like a squaw in some squalid hogan—"

"A true artist—"

"A true slut," Stuart mouthed, grinning lewdly.

He heard a soft footstep.

"They're jealous," taunted a soft purr from the dark. "So are you."

He jumped.

She stepped forward, but not into the light. "My, my you're just a boy."

"Who the hell—" Stuart croaked, shamed by this mysterious creature.

She moved closer. Half her face was veiled with wild black hair. One green eye stared. She swept the lush dark mass aside.

Two green eyes now stared at him, through him. Low-cut black satin was so tight, it had to be sewed on to her.

Wow.

"Damn. Damn. Damn."

"You got it."

Indiana Parsons.

The flower beds beyond the porch and patios where she stood were rampant with color in the evening light—lilacs, iris and hollyhock. Smiling at him, she leaned down and inhaled their perfume.

He could see her breasts.

She could read his mind.

Adrenaline. Panic. If this rich famous bitch said anything to his mother....

She smiled darkly.

His brain dissolved. Total regression. He was scared enough to pee in his pants.

Car doors slammed, and two black-haired boys about his age—one tall, the other plump—got out and raced to the swings.

"Slut?" she whispered, toying.

"I didn't mean you—"

Green eyes sparkled in the dark. "I was hoping you did." Playfully she touched his cheek.

He jumped.

She licked her lips, and he burst into flame.

"Why aren't you inside, *little* boy?"

"Baby-sitting," he choked.

The twins shouted at her sons when they tried to steal their swings.

"Oh." She turned, remembering her children. "Sando! Raymond! Come here! The girls already have a baby-sitter."

His humiliation was so great, he wished he could be swallowed by some black hole.

If she ratted to his mother, he was dead meat.

Indiana Parsons laughed at him when her sons stormed onto the porch. "Enjoy yourself...out here." Then she stepped past him as if he were nobody, and joined the glittering throng awaiting her arrival.

Stuart was staring down at the burnt-orange tile floor when his mother's shadow fell across the arched doorway. Behind her, Indiana watched slyly.

"Is that odd, shy creature...yours—?"

"Was he rude?"

"Aren't they all at that age?" Her own sons were galloping about inside.

His mother banged the doors shut in his face with a look that said *I'll deal with you later.*

Shit. Shit. Shit.

Slut.

Darkness swallowed him. The light was going out of the sky. When he turned, all was still.

Too still.

Then, his mother's Arabians whinnied. Above, black vultures soared, circling, looking for their nighttime roost.

Vultures always made him think of death. Which was why he liked them so much. They were ugly on the ground, creepy hunched figures with those awful curved beaks…feathered undertakers. But in that dark blue, opalescent sky, gliding together in a sort of weird ballet of dancing black feathers, they were graceful and gorgeous.

Omens?

He shivered.

Beyond the walled estate, wild desert rolled away to the mountains. Juniper and piñon pine cast long, purple shadows across the sandy ground.

The growing dark held latent menace.

Stuart wanted to rush inside, to lose himself in his computer, to smoke till he turned green and puked. For no reason at all, he thought of those white boys killing those Navajos.

Maybe they were out there, their guns pinned on him. Maybe they had him in their crosshairs. With scopes, they could pick him off from a long way off.

Frantically, he shrank deeper into the shadows, all the time scanning the grounds for unseen attackers.

Maybe with their scopes, they could see in the dark.

His blood turned to ice. His heart thumped.

He couldn't see a damn thing. Nothing but glowing gold sky. Green lawns. Adobe walls. Swings. White pipe fences.

All was silent.

Like a joke he couldn't catch, it took a while for the meaning behind this new stillness to penetrate.

He went cold to the bone.

The swings behind the shimmering sprinkler were empty.

The twins were gone.

Mother would kill him.

3

"Kara!" Emma's heart pounded as she stumbled over fallen boulders and gravel in an attempt to find her twin. It was getting dark, and Emma was afraid of the dark. She was thirsty, too.

Suddenly a huge red rock squatted right where the much-used path took an abrupt turn. Above her, high against the red face of that rock, Kara arched her body to find handholds and toeholds. Slowly, inch by inch, she was pulling herself to the top.

"Come on," she yelled when finally she made it. "So you can see how far we've come!"

Despite the crisp coolness of the thin, dry air, sweat dripped from Emma's forehead. Her throat burned. Panting, she sat down and stared glumly up at her more adventurous twin.

"Do you have water in your backpack?"

"No! You coming up or not?"

Emma got up. Her palms began to sweat as she wedged the tip of her left sneaker into a small crevice, stuck her bare fingers in a crack and tried to pull herself up.

When she finally got to the top, Kara was standing on

the edge. Less than an inch beyond the tips of her worn sneakers, pink sandstone sheered off into nothingness.

The twins were used to wandering about in the desert, used to climbing cliffs and rocks. But not this late in the day.

"Kara! Not so close!" Emma squeaked.

"I'm not gonna fall."

Taking prissy little sidesteps, Emma moved closer to the edge, stopping well behind Kara. There, perched like a pair of eaglets high on that talus slope that led to the ancient kivas and caves, the twins' dark eyes widened as they peered breathlessly over the ledge.

The daunting view squeezed Emma's lungs and left her gasping for oxygen. Never had the trees and houses looked so little. The big hills behind their backyard were pathetic lumps of bald stone.

In the distance a slanting sun slid beneath purple mountains, bathing the sky in a tangerine glow. Then, beneath her, the trees seemed to swim in a strange white sea. Dizzily, she searched for a glimpse of their mother's walled kingdom, but found only tiny boxy shapes fast being swallowed by deepening shadow and thickening ground fog hundreds of feet beneath her.

When Kara let out a piercing war whoop, a tingle of raw fear shivered down Emma's spine.

"How'd we get so high?" she whispered, moving back. "When did the path get so steep? So dark? My legs hurt, Kara. Do your legs hurt? I'm tired. And hungry. Are you hungry?"

Kara jammed fists on her hips. "We can't quit now! We're nearly there!"

"Kara, if we can please, please, let's go home, I'll sneak inside the kitchen and steal some chocolate cake for you."

"You're such a ninny. How come my necklace isn't making you brave?"

Emma patted her blue collar above the golden *K* that Kara had traded for her necklace with the golden *E*.

"So? You're 'sposed to be me—Kara. I'm 'sposed to be you. Wimpy and nice. Yuck."

Emma flushed. "Then," she began timidly, "you should be scared to death and want to go home!"

"Auntie Z showed me an old bowl up there with black marks on it. I want to get it."

"You're not 'sposed to take stuff—"

"We're not 'sposed to go, either." A nasty edge had crept into Kara's voice. "We're not 'sposed to change necklaces. We're not 'sposed to pull twin tricks." She smiled. "What's one old bowl?"

"But if everybody takes a bowl…"

"Go home, then! See if I care!" In a single leap Kara jumped off the rock and hit the trail, skidding, sending rocks tumbling hundreds of feet down the slope, catching herself just in time.

Emma slipped the golden *K* out of her neckline and said a frantic prayer. When Kara bounded out of sight, Emma stared down at the purple shadows cutting across the stark landscape of the canyon. Now only the tips of the roofline and chimneys of their mother's mansion were visible above the strange mist.

The view seemed eerie, unearthly, scary. More white streamers swirled up from the creek bottom, blanketing juniper and piñon, rising higher and higher. When their mother's house disappeared, Emma shivered.

"Higher, Emma. Climb higher."

Close to tears, Emma wiped her eyes, but her gritty fingers only made them burn. "I want to go home."

"You don't ever want to play with me." Kara's hurt tone held betrayal.

"I do, too. You're my twin."

"Prove it!"

"I want to go to Auntie Z's shop and play princesses."

"Shop" was a euphemism for the adobe ruin their aunt had stuffed with dusty Stetsons, peacock feathers, old wagon wheels, saddles, all kinds of antique bottles, glassware, old-fashioned jewelry and clothes. Junk, their mother called it. But Emma loved wandering through the large rooms, her neck dripping with long ropy necklaces, or wearing some huge hat, with a dragging ostrich feather.

"Her ol' shop stinks of cat pee. Last time I was there a cat bit me. My finger swelled double."

Kara hurried up the unstable talus slope, every footstep causing rocks to tumble downhill.

"Kara!" Emma called in mortal terror when Kara raced ahead.

By the time Emma neared the top of the mesa, it was nearly dark, and Kara had vanished somewhere in the cliff ruins cut into the side of the high sandstone ledges. Fearfully, Emma stared at the cozy, little one-room houses made of mud and rock. And into the caves and kivas, too.

As she hurried past the tumbling adobe walls to catch her sister, gravel and loose chunks of rock and pottery shards slid beneath her, and she fell. Blue silk snagged. Her knees hit hard, sharp rocks, biting deep.

An owl hooted.

"Kara!"

For several long minutes, Emma pulled at the loose threads stuck in the bloody scratches on her dirty legs. Kara had said Stuart would follow them if they snuck out of the walls. She'd said he'd take them to the ruins. Kara had said if he didn't come, they'd watch wild deer or turkeys; she said the boy turkeys were doing their mating dance. Emma had wanted a turkey feather. Only there hadn't been any turkeys.

Emma wouldn't feel scared if Stuart were here. Her big brother wasn't afraid of anything. He laughed at monsters in the dark.

The owl hooted again. Or was it a ghost? A gust of air brushed her cheek, and she screamed. Emma pushed herself up and climbed the ever-steepening trail that carved itself into the mesa's rim. A maze of crumbling walls that had once been rows of adobe homes built around some sort of plaza littered the mesa, spilling over the cliff.

A lizard scampered in the shadows. The wind moaned.

Anasazi. The ancient ones. That's who used to live in these roofless huts and work magic in their dark circular pits. They'd farmed and fought and vanished.

Vanished. Just like Kara.

The cold wind blew harder up here, whipping her thin skirt and untying her ribbons, sending them fluttering away. Emma raced after them, but a gust of air caught them and hurled them over the cliff, which fell twenty feet into a black pool. The pool made her remember how thirsty she was. Far below Emma saw the dark land of pine and stunted juniper...where Mother was.

Emma stared down past the pool, wishing there were some magic way, other than the steep path she'd just taken, that would take her home. Like a magic carpet. Like Aladdin... With her hands outstretched, she moved to the edge.

Kara screamed, "Don't jump!"

Emma whirled and was blinded by a white cone of light.

Kara burst into laughter. "Flashlights!" Kara switched on a second beam, waving it around, so that she looked like an alien with two light-sabers. "Did you think I'd come up here in the dark without—"

"Where'd you get 'em?"

"Outta my backpack."

"But you said you didn't—"

Then they heard it. A low, pitiless groan echoing from the black bowels of a circular chamber directly beneath them.

Emma ran to Kara, hugging her tightly. The two of them jabbered excitedly in terrified whispers.

"What's that?"

"Maybe a spirit."

"Or a dead person."

"An Ana...sa...zi...."

"Same thing, stupid."

"Shut up."

Clinging to each other, their round eyes stared wildly at the rugged, gouged rocks, at the lone dwarf pine bent double from the prevalent wind. At the same moment they both saw the rickety spruce ladder sticking up out of that black hole a few feet away.

In the rapidly fading light, where every shadow held a ghost or something worse, that black hole sucked in all the evil in the universe.

"Who put that there?" they whispered. "It wasn't here last time—"

"A ghost."

"Don't say that—"

Their whispers floated away on the wind; they expelled quick, hushed breaths.

A single scream cut the thin, dark air like the sheerest blade. Absolute silence followed this blood-chilling cry.

The girls clutched each other harder, their sharp little nails gouging deeply.

United in mortal terror, they truly were two beings of one mind. They began to babble in their twin language, using words only they knew.

Oh, God. Oh, God. Emma felt shriveled and lost, a tiny little girl, growing smaller and smaller in an unfamiliar world that mushroomed larger, darker and more dangerous.

Sick with fear, Emma wished she hadn't run away. Their mother was powerful. She had rules. What chairs they could sit on. What rooms they could eat and drink in. What they could eat and drink. No sugar except on Sundays. Now the thing she'd run from—her mother's dominion—was what she most wanted.

What were they going to do up here all alone?

Strangely, though her mind formed this question, Emma could make no sound. The ability to speak had left her. In mute frustration, warm tears seeped from her eyelids.

"I'm getting outta here," Kara said. "If it—whatever it is—was gonna fly out of that hole and eat us, it would have. Here's a flashlight. Follow me."

As Emma pulled herself to her feet, something scuffled in that underground kiva. For no reason at all, she imagined a giant scorpion, tail curled, climbing that ladder, sticking those big claws out to pull her down into the dark. Next, she envisioned a mountain lion ready to pounce.

A tangled scream flew out of that hole.

"Help…" The plea was faint, pitiful, broken, and it tore something in Emma's heart.

Maybe *it* wasn't a monster or a ghost or a scorpion. Maybe *it* was somebody who was scared and helpless.

"Kara, wait! Stop!"

Later Emma had to rely on Kara to tell her what had happened, because she couldn't remember.

Kara's eyes glowed like coals. "Would you come on? I'm hungry. For that chocolate cake you promised me."

"Chocolate cake?"

"Milk, too."

I have to see who's down there. I can't just leave her or him there all alone."

Emma's fear was gone. It was as if some force, outside herself, something stronger and wiser even than her mother, made her feel utterly safe—even up here.

She crawled on bleeding hands and knees to the *sipapu*, or spirit hole. Leaning over the edge, she shone her flashlight down inside.

She jumped back, her heart racing.

"What's wrong??" Kara demanded.

"Big black cats. Lots and lots of them."

Kara shone her light inside. Sure enough, there were dozens and dozens of them. Leaping and dancing on the earthen walls. Painted panthers, the kind that gobbled little girls whole in a single bite.

When Emma shone her light into the cave again, her beam hit a pair of mud-caked feet sticking out from filthy denim cuffs. Her light traveled the length of jean-clad legs; up a lean, male torso in a dusty white T-shirt. Then she gasped at the lethal beauty of the boy's darkly dangerous face.

"Kara!"

Emma began to shake. She clenched her flashlight and pointed it straight at his eyes.

Green eyes shone in the dark with a fierce and palpable hate.

"It's a boy," she whispered.

Kara aimed her light at him. "He looks mean. Yuck. He's dark. Dirty. Horrible. Why, he's some sort of...Indian."

Emma couldn't take her eyes off him, even when his face hardened. He was quite old. Maybe even older than Stuart. His shoulders were wide; his lean brown arms bulged with muscle. His brooding face, with its high, sharply defined cheekbones and squared-off edges, was tough and suntanned under a thick straight mane of blue-black hair.

He squeezed his hooded eyes closed. When he opened them again, the look he gave her stole her breath away.

Then the strangest thing happened. It was as if he hypnotized her with those emerald-green eyes that sparkled in the dark. Or maybe she hypnotized him. She couldn't seem to stop staring at him any more than he could stop staring back.

"Hey, Kara," she whispered. "You remember that Navajo boy we saw on TV that's missing…"

The boy closed his eyes. His lips moved, and a low tortured moan rose from the depths of the cave.

"Get up," Emma pleaded with him. "Climb the ladder." Then she saw that his leg was oddly twisted.

She couldn't leave him. Suddenly nothing mattered but going down there and making sure he was all right. When she reached for the ladder, the rough spruce stung her bleeding fingers. She put a toe on the first rung, and it wobbled.

Clinging to the rough spruce, she lowered herself over the edge. The sky blackened. A gust of cold wind lashed grit against her cheek and whipped her skirts around her legs. She was hungry and thirsty and cold. She wanted to go home.

"I'm coming," Emma called.

He glared coldly, his silence thick and oppressive.

When Emma's sneaker trembled on the second rung, rotten wood cracked, splintered.

"Kara…!" She screamed all the way down to the third rung—which wasn't there, either.

"Oh, God! Oh!" She tried to hold on, her legs dangling.

Kara's eyes bulged. Paralyzed, she could only watch as Emma's bleeding hands slipped greasily out of reach into the darkness. Then there was nothing but that trail of blood.

That final scream.

That final *thump*.

Kara put her hands over her ears. Still, she heard that dull *thud* her sister's body made when she hit rock below.

Kara shone her light down. Green eyes blazed up at her from that dark pit. They stared deep inside her, saw her every flaw. She hated him for seeing. Even as she was fascinated that he could.…

He scared her. It was as if he pulled her soul out of her, and she became who she really was. He saw the cruelty in her heart. He understood it. He despised it. Odd, how his seeing it set her free. But the longer he watched her, the more he frightened her. Would he tell?

He closed his eyes.

With a little shiver, Kara came back into herself.

She saw the long silver tube-like flashlight beside her sister's lifeless hand, and wished she had it for the long walk home.

Just in case her own batteries gave out.

After all, Emma wouldn't be needing it anymore.

4

The ground fog was gone when Kara climbed down from the mesa. A full moon turned the desert luminescent. But to Kara, who was scared and running softly down that narrow, winding path, the delicate, white brightness made weird, ghostly shapes of normal things like rocks and trees. Things that had looked so wonderful in the sunlight when she and Emma had climbed this way earlier.

Running through rough scrub and cacti, she found nothing to admire in the strange beauty of glinting thorns or the silver lace of a spider web. Not when every leaf that crackled or every snort she heard in the dark beyond the path made her think of ghosts and goblins, or of the stories Stuart told about bears and cougars eating little girls. Not when she knew that those dry rustling sounds underfoot could be snakes or scorpions.

She was hungry and thirsty. Her feet were blistered from the rough rocks; her legs ached. Her tangled curls were matted with leaves and dirt, and her tummy gurgled. During lulls of anxiety, she pictured a big moist slab of chocolate cake.

Anger toward Emma swelled in her heart. If Emma hadn't climbed down into that kiva, Kara wouldn't have to walk home alone. Emma's fear wouldn't have gotten inside her. Not that she was the least bit afraid. No, not she, brave Kara. It was the necklace that made her think like Emma.

Shakily, she shone her flashlight along the rocky path. Sometimes she directed it in fierce, sweeping arcs through the stunted juniper and piñon, where more than once a pair of yellow eyes had gleamed. She'd shrieked, but that was only because she'd remembered what Stuart said.

How Kara longed for her sister as she remembered Stuart's exact words. "To a big cat, you'd taste better than chocolate cake. If he doesn't finish you off with one bite, he'll stash what's left of you in a tree and eat you for leftovers till there's nothing left 'cept bones. Buzzards'll come and eat out your eyes."

Buzzards swirled above her. Kara began to run in earnest when they swooped lower, almost falling into the branches.

Kara ran harder. Even when her heart was pounding and she was utterly breathless, she didn't stop.

At least not till she rounded the last turn and heard raised voices and saw the sheriff's car, its lights flashing, in her mother's drive. Not till Mother's adobe mansion loomed out of the stunted, black trees, every single window ablaze.

Skidding to a halt, she stared. Now how come Will Gentry, the sheriff, Auntie Z's special friend that nobody was supposed to know about, was here?

Did he already know…about Emma? Had buzzards told him where she was? Had he found her in the cave? Had he told Mother?

Would they blame her? Would Will carry her off and lock her up in his jail?

How could she defend herself?

Oh, dear! How could she ever tell them Emma was dead? They'd blame her, say it was her fault because she'd had the idea to sneak...

No! Kara chewed her lip. That wasn't the way it had been. A smile spread across her face. She'd say Emma had wanted to go to the mesa, not her.

Unbidden came the ghastly image of Emma's lifeless body lying on that dark cave floor, her thin white legs and arms twisted in those strange, painful angles, her gentle face turned toward that dark horrible boy, her once-beautiful red curls dark with blood and dirt. And her eyes, those big, brown, trusting eyes, closed forever.

The horrible vision dissolved when she heard the piano music. She was glad for the dazzling brightness of her mother's house. Glad she wasn't lying dead in a cave.

She switched off her flashlight and kept to the shadows. She needed time to think, time to make up the perfect story.

People spilled out of the adobe mansion. Her mother's party must still be going on. She couldn't possibly tell her story to such a large audience. She might get nervous, mess up.

Anyway, if Emma was dead, she was beyond help. The smartest thing was to sneak inside, have her chocolate cake, and pretend to come home later. That way she wouldn't spoil her mother's party. But it was hard to get close to the house without someone seeing her. People milled, so Kara crouched in the shadows.

Will and his deputy were talking to a clump of people on the porch, a man and a woman in particular. The same woman who'd made such a stink when she got all wet in the music room. The couple had their arms around each other. The woman was crying. Something about this desperate, hushed little scene was as horrible as Emma's twisted body in that cave.

Other big people were trying to hear what was being said on the porch, but staying just far enough away to show respect. Kara could hear, but she wasn't the least bit interested. It was big-people stuff.

Will's voice was stern. "You are the parents of—"

"Yes..."

"Terrible. Accident... Dead, I'm afraid."

Like Emma.

"Both—"

"Instantly—"

Like Emma.

"The tribal police gave chase. The boys ran straight onto the highway, straight into the path— Hit by an eighteen-wheeler. Six more cars."

"—hamburger meat—"

That got Kara's attention. She'd seen a rabbit on the road once after Mother ran over it in her truck. Kara had gone out to the road every day for two weeks till there wasn't much left of its flattened corpse but a few scattered bones. She'd kept a bone as a souvenir.

"My Davie? Rick, too?"

Will touched that gun holstered in black leather—the one Stuart was always pestering him to take out—and nodded.

"Why? Why was the law after my boys?"

"The rez murders."

"Not our boys..."

"We've got them at the scene. Triple homicide. The ballistics match—"

"When can you release their bodies?"

"Now, ma'am, that may take a while. People are pretty riled. There's that Navajo boy that's still missing. The victims' son and grandson. Every damn Navajo on the rez thinks he's dead, too. They've got a huge search party out looking for him. The whole rez is up in arms. They've got dogs…but you know what this country's like. He might never be found.

"The victims, well, ma'am, they weren't just anybody. The old man, Calvin Greywolf, was a World War II hero and a code talker. The old woman was Bessie Greywolf, the weaver—internationally famous in her own right. Their son is Shanto Greywolf, the jewelry designer who does all that mosaic inlay stuff with lapis lazuli and Australian opals."

Kara wished Will would shut up. Then everybody would clear out, and she could get her cake. Instead, he began a boring lecture about kids having too much money and watching too much television.

By the time the group on the porch ran out of words, Kara's throat was dry, and she was so hungry that all she could think of was a giant-size, triangular slice of sugary, moist, dark, rich, gooey, melt-in-your-mouth chocolate cake. And a tall foamy glass of milk.

Frances had been looking forward to this moment all day.

Time to reward herself with that second drink.

Frances Shayne nearly glowed. Aside from the usual minor difficulties—the twins' mishap in the music room, and then Will's truly shocking news that *the* Dobsons, *her* Dobsons of impeccable breeding, *her* guests, were the parents of teenage murderers—her party was an unqualified success.

The poor Dobsons. Children—especially *sons*—were as unpredictable as husbands. When you had children, you could never be sure what you were getting.

Still, her children hadn't embarrassed her too terribly. But she didn't want to think about them. Motherhood, except where it concerned Emma, was her least favorite duty. Children were such wretched little savages. They thought if they screamed or sulked, they could run the world.

Not *her* world.

She pushed such thoughts aside. She wanted to savor how that sweet, young governor, Steven, had patted her hand and kissed her cheek as he left. "Wouldn't have missed this for the world. So dramatic. Indiana. Her paintings. And then your grand finale—the solution to New Mexico's biggest murder mystery. Frances, only you could have pulled this off with such style. What a party!"

She'd actually blushed.

Her eyes fell to the precious weaving she was standing on. With a tight, little smile, she sidestepped off a blue woven corn plant.

Imagine. This very rug, *her* favorite rug, with its four Dontso figures and two corn plants and Rainbow God, had been woven by that poor dead woman, Bessie Greywolf. Frances had been shocked when Will had said the poor creature's name. She'd recognized it instantly. Bessie's pieces would quickly be priceless. After tonight, she would have to have the rug taken up, hung on a wall, maybe even put behind glass for safekeeping.

Indiana's bold paintings blazed on Frances's high walls, the brilliant colors dancing as if alive. Frances still couldn't make up her mind which one to buy.

Maybe the trees. Frances studied the violent brush strokes that made the twisted tree trunks explode in a sundappled forest lit by pink radiance. Indiana was so good with light and shadow.

Choices.

She frowned when she saw Z talking animatedly to Indiana. Z was wearing hiking boots and thick socks. And that awful black cape!

But tonight Frances could forgive Z for almost anything, for she had saved the day. When Will had driven up, his lights blazing, demanding the Dobsons, everybody had abandoned Indiana for his little show outside.

Indiana had querulously requested her car. If she'd left, the lovely party would've been ruined.

Z had been rushing out to Will. Frances had seized her cape. "She's leaving! Indiana's leaving! Stop her."

"And miss Will's big moment?"

Indiana slipped out the front doors.

"Z! Everybody will leave if you don't stop her!"

"Oh, all right."

Z had told Indiana that Will had come because of the Navajo murder victims. After that, marauding Navajos couldn't have dragged the *artiste* away. Which made Frances wonder if that nasty little rumor about Indiana having a Navajo lover was actually true.

Indiana. She slept around. Her husband turned a blind eye. Again, Frances scanned the paintings on her walls with a collector's scrutiny.

Which painting? The red? Or the cross with the flower petals that looked like blood? Or was that too much like O'Keeffe? Frances wanted a painting that was the essence of Parsons. She already had one of O'Keeffe's flowers.

Frances surveyed her lovely room with its museum-quality contents, delighting in her lucky little investment with the rug.

When the clock on her mantel chimed, she almost felt content.

A caterer rushed by. Frances's rigid aristocratic features

relaxed as she lifted her second glass of champagne from his silver tray.

She sipped, and the cool, bubbly wine floated her cares away.

Another caterer came by.

A third champagne? Just this once.

Her eyes met Z's.

No. She couldn't lower her standards...in public.

With a frozen smile, she gave him her empty glass. She was looking forward to her flask upstairs—when it happened.

A bedraggled figure in dirty blue silk streaked down the hallway into the kitchen. The blue ribbons Frances had carefully bought and tied were gone. Filthy tangles had replaced shining red curls. But it was the child's enormous eyes and ashen face that made Frances clutch at her throat.

Frances waited for the twin's partner in crime to sneak across the hall.

But she didn't.

There was only one.

Champagne no longer sang in her veins. No longer did she hear her guests' laughter, or the piano music filling her beautiful rooms. She didn't care in the least about the value of her Navajo carpets or which Parsons to buy.

Every cold ambition in her adult heart died.

Some people love, truly love, only one person. For Frances that person was Emma.

With a mother's instinct that this most precious being was somehow threatened, Frances abandoned her moment of exquisite triumph and headed quickly after the little girl.

All that mattered, all that had really mattered since her husband had left her, was Emma.

She had to make sure that Emma was all right.

5

Kara was stuffing chocolate cake into her mouth by handfuls and chasing it down with milk.

"Young lady!"

Mother.

Gooey chocolate clogged her throat. Choking, Kara put her fingers to her lips so she wouldn't spew black crumbs everywhere.

"Don't be afraid," Mother said, gently fingering the golden *E* at Kara's throat.

"Emma?"

Kara nodded fearfully.

"Precious, what's wrong?"

Never ever had Mother spoken to her so sweetly.

Then Auntie Z was there, her honey-blond braid hanging limply over a cool black cape. With a jingle of silver bracelets, she, too, touched the golden *E*.

They were so stupid.

"Where's Kara?" Auntie Z asked gently.

Kara remembered Emma lying twisted and broken in that cave, and amazed herself by forcing warm tears from under her eyelids. They were her first ever.

"Where is she?" Auntie Z demanded.

Kara put chocolate-covered fingers to her temples and squeezed, as if straining to push out thoughts the way one might juice an orange. The frantic gesture was pure Emma.

"Can't you see, she doesn't know. She can't remember," her mother said. "She's having one of her spells."

Emma's spells were how come they could get away with so much stuff and Stuart couldn't. When Emma got really scared, she forgot. Then Kara got to tell everybody what happened.

Once, Kara had tried to get some peppermints out of Auntie Z's candy jar in the kitchen. But the dumb old china frog had fallen to the floor and smashed. Kara had talked Emma into burying it in a pile of cottonwood leaves. Only Emma got scared when their mother came out. Emma had raced up into their tree house, holding the frog's blue china eye.

Later, when Mother asked her what happened to the candy jar, Emma could only shake her head. After Z opened Emma's fist that held the bulbous blue eye, Kara had pretended the last thing she wanted to do—while Emma cried—was tattle or lead everybody to the pile of yellow bits of china frog buried under the leaves.

Not long after that Mother had taken Emma to a psychia...psychia-a-something. He'd called Emma's forgetfulness "losing time." Emma had told Kara all about the visit, about the big red armchairs that almost swallowed her up whole.

"Did he cure you?" Kara had anxiously demanded. Lucky for her, all he ever did was talk. And convince everybody Emma forgot when she felt guilty. Sometimes Emma forgot whole days.

"Where's your sister?"

Kara shrank lower, the way Emma often did. She imitated her sister's blank, stupid look.

They bought it.

"Oh, dear," said Auntie Z.

Her mother picked her up, brushed chocolate out of her hair, carried her to the sink and got a nasty wet rag to wipe her face.

"What will happen to that precious baby," Auntie Z began, "if we don't find—?"

"Where's Stuart? He was supposed to be watching them."

Thankfully Stuart, the skunk, had disappeared. So, Auntie Z and Mother fairly smothered her with love. When they didn't ask her any more questions about Kara, something mean and hateful coiled around her heart. How little they cared that Kara was missing!

They tucked her into Emma's clean sheets, kissed her brow, and were gone. They must have dispatched some of their guests to look for the missing child, because Kara fell asleep to the frantic, singsong cries. *"Kara! Where are you? Kara..."*

She supposed she'd have to tell them in the morning.

"Kara!"

Kara sat bolt upright in her bed, her eyes searching for some monster in the dark.

He sprang on top of her.

She tried to scream, but a hand closed over her mouth. She sank her teeth into thick fingers that reeked of nicotine and chocolate.

Stuart yanked his hand loose.

"Kara!" he yelped.

Kara tried to cry.

"You can't cry! You aren't Emma!"

"Shut up, Rodent Nose!"

"I'm going to tell."

"Who's gonna believe you, huh? What difference does it make whether I say I'm Emma or Kara? We're identical. Two beings in one body. Inseparable."

"You have the cold slimy heart of a snake."

"If I did, I'd have poisonous fangs to bite you with."

"See, you are her."

Before she could think what to do, he ran out the door. He was downstairs before she reached the landing. Their stunned mother and Auntie Z and everybody else were staring up at her. Then her mother came flying up the stairs.

Kara sank to the floor in tears, dragging her hands down the railing, crying just as Emma would have. Stuart streaked past their mother and lunged, tackling Kara, rolling over and over, pounding her with his fists.

"Tell 'em who you are, you fake! Tell 'em."

"Emma. Emma," she sobbed.

The harder he hit her, the louder she wept, but she didn't hit him back, the way Emma never hit back. Gritting her teeth, she let him pound her. When his hand got near her mouth, she felt tempted to bite him.

"I am, too, Emma. I am."

"Go to your room, Stuart. I'll deal with you later."

Frances picked Kara up and stared at her. Kara lowered her gaze.

She carried her into the bedroom and laid her back in Emma's bed. "You must sleep and try to remember all about Kara. Where she is. Then we'll find her."

Kara stared up at the dark ceiling. What difference did it make who she said she was? Emma was dead. She must have hit her head when she fell. Kara had shined her light on her for at least five minutes. She'd called her name again and again.

They weren't inseparable, after all.

She was the only twin.

She was Emma—the favorite.

When Emma opened her eyes, she was in a close, dark place that was as black and airless as the inside of Mother's cedar chest. But the strong, moist, earthy smell wasn't mothballs. It was guano.

She hurt everywhere. Walls were closing in. She could feel the sickening suffocating closeness of not having enough oxygen…like before. In a panic she began to pant, but the faster she breathed, the less air she got.

She was in the chest again in Mother's bedroom. They had they been playing hide-and-seek. Kara had explained that Emma must have taken the blankets and mothballs out and climbed inside. That the heavy lid must have fallen shut.

The airless coffin had reeked of wool and cedar and mothballs, as she'd lain there, afraid that they'd never ever find her and that she'd be buried alive.

Emma had been unconscious by the time Kara had brought Stuart and Mother. She remembered opening her eyes to Mother's sparkling face. Mother, who never cried, had sniffled quietly and then hugged her so tightly that she couldn't catch her breath again.

"What happened, darling?"

Emma had stared at her mother, Kara and Stuart, her mind curiously blank.

"Mothballs," she whispered. Emma got down on her hands and knees and pulled one of the nasty white balls from under the chest.

"It's all right, darling. We'll pick them up later."

That's when Emma had first "lost time." She never did remember how she'd gotten into the trunk. Kara had told them. Thank goodness Kara was always there to re-member.

Waves of darkness lapped her. Cautiously, she moved her hands, groping the hard, dirt floor. Even those tiny movements made her bruised arms ache and her head throb.

Slowly her burning eyes grew more accustomed to the dark. There seemed to be a smoke-blackened hole in the rock ceiling above her. A ladder with only one rung led up to the stars. The constellation Scorpio shone bright and true above the ladder's spruce poles, reminding her of happier nights when Auntie Z had held her high and pointed it out.

Hole in the ceiling... Kiva...

Emma wished she were home, wished she'd flown home on Aladdin's carpet. Maybe there was another way out. But when she tried to lift her head to sit up, pain burned down her neck and spine.

She began to shake so hard her teeth chattered. It was freezing cold. She closed her eyes, then opened them again, hoping this was a bad dream.

But it was real.

Then somebody coughed, startling her nearly out of her wits. She jumped, which hurt so badly that she fell back onto the hard earth, weeping a little, but holding herself very still. Opening her eyes just enough so she could see through the slits in her lashes, she stared into the darkness where the cough had come from.

Awareness spread through Emma. She felt him even before she could see him.

He was real.

Tall and dark, but hunched in on himself like a

wounded bear, a savage-looking boy with clumps of long black hair watched her with deliberate, narrowed eyes.

"Who are you?" she whispered.

He didn't answer. He just stared like a big dark cat, his tangible, wild-animal magnetism compelling her.

"My name's Emma," she said fearfully, after an awkward interval.

His lips thinned, his cruel eyes hardening with unstudied insolence. "So what?"

"Are you mean?" she whispered.

This brought a faint smile, but he didn't answer.

"You have the worst manners in the whole world. Did you know that? I climbed down here to help you."

Again, that thin smile.

"I said, I'm Emma."

"I guess I don't think names matter much, *Emma*," he whispered, his voice raspy as if it hurt him to talk. Yet it resonated inside her.

Then they simply watched each other a while, till he got bored and wearily closed his eyes.

"Are you that boy whose daddy got shot?"

His eyes snapped open then, burning her, devouring her now with such contempt that she was almost glad he was hurt and couldn't stalk over and hit her.

"How do you know about that, *Emma?*" He emphasized her name as if it were something dreadful.

"Everybody knows."

"Whites killed them. Did you know that? Whites…like you, little rich girl."

"How do you know I'm rich?"

"'Cause of your silk dress and your gold necklace with that curly *K*. 'Cause of your pretty red curls. 'Cause of your voice, the way you speak. 'Cause of those manners you're so damn proud of. I just know, that's all. Our kind, you and me, Navajo and white, we don't mix—I'm the living, mongrel proof of that. You shouldn't have crawled down here, white girl. You should have left me to die."

"Die?"

"There are things way worse than death, and if you're not careful, I might just show you." He leaned closer, the threat in his dark face so terrible, she was afraid he really might strike her, or abuse her in some other, even more humiliating, unimaginable way. But his savage words and glare were a bluff.

She fell asleep again, and the next time she woke up, she was so thirsty, she thought she'd die for sure if she didn't get a drink. "Water... Water..."

He was asleep, moaning words in a language she didn't understand, crying out, his terrors more profound than hers.

Feeling sorry for him, she edged closer to him, even touched her hand to his hot cheek. His long lashes fluttered open. He stared into her eyes. Nobody had ever looked at her like that, really looked at her, absorbed her. She was surprised that he didn't push her hand away, that he let her lie there, beside him, that he kept looking at her.

Then they both lapsed in and out of consciousness for a while. Once—and she held onto this memory as if it were as precious as a jewel—yes, once—this wasn't a dream—she was licking her parched lips, and the boy wasn't mean like before. He was awake, too, his powerful arms wrapped around her. He was pouring water from his canteen into her mouth, holding her head up so she wouldn't choke as the liquid dribbled over her lips and down her throat.

"Enough?" he finally whispered, his own lips dry and very close to hers. She thought he had about the prettiest mouth she'd ever seen, which was strange, since he was such a wild, dirty boy. He gave her another long deep stare. Only this one wasn't nearly so scary.

"So your mother did teach you to speak and be nice?" she said.

"I don't have a mother," he replied darkly. "But, yes, I can still speak...and be nice...but only sometimes."

"When?"

"When I feel like it."

Something rustled in the dark above them. Edging closer to him, she asked softly, "Do you believe in ghosts?"

He didn't answer, but when the wind began to moan, he held her, as if he, too, were a little bit afraid, more than he let on.

They heard a terrible hooting sound, then the baleful yapping of coyotes. She grabbed his arm. "What's that?"

He stared into the darkness with wide frightened eyes, seeing things, seeing horrible things. She knew this without knowing how. But when he turned back to her, he said, "It's just coyotes, baying at the moon. Try to sleep. You'll feel better in the morning."

She woke up again and again, and every time she did, he was there. She wondered how long they'd been in this cave, and how long it would be before Kara came back. Then she fell asleep, only to be startled into wakefulness when something leapt at her from the ceiling, flapping cold and clammy wings against her cheek. She screamed and screamed, and the boy woke up, waving his arms at the thing, shoving the awful creature away. When it was gone, he pulled her close.

"Bats," he whispered. "It's only bats. They've been out all night. It's nearly morning. They'll settle down if you quit your hollering."

"I can't quit screaming. I can't."

"You can do anything you want to do!"

"I can't."

Then he said, "Be still. I broke my leg when I fell—"

She saw how white he was, how he bit his lip in pain.

"Oh. Oh. I'm sorry if I hurt you." She burrowed her head in his chest to get away from all those wings beating above them, from every other nameless monster she could imagine up there in the dark. Or maybe, even then, she just wanted to be near him.

And she was still.

Another time she was lying on her back, staring up at stars, wide-awake, starving now. "Why don't you close your eyes?" he murmured.

"'Cause once I got shut up in a chest. I'm scared if I close my eyes, scared I won't be able to breathe. Sometimes I have nightmares about it."

She told him every detail of that awful experience. At least, she told him what Kara had told her.

"You're not in that chest. You're with me, Mike Greywolf. I'm not gonna let anything bad happen to you, ever."

Greywolf. So that was his name.

"Shut your eyes, and let me watch the stars for you."

He dug for something in his buckskin bag. Then he put a smooth, cool object in her hand.

"What is it?" she asked, holding it up, turning it round and round in wonder.

"Something I carved a long time ago. A big cat…like the ones on the wall. A howling lioness I call it. Lionesses are brave, like you. This one tried to get my lambs."

"I'm not brave. My sister's brave."

"Kara. The *other* one." His snort held that nasty edge he'd first used with her. Only it wasn't meant for her. But he said only, "*You* were the one who crawled down that ladder."

"I fell."

"Same thing."

"You really think I'm brave?"

"You've got definite possibilities."

"And you won't tell anybody ever...how I screamed about the bats?"

He smiled. He was so beautiful when he smiled. "You should smile more often," she said.

Which made him stop.

"Promise you won't tell," she said.

"Word of honor."

She closed her eyes, almost happy to be lost in a kiva with this fierce dark warrior to watch over her, in what now seemed a strange new world, a mythical, mystical world, a world outside her mother's realm where new rules applied.

Here she wasn't a twin, wasn't a Shayne.

She was herself, and Greywolf was her friend.

Hers *alone*.

He was too precious to share.

Even with Kara.

6

Why did it take so long to die?

His leg pulsed with pain.

Murder had turned Greywolf's heart to stone. He'd been lying in this tomb-like cavity, a living corpse, more dead than alive, waiting for death, ready to welcome it. Then she'd come—the girl with the red hair…from the vision he'd had after the deaths at the hogan.

The raspy sound of Emma's shallow breath made shivers race up his spine. She was hurt, maybe badly. The cave was too cold and clammy for her. He didn't like the way she trembled, the way her teeth chattered. She needed food, shelter, the magic of white doctors. She'd come down here to save him; she'd hurt herself for him, and for some ridiculous reason that touched even his hard, grief-stricken heart.

Till she'd come, he'd been half out of his mind with pain and grief. Funny that he could care for her so quickly when he hardly knew her, when she was from some wealthy white family. When she was from a world that had nothing in common with his.

But she was a comfort. It was as if he'd always known her in this life—maybe in others, too.

Or was she simply a gift from his grandfather?

The wind began to howl, and Greywolf, thinking of ghosts riding the wind, ghosts crying for vengeance, clutched Emma closer. Her eyes were closed, her face still, but when she'd looked at him earlier, he'd thought he'd never seen anyone so beautiful. As in his vision, her entire being had seemed to shine out of her soft brown eyes. She had the trusting, open face of a little girl who was much loved. Her family would miss her, look for her.

Before she'd bravely descended that spruce ladder, Greywolf had wanted to die.

Now he had to live—to save her. If he wasn't so worried about her, he would have hated her for that. Because to live meant his grief would go on and on, till it ate him alive.

He couldn't get the images of his family's blood-soaked bodies out of his mind. Even when he slept he saw them. When he woke he saw them.

First he saw the trickle of blood staining the sand outside the hogan's door. Then came vivid horrible images of his grandmother's slashed, handwoven rugs, of his father's scattered silver-and-turquoise jewelry. All the things they'd been working on had been left untouched by their killers. None of his family's stored goods—their spices, herbs or extra food, their clothing, guns or money had been touched, either. Their sheep still grazed peacefully.

The killers' motive hadn't been robbery.

It had been blind, racial hatred.

If he'd been there, he'd be dead, too.

He'd been too weak and upset to do a good job of burying the bodies, and afterward he'd collapsed on the hard ground. He'd lain near the coals of their last campfire, where his father had once sung to him of the clan's

Long Walk and imprisonment at the Bosque Redondo, instructing him always with such stories. Even when he'd been a small boy, he'd been taught that he was a future warrior. Warriors were men of compassion, courage and endurance. Warriors did not long for death.

Then the coyotes, smelling blood even from the cliffs, had begun to howl. His breath had stalled. Then Mike had jumped up, shaken to the core with fear.

Fear had propelled him from the red cliffs and the deep gorges of the Navajo reservation where he'd herded sheep, away from the only home he'd ever known, in search of somewhere new. Not that he thought of seeking the family of the white mother who'd abandoned him, the amoral witch with wild black hair whose infamous name his father had never allowed to be spoken, saying only, "She bewitched me. She is dead...*chindi*."

Mike had taken the silver jewelry box she'd left behind, the one his father had kept hidden deep inside a drawer, and had stuffed it into his buckskin bag. He'd filled the bag with food, too, and a few valuables.

His grief was so powerful that the long, arduous journey across miles of pathless cliffs and tangled canyons were a blur. Forgotten were the rides he'd hitched. Forgotten was the sandstorm that had peppered him with sharp rocks the size of beans until his arms and legs were bloody. Forgotten was the quicksand beside a dry riverbed that had nearly sucked him under. Forgotten was the hunger gnawing his empty belly that had driven him to eat what he could find along the way—wild carrots, wild onions, wild potatoes, fruit from the yucca plants, piñon nuts and berries. He'd carried a canteen and an old can to scoop muddy water from stagnant ponds or watering holes. He'd sucked the milk from milkweed. All the while his fierce determination had forced him to take another step and still another, until he'd found himself in a cave filled with skulls. Then he'd run, trying to climb down to get out of the icy wind, and had fallen into the kiva.

The third rung of the ladder had given under his weight, and he'd plunged to the floor. The tibia in his right leg had shattered; his bare feet had been cut to ribbons by rocks and thorns. The black circular room had soon made him feel claustrophobic, as if he were buried alive. Hungry and freezing, he had lain shuddering and hallucinating in that silent chamber, seeing that pile of skulls again, imagining prancing panthers and dead spirits swooping around him. The people who had lived here and gathered food here and put their children to sleep here had departed hundreds of years ago.

Then, slipping in and out of consciousness, he heard chirping voices high above him. That's when he'd known he was dying. Believing those cries to be the chants of his murdered family who had come to lead his spirit deeper into the underworld, he'd opened his eyes and squinted into twin blinding cones of white light.

The flares had bobbed wildly over dark walls painted with giant mountain lions. Then the lights went out. In total blackness, he heard laughter and smothered whispers.

"Don't tell Mother—"

Ghosts? *Chindi?*

When his eyes grew accustomed to the dark again, instead of his father, grandparents, uncle and cousin, he saw two identical, elfin faces, backlit by the moon.

Two little white witches with hair like fire. Younger and smaller than he was, their eyes huge and dark, they stared down at him with astonishment.

Always the pretty face in the deeper shadows blurred and the more angelic—Emma's face—brightened. He could feel the warmth of Emma's sweet smile and her kind, long-lashed brown eyes even then. He knew her from the vision. She'd led him here. To this place. To her.

Her twin's eyes glowed like molten orange coals and yet gave no light of their own as she shrank against a wall. "He's dark and dirty and horrible— Emma, let's go!"

Disdain from whites had already hardened him. Even so, he had concentrated on the other girl.

Emma.

When she'd told him her name, she'd carved it into his soul and heart—forever. For a Navajo does not think and learn as a white man. He memorizes and claims instantly that which is vital.

That which is his.

Emma.

Even as he thought of her, her teeth began to chatter. He wished he had a blanket to cover her. Since he didn't, he enfolded her white, small hand in his larger, rougher one.

"Hold on. They'll come for you," he whispered.

She was so soft—as soft as her silk dress. Even in the dark he saw how white she was compared to him. But he liked touching her. Maybe that's why he dropped her small hand so abruptly, letting it flop to the ground.

They didn't belong together. Not even here.

He couldn't stop staring at her. Her long red hair floated over his arms and chest. Her dark lashes seemed oval feathers against her bloodless face. Her blue silk dress— or was it her skin?—smelled of lilacs. Not like him. He was a dirty, sweaty Navajo...like her sister said.

Gently, he lifted a soft red strand from her face, feeling the silken texture against his callused palm. When the back of his hand accidentally brushed her delicate cheek, he jerked his fingers away.

She was a mere child.

But a beautiful child. A woman-child.

Someday she'd be a beautiful woman.

Some man would love her.

Not him. Never him.

For him, there could never, ever be someday with a girl like her. He remembered his father, and then with a frown…his mother.

White and Navajo could not mix. He was living proof of that fact.

But the gods had brought this beautiful woman-child to him in a vision, like an offering.

He'd seen her during his Long Walk. Seen her growing up, seen her falling in love with him. He'd seen them old—together. They had a child with red hair, like hers.

But other, darker images washed that foolish fantasy from his mind. He saw his father, spread-eagled in the dirt, the silver bracelet he'd been working on in his stiff, outstretched hand, his black eyes opened in a horrible death stare, his thick throat slashed, black flies buzzing above the fetid line of dark congealed blood above his collar.

The vision about this girl was a lie.

His gods had forsaken him.

He closed his eyes and dreamed not of death, but of her. If ever there was such a thing as natural goodness, it lived in this child. No amount of money, fussing of servants, limitless adoration of parents, not even her white blood had spoiled her—

Suddenly the kiva was filled with blinding light. In his dream, he saw Emma's enchanting face with its glorious red curls in a golden halo. He opened his eyes, squinting.

She was still there, nestled in his arms. Above, someone was shining lights down at them.

Emma stretched, clinging to him. Then she moaned.

"Emma!" shouted a woman from above.

Louder: *"Emma!"*

Emma rubbed her eyes. "Mother—"

Then she stared at Mike in embarrassed silence as the excitement above them mounted. There was so much nervous laughter up there, so many questions, so much hope, so many decisions. Unfamiliar faces peered down at them, more lights flickered over the walls. A bundle of food was lowered, and he and Emma had a picnic.

Finally someone brought a ladder. There was the sound of metal extending against metal, and a new aluminum ladder was lowered into the cave. José, a man with a red rawboned face climbed down. Carefully he lifted Emma onto his shoulder and carried her up, leaving Greywolf behind.

The kiva seemed so empty and cold without her. His muscled arms felt so heavy and drained. Hot and achy, he closed his eyes.

His throat was dry, so he swallowed hard. Reaching for the plastic bottle they'd lowered, he remembered he'd let Emma finish the water.

She was gone. He was alone again.

Just like before.

She'd forgotten him now that she had her family again.

Damn it, she was white.

He couldn't care about a white girl.

He was glad she was gone; he wanted to die.

But at the thought of being separated from her, a heavy weakness descended upon his heart. A sullen, numbing fear gripped him.

He did not want to die.

Not if she was alive.

7

Scarcely conscious, Emma lay shivering on the cold, rocky ground beneath black sky and brilliant stars, amidst family, strangers, bustle and much excitement. Everybody except Kara hovered near.

As always, her formidable mother had taken charge. She was kneeling over her, covering her with a thick, wool blanket.

"He's down there," Emma murmured anxiously. "Down there all alone and cold with only bats and ghosts to keep him company."

"You are so brave, my darling. Hold on. A great big helicopter's on its way to take you to the hospital."

Her mother could think only of Emma. Emma could think only of Greywolf. "I don't want a helicopter. I want Greywolf."

"There. There." Mother frowned and looked up worriedly at Auntie Z. "She's delirious, poor child. Can you understand her?"

"Greywolf," Emma whispered fretfully, her dry throat making her scratchy voice almost inaudible.

Other people circled, knelt down, gently touched her

face or pressed her fingers. Auntie Z, Stuart, everybody came except Kara.

Emma's lips cracked when she tried to smile at them. Kara stood apart, not smiling back. That boy named Raymond and his brother Sando stood over her, too, their faces wavering in the dark as if they were swimmers in a murky sea. Brightened by flashlights, their eyes glimmered like bats' eyes, and Emma screamed.

"Everybody, all of you, stand back," said Mother.

"Greywolf... Please... Please," Emma sobbed.

But her voice was too faint, and they turned away, unable to understand, until the great painter lady, Indiana, bent over her. With fingers that smelled of paint and varnish, but of flowers, too, she stroked Emma's matted curls.

She had the most expressive eyes. They were green, jewel-bright, intense. She had *his* eyes. She stared deep inside Emma as Greywolf had done. She saw.

"Make them get him," Emma whispered, feeling strangely reassured. "Make them get Greywolf."

"Greywolf?" Indiana stilled, leaning closer, really listening as the others could not.

Emma nodded. "Greywolf."

"If you know what's good for you, you'll forget him," said Raymond, his mouth curling, after his mother rose and went to Frances.

Emma heard her mother's sharp retort. "A boy? Down there? Are you sure?"

"It's the missing Navajo boy. He's in the kiva," said Indiana.

"That's what I was trying to tell you. A boy, fifteen or sixteen years old. And he's busted up pretty bad, too," José confirmed.

"My poor baby was down there with a savage all this time!"

"Like I said, he's busted up," said José. "Nothing to be scared about as far as your daughter's concerned."

Frances snatched Stuart by the collar. "This is your fault."

"I told you they wanted to come here. Kara lied about everything."

"I'll deal with you later."

Then Frances bent down to Emma again and pressed cold fingertips to her brow. "Hold on, darling."

Kara began to whine about a thorn in her foot, but nobody paid her any attention.

"You mustn't think about that boy," Frances said to Emma.

"But he held me when the bats came."

"Did he touch you?"

"He watched out for ghosts. He gave me a present, too."

"Emma Claire, did he touch you where a boy shouldn't touch you?"

Emma wept in frustration and shame that her mother could think such a thing. Her mother misunderstood.

Mother breathed deeply. "Emma, he…is little better than an—an animal. You must forget him, what he did…everything. Forget him."

Emma pressed her lips together. She wouldn't forget him. Nobody could make her.

Greywolf's breath came in shallow gasps. The brawny-chested José who'd heaved him out of the kiva had hurt him badly. He knew he must have a broken rib or something, 'cause every time he breathed, it felt like a bone was going in and out of his lung.

When they laid him down beside Emma, he groaned. Not that he twisted his head to look at her. From the hateful way they stared at him—especially her mother and her twin—he knew better than to show the slightest interest in their fancy little white princess.

"Don't let him die," Emma whispered.

Her mother leaned down to him and said softly, "I know what you did. And I'll make you sorry."

The harshness of her words and scowl stabbed more deeply than did his broken rib. The puncture felt so bad, he began to shake.

"Greywolf," Emma whimpered.

He stared straight up at the starry sky, exhausted, gulping mouthfuls of air. Her mother glared at him, her eyes bluer than icebergs.

"Greywolf," Emma pleaded.

Her voice sounded thready and desperate. He never showed how her fragile plea almost cracked his heart. He stared sightlessly, silently, at the sky.

Emma. What have you done to me, girl? He felt weak, unmanned.

He lay beside her, as still as a statue. When she began to weep in earnest, his dark face hardened.

"You hate me, then?" she whispered brokenly.

"Yes," he growled. "Yes. Yes. *Yes.*"

"Greywolf, don't shut me out."

"Just shut up."

Kara watched him from a distance, her grim eyes golden.

Then rotors chopped through the night-black sky, roaring, whipping Kara's red curls and skirt. Before the monster even set down, a girl in white jumped out, and ran to him. Squatting near his head, she plastered a cold stethoscope to his bare chest.

When he jumped, she laughed. "So, you're the famous

Mike Greywolf. We've been looking and looking for you. Good pulse.'' She smiled encouragingly. "You'll live.''

He thought of the blood trail leading through the hogan door, and closed his eyes.

Weeks later, he couldn't believe he was finally off all those tubes. Z drove him home from the hospital in her dusty brown Bronco plastered with tattered bumper stickers. She brought him home to her ranch—*La Golindrina.*

She pulled up to a rambling ranch house from which spilled stray cats and dogs, parrots—and flowers.

Furious, not wanting him to stay, Frances sent a message to the rez for his people to come get him.

But instead, his grandmother's clan sent strange Mabel Blackgoat, the prophecy weaver, to fetch him. Mabel had a penchant for riding the bus all over the Four Corners area to trade. Once, she'd started off with fifteen drums, and returned after a long meandering journey with two cows and a mountain lion cub.

The avaricious witch came on the bus, carrying a sack of black pottery. She inspected him. Then she went out with Z to the porch and sat in the shade of cascading lilac and wisteria vines.

Mabel and Z shared a pot of Chinese green tea filled with nasty-smelling herbs on Z's porch. They also shared a vision. A faintly luminous figure curled out of the teapot like steam, his head orbiting his body like a tiny blue moon. This powerful spirit told them that Greywolf belonged with Z now, that the Shaynes were his destiny. The spirit also convinced Z to buy all the black pottery in Mabel's sack for her shop.

"A vision? You're as insane as Mabel," said Frances to Z after the prophecy weaver left on the bus to the rez without "the savage," as she called him.

For once, Greywolf sided with Frances.

Z proceeded to rake gravel in her Zen garden on the edge of which sat twenty shiny black pots. "If you'd seen the spirit, you wouldn't argue."

"Your tea was bad."

"I'd be scared not to keep the boy."

"You can't let some—some *hallucination* in a teacup guide you into making a terrible mistake. She's paying you, just as she's paying that witch from the rez to give him up. Just because *she* sleeps with her gardener doesn't mean we have to—"

"I've taken a fancy to the child. I've envied you your three children. I consider Greywolf a wondrous gift. Maybe he's a little wild right now. But kindness will tame him. He's got talent, too. Have you seen his carvings? His drawings? He has a fine, pure spirit."

"You're doing this to upset me."

"This isn't about you. My animals like him. So do your Arabians. The trouble with you is that you're motivated by fear...and I'm being led by love."

"I love my daughter."

"You're afraid for her."

"He did things to Emma in that kiva...."

"What things?"

"Nasty, sexual things."

"And we know this, how?"

"Emma."

"I don't believe he'd do that. I don't believe Emma said that. Not the way she checks on him all the time."

"Emma—here?"

Z hacked at the gravel as if she held an ax and was chopping wood.

"Then you've got to stop her! Do you understand? I won't have her near him. He's low."

"He's poor," Z said. "And Navajo. Which makes him unsuitable in *your* book."

A long pause.

"If you keep him, I won't speak to you."

Z pounded her rake so angrily that bits of rock flew. "Fine. Fine. Triple fine."

A Zen statue toppled. Doors slammed. House doors. Car doors. Engines roared. Another sisterly feud had begun.

Emma had said he'd done things? Greywolf's heart pounded so hard, he was afraid it would pulverize his broken rib.

Why did she come around so often if she told her mother he did things? Why did she bring all those pretty little rocks and feathers, and that broken robin's egg that was the same saturated blue as the sky?

He smashed the robin's egg and threw the little blue bits and the rocks and feathers outside.

When Z came to tend him that night in her battered fedora and her diaphanous gown with the huge flowers, trailed by a dozen cats of all sizes and colors and shapes, he shoved her tray with homemade bread, apples, grapes, vegetable soup and nuts off his lap.

"I want to go home."

"This is your home."

"Who's paying you to keep me?"

Just because someone asked a question didn't mean Z would answer it.

A fat yellow cat jumped onto the bed, rolled over, and, stuck all four paws in the air. He was huge and big-bellied, but his kittenish eyes stared brightly.

"I don't belong here."

"You will."

The next morning, as he lay in Czarina's huge canopied

bed with three of her favorite cats plopped all around him on pillows, he dreamed of the twins. Their identical pale faces were framed with bright, burnished curls. They were always sneaking into his room when they thought he was asleep. Kara watched him. Emma tucked little gifts under his pillow or set them on his bedside table. Their images blurred, ran together, fusing into one—Emma's.

"Greywolf," they whispered. "Are you awake?"

No. There was only one voice—Emma's.

When he opened his eyes, he found her peeking at him through his bed curtain. He didn't have a stitch on under his blankets.

Only one emotion—fury—ruled him. Fury that his family was dead and he'd been sold like a slave to Emma's aunt. Fury that she'd saved him from the ghost sickness and then told lies about him.

Fury that she'd made him care about her.

"Greywolf." She smiled brightly.

"Get out."

When the bed curtain fell, the fat yellow cat got curious and stretched, snagging it with a claw. Through this crack, Greywolf saw Emma, standing on her tiptoes, pouring more water into the glass beside his bed.

She glanced toward him when the curtain moved.

"Why are you mad at me? Why did you throw out all my things—"

"Go away and don't come back!"

"Why?"

Frances's car roared in the drive. Doors slammed as she stormed into the house and down the long hall, shouting, "Where is she?"

"We aren't speaking," yelled Z at the top of her lungs.

"You have something of mine—"

"You mean Emma? I haven't seen her."

"Because you're so damn inattentive and incompetent."

"I am raking my garden. Now I'm watering my sweet peas."

"Did anybody ever tell you that big orange flowers and huge skirts make you look very, very fat? And that old hat. It mashes your hair and makes—"

"Yes—you!"

Greywolf's gaze followed Emma, who was desperately scanning every nook and cranny for a hiding place.

"If Mother finds me…"

"You'll get what you deserve. Maybe it'll teach you to stay away from me."

But when she began to shake, he felt sorry for her.

He finally relented. "In here."

Quick as a flash, he whipped the bedspread up. But when he peeled back the sheet, and she saw the brown length of him, she froze.

He swore under his breath and gave her a nasty smile. "Are you thinking I'll do all those dirty things you told your mother I did?"

"But I didn't—"

When her mother's footsteps quickened outside the door, she dove against his naked brown body. He barely had time to roll her on her side away from him and sling the covers over them both before Frances barged into the room.

"Where is she?" she demanded, ripping the bed curtains open.

The fat yellow cat and his scruffy companions watched Frances lazily. Greywolf yawned.

Even though Emma had scooted as far from him as possible, and they weren't touching, Mike was instantly warmed by her body heat. "What do you want?" He had to get rid of Frances, and her kid, or go crazy.

"Emma." Frances grasped the edge of the top blanket to peel it off.

The heat from Emma's body was burning him now. "Careful. I don't have much on."

She glared. "You *are* a savage."

"I gotta pee. Bad." When he flung his cover halfway off, she bolted.

Beneath the blankets, Emma giggled.

"Damn your hide," he said gently. "You're gonna get us both killed if you don't stop coming in here. Now scat. And don't come back. And don't you ever, *ever* crawl in another guy's bed, either...or he'll do what you told your mother I did."

"But—"

Frances's car started up outside in the drive. "I don't want you here—see?"

Emma scrambled out of his bed. "But Greywolf—"

"Would you *get?*"

His harsh tone made her eyes brim with unshed tears. She crossed her arms. "I wish the bats had gotten you."

He stared bleakly past her. "So do I."

"You're mean. You have bad manners. I saved your life. You don't thank people. You didn't thank me."

"I just saved your ass. So, we're even. But we can't be friends. You're white, and I'm not. Understand?"

"Where is it written we have to hate each other?"

"It just *is*. Like the sun and the stars and the moon. It just *is*. Ask your mother."

They shared an endless breath.

She studied him with some confusion. "Don't you care about anybody, ever?" She laid her head on the edge of his bed and stared.

She was so pretty.

"I—I thought we made friends in the cave," she whispered. Then she buried her face in his sheets so he couldn't see her cry.

He leaned closer. When he gently touched her hair, she stilled.

"We're not in the cave now. We can't care. Not about each other. After I saw my daddy…shot, all I wanted was to run, to hide from people like you. To be alone and die. You found me. I ought to hate you for that."

Emma held onto a breath. Her big, luminous brown eyes held on to his heart.

"What do you need me for? You've got lots of friends," he lashed out.

A single tear dripped from her long black lashes.

"Oh, God, don't—"

Suddenly his rough, dark hands were on either side of her wet face, gently smearing the tear with his palm. He felt again that strange pull toward her, that strange unearthly connection to this white child who would someday be the most beautiful of women.

Her skin was so warm and soft. She was crying for him, crying because she liked him so much.

She held her breath.

So did he.

He *couldn't* like her. But it was as if his brain had gone into hibernation in that cave, and she'd slipped through the cracks in his broken heart. He couldn't get her out.

"You threw my gifts away," she whispered.

You told lies.

In a rough voice he said, "You wanna know something crazy? I liked your coming, your leaving all those weird things on my bedside table. I—I kept the dead beetle. I didn't throw him out."

Emma laughed through her tears. It was a soft, throaty sound that filled him with happiness.

"Now get."

She didn't.

Then Z waddled inside and put her hands on her wide hips. "Now looky here, Emma. What's going on between you two?"

Mike stiffened. "I was telling her to get. She won't listen."

"Child, you run along. And don't come back. Greywolf's too old for you, and too...too— Your mother doesn't like him. She's a powerful woman. If you keep coming around, your mother will find a way to make me get rid of him."

Emma ran.

When she didn't come back, it surprised him how much he missed her.

8

When Mike was better, he marveled at how much stuff white people had—even Z, who didn't have nearly as much in her tumbledown ranch house as Frances had in her mansion.

First he was interested in everything electrical and in the running water that gushed straight out of the faucets, in the toilets that flushed with the touch of a finger. Z had so many clothes locked away in tiny rooms she called closets. And there were so many rooms—bedrooms, bathrooms, living rooms, dining rooms, and the kitchen, too. There were so many dishes in the kitchen, and more in the dining room. Stacks and stacks. All different kinds. China in the dining room, and pottery in the kitchen.

White people thought in English. They used long words he didn't know. They read fast, silently, and not with their lips. He'd never realized before that he was so poor or so uneducated. Now he saw that he was both, and that there was a wide gulf between their world and his. Between Emma's and his. He had a new understanding for his dead father, for his cares and worries, for his wisdom, too. A gifted silver designer, he'd loved a rich white woman. But he'd understood he had to let her go.

Some things were the same in both worlds, though. Z grew all her own vegetables the way his grandmother had. She had a grapevine that produced the sweetest blue-green grapes. She made wine and her own wholesome bread, as his grandmother had.

The animals were the same, too. Z's cats and dogs and pet crows quickly grew to love him, 'cause in his loneliness he started feeding them and petting them and talking to them. He helped Z's hands work cattle. But more than anything, he loved the horses. No matter how many times Frances ordered him not to go near them, he couldn't stay away.

At first Frances ran him out of the barn every time she caught him there. She and Z broke their silent feud, and had a terrible fight about it. Then Frances's trainer quit, and she stopped minding his brushing and combing and talking to her prized Arabians so much. After Emma, Frances loved these big pedigreed babies more than anything.

She strode into the barn one afternoon and was about to order him to leave, only to be struck dumb that he was in the stall with Rio. Rio was wild and unbroken, but was standing as calmly as a lamb beside Mike, his back white foot in a bucket of warm water.

"What are you doing?" Frances whispered. "He'll stomp you to pieces."

"What do you care?"

"Get out now."

"Be quiet. You'll scare him. He cut his foot. He's kinda grumpy 'cause I've been cleaning it."

"He'll let you do all that?"

Suddenly the wind blew a stall door open. A horsefly buzzed into the stall right at Rio's eyes. Rio reared, kicking the bucket over. The fly circled Rio's ears, and the big animal stomped down on the side of the bucket, slipping on the wet concrete. When the big bay felt himself falling, he neighed in terror.

Greywolf pushed lightly against his shoulder, "Easy, fella. Easy. That's a little bitty bug, you know. You're just one big accident waiting to happen."

Rio scrambled to his feet, dancing skittishly, while Greywolf stroked and soothed.

"My goodness." Frances was further amazed when Rio quickly calmed. "He gives to your slightest touch."

"I've been working with him."

She watched Mike refill the bucket and marveled at how easily he coaxed Rio into putting his foot in it again.

"You're good," she muttered grudgingly. "Very good."

"I didn't do much. When a horse is pushed or pulled, his nature is to resist. I've been gentle with him, and he trusts me. He's learned to give."

After a few minutes of soaking the bad foot, Greywolf patted Rio and offered him an apple.

"You stay away from Emma," Frances said. "I know what you did. What you'd do again, if you get another chance."

"Do you?" He glared at her, not bothering to defend himself.

Which confirmed her bad opinion of him. She glared back. "You can come to the barn…anytime. But don't go near my house. Do you understand?"

He picked up Rio's brush and then the bucket, turned his back on her and walked out of the barn.

Once Emma was well, she was more interested in Greywolf than she was in Kara. But that had to be her secret. She could write about it in her journal, but she knew better than to tell anybody, especially Kara. When no one was watching, she followed Greywolf everywhere. For she'd taken Auntie Z's words to heart. Her mother could find a way to make him leave if Emma kept going near him.

Emma marveled at the way all animals trusted him, came to him. If he didn't shut the door, the cats all slept in his room. If he shut it, they scratched little flecks of paint off it at night.

He had only to walk outside, and all the dogs ran to the porch, trailing him everywhere. When he stood at the edge of a pasture and said an individual horse's name, the proud beast would lift his head and gaze at him as if to consider the invitation. And always, the animal would head toward Greywolf, slowly at first, then breaking into an eager trot.

Greywolf would circle the horse's neck with his brown arms, hug him, leap astride sometimes. And when he rode, he rode like the wind.

Watching them, Emma envied the horse Greywolf's affection, though she could say nothing, reveal nothing. Not to anyone. Greywolf didn't want her love.

Kara sensed Emma's fascination and resented it. She constantly belittled Greywolf to Emma, who pretended not to care. When her mother criticized him, Emma did not defend him. Nor did she agree with Auntie Z when she bragged about him, saying how indispensable he was when it came to the cattle or describing the cages he made for injured wild animals he found on his walks and brought home to tend till they were better.

Emma wanted to please everybody, so her secret was a necessity to protect the emotion that was so sacred, from those who would have oppressed her. Secrets are the freedom of the soul; all prisoners know their power. She couldn't find her freedom without, so her refuge was within.

Thus, what was suppressed and forbidden grew stronger in both Emma's heart and his. She could no more forget what they'd shared in the kiva than she could forget the warmth and comfort and strength of his long bronzed body beneath those covers. Everything good or wonderful that he did, she added to her secret store of love.

Nor did she forget that Kara had left her to die, not telling where she was. About all these things, she wrote in her journal.

Greywolf grew taller and leaner, and his maturity only made him more breathtakingly handsome. His shoulders were powerful, and he exuded virile, animal magnetism.

She wrote of her dreams that someday he would hold her in his arms and kiss her and love her as she loved him. He had an alert mind and did well in school, especially in science, math and art. She marveled at the animals he carved out of wood, at the wondrous shapes he sculpted from stone. He drew and painted, but talked little. With quiet strength, he shouldered more than his share of ranch responsibilities.

But no matter how busy he was, that haunted look in his eyes remained. Emma knew he hadn't forgotten his dead family. That secret pain must be why his skin was so tight across the high, chiseled cheekbones of his dark face. She imagined how terrible she'd feel if something like that had happened to her family, and she cherished his pain and prayed for him every night. More than anything she wanted to touch his cheek with her hands, to ease his tension, to make him forget, to tell him he had a new family, to tell him he still had her. But she was too scared to reveal her secret, profound love even to him—

especially to him. So every night she wrote what she felt…and was careful to hide her journal.

So she watched him from afar, her feelings for him mounting as the years passed, and he watched her, too, waiting with the steely patience that was his nature, keeping his distance, guarding his secrets. And like seeds buried deep in the fertile soil of her affectionate heart, and his wilder, darker, more troubled one, their passion took root long before either of them realized how stunning and tragic the full-grown blossom would be.

Once, only once, when she was a little past sixteen, did she nearly reveal what she felt. He'd carved a little bird for her. She'd thrown her arms around him, and he'd kissed her. Her first, trembling kiss. As caught by surprise as she, he'd run from her. After that he'd worked doubly hard to avoid her, as she to avoid him. But after that she *knew* he was the most wonderful man on earth.

Meanwhile, Kara's life had gone wrong after she'd left Emma for dead. Although everybody wanted to believe she'd been young, and that the shameful deed was best forgotten, again what was hidden was not forgotten. Although people said little, they noted a darkening in her nature. Sensing her own loss of stature, Kara blamed Emma and Greywolf.

Then one day Kara found Emma's journal. Crazed with jealousy that Greywolf had this mysterious hold over her twin, Kara determined to find a way to break that bond. At first she attacked him directly.

"It was your fault *she* fell, and I got into trouble," she accused Mike. "If you'd go, they'd forget."

"You lie to cover your own lies," he said.

Kara forgot the journal for a time. She became bolder and more sexually precocious, while Emma grew shier and less confident with boys, especially with Mike. Kara flirted with him to torment Emma. Other girls noticed him, too.

He went away to college to study art, and became a fledgling sculptor. Emma's secret longings became shadowed by uncertainty and jealousy. His sculptures began to win awards. She was proud of him and yet afraid he was climbing beyond her reach.

When she was seventeen, her heart felt near bursting. She pined when he was away in graduate school. When he was home, it was worse. He lived in the loft apartment above the stables now, dividing his time between sculpting and ranching chores…and Kara. Kara followed him everywhere. The one place he never went was to the mesa, to the ruins he believed still held the spirits of the dead. Kara went there often. She was fascinated by the place and frequently climbed the cliffs and spent whole afternoons there, puttering or swimming in the pools.

On the surface, Frances's identical daughters were inseparable; in reality they were worlds apart. Sensing that whatever was amiss worsened when Greywolf came home, Frances wished time would go backward. She wished her family to be what it had been before he'd disrupted the balance of her well-ordered life.

"Greywolf is grown and gone. As far as you two are concerned, he no longer exists," Frances said.

But he does, Emma thought.

Maybe he wasn't around all the time, but he was like the sun, the center of her entire universe, especially when he came home on weekends or on holidays, or in the summers to help Z with her cattle. Emma lived for his visits, even though Kara made them agony. When he went away again, Emma wished him back, even though Kara threw herself at him.

Kara grew wilder, flirtier. Except for Raymond Parsons, who rumor said was Mike's white half-brother, she made the wrong sort of friends. She lost her temper quickly. She flirted with every man who was near. When Mike came home, she dropped her usual male friends and chased him shamelessly, a habit that brought Raymond and Mike to blows.

One Saturday evening when Mike was home and Kara was chasing him, Emma dashed up to her room to vent her heartbreak in her journal.

But her little green book wasn't there.

She remembered taking it out to the cottonwood tree by the swings and writing there. But when she looked for it, it was gone. She searched everywhere. Later, she saw Mike returning from a desert walk with Kara and his black Lab, Lucy. Kara wore her prettiest lavender dress. Her eyes were brilliant, her cheeks flushed. When she saw Emma, she threw her hands around Mike's waist.

Greywolf was *her* Greywolf, Emma thought. *Hers. She'd found him, saved him.*

Greywolf stopped and moodily contemplated Kara and then Emma. Then Emma's gaze fastened on the green leather journal he was holding.

When Greywolf saw Emma, he tried to shrug Kara loose, and quick as a flash he hid his hand behind his back. But not before Emma had seen her book.

He studied her, his quiet stricken eyes probing. Then he turned that sharp gaze on her twin.

He knew.

Dear God. He knew. Everything.

She flushed.

"I was just looking for you," he said stiffly.

Emma eyes turned to solid ice.

Kara must have stolen her journal, given it to him. They'd read it together. Laughed, probably.

He knew how much she loved him, and despised her. Kara knew, too.

Emma felt frantic, as if her soul lay exposed. She felt like an oyster without its shell.

"You're both contemptible," she exploded, throwing herself at him recklessly, yanking the journal out of his hand.

"I'm sorry," he whispered, holding on tightly.

When he let go and she fell backwards, Kara's triumphant eyes burned bright and golden.

As Mike guiltily watched Emma's frozen face, he seemed to turn to stone. Then Emma saw the rush of blood to his face.

"Quit staring at me!" she said. "Just go!"

"Maybe I will." His eyes darkened. Then he shook Kara loose and walked swiftly toward the barn.

Emma couldn't go down for supper that night. And when Kara came up to their room, she squeezed her eyes shut.

Kara made a lot of noise getting ready for bed. Finally she said, "Quit sulking. It's better he knows. I did you a favor."

Emma didn't reply.

"You want to know what else we did in the desert…which was way more fun than your old journal?" She laughed.

Emma wished herself dead.

Her twin shrugged. "He kissed me." She laughed again. "Yes. He kissed me, lots of times. He's good at it."

"I don't want to hear about it," Emma said dully.

"A man like him can't do without."

"Why are you telling me this?"

"So you'll know what he's like. He's not like your stupid journal. You don't really know him. I know him," Kara said.

When Kara wouldn't shut up or leave, Emma flung herself from the room. She dashed headlong down the stairs, slamming out of the house.

Where, oh, where could she hide?

Mike stepped out of the shadows, looking lean and tanned and so handsome, she knew just how crazy she'd been to hang onto her dreams. It never occurred to her that he might have been concerned about her, that he'd been waiting for her, that he was just as upset as she was.

When she raced past him, he fell in behind her.

"You okay, Emma?"

"Terrific. I love being made a fool of."

"I didn't know it was your journal. Not at first—"

"You read it, though."

"I couldn't stop myself," he said in an odd, strained voice.

"So why aren't you with Kara?"

He caught up to her. "Because maybe I want to be with you."

When he smiled, the night sounds died to nothing. He was so bronzed and handsome.

"What for?" she whispered. "You think I'm an idiot."

"You're wrong."

She wanted to throw herself into his arms, to bury her face against his broad chest, to cling to him forever. But she'd already made a huge fool of herself. He would only laugh at her.

"No! You were wrong...to do what you did."

"Forgive me, then."

"Never!" On a soft, shattered cry, Emma ran toward the apricot orchard.

She was surprised when he followed. He shouted her name, but she cringed, hiding in the shadows.

"Emma. Can't we at least talk...about what you wrote?"

"I wrote that for myself. Not for you. Certainly not for you and Kara to read together."

Emma spun and ran farther into the orchard.

His voice followed her. "For God's sake, Emma—" He waited. "Don't you want to know how I feel?"

She could see him through the trees. His face was hard and set in the fading light.

Her heart ached.

She knew how he felt. Kara had told her.

Emma drew a shuddering breath and kept still.

9

She had to know what he would have said!

The next morning, as the light in the eastern sky behind the barn began to burn, Emma came to a sudden, breathless standstill. It was a cool fall morning with a fresh breeze gusting across the desert. She shivered, wondering if he was still asleep.

Damn you, Mike Greywolf, for making me love you. For making me wish I hadn't been too hurt and stubborn to listen last night.

She'd fretted most of the night. So here she was, tired from tossing and turning, scared of her feelings. Summoning her courage she headed straight into the shadowy barn, up the stairs, only to stop and blush at his door. When she knocked, it gave to her slight touch, slanting into darkness.

Sunlight spilled across an empty bed with covers askew. His wooden floor creaked with every step. She picked up his pillow, pressed her face against it, and inhaled his clean fresh smell. Then she threw herself full length upon it and pulled his covers up to her chin. She remembered the other time she'd lain in his bed. Only, that time he'd been with her.

His art books were piled high by his bed. When she thumbed through a few, a set of drawings fell out.

Two faces, alike but different—one hers, the other Kara's. He had made her, Emma, beautiful. But to Emma somehow her own sweetness seemed dull compared to Kara's dark fascination.

Emma put them back and rose from the bed. All his things she touched—the little animal carvings, the rocks and bones and feathers he'd gathered from the desert. He had a gun, which surprised her. Some sort of pistol. She could see the bullets in the cylinder.

Last of all she went into the bathroom, where she found his shower and a damp towel on the floor. She picked it up and smothered her face in the deep cotton thickness. She wanted to take it home, keep it. No sooner had this desire taken shape in her heart, however, than the horses began to whinny and stomp below.

She stuffed the towel onto the towel rack and fled, running all the way to Auntie Z's, where she slipped into a kitchen that was redolent with the yeasty smell of rising bread.

Auntie Z's thick braid swung about her waist like a red rope as she bustled about in her kitchen. Cats swirled around her ankles, milled around their bowls, sprawled on the red tile floor, lazed on high stools. The counters were cluttered with old newspapers Z intended to read someday, dirty cups, saucers, clippings from catalogs, and goo-spattered recipes. Grassy herbs gone to seed stood in pots by the door, overdue to be taken outside and planted.

Emma began washing dishes. What she wanted to know was where Mike was. But naturally, she talked to her aunt about everything else—school, her prom, and her cats.

Emma finished the dishes, while Auntie Z took the bread from the oven and made sandwiches. She poured chili and beans into plastic containers and wrapped the last brownie in tinfoil. Her eyes twinkling with mischief, she then asked Emma to take lunch to the men. Emma usually didn't like to be anywhere near cowboys working cattle, but she had to see Mike.

How would she face him? What would she say?

By the time she got to Camp Bonito and its pens full of dust and bawling cattle, she was a bundle of nerves. Horse trailers and cattle trucks littered the pasture. The cowboys were causing so much confusion and noise, she didn't see Mike at first. Then the men got some of the cattle loaded, the dust cleared, and there he was.

Tall and dark, he stood on a catwalk above a rusty metal shoot. Caked with red dirt from the tip of his black head to his scuffed leather toes, he wore a denim work shirt and skintight jeans. His long legs were spread widely apart. It wasn't even noon yet, but the day had warmed. Already his Stetson and the armpits of his shirt were stained with sweat.

Standing above the fray, so he could personally inspect each animal up close, he was dehorning a cow with a handsaw to prevent a deformed horn from growing into her head. The cow was bawling louder than all the others, her tongue lolling, her eyes rolling backward. When her horn fell off, blood spurted out of its center, spraying Mike's shirt.

Another farmhand, Randy Lee, jammed a syringe into her.

"Easy," Mike said, patting the animal, "don't want to overstress her."

Then Frank opened the triangular gate, and Lucy, Mike's chocolate Lab, leapt at the cow as she stumbled dazedly out of the chute.

"Lucy!" Mike yelled. "Get back here."

Lucy ran up to him, hung her head for a moment, but quickly forgot her shame and barked excitedly when another cow was prodded into position. Again the cow bawled, lunging forward, kicking, when Randy Lee shoved his arm deep inside her to check if she was pregnant.

"*Whora!*" he jeered—*pocho,* border Spanish, for whore. The arm he pulled out was gummy all the way to his elbow. This cow would be rebred if she was young, turned into hamburger meat if she wasn't.

"Working cattle," they called it. Emma hated this part of ranching. No matter what Auntie Z said to the contrary, it seemed cruel, inhumane. But Mike and his men loved it.

Emma shuddered at the sight of pliers, the bloody saw, huge syringes and boxes of medicine that lay on the ground for inoculations.

Randy stuck his hand inside the next cow. "*Buena vaca.*" Good cow.

Two more good cows followed, one of them kicking so hard that Randy was slammed against the chute. "*Whora!*" Randy whooped after the next cow.

Emma climbed down from her aunt's truck. Then Mike's bright, insolent green gaze chanced on her, his eager smile sending her heart skittering.

Blushing, Emma scampered off to the shed to set the sandwiches and pot of chili and drinks on the long picnic table under an arbor tangled with grapevines. Her eyes were downcast, so she jumped when Mike's long shadow splashed her with darkness.

He stood silently outside the dangling leaves of the arbor in his dirty, blood-spattered shirt, his bold gaze inspecting her as carefully as he had his livestock.

"What?" she whispered, embarrassed. "*What?*"

He stared wordlessly. Where had the wild boy gone? The one she'd written so many pages about? When had this dark, dangerous man with the bold, black-lashed eyes, with the carved cheek and jaw, the strong chin taken his place?

"So, you've finally grown up," he said softly. "You've grown a woman's heart, too. You write all that hot sweet stuff in your book...about me. But I've been home three days. How come you haven't even said hi?"

"I—I didn't think you'd care."

His smile was frank and easy. "That's a damn fool thing to say."

"Hi," she murmured shyly.

A crooked grin appeared. "Why'd you run last night?"

With meticulous care she set out plates, flatware.

When he moved nearer, she felt a funny little dart of pleasure in her stomach.

"I missed you," he said, "while I was away. While I was here, too. I can't write it down...I mean, what I feel—what I feel for you...."

She wished she could look at him without feeling so afraid and fluttery that she was almost sick to her stomach.

"That's hard to believe...I mean, that you missed—"

He lifted one eyebrow quizzically, and her tension built. Flustered, she picked up the tea pitcher.

"I did write you," he prompted.

She set out glasses and began to pour. "I—I never got any letters," she blurted.

He laughed. Her hands shook so badly that tea went everywhere. "Careful," he whispered, his voice deep and husky. Taking the pitcher from her, his big brown hands poured, filling the rest of the glasses. "Not letters. Postcards."

"Postcards? Really?"

''Yeah,'' he whispered, setting the empty pitcher down, leaning closer. ''I told you about an award I won. A big one, for a cat I carved—sort of like the one I gave you in the kiva. I like what you wrote about the cat…about your taking it to bed with you.''

''Did you write Kara, too?''

He moved back. ''So that's it. What's she been telling you?''

''I didn't get your postcards.''

''Maybe she took 'em.'' His face darkened. ''I want to know something, Emma Shayne. All these years, you've filled a book up about me. But you hardly look at me or speak to me when we're together. Is that because you're ashamed of your feelings because…I'm half Navajo?''

She wanted to sob, ''Yes, yes,'' because it would cut him, and she'd be safe to go on loving him in secret. But the cruel retort stuck in her throat.

He touched her arm, which made her shake. He smiled as if he liked that response. It had been years since he'd kissed her. As experienced as he was, he probably knew his light fingers falling gently on her sleeve burned through her cotton blouse like a live current.

''What do you want from me?''

''The same thing you want from me,'' he said quietly.

''You could have anybody.''

''I've been waiting for you to grow up.''

''You've made love to lots and lots of women.''

His face grew dark, but he didn't deny it. ''What else did *she* say?''

When Emma whirled and raced to her truck, he stormed after her. She jerked at the door handle, but he grabbed her by the waist and spun her around. There was nowhere to run, with the truck behind her and his big body in front of her.

"It's time you stayed put and heard me out."

"I already know the truth."

"I'll give you truth." His big hand tightened around her waist, and he pulled her against him. He felt so hot and solid and powerful. "Maybe I can't write like you, but that doesn't mean I don't care—"

"And Kara?"

"You—you're everything. She's nothing to me." His voice was faintly rough. "You're everything." He swore under his breath. "I shouldn't have had to read it. I should've seen it on your face. I guess I was too scared to look."

His fierce gaze locked on her eyes, her lips, searing her from the inside out. "Yes. There've been women. I used them to try to forget you."

She thought of how terribly she'd missed him.

"I've had a secret benefactress—an unlimited source of funds...to study art...to travel. I imagine your mother shelled out big bucks to keep me away."

Emma said nothing. Unconsciously she registered how hot his skin was, how the odor of leather and dust clung to him.

"Sometimes I almost hated you...because I wanted to forget you so much. I never felt poor till your family took me in and showed me that no matter what I might do, I could never be good enough for you. They gave me everything, in a way, except the one thing I wanted." He ran a callused fingertip down the pale white curve of her neck, and sighed. "Your mother doesn't care that I've got a job, that my work is getting noticed—"

"Mike, that's wonderful. I'm glad—"

"I'm not white. I wasn't born rich."

She flung herself at him, burrowing her face in his soft, denim shirt. "Stop—"

He stood perfectly still. He didn't put his arms around her or draw her near. When she pulled herself together again, the blaze in his eyes both thrilled and terrified her.

"Emma," he whispered tenderly. "I can't hold you— or kiss you—here…in front of the men with the cattle bawling their heads off. I'm filthy and… But I'm leaving tomorrow. Going to New York."

"You are?" she whispered, stung by that news.

"To study under somebody important."

"Are you ever coming back?"

"It depends."

He stared at her from beneath the deep shadow of his hat brim.

"Come to me tonight," he murmured huskily.

She shook her head, but as his gaze lingered over her face, she felt as if her eyes glowed softly.

When he kept studying her, she turned pink, even as hushed embarrassed denial bubbled up like laughter in her throat.

He drew in his breath. "See ya."

Then he opened her truck door, and lifted her into the cab. With a wink, he asked, "Did you bring me a brownie?"

10

Her pulse humming, Emma stared at the silent barn beneath the brilliant moon.

Go home, her brain screamed.

She took a step backward. A mournful whimper came from the barn. After that piteous sound, a shrill bark pierced the air.

"Lucy?"

Limp tail wagging, her four-legged black shape slunk from the barn.

"Over here, girl—"

The black Lab trotted over and whined.

"What's wrong?" Emma extended her hand.

Lucy stayed where she was, just out of reach, big soft eyes pleading for help. When Emma hesitated, the dog whimpered and barked again.

Lucy shuddered and lowered her head in shame, attempting to hide the nose and gums and tongue jammed with porcupine quills.

She had to find Mike.

Quickly Emma dashed across the moonlit yard to the barn. With new courage she climbed the ladder and tapped gently on his door.

"Mike?"

Quick hollow steps. His door swung open. For a long moment he just stood there, his chest bare, green eyes glittering in the dark. He seem edgy, almost shy, which surprised her.

She wrinkled her nose. "You smell like a brewery."

He set the whiskey bottle on the floor. "I'd given up on you." His brilliant eyes moved over her. "You paid me a visit this morning while I was gone, I see."

She swallowed nervously.

"Your perfume was on my pillow…my towel."

Swaying unsteadily, he backed a safe distance away from her. The carved lines of his face were made harsher by the shadows. "Look, Emma. I've had a few. If you're smart, you'll go."

"Lucy's hurt. Downstairs. I think she tangled with a porcupine."

"I've told her and told her—"

He grabbed his shirt, buttoned it, rushed down and called Lucy. The dog came, whimpering softly, head sheepishly lowered. When Mike knelt, she wagged her tail.

"Sit," he ordered. Rummaging clumsily in a drawer, he pulled out a pair of pliers. Then squatting on his haunches, he grabbed one of the quills with the needle-nosed tool.

Lucy growled.

"Now, Lucy, you gotta sit still, girl. This thing's got a barb, and it's gonna hang when I pull on it. It's gonna hurt like hell, girl—"

Lucy yelped when he gave it a tug, and scurried off. "See what I told you? If you want me to pull 'em, you better come back and sit still."

Lucy whined, but she returned and sat as still as stone.

He grabbed another quill, yanked harder. It slid through the dog's flesh, hung on the barb, then pulled free. Lucy yelped and shook her head, dog tags jingling, tried to lick her nose, then yelped again.

"Lucy, you gotta let me do this."

With a weary shudder, Lucy laid her head obediently on his lap, her big brown eyes watching him.

"I told you not to mess with porcupines."

The dog somberly studied him. His pliers grabbed another quill, plucked it. Then another. Lucy didn't flinch. It amazed Emma that the dog trusted him enough to endure the ordeal, sitting still, her head on his knee, her mournful eyes glued to his face. The animal didn't utter another yelp until Mike had removed every quill.

"There you go!" He stroked Lucy and then turned to Emma. "I'm glad you told me about her," he said. "She'd have been worse off in the morning. I gotta find some steroid salve so her nose won't itch."

After Lucy's nose was gooey with medicine, he turned back to Emma. "You want to go for a walk or something?"

She hesitated. "I—I'd better go home."

"Suit yourself." He stood up, his mood now seeming more bitter than noble.

"Maybe I shouldn't have come."

"I'm not your kind, am I?" he whispered. "I'm not safe enough? White enough?"

"That's not it."

"Then what is?"

His eyes held hers. When she didn't answer, he turned and headed toward the barn.

She stared after him, not knowing what to say or do, as his long strides rapidly carried him away. Tomorrow he was going to New York. She thought of those other women. He was never coming back.

When he vanished into the barn, a stillness descended upon her. She felt lost in a huge dark world.

And then it just happened.

Heart over mind.

She was running, crying his name, her entire being in the husky sound.

He stopped, his tension uncoiling. Then he was loping from the barn toward her. When she threw herself into his arms, he caught her, lifted her, swung her around and around beneath the stars. Then his mouth came down hard on hers. Not like before, when she'd been a girl in that field with the butterflies, when he'd given her the little bird carving. He'd been so gentle that day when he'd first opened her up to love.

This was different. Utterly and completely and wonderfully different.

Pulled flat against the solid wall of his muscular chest, she thought of Kara, of those other women, of her mother's warnings. She was probably throwing her whole life away. But the carefully guarded secrets of her heart had been revealed. He knew her weakness for him, and she couldn't stop herself.

"Do you want to go upstairs?" he asked.

No.

She let out a deep sigh. Then her arms slid around his neck, and her mouth opened. At first his mouth merely skimmed hers, but even that made her fingers curl tighter. Then, he tilted her head back, and his lips explored hers thoroughly. Neither of them was prepared for what a soul-jolting experience a single kiss could be.

Afterward they were both silent as the enormity of what they were about to do sank into their consciousness.

Taking her hand, he slowly led her upstairs. His eyes blazed as he bolted the door. Then his arms wrapped her so tightly that she felt the ridge of every hard muscle through her clothes. He pushed her down on the bed, his mouth all over her, low rumbles of arousal purring from his throat.

Suddenly she was scared. What if he'd read her journal and only saw her as a conquest?

Everything was happening too fast. But she wanted him. Whatever else was false, that was true. From that first moment in the kiva, tonight had been destined.

She knew nothing of men, nothing of what her presence in Mike's bedroom did to him. He didn't bother to undress her or himself. His flushed face seemed to loom over her, his eyes dark and wild. When he moved closer, Emma squeezed her eyes shut and tried to turn her head away. But his mouth found hers, and he kissed her as if he wanted to draw her entire essence into himself.

His kisses went on and on and were terrifyingly ardent to a girl of so little experience. But she was too unsure to protest, too afraid of displeasing him to let him know how uncertain his forceful eagerness made her feel. She wanted so much to compete with all those other sexier women. So she lay there and kissed him back, the thrilling need she had felt earlier giving way to fear.

He pushed her onto the mattress, his body pressing down onto hers, his mouth so hard that she grew increasingly terrified. And still she let him go on. The harder his hands and arms gripped her, the harder she gripped him, thinking that was what was expected. He was panting above her, his eyes wild, when he straddled her and unzipped his jeans. She froze, and still she didn't stop him or slow him.

Not bothering to undress, she heard the *swish* of fabric

as he hiked her skirt to her waist and peeled her panties
down. When his hand slid between her legs, instead of
desire, she felt a burning shame to be touched there. But
she let him. She let him do everything, anything. Only
when she felt her soft, wet, untutored tissue parting as his
manhood slid inside, only when the bedsprings began to
squeak as he rocked back and forth, only when she felt
the sudden tearing pain, did she scream.

But his mouth fused to hers as tightly as they were
joined elsewhere, muting her cries as he drove deeply.
Pain shattered her, and she writhed to free herself. But
her every movement only excited him more. He began to
rock in earnest, and little by little the agony dulled. As
he thrust, he caressed her cheek and throat, her plump
breasts, moaning her name as if she were infinitely precious.

"Emma. Emma. Emma."

Her breath came in fitful sobs. More than anything, she
wanted to learn, to please him.

Then, slowly, her pain gave way to the warm tinglings
of pleasure. She gasped in awe and kissed his cheek. And
her timid response sent him over some edge. For he stiffened too soon, slumped forward, into her, drawing her
closer, closer in a final, savage thrust. He ground his hard
mouth against her lips, then against her throat, holding
her tightly, so tightly, his body joined to hers. Then his
wide shoulders shook, and she knew it was over. He held
her against his long body and kissed her sweetly.

"Did I hurt you?" he whispered.

"No."

Then he saw the blood.

"Oh, God, I—I got carried away. I'm sorry." He
stroked her hair. "Next time, next time, I swear it will be
better."

Next time.

She lay in the dark, staring up at the ceiling, savoring his promise, dreading it a little, but wondering about everything.

She was a woman now.

Mike Greywolf's woman.

How many others had there been before her? What made a man value one woman more than another?

"Emma?"

"Hmm."

"Don't write about this, okay?"

"As if I could."

"This is our secret…for now. Just ours. You're too precious, infinitely too precious to share." Then he said, "Don't be sorry."

But she felt let down, and he could tell.

Neither knew what to say. Finally, he gathered her close, his open eyes gazing at her profile. They lay like that for what seemed an unending time, while her heart thumped painfully. When at last he fell asleep, she lay in the dark, filled with even more doubt.

Should she have let him take her, let him hurt her, let him do those wild, terrible, wonderful things that made her blush to think about? At the thought of her mother, fresh shame swamped her.

She had to get away, put this reckless, wanton act in perspective. He was right about one thing. Nobody must know.

When Mike came awake, his first compulsion was to touch her. His large hand groped.

Emma wasn't there.

That made him remember how she'd stared back at him

afterward, with huge fearful eyes that earlier had been as
bright and warm as candleglow.

She was afraid of him now.

She'd been a virgin. He sat up, combed his fingers
through his long black hair. Oh, God. Had he hurt her?
He had. He knew he had.

He'd never wanted anybody so damn bad. Only her.
Her. Always her. Ever since the hogan, when his vision
of her had instilled new life.

God. Had he now lost her?

All the time he'd tended Lucy, he'd felt on tenterhooks,
wondering if she'd stay with him afterward.

Dear God. He hadn't meant to take her to bed. Just to
kiss her, hold her.

All he wanted was one more chance.

No sooner had that thought formed than his door
creaked, and she was there, her red hair glinting around
her pale face.

"I'm sorry," he whispered in a broken voice.

She laughed and then ran to him, tearing her clothes
off in the dark. Soundlessly she pulled back the sheets
and slipped into bed.

She was warm, perfumed, her mouth eager. She was
bolder, too. She put her hands all over him and he instantly got hard. Her eyes were mesmerizingly dark with
desire. She climbed on top of him and guided him inside.

Emma. Emma. Oh, God, Emma.

With a shudder, he plunged, wild with joy because he
had thought he'd lost her forever.

Beneath them the horses neighed. He imagined a man's
voice, but he ignored the uneasiness that prickled down
his spine. He was too caught up in Emma's miraculous
return, too determined not to disappoint her this time.

And then the woman on top of him began to laugh with

contempt and triumph, and even before she told him who she was, he knew.

"I'm Kara," she said, wrapping him tightly with her arms and legs, climaxing as he fought to break free.

He felt violated. Raped.

He swore, pushed at her, clawed to get free.

But she clung tightly and was still laughing when the door creaked open, and Emma tiptoed inside.

He threw Kara off. Frozen, Emma stared at him through a sheen of tears.

Emma.

He'd never felt so helpless or so ashamed in his whole life.

He'd been tricked, terribly wronged, and yet he hated himself.

He stood up. Sheets with Emma's blood spilled to the floor.

"Emma," he pleaded.

With a tortured moan, Emma fell against the door.

He wanted to throw himself at her feet, kiss them, beg her forgiveness. But it was no use—she wouldn't believe him.

"I love you," he mouthed hopelessly.

But she was already stumbling out of the room.

Stall doors banged below. The horses screamed in panic.

But what tore out his heart was Emma's single cry.

By the time he reached her, the horses were gone. Emma lay in a crumpled heap beside Rio's stall door, a bloody gash across her temple. Her face was waxen, her body limp, blood all over the concrete.

Awkwardly he gathered her in his arms and cradled her to his chest.

Kara came down.

"Go get your mother!"

"Do you want a blanket?" Kara asked, her voice hideously calm.

Mike realized he was naked. He nodded vaguely. "But hurry."

Kara brought down a Navajo blanket. After draping him in its fluid folds, she glided out the door.

It seemed an eternity before Frances came, even longer before the ambulance arrived.

And because he was terrified for Emma's life and of what he didn't see in her dazed, blank eyes, he was in hell.

"Give her to me and go," Frances demanded.

"Emma!" he whispered. "I didn't know. I didn't know."

"She's my daughter, damn you!"

With his strong, brown hands he pressed Emma's bright head against his hard chest, refusing to release her till the ambulance came.

"Emma, my God. It was dark. I wanted you so much. I thought she was you."

Her long lashes flickered open. Her eyes were glazed with pain and disbelief.

As soon as the ambulance was gone, Frances said, "I don't want you here, Mike Greywolf, when I get back from the hospital. And don't ever return."

Emma had no sense of time after Mike let her go. She didn't care if she lived or died. Vaguely, she knew she was in ICU with IV needles taped to her hands. Vaguely, she sensed the presence of nurses in scrub suits as they came and went.

Always her mother was there, standing guard, determined that Mike Greywolf would never bother her again.

Although deeply disturbed by what had happened, Stuart rarely came around.

Frances told her that Kara had run away to Hollywood, that Mike Greywolf had gone home to his people. Every time her mother said his name, she became stern and hate-filled. Once though, when she was in a strange mood, she confessed that Emma wasn't the first Shayne woman to fall for the wrong man.

Emma began to doubt everything she'd felt and everything Mike had said he felt. Her mother said what had happened proved she was right, and her negative harpings had a withering effect on Emma. Maybe her mother *was* right. Maybe the best thing was to forget him. To do that, though, she would have to leave New Mexico. And she didn't know how to tell her mother that.

When she was better, Emma began to write in her journal again. Only then did the pain flow from her heart, only then could she imagine a new life far away, without Mike.

When she told her mother she had to go, Frances fought the idea fiercely.

"You're too young. You'll just get into more trouble."

"Maybe so."

"You need to finish your education."

"I can do that anywhere." *But if I stay here, all I'll do is think of Mike Greywolf.*

It was Z who figured out the perfect place for the listless Emma to recuperate. Z had a younger friend, Katherine, a doctor, who ran a clinic for poor children in Isla Mujeres, Mexico. Z convinced Frances that helping others would be the best way for Emma to help herself.

Yet Frances was still reluctant to let her go. She blamed Z for everything. "It's your fault she's obsessed with that savage."

"It'll be yours if she doesn't get over him. She won't get better staring out that window, waiting for him to come back."

"She'll stop."

"You didn't. You're still waiting for Court."

"Don't be ridiculous."

Frances went to the window where Emma often stood. In her mind's eye she saw a man with golden hair and that easy smile that had thrilled her and too many other women. Court Shayne. How wildly, how foolishly she'd loved him. She thought of all the wasted years.

Her life.

"Sooner or later Greywolf will return," Z said. "How will you keep him away from her when he does?"

Frances didn't answer. Later, though, she marched upstairs and wrote to Katherine to see if she needed any help in her clinic. And not long afterward, she helped Emma pack her bags.

Part II
THE PRESENT

"Two stars keep not their motion in one sphere."
—William Shakespeare
Henry IV, Part I,
V, iv, 65

11

Mike Greywolf's bedroom stank of sex, lilacs and tequila.

A brand-new sun peeped over blue mountains and beamed fire through a pair of red bikini panties that dangled from his bedpost like an ill-gotten trophy.

He rubbed his eyes and winced from the brightness without knowing why. He hadn't expected New Mexico to feel so alien even after so many years. He was beginning to think he'd never settle in.

Jumbled flashes in his brain. Twin figures, so alike he could not tell one from the other, swung back and forth in his imagination. Silent ghosts, their long red hair swept the earth, their eyes shining as brightly as jet. He shook his head to erase the vision. But the ghosts lingered.

He'd come back a few months ago, in the dead of winter—to be alone. He didn't want to feel connected to them. He hated remembering them, hated the Anasazi ruins in the cliffs where they'd found him. Hated remembering feeling poor, feeling less than them. Most of all he hated being caught between them. That final scandal when they'd been older had damn near destroyed him.

He had come back and had bought *La Golindrina* to be alone. To find peace.

But this wild place—for Z had let the ranch go wild, even though it was now surrounded with ritzy development—bound him to the past, bound him to the world-famous twins. To Kara, the movie star and to Emma, the author. Everything that had happened between them here seemed to shade his future. New Mexico, he now realized, was the last place he should've chosen.

Navajos believe cooperation and consideration between kinsmen to be more important than any one man's needs. Upon his return, his father's people came from near and far to be with him.

First, the maddening Mabel Blackgoat of his grandmother's clan, who'd sold him to the Shaynes, had appeared. Mabel's wrinkled face was as dark as mahogany, her hair the color and texture of steel wool. Her cherubic smile belied a greedy nature. Although she scarcely came up to Mike's chest, she possessed a stubborn will and the boundless zeal of ten chiefs on the warpath.

Somehow, he still wasn't sure how, she had forced him to rebuild a ruined hogan for her. Then she'd set up her loom inside and had begun to weave one of her famous prophecy blankets. She said it was about him, the famous Navajo sculptor, finding his true wife, and about Lilly, his daughter, finding her true mother.

"Lilly doesn't need her mother," Mike had proclaimed fiercely. "And I damn well don't need another wife. Weave your own story—not mine."

"I had a vision."

"To hell with your infernal visions. That last one nearly killed me."

"Lilly's fourteen. She must have a mother—to teach her how to be a woman. She needs her father, too."

"She's got me."

"What's left of you...which isn't much." Mabel's

deep-set eyes narrowed to dark slivers of charred wood. "No, I must teach her the Navajo way—to live the good life, to live in beauty, to respect all things…especially her relatives."

"That path doesn't work in today's world."

"How would you know? You sold out to the money and fame gods."

"You do not weave your rugs for nothing."

"One must eat."

The harder he objected, the more quickly Mabel entrenched herself. Now she was a constant irritant, seeming to be everywhere in her layered skirts, her velvet blouses. She watched him slyly—watched Lilly, too. And always, always, her nimble brown fingers wove.

Her gloomy stares made him nervous, as did the colorful designs of her loom, but he couldn't send her away. Worse, no sooner had Mabel settled herself in than she got lonely and had to have friends join her. It wasn't long before more old spies from his grandmother's clan—clad in similar velvet blouses, their hair pulled back in buns and wound with yarn, laden with heavy bundles and looms—bustled about everywhere.

"I need help with the weaving," Mabel explained when he asked when they were leaving. "This tapestry is about twins. One man and two women go to the mountains. Only one woman returns. When I am done, my rug will be your wedding gift."

"I'm not getting married."

"You are. Soon. That's why I need help to hurry the weaving along."

"We honor you," the women said in unison. He hated their dark stares, as they watched and judged him. But what could he do? These women were esteemed weavers, although not so highly esteemed as his grandmother had been.

"I'm not getting married," he repeated.

Next, the infamous Nigel Galbraith had roared up the steep red hill in a truck laden with dusty archaeological tools and maps and a permit to dig a nearby site. He'd flung himself out of the truck and knocked down the door of an abandoned cabin as if he owned the place. Mike had been away because Lilly, ever the compulsive shopper, had seen a down-filled vest on sale in Santa Fe she had to have.

When Galbraith had stormed out of that cabin, yelling, "Anybody live here?" Mabel pounced, offering to rent it. He'd opened her palm and slapped a thick wad of cash in her fist.

She'd smiled.

By the time Mike got home, Galbraith's stuff was everywhere, stacked inside the cabin, spilling out the doorway. Bart, Frances Shayne's prized Arabian, was tied to a post that held up the roof of the cabin's sagging porch.

Mike went up to the horse. "You gonna tell me where your high-and-mighty mistress is?"

Bart shook his head and snorted.

When Mike called out, Frances clanged something inside the cabin, so he stomped up to the door. Sure enough, she was inside, a lace handkerchief pressed delicately to her skinny nose as she picked at Galbraith's shovels and picks, and boxes piled high with bone shards.

From the doorway Mike tilted his black Stetson. "Excuse me?"

Frances, slimmer than ever, whirled. She was holding a dusty, ill-shaped ball, turning it around and around in the shadows. She frowned in disgust.

"I should've guessed. Cut marks from a stone tool.

Fractures to the cranial vault.'' She looked up, her sharp, blue eyes narrowing at the sight of Mike's huge, broad-shouldered frame. ''I wouldn't have believed even *you* would stoop to rent my cabin to a villain like Galbraith.''

''*My* cabin now.''

Her unblinking gaze regarded him with icy contempt.

''Why'd you have to come back?''

''Stay out of my way, and I'll stay out of yours.''

''Not so easy…when you do something this stupid. I have investors, seeking to buy part of my ranch. Tell Galbraith to leave.''

''You can't tell me what to do.''

That made her angry. Lifting her head, she strode past him, jamming the dusty bowl she'd been holding into his hands. ''Then…enjoy. He's your tenant.''

Grabbing Bart's reins, she swung herself into the saddle. For a lengthy moment, she cast a critical eye over his property.

''Z let things go.''

Frances frowned at the dirty walls of his ranch house. His gardens were wild. Dozens of statues lay on their sides in dust and withering weeds.

''Why don't you tear those old school buildings down?''

''Lilly and her friends roller-skate in the gym.''

''And the ruined school?''

''I'm going to use it for parties and exhibitions.'' Which was why he'd built the amphitheater with its pink columns supporting nothing but vast sky.

She stared at the flat on his eighteen-wheeler.

''I was going to change the tire. But I don't need to haul granite anytime soon.''

''Never mind,'' she said. ''You haven't done a damn thing to improve the place. I don't expect you will.''

All of a sudden he realized he was holding crumbling bone. Whatever he might have said died in a gurgle-like sound in his throat. Superstitious to the extreme about death, Mike stumbled outside, off the porch, air exploding from his lungs. Frances pressed her heels into Bart's flanks and took off.

The bowl-shaped object was a human skull. A dozen more were heaped atop Galbraith's boxes. *Mabel.* He knew Mabel had been up to more of her mischief.

When he found her, she was about to catch a bus to go trading. When he began to rant, she sat at her loom so as not to waste time. It was most distracting the way Mabel's nimble fingers flew, slamming down on the wool yarn, the thumping drowning out his lecture. The louder he ranted, the louder she banged away. When he was done talking, her brown hands stilled. The hogan, with its Pendleton blankets and sheepskin bedding rolled against the wall, was suddenly mercifully silent. After all, now she wanted to talk.

"How can I feed so many mouths with no income?"

"You should have thought of that before."

"I'm thinking of it now. You have no use for the cabin. Nigel has need of it. I have need of his money."

"He dishonors the dead. He can't stay here."

"He was in your vision."

"*Your* vision."

"It would be a dishonor to go back on my word."

"You can't rent my cabin to him!"

"Tell him so, then."

"I will."

But somehow Galbraith wasn't ever around when Mike got up the nerve to evict him. Then the local press began blasting Galbraith's unpopular theories about the Anasazi being cannibals and Mike's neighbors started harassing

Mike for renting to the scoundrel. Mike had peculiar sympathies for any underdog. So, Galbraith stayed.

If Mabel and Nigel made him tense, the spring winds made him more so. The dust storms were worse than usual. Mike had been spending so much time inside, he'd gotten too crazy to work.

Not that he could blame his artist's block entirely on the wind or Mabel or Nigel. He'd even had problems back in New York. His block had simply worsened here. The delivery of the bronzes hadn't helped. If not-sculpting made him edgy, the bronzes of the twins made him edgier.

On a sleepy groan, Mike rolled over. Yesterday afternoon, Sara, his ex, had shown up, probably to see how poorly he and Lilly were faring without her.

A few glances at the Navajo women around Mabel's hogan, at his messy house, at Lilly's tangled, waist-length hair, her six silver earrings, her Birkenstock sandals, and her morbid, black toe-polish had told Sara too much.

"I hadn't expected this place to be so wild. It needs a woman's hand."

"Mine will have to do."

"I read about Galbraith living here. Who are all these old women? You said you wanted...space."

"Believe me, Mabel and her spies weren't my idea."

"You and Lilly have been here four months. How come all these boxes—"

"Lilly likes to shop for new stuff."

"How many times have I told you, you can't let a fourteen-year-old dictate to you?"

"Have you told Lilly?"

"Lilly—" Sara called, slipping smugly into her old role. When Lilly walked up with a frown, Sara said, "You simply must unpack one box a day—"

Lilly's mouth twisted sullenly. "We were going shopping before you—"

"You won't need to shop, if you—"

"You divorced Daddy, am I right?" Lilly's voice held a motherly tone, pleasant yet firm.

"Lilly—" Mike said warningly.

Lilly smiled. "I only meant that she and I can be real friends now that you're the disciplinarian, Daddy."

"Some disciplinarian," Sara said.

Lilly smiled.

"What's with that nightgown of a dress? And all those rings in her ears?" Sara asked later.

"There's a fringe element in Santa Fe. I'm afraid Z isn't the best influence."

As soon as Lilly had floated off in her gown to sulk, or to meditate on cosmic love, or give her funeral nails a second coat of ebony varnish, or visit Mabel, or do whatever the hell she did these days other than help him, Sara had stuck her tongue in Mike's mouth and attacked him like a love-starved lioness. Not that he'd fought very hard to fend her off.

No, he'd been too lonely since their divorce. His immense male ego had needed her special brand of flattery. He'd laughed when Sara had pulled a scratchy, handwoven rug out of a box.

How many times had she made him do it? Once on the valuable rug, with the rough wool fibers burning into his back as she straddled him. Then clumsily on the staircase, which hadn't been one damn bit more comfortable. Then outside beneath the cottonwoods in the moonlight near Lilly's tree swing. His eyes had been wide-open, scanning the silvery darkness for any sign that Lilly or Mabel or that bone-digger might be hiding behind a juniper, snooping.

Their lovemaking had had the sad, panicky fierceness of denial in it. Their marriage was dead. No amount of sexual fireworks could reignite it—at least as far as Mike was concerned. Which was good. He wanted to be alone.

Still, this morning he was dog-tired.

And spiritually depleted.

As he hadn't been after making love to...

Emma—

Damn it.

Forget her. She's gone. Forever.

So was Kara.

Once so inseparable, the twins were now estranged.

Because of him, everybody said.

Whatever. The connection—between the three of them—was broken.

Emma, the writer. Kara, the movie star. Mike, the sculptor.

Damn the twins to hell. Time and again they'd used him for their own devious purposes. They'd both been after him when they'd been kids—Emma, sweetly; Kara, more brazenly. But always, he'd been a pawn in their jealous little game.

As adults, the stakes had gone up. The twins hadn't known how to be individuals; they'd had to share everything, even men—him.

He'd never forget that night in the barn.

Later, he'd tried to see Emma, but her family wouldn't let him. When she'd gotten better, she'd left for Mexico to heal, to write. Thinking Emma was through with him forever, he'd gone home to his own people.

Nine months later he'd seen a picture in a celebrity magazine of Kara leaving a Hollywood hospital with a baby girl. The gossip was that she'd been having an affair with a leading male star, a married man. No matter how passionately he denied paternity, the rumormongers said it was his. His wife left him. She didn't come back till blood tests proved he wasn't the father. That's when Mike had flown to L.A. and claimed his daughter.

Kara had been glad to get rid of Lilly. Mike had sworn to forget the twins and pursue his career. By the time Lilly was seven, he was an emerging sculptor. He'd returned to Santa Fe to do his first important show. He'd been browsing an art show on the town plaza when, out of nowhere, Emma had appeared.

The square had felt magical that afternoon—or maybe he'd just felt newly alive when he saw Emma. The trees were lime green; the light, clear and pure, had dazzled him—or maybe Emma had been the dazzler.

Emma had glowed as she'd walked through that bright shower of flickering gold and purple shadow. Her eyes fastened on Lilly, who was watching a green-haired skateboarder, Emma had breezed past the finest art and the tackiest schlock without so much as a glance. Kneeling, she'd touched the child's red curls.

"Who are you?" Lilly had asked as the teenager jumped a curb and skated out of sight.

Emma had sunk to the ground, tears streaming down her face.

"Nobody. Nobody important."

Mike had taken Emma's hands, lifted her. The trees had seemed to whirl as he and Emma had stared into one another's eyes. Then the world had stopped spinning. The Bermuda-shorted tourists snapping pictures, the traffic, all the artists dashing about on the lawn, the Native Americans selling their exquisite handmade jewelry beneath the portal in front of the Governor's Palace—everything had stilled and gone quiet.

After her long absence, Emma had unlocked something

inside him, and he'd been overpowered by his feelings for her.

"I saw you with Lilly." he said.

"Lilly," she repeated softly.

A long shadow swept the plaza. Then a limo stopped, and Kara stepped out of the darkness. One glance from Kara sent Emma running for cover. He started after her, but Kara stopped him. She was all over him, and totally indifferent to Lilly.

"So why are you two in town?" he'd asked.

"Won't Emma tell?"

He waited.

"Emma wrote a book, *Betrayal*. I optioned it so I could star in the film. I thought it would be fun to do the premiere here. I'll get you and Lilly tickets."

"I'm pretty busy with my show."

"Our film's about twins who share everything...till they fall in love with the same man. It has a twist. The married sister dies. The sweeter sister impersonates her. Only...the husband kills himself. See, he thinks the sweet single twin whom he secretly loves was the one who died." Kara's eyes turned gold.

Later, Sando told him that Emma had come to his show. That she'd wandered through the rooms, her eyes streaming with tears, as she'd beheld the busts of his daughter.

He'd tried to call her. When he couldn't reach her, he'd called Kara and said he wanted tickets, after all. At the premiere he'd watched Emma. She'd watched him...and Lilly. Afterwards, when he tried to talk to her, the crush of too many people prevented any privacy. Kara had invited him to a party at her hotel suite. He'd gone because she'd sworn Emma was the guest of honor. Only, Emma hadn't been there. When he'd demanded answers about Lilly, she'd led him into her bedroom. Their quarrel had

escalated into a seduction scene that had degraded both
of them and destroyed his last hope of ever winning
Emma's love. He would never forgive himself for that
night. He'd said such terrible things to Kara afterward that
she'd cried. And Kara never cried. But no one had hated
him more than he'd hated himself.

The premiere had gotten raves. When neither Emma
nor Kara appeared at their scheduled interviews the next
morning, the press went crazy. So did Frances. The rumors were ugly. Kara's party guests remembered how
livid he'd been with Kara at the hotel. Frances wanted to
know if he'd killed her.

She sent people to the police who accused him of murder. Fortunately for him, both twins returned a few weeks
later, just as things were getting ugly.

In the aftermath, Kara had become the movie star of
the decade. Reclusive Emma shot to the top of the best-
seller lists. He'd hadn't done so badly himself—if one
wanted the reputation of being a big, bad, sexy sculptor.

Fame had a black edge. Sure, he sold all over the world.
But fame and fortune had created more problems than
they'd solved. He'd felt invaded, devoured.

Navajo warrior. Perpetual outcast in the white man's
world. In the Navajo world, as well. His people were poor
on the rez. He was rich, famous. His fame was partly why
they didn't trust him.

Too late, he learned that the love of strangers could
strip you of your humanity, your privacy; that fame cre-
ates a false image. The mythical being everybody loved
wasn't Mike Greywolf. Fame wasn't love. All it did was
make him feel colder and lonelier.

The world couldn't give him what he'd been looking
for. His dreams had gone as dead and cold as ashes.

* * *

Usually he was up with the morning star.

For a rancher with a drop of Navajo blood, mornings are the most beautiful, the most magical times in New Mexico. For at that hour, when the wind dies, the sleepy desert glows fuchsia and gold and purple under an opalescent sky brushed with lavenders, reds and golds. The bald mountains, so dark and forbidding at night, become a radiant mauve.

Such mornings could spell hell for him when he slept in the way he had today. At this particular hour his defenses were down, and he dreamed.

The wind had howled last night. Navajos believed ghosts rode winds like that and cried. Maybe that was why he'd dreamed again. White men would say it was only the wind he'd heard and not the cries of his father and his uncle and his grandparents. Navajos believed dreams told truths.

His dream always began after the random, racist murders—the ones that had made him an outcast in two worlds and started the slow, incessant festering in his soul. That festering had ignited into the ambition that had driven him to the top, but left him hollow.

Awake, he was too Navajo to think of the dead.

In his dream, he was freer, darker.

He was always fifteen years old and lost and alone.

Orphaned, Navajo—and thus, even more terrified, on some primal level, of death and ghosts than a white, he'd stumbled blindly away from his family's blood-soaked hogan. The killers had been boys; their parents, friends of the mighty Shaynes. Their motive hadn't been robbery, but blind, racial hatred. Since those murders Mike had felt half-dead himself, alone. Always alone.

Mike, the boy, had sat outside in the dirt for a while

till the coyotes had begun to howl from the rim of the mesa. Mike had jumped up, shaken to the core.

They were ghosts, crying for vengeance.

Mike's nightmare skipped over the long, arduous miles.

Always he was lying in that ancient, Anasazi kiva where he'd found shelter from the wind that icy night.

Slipping in and out of consciousness, his leg broken, he heard chirping voices high above him. Believing those cries to be the chants of his murdered family, he'd opened his eyes and been blinded by flares bobbing wildly over dark walls painted with giant panthers.

Then the lights went out. In total blackness, he heard the witches' laughter and smothered whispers.

"Don't tell Mother—"

Ghosts? *Chindi?*

No. Two little girls with hair like fire.

Always the pretty face in the deeper shadows blurred and Emma's face brightened. Her sweet smile, the warmth in her long-lashed brown eyes, charmed him in his dream.

Kara had called him bad names, so he had concentrated on the other girl.

Emma.

Somehow she'd claimed him that night.

Emma. The name had come to mean sweetness and passion. Only later had it signified betrayal and rejection.

He had not known then that for all her outward sweetness, Emma could be as stubborn and willful as her theatrical sister. Nor had he known how deeply Emma, who was like her aunt Czarina in that respect, felt the pain of any lost and abandoned creature—even a Navajo.

Once Emma had told him she would never leave him.

But she had.

Just like his white mother had.

The dreams would stop.

He saw a bronze statue of a girl with closed eyes and tears streaming down her gleaming cheeks.

He saw Emma touching Lilly in the plaza.

In a spasm, half awake, still asleep, he grabbed his pillow, burying his head in its softness, and, maybe because it smelled of lilacs, he clenched it tightly. Then he moaned Emma's name.

"Emma. Oh, God, Emma— Come back to me."

Sara leapt up. "You savage! You—"

Sara's frizzy red hair was a blur. Her vengeful, pain-glazed eyes drilled him.

Poor Sara. He'd hurt her—again,

For what? He imagined Emma as he'd first seen her in that vision. The hateful memory of her incandescent smile triggered an unwanted, raw ache.

It was the damn delivery of the statues of the twins yesterday.

Angrily Sara tossed off the sheets. "I thought this time—maybe this once—we could be together.... But no, you want Emma! Always, always Emma! Damn you, Mike!"

Just as angrily, he grabbed Sara.

12

"Let me go, you bastard!"

"Sara, baby…"

"How could you do that—scream Emma's name—when you're in bed with me?"

"Sorry." He paused. "How come you came to visit me?"

Her eyes shuttered, Sara slid away from him.

Instinctively he caught her wrists again when she tried to get up out of his bed, rolling his powerful, muscled body on top of her slim frame. Why *had* she come? What did she really want? Guiltily he remembered the trucks yesterday. If she'd come then, seen the statues, there would've been hell to pay.

"I said I was sorry," he whispered huskily. "I meant it. I—I hate her. You know that."

Sara had been good to him, true to him, at least in her way. They'd been married for more than six years.

"No. I don't know that. Maybe it's time you quit kidding us both. She was always there between us, wasn't she?"

"No," he lied.

"Even during the good times."

"Not true."

"You locked yourself in your studio, for days... months."

"I was trying to make a name for myself."

"That faraway look you used to get in your eyes made me sick. Maybe it's time you dealt with the twins. For Lilly's sake. She misses her mother."

"Well, there's not a damn thing I can do about that."

"I called you five times this week. Why didn't you call back?"

He frowned. *Lilly.* She hadn't told him Sara called.

Mike squinted against the lavender dawn light that lit his swarthy features. He had banded his long, black hair Navajo-style with strips of colored silk.

"I was busy," he hedged.

Sara saw.

"So, Lilly's up to her old tricks. And you're protecting her." Sara sighed. She lifted his inky braid. "Don't scowl. I didn't mean to make you feel guilty about Emma...or Lilly. Did I ever tell you Mother calls you The Barbarian?" Sara spoke absently. It was her way of saying good-bye.

He nodded.

"It's 'cause you stare so intently, like some wild animal. You're so deliberate. You see inside people. You absorb them. You get too close."

"It's a gift. It's gotten me into a hell of a lot of trouble." With white men over white women. With women, too, especially the twins. Kara had seen something in the way he looked at her that wasn't there. And with their mother. It was partly why everybody had believed he'd killed them.

"You always hold yourself back, Mike. What did I ever mean to you, really? You never said."

"You and your journalist friends said and wrote enough words for both of us."

"And you hid behind them."

"I am what I am."

"Big hunky sculptor."

"Blocked sculptor—" He didn't admit that to just anyone.

"Macho rancher. A guy who only socializes to sell Mike Greywolf, hot-shot sculptor. You don't share your real self, ever, not even with your wife."

"You divorced *me*, remember?"

"You were never there, Mike." She tried to smile, but her eyes glimmered with pain.

"Maybe you should have married an intellectual—a popular, sophisticated guy who likes to party."

Her voice hardened. "Did you marry me for my money—to sell yourself to collectors...to museums?"

"Why does it always come back to your money?"

"Because everybody constantly throws that up at me. Because you never—"

"Feel what you feel. Believe what you believe—not what they tell you. You're the one who's into fame and money. You and your fancy friends. Not me."

"You're the one who's famous."

Again he saw that hard glimmer in her eyes. "Fame's not so great. Mostly people think you're something you're not, something you don't even want to be. And you feel like a fraud."

She flushed. "I want to know if you deliberately used me to get where you are."

"Everybody uses everybody." He pulled her into his arms and buried his lips in tufts of wiry red hair. "You used me. When you didn't get what you wanted, you divorced me.'' He pressed her close. ''I'm going to miss you, Sara. Whatever else we weren't, let's be friends.''

''You loved her, though. Not me. You came back here—to her.''

''No. To be alone. To allow Lilly to know her family. You thrilled to the frenzied pace of white men's cities. You sparkled at my museum exhibitions and sold-out gallery shows. You couldn't stand my drive to sculpt—the long, arduous hours I had to spend alone.''

''You shut me out.''

I was trying to shut out the ghosts. Aloud, he said, ''I have this half-wild, motherless daughter who was getting lost in our glitzy life-style. There was so much in New York I didn't give a damn about. I felt like a beast in your cage. It was getting harder and harder to get inside myself and create.'' *Harder to hide.*

''I made you.''

''Maybe you think so. You damn sure tried.'' He smiled. ''People are made of lots of bits and pieces.'' He remembered his father, taking him into the cornfield as a boy, teaching him which ears of corn were ready to be picked, his grandfather pulling him up onto the creaky, old saddle, handing him the reins. His father and grandfather sending him out to herd sheep, to spend night after night alone when the sheep refused to come home at bedtime. His family...sprawled across heaps of silver jewelry in the hogan, the red dirt black with their blood.

''I was forged long before we met. But you damn well got yours in the divorce. I'll give you that, Sara.''

The bitterness in her face matched his voice. ''You took more from me.''

''You got the apartment on Central Park West, my villa in Laguna Beach.'' He grimaced. ''And my car—''

''You took my heart.''

''I should've married a Navajo—a simple girl who busied herself with children, livestock and weaving.''

''Next time.'' Sara fluffed her auburn bangs out of her eyes. Then she got up, grabbed her bikini panties and began to dress.

He stared at her, memorizing the way she looked this last morning, just as he'd done the first morning he'd met her.

Marriage.

Divorce.

They'd been through a lot.

How could he feel so little when she still seemed to feel so much? Why did Emma...haunt him?

Sara, always wanting what he couldn't give, never wanting what he could give.

Seven years ago Sara had come to see his work at Sando's gallery, right after the twins had vanished. The cops wanted to know where their bodies were. The press had dogged him. Frances had called him a murderer.

Twin-killer. He'd been an outcast—with whites, with his own people. He'd been scared to death for Emma. Then the two had turned up alive, both of them furious. At him. At each other.

The press had gone wild. The scandal had made all three of them even more notorious.

Sara Gold had worked for an Albuquerque newspaper. She'd come to his first show, wanting to know about the missing twins. He'd refused to answer any questions that hadn't dealt with his sculptures.

Sara had moved arrogantly through Sando's gallery. ''Of course, I want to know about the twins.'' She'd reached out and rested her hand on the forehead of a mustang stallion that had been made of chunky coils of bronze. She ran her hand down the length of the horse.

"Nice. Spirited. Explosive. Maybe you have promise, yes? But who cares about Mike Greywolf, the sculptor? He's nothing compared to the twins. Where are they, Mike?"

"Get out."

"My readers want to know if that nude scene in *Betrayal*, where the hero smashed the glass to get the heroine, really happened. They want to know about Kara Shayne's Navajo love-child—your Lilly. They want to know if you resumed your affair—with both twins. They want to know if you did it to them both at the same time and then killed them. They want to know where you hid the bodies."

"Stop."

"You have huge hands."

"Voyeur!"

"Barbarian! Murderer!"

He'd hustled her toward the exit.

"I've dug up things about your past *you* probably don't even know!"

He'd started to close the door in her face.

"It's my job…to tell the truth."

"Ha!"

Slam.

When Kara showed up alive, a contrite Sara drove out to *La Golindrina*, where he'd been staying with Z. He'd found Sara wandering along the gravel paths in his sculpture compound. She'd focused on his art, but she'd rattled him with her bossiness and frenzied, nonstop questions.

He hadn't known that she was new at her job, that her brashness masked shyness and guilt. That false pride wouldn't let her apologize. He'd lost patience and poured himself a tequila.

"You say you tell the truth, but you don't," he'd said.

"You know what you're like? You're like the worst kind of tourist on an Indian reservation—shoving your camera in my face, scribbling stuff you already believe instead of what's really true, and then writing what I say as if you don't have a brain to remember it with."

He'd leaned toward her and punched a button on her laptop that turned it off. Maybe they never would've gotten started if he hadn't been so wrenched by what he'd done to Kara in her suite, if he hadn't noticed that Sara had smelled of lilacs, just as Emma always had.

"Why won't you talk about *them,* Mike?"

"I want to forget them. They damn near destroyed me—twice!"

"Liar."

"Be with me, Sara. Put your notebook and your laptop away." He'd shut her laptop and seized her spiral notebook. "Know me. Carry me inside you... Then go back to Albuquerque and write what you know."

He'd poured her a tequila. He'd taught her to drink it with salt licked off her hand.

Maybe the tequila had made him speak too frankly, reveal too much about himself, about the twins. She'd drunk too much and then, almost casually, blurted out secrets he hadn't wanted to know.

"Are you going to the opening of the Indiana Parsons Museum in Santa Fe next week?"

"Hell, no."

"Why are you so defensive? After all, Sando Parsons is your half brother."

"No—"

"Why do you think he took such a particular interest in your stuff when he has a reputation for being prejudiced against Native—"

"Liar!"

"Indiana Parsons is your—"

"Shut up—"

"She gave you away because you had a Navajo father."

"I said—"

"I researched this, Mike."

"I don't want to hear." So why had he listened?

"I talked to a nurse who used to work at the hospital where you were born. She told me that a woman can give birth to twins with different fathers. Indiana gave birth to fraternal twin sons—you and Raymond. You were too dark, too Navajo, to be her white husband's. Parsons threw her and you out, so Indiana took you to Shanto Greywolf."

"Get out!"

"After her husband calmed down, Indiana went back to him. You grew up herding sheep. You hardly knew how to read when Czarina.... Indiana paid Czarina to adopt you."

Mike stared past her. "I told you to go," he said quietly.

But there was no way Mike could muzzle Sara. He'd gone to her office and begged her not to write what she knew.

"Mike, I believe in a free press, in the public's right to know."

"Some things are private."

"Not in my world. Not anymore. You're Indiana's son. And Kara's lover."

"Kill the story."

"This is my big chance."

"Kill it. Let me be your big chance."

"How?"

"I'm not sure." He'd softened his accented voice. "Do

you get lonely?'' She'd nodded. He'd added, ''Well, damn it, so do I.'' He'd run his hand along her shoulder. ''I'd like to sculpt you. Would you sit for me?''

''What else do you want?''

''More. Much more.''

13

Sara hadn't called that night or the next. He hadn't wanted to think about her, but he had, especially when he was in bed. During the day he had begun to dwell on what she'd said about Indiana Parsons.

His mother was dead.

To even think that she wasn't, opened up some dark, unexplored but wildly exciting side of himself.

Raymond, the white boy who looked like him.

Indiana, the artist.

Mike despised her stuff.

She was good.

If she weren't, he would merely have been indifferent.

He never knew what made him drop by the opening of the Indiana Parsons Museum several afternoons later. As luck would have it, Indiana was at the podium, speaking to a crowd, when the museum doors banged noisily behind him. Her bold, voluptuous canvases that had been banned as blasphemy ten years earlier splashed the white walls with scarlet, gold and purple.

So much passion.

The one nearest to Mike was of Marilyn Monroe, wearing a crown of emerald thorns that dripped rubies. Her semi-nude body hung in chains from a crucifix. The expression on her face was exactly the same as Shanto Greywolf's lying dead. Indiana's painting repelled and fascinated him more than anything he'd ever seen.

Bitchy, controversial, misunderstood, notorious, Indiana was an icon in the art world. She didn't give a damn for anybody but herself.

But she was good.

That day Indiana had been thin and sexy in black riding boots and tight riding pants. Her blouse had been low-cut. She'd seemed taller than a flesh-and-blood woman, larger than life. Her voice had rung with arresting, raw passion as she spoke about her work.

Suddenly she'd stopped and stared straight at him. Sara had been in the crowd. Raymond, too.

Adrenaline, rage and fear pumped through Mike's veins.

"We have another notorious person in our midst," Indiana purred.

A thousand faces turned. Sara stood up. Raymond stormed out.

"Maybe it's time I introduced you to a young man who's special to me—"

Humiliated, Mike had run. Outside, he'd panicked when he'd slid behind the wheel, stomping on the gas and peeling out of the lot. A cop had given chase and ticketed him.

For days he'd been terrified of what Indiana or Sara would do. But it had been okay. Indiana had ignored him, and Sara had written about his work.

After Sara's article had come out, he'd waited a week before calling to thank her. "You still want to date me?" she'd asked.

"Call it whatever you like."

Wearing skimpy black shorts and a tight halter, she'd driven to his house and made her play. That night when they'd shared tequila, she'd poured the salt from his hand onto her thighs and suggested he lick it off. After he'd finished, she'd wrapped her legs around his head.

Afterward, that very same night, she'd asked him to marry her.

"You're fast," he said.

"I don't sleep around. I know what I want. What do you want, Mike?"

"I'm lonely. I want to move on." He wanted to put Emma, the Shaynes, New Mexico and Indiana behind him. To forget all the Parsons, including Sando.

"I want a new start," he'd said. "I want to be somebody—but on my own terms."

"Marry me. I'll help you."

"There's something I've got to get out of my system first."

For once, Sara hadn't pushed.

He'd escaped into his art, hiding out in his imagination, sculpting the bronzes of the twins to rid himself of their hold on him. A year later, when he was done, he'd returned to the U.S., and Sara had proposed again.

"Why the hell not?" he'd whispered.

Weddings never made as big a difference as women want them to, Mike realized. Sara had been sexy. She'd said she'd given up her big chance for him, that she was rich, that she was going to launch him.

Even on their wedding night, he knew he'd made a terrible mistake. No matter what Emma had done, Sara wasn't the answer. She was pushy and materialistic. And an untalented stepmother. He'd tried to stick it out. But, over time their marriage had unraveled.

Lilly had resented Sara, resented the fancy private

schools Sara enrolled her in. When she hit puberty, Lilly hadn't fit in with other girls her age. She'd pierced her ears and started wearing combat boots.

Six months ago Lilly had gotten a crush on a bald guy named Nafu who'd pushed his New Age philosophy on her. Worse, he'd shown her old clippings of the twins.

Starstruck, she'd grown obsessed with Kara and the rumors that she was her mother. When he'd refused to discuss Kara, Lilly had run away to Malibu to ask Kara herself.

Fortunately, Kara had been away on one of her mysterious trips. Her maid had called Czarina, who'd flown Lilly home to New Mexico before dialing him.

"I'm sorry you're worried, Daddy," Lilly had said in her wisest New Age voice. "I love it here. I love Uncle Sando and Uncle Stuart and Grandmother and Auntie Z. I don't feel this kind of magnetic energy around you and Sara in New York. You two aren't aligned. You won't talk to me about…about my real mother. Auntie Z will."

"Damn her hide."

"I don't want to hurt you, but if you try to make me live with Sara, who's jealous of Kara, I'll run away. Only next time, you won't find me."

He hadn't told her that if she stole his credit card again, it would be damn easy to trace her.

"Sara's gone, honey."

"That sucks. That really really sucks."

"I can't believe you said that. You two fought all the time. You just said—"

"We fought 'cause she was on my case about school and stuff. 'Cause she wanted me to be the same boring, uptight, high-achieving nerd she is. But at least she cared. *You* don't! You're always in your old studio!"

"Is that Nafu character with you?"

"If you don't learn to be nonaggressive and nonjudgmental of my friends, Daddy, I won't ever come home. Uncle Sando loves Nafu."

Mike had gritted his teeth until he heard Czarina's soothing voice on the line, suggesting that Lilly needed roots. "Maybe she'd have less temptation here than in the city. Maybe she needs her grandmother and me and Stuart...."

"Frances hates my guts."

"What do you care what that stubborn old fool did? She'll leave you alone. With the twins estranged and gone for good, she's lost some of her arrogance. I'll lease you *La Golindrina* with an option to buy."

"Why would you do that?"

"I raised you. Lilly is family."

"People thought I killed—"

"Fools.... You can see after my cattle again. You can use the outbuildings for a foundry and a huge studio. There won't be any city ordinances to silence your saws and hammers out here. You can use the ruined school and the gym for warehouses, too. Or if all you want is to hide from the world, you can. I'll see after Lilly."

She sure knew how to lure him. In New York, he had to commute an hour to a foundry in New Jersey.

As a kid he'd loved that place. Maybe Z had let him run a little too wild. He'd spent a lot of time wandering the parched pastures of *La Golindrina* as well as the juniper and pine forest and the desert that fringed the property.

"You fought awfully hard for Lilly fourteen years ago. But it's easy to mess up with teenagers."

"How come she's gotten so impossible? Lilly and I used to do things together. I fed her breakfast, drove her to school. She'd come into my studio and watch me for hours. Now she lectures me if I so much as fry bacon. She's a vegetarian—"

"Girls aren't puppies that follow you around forever. She's fourteen. She's a Shayne. In this family we go crazy at that age. It's our nature. I could tell you stories."

Mike felt grave doubts about the wisdom of exposing Lilly to Aunt Z, herbal guru of dubious philosophy. "Is Nafu there with her?"

"Bottom line, I'll help you with Lilly if you come home."

Lilly was a charmer when she set her mind to it, and the besotted Z hadn't let up.

When Z ran Nafu off, Mike decided maybe the old windbag could be more help than menace. He and Lilly had ended up here.

Not that they were getting along any better. Hell, she got more difficult by the day. He got edgy every time she added a new earring, every time he saw her flowing red hair or her gauzy skirts.

It was all he could do not to shout when she started in on him with her half-baked ideas. He wanted to yank Nafu's obnoxious, Coptic cross from her throat. He loathed the smell of incense and the sound of those African drums. He had to bite his tongue when she mentioned shopping.

At least they had more room. The main house, which stood beneath tall cottonwoods not far from the river, had high, wood-beamed ceilings and lots of spare bedrooms. Lilly could run off to the desert and sulk to her heart's content.

When she finally decided she wanted something, she would come slinking into his studio, the way she had yesterday afternoon before Sara's arrival, bestowing her forgiveness in that airy manner he distrusted.

As always, questions about his art preceded an outrageous demand.

She'd been wearing a long, loose-fitting dress of several shades of pink over clumpy sandals.

"What are you doing in here all by yourself, Daddy?"

What he always did.

His hands were wrist-deep in wet clay. When he groaned, she said, "Mabel got back from her trading trip. She brought us the most wonderful rugs."

"Spendthrift."

"You were going to tell me what you're doing in here."

"If you can't tell for yourself, then I'm a total failure."

"And you're not that. Why did you quit working on the granite?"

"This is sort of a warm-up. I was afraid of making the wrong cut."

"Oh. The wind. You said it was bothering you. I remember. You're blocked."

Why did his daughter have to look so haphazardly sexy with her wild red hair? And yet look like an intuitive child, at the same time? She had a maddening, artistic temperament, but without a trace of talent.

When she circled him, picked up an art book, flipped pages noisily, and then set it back down on top of a stack of dusty art magazines, he grew nervous. Is there any creature on earth more disdainful than one's own teenager?

Her green eyes drank in everything in that high-ceilinged studio—the charcoal life sketches tacked everywhere, the huge bridge-saws with their diamond blades, the pneumatic hammers and steel wedges, the unsold pieces from his last show tour, the newly torn, half-done huge slab of pink stone he'd only recently wrenched from an even greater slab of raw granite.

As he rolled a piece of clay into a ball, Lilly tentatively tiptoed up behind the latest clay bust he was working on. It was awkwardly perched on its armature.

"It's—it's ever so wonderful, Daddy. I mean…whatever it is."

The clay in his hands was drying fast. "It's abstract."

Unimpressed, she frowned. "Is it Sara?"

"God, no!"

"I wish it was."

"So, you don't like it."

"Do you still love her?" Lilly asked.

"Who?" His big powerful hands began to knead a hard lump in the center of the clay a bit too thoroughly.

"If you have to ask, I suspect you don't. Poor, poor Sara. She's called several times, you know, while you were hiding in here."

"I wasn't hiding."

"I don't see anything new."

He threw the extra clay into a bucket of water. He grabbed a pointed sculpting tool from a sideboard and dug into the bust, tearing out an angle for the nostril, making another rip where the upper part of the ear would be, a slash where the mouth would be.

"Ouch," Lilly said carelessly.

He pitched the tool onto his worktable. "Why didn't you tell me she called?"

Lilly had the decency to blush. "I sort of…I forgot."

Her manipulative pause lacked even a hint of remorse. "Did you?"

"Well, Daddy, aren't you going to call her, now that you know—"

"I thought she drove you crazy."

"Oh, definitely. But then that's what any good step-mother would do."

"So, she was good, was she?"

"I suppose you think I'm a pain."

"I guess it's your age."

"That's not very flattering. I came in here to try to make up."

"Oh. So that's what you're doing." He tried not to sound skeptical. "That's very kind of you."

"I, er, I also sort of have a...an emergency. I really, really hate to interrupt you if you're finally working, but there's something I simply have to have. And I can't find..."

He wiped his hands on a rag. "What?"

"It's...in town. You know how you're always complaining about my weird clothes."

His gaze ran over her sloppily dyed pink outfit. "You want to go shopping on the Plaza? Again?"

"No, silly, the mall. There's the cutest dress. You will simply love it, Daddy. You could drive me, and we could talk. We never get to."

"I drove you yesterday. You wore headphones."

Her face lit up like a candle. "But didn't we have fun?"

"Lilly, you can't shop every single day."

"Why on earth not?"

"You spend so much. I'm a bad father to indulge—"

"Uncle Stuart says, 'If you have the money, there's nothing wrong with me spending it.'"

"He's rich. You haven't earned any money."

"You're so old-fashioned." She sighed. "There's nothing to do out here when you're holed up in your studio—except visit Uncle Stuart or Aunt Czarina or Grandmother. Bor-ing."

"You could unpack. I could pay you for each box."

"Oh, I don't need money. We have credit cards."

"*I* have credit cards."

"Same thing." Her eyebrows rushed together in excitement at something she saw beyond him. "Maybe Nafu—" She flew hopefully to the window and then let out an anguished yowl.

A flame-red rooster tail of dust whirled toward them like a tornado. *His* bright blue Corvette was the head of all that billowing dirt. The washboard road leading up to the house was under construction, and Sara—she paid no attention to the lower speed limits, cones or warning signs—was bouncing the guts out of *his* car.

"Do me a favor," he growled. "Keep that maniac busy while I clean up."

"But you promised to take me shopping for that cute little black dress."

"I did not—"

"You did, Daddy."

Damn it! Had he? "Tomorrow, then."

"Today."

"Lilly!"

"Uncle Stuart keeps *his* promises. And he's a whole lot busier than you. He works all the time, especially now that he's buying out that other tech company."

Right. Throw up Uncle Stuart, electronics wizard, the multi-F-ing-millionaire—or was it billionaire—with the plastic face.

"Maybe you should have told me Sara called. Then she wouldn't have driven out."

In a furious whirl of pink skirts, Lilly flounced out.

Which was the way she usually departed these days.

14

Teenagers had to be the most infuriating breed on earth. When they were around, they drove you crazy. When they weren't, you worried about what they were up to.

Where the hell was Lilly?

"...*Wall Street was stunned today when computer giant Stuart Shayne announced the imminent hostile takeover of Benedek Tech—*"

Mike snapped the radio off, Stuart being the last thing he wanted to think about. Mike didn't know what to make of the new Stuart, who was now incredibly handsome thanks to a nose job. He was suave and fantastically rich, as well. Stuart, former nerd, now the zillionaire, the paragon uncle. Suddenly, the electronics genius had become a ruthless corporate raider, too. Who the hell was he?

Thank goodness the wind had died down. Lilly's rope swing barely swayed in the faint breath beneath the leafy cottonwood. If Mike only knew where Lilly was, maybe he could settle down and work.

The afternoon was cloudless, the immense sky deep blue above the purple mountains and tall red cliffs, the horizon endless, and the silence almost total. Not that the stark beauty moved him as it had when he'd been a kid, herding sheep, following them into the great unknown, living off the land for whole days and nights. The white man had taught him a great deal, but had cost him as much.

A faint drift of air moved across the vast stillness, ruffling Mabel's penstemons and hollyhocks. The sublime spring afternoon smelled of apricot blossoms.

The first purple buds had formed on the lilac bushes beside Mabel's hogan. As a kid, he had felt the isolation of the desert landscape had expanded into something grand inside him. Growing up outside, he'd taken such feelings for granted, little realizing they were a life force.

It had taken him years to learn that no matter how rich or famous he was, no matter how many of the white man's games he won, he'd never feel as grand as he had as a kid chasing sheep.

As a man, he'd stared down at the bustling city of Manhattan, listening to its roar, watching pedestrians darting along sidewalks and streets. The people had seemed like ants, the taxis and buses toy-size. The ants thought they were so damn smart, so sophisticated, but they were out of touch with themselves. They were all racing to get nowhere special faster than somebody else. They were dead to what really thrilled them.

He was no different.

He'd thought he could leave the deadness behind. But the nothingness of this huge, silent land magnified the nothingness inside him....

Where the hell was Lilly? How could she sulk about the divorce, about needing Sara to unpack, and not bother to say goodbye?

Mike wanted to enjoy Lilly. What was it with teenagers? He didn't buy the hormone bit. She was rude, extravagant, selfish, willful, reckless, defiant—when she stuck around. When he needed her for the least little thing, she was gone.

She was the reason he stood scowling at the slanting sunlight beyond the shade of the tall cottonwood and elms behind his adobe ranch house. He blamed her for Mabel's arrogant peafowl now wandering about, preening in the shimmering brilliance and dark shadow. One of them spread its wings and sprang on top of his truck.

Messy birds—peafowl. Multiplied like jackrabbits. Jackrabbits with wings that shit on his truck. Lilly had said they would be awfully pretty and she'd care for them.

He tried not to think about Lilly.

A bank in Tucson had commissioned a monument. His men had trucked in a three-ton slab of pink granite from a Texas quarry and set it up in a studio. Last week he'd torn into the raw stone with drills and wedges and pneumatic hammers. Then the wind had rattled the windowpanes, and he'd stopped, unsure.

But this morning, he'd started to mull over that project again. He'd put his ear against the cool pink stone. Nothing. He'd felt nothing, heard nothing. So he'd carried his frayed notebook, heavy with ideas, quotes and sketches, out here.

Now he was staring down at his easel under the cottonwood. He picked up a charcoal stick. Then his hand froze, his mind as blank as the page. Maybe he needed to go off by himself—to his hunting hogan where he hid out when he needed solitude.

Draw! Something! *Anything!*

He sketched a face that was too damn beautiful and mature and willful for its fourteen years. The spirited young girl had high cheekbones and a contrived, yet saintly, otherworldly smile. She had reckless eyes that were somehow both innocent and self-absorbed. Her long, unkempt, red curls flowed off the paper. Nafu's much-hated, intricate Coptic cross dangled from a black ribbon at her neck. Tall and slim, she flitted off his page with breezy contempt.

Mike's charcoal hesitated above her ears. Those damn earrings! He ripped the sheet from the easel. Her image was too bold and sensual.

Mike knew very well what Nafu saw in her.

Mike forced himself to study his notebook. To his surprise, his next image wasn't his daughter. An elusive, mysterious spark had been ignited, and the frustrating, creative process began.

His strong brown hand raced across the paper. Soon a dozen wadded sheets littered the lawn. His charcoal slashed another sheet. He felt a building, intangible tension. Still, what he struggled to capture remained hidden in the mists of his mind.

He ripped the last sheet from the easel.

Give it time. Have faith. It will come.

Lessons learned from his father whose designs in silver and turquoise had made him famous.

Believe in yourself, Mike. Emma's voice.

Where the hell had that come from?

Unlike Sara, who'd been so good at promoting him, Emma had been able to sit beside him in silent harmony. Sometimes she'd read or written; sometimes she'd shut her book or notebook, propped herself on an elbow and simply watched him.

He had liked working with her nearby. His first really good bronze had been of her. He'd never shown it—nor any of the others of her. Nor the nude of Kara.

He never would. He'd changed his style since that sentimental, overwrought garbage.

He worked two more hours, and still no Lilly. Only

when she was up to real mischief did she stay away this long.

One minute his charcoal flew across the paper. The next, he felt a thrill of clarity as he accidentally discovered a fresh angle. The mists parted. He forgot Lilly and Emma. Instead, he saw a waterfall, horses. He looked up, concentrating....

His imagination saw a lone Arabian stallion, nostrils flaring, hooves flying across the desert—

The sound of rollers from his warehouse jarred him. A raven shot out of the cottonwood. Mike's eyes followed the flutter of black wings as the bird soared above his warehouse.

The doors of that warehouse gaped open.

His first thought was Sara.

Hooves froze. His vision dematerialized.

Grim shock replaced creative quandary. Charcoal hit the ground and shattered. For several long seconds, he glared at the yawning, black rectangle that punched a huge hole in the north wall of his warehouse.

"Lilly."

His heart raced. She'd been playing hooky from school when the trucks had come with the crated bronzes of the twins.

Than evening she'd found him in his studio. "Mabel said big trucks came—"

"The principal said you didn't go to school."

"Mabel said the trucks stayed for hours," Lilly had said almost carelessly.

"Lilly, why didn't you go to school?"

"I was sick. I didn't want to worry you."

She had seemed to forget all about the trucks. That should have made him suspicious.

Mike sprinted past the foundry to the warehouse.

"Lilly!"

Lilly poked her bright head into the sunlight. "There you are, silly."

Three sets of earrings gleamed. She'd done her hair up in a series of tiny braids, intricate loops and knots.

At the sight of his scowl, her sweet face beneath the bright purple headband took on an unhealthy pallor. Somehow she managed one of her infuriating, whimsical smiles. "I hope your sketches aren't going badly—"

She didn't give a damn about his sketches. "Why aren't you in the house? Unpacking?" His voice rasped fury and other long-suppressed emotions, not the least of which was fear.

"You simply *must* see these—" Still smiling, she vanished, ankle bells jingling.

A bar of sunshine streamed into the dark, musty, building, illuminating the wide central aisle all the way to the rafters with dazzling light, but leaving in shadow the north corner where Lilly knelt over an open crate. Only when she snapped on the overhead light did he see she'd pried the lids off all the boxes.

From every crate, pairs of identical bronze faces shone like pure gold.

For the first time he noticed the dead, rank odor in the air. The hairs on the back of his neck spiked. He'd created these pieces to exorcise the twins, not to bring them back.

Outside, the sunshine was blindingly bright; inside, the warehouse was as eerily dark as an ancient death chamber. The Navajo spirit in Mike felt an evil force mushrooming out of those crates, ghosts rushing at him like a stagnant breath.

"They're of Kara and Emma, aren't they?" Bells jingled as Lilly careened recklessly among the crates, tossing lids askew. She whirled. "Oh, Daddy, you should be ashamed of yourself, not telling me. They're all so beautiful." Her face was rapturous, her voice breathy. "You're so good. Why didn't you ever show me these pieces? They are so much better than those blobs and slabs you do now. Oh, sorry…abstract, they call it?"

He'd been dead, lost, when he'd created them. He'd been ridding himself of ghosts. He should have opened the crates and destroyed them when they'd arrived.

Some indefinable stench was suffocating him. What was it—rats? The evil souls of the dead? He felt as claustrophobic as he had in that kiva, when he'd held Emma in his arms when the bats had come.

"You shouldn't have come in here."

"Daddy, stop treating me like a child. I'm tired of all your precious secrets. I think that's why we aren't aligned. You shut me out."

It was the ghosts he wanted to shut out.

"Sara—"

"Sara?" He moved toward Lilly. The warehouse felt *chindi*—bewitched. He felt a fierce compulsion to lock the statues back up and leave them in their boxes where they belonged—untouched, unseen. Or to destroy them.

It was too late.

"I told Sara about the trucks, and she said…"

Lilly shifted the top off another crate. A whorl of dust motes danced above the sexually provocative nude he'd created of Kara.

"Wow?"

The statue splashed light back at him as if it glowed from within. Captured forever in bronze, that private little half smile of Kara's that had enticed men to their doom, that had enticed him that last night in her hotel suite, both taunted and shocked him. The statue was so blatantly erotic, it could only have been made by her lover.

That smile had destroyed him, tempted him to that final, ultimate betrayal that had made him loathe himself even more than he loathed her, gotten him accused of murder, made people condemn him without a trial.

Mike mopped the perspiration from his brow with the back of his hand. His throat felt too tight to speak. Never again did he want to feel such rage, fear, grief and heartbreak. And regret—so much regret.

Kara's statue stabbed him in the heart as nothing else could.

Lilly understood none of what he felt.

"Wow! Wow! Wow! Daddy, you must have loved Kara…as I loved Nafu."

"Have you been in contact with that damn guru?"

"Not…this week, Daddy."

Something in her too-innocent denial worried him.

"Love in your mind produces love in your life," she continued wisely, patting her Coptic cross. "No wonder you and Sara weren't in harmony. How could you be, after loving the twins?"

A ceaseless loneliness closed over him. "You don't understand."

"Kara is really, really famous now. She's so mysterious, too. If you showed these, especially this sexy one of her, everybody would come. Maybe even Kara and Emma would show up…together. Maybe they could become friends again. And—and I could meet Kara."

"That's the last thing I want," he thundered.

"It's what I want, though," she whispered.

"No!" he exploded, slamming the lid down. He hurled the next lid down, then the next. The loud bangs cracked like gunshots.

Again, Lilly's soft voice attacked. "You came back here because of them. You loved them. Both of them."

''No.'' He stared at his daughter.

No longer did Lilly use that false, breathy tone. ''What I want to know is, which one of them you got pregnant.'' Her pretty face reddened prettily. ''I look just like Kara.'' Her voice was both hopeful and awe filled.

He banged another lid down. ''Who told you that? Kara and Emma looked just alike.''

''You got famous because you slept with both of them.''

The heat in his own cheeks matched hers, only his was due to rage. He crashed another lid over a pair of golden faces, sealing them in dank darkness.

''Leave it alone!''

''I want to know who I am.''

He felt battered, deafened, blind. Maybe he was crazy, but now, even when most of the crates were shut again, he felt she'd unleashed some destroying force that could not easily be contained.

''Which one did you really love, Daddy? Which one is my mother?''

Again Mike saw the color drain from Emma's incandescent face when she'd discovered Kara and him in the barn.

''I want to know my mother. I want to know why you made the twins hate each other. Why everybody thought you'd killed them, till they came back. Most of all, I want to know why you made them hate me...and each other.''

The warehouse was so big and empty, the silence after that last question seemed to echo.

For a second he was in Kara's hotel room again. He could almost hear her voice. *''Mike, Lilly's mine. I'm sorry.''*

He was sorry, too. So damn sorry.

His heart throbbed. ''They hate me—not you.''

"I want my mother. I need more than just you."

Did Lilly feel none of the evil around them? Was she too white?

"Daddy, your aura's a bright, tingly red."

"Maybe because I'm on the verge of a stroke."

"Silly. If you don't tell me who my mother is, I'll call Uncle Sando."

Mike exploded. "Leave him out of this!"

Lilly smiled her most worrisome, maternal smile. "There will be no stopping Uncle Sando when he sees these."

Mike rushed toward Lilly. Grabbing her elbow, he propelled her forcefully farther away from the boxes.

"Daddy!"

"Lilly, there are reasons why I hid these."

"Why did they both run after *Betrayal*? Kara to Hollywood? And Emma to Mexico. Why won't Emma ever come back here if everybody, especially Grandmother, loved her the best? At least, that's what Uncle Stuart says."

Mike went white.

"You made all the statues look just alike, Daddy. I can't tell them apart."

"Because they were just alike…in appearance." *God. What that had cost him.* "When they wanted to be. When they were older they didn't dress alike or try to look alike at all—which was why they could trick people when they wore each other's clothes when they did try."

"They were close, too. I've read that. Too close, Uncle Stuart says. Like two beings in one body."

"Identical—" Mike swallowed against the dry lump in his throat. "Inseparable." He choked out the second word in a dark, helpless voice. "They were closer than mother and daughter. Closer than lovers. That was their problem.''

''But they did separate.'' Lilly hesitated. ''Because of you.''

He shook his head.

Her gaze was rapt. ''It's all so romantic.''

One last golden figure lay uncovered. Suddenly that bronze face in the nearest coffin-like crate captured his gaze.

The long narrow box had been shoved against the wall, away from the others.

Transfixed, he stood without moving. The box held the supine figure of a girl lying as still as death. Her exquisite bronze face appeared expressionless, all its passion spent. Her arms lay limply at her side, heavy and yet weightless, too. Her eyes were closed, and tears of sparkling gold ran down her cheeks.

Kara's face.

Emma's tears.

Mike recoiled. That night had ended everything. Kara had seduced him so easily. He blinked, hating the memory of wild sex, their quarrel afterward.

The press had crucified him. He'd crucified himself for destroying Emma all over again, for destroying his belief in himself.

His face paled. The ghosts *were* too real.

''Daddy— I have to know. Which one is my mother?''

His fists knotted. Then he picked up the hammer Lilly had used to pry off the lids. Swinging it over his shoulder, he smashed it down on the supine statue's face, gouging out a chunk of bronze. He hit the statue again and again. Bits of bronze flew everywhere. He didn't stop until the face was unrecognizable.

He threw the hammer down and looked into his daughter's stricken eyes. "Get out!"

For once she didn't talk back. When she was gone, he sank to the floor beside the crate.

Emma. Just her name could conjure a wealth of unwanted memories. How many times, when he'd been a shiftless boy with too much time on his hands, had he scribbled it into hard sand lots with a long stick. Into how many rough-barked cottonwood trunks had he carved it, into how many school desks, his knife sometimes digging savagely, most times tenderly?

Emma—sixteen, in a field of red admiral butterflies. They had landed in her red hair. She had risen slowly, like a magical creature, with them swirling around her. Then she'd thrown herself into his arms and kissed him, stunning them both into blistering sexual awareness.

Emma—older, after that kiss, with her hot dark eyes. Emma—always wanting him, always loving him, no matter what kind of badness he got into. Emma—understanding him so that her very soul felt welded to his. Emma—her eyes burning with unshed tears when he'd read her diary and discovered the secrets of her heart.

A deep cold closed over him. Mike had lived in darker places than Lilly had. Or maybe they just felt darker because he was a man, and half Navajo. He'd spent a lot of years battling heartbreak, prejudice, ignorance and poverty. Grief and loss, too. Lilly didn't know what it was to feel less than nothing, to have nothing, to have no one. He hadn't done much, but he'd protected her from that.

He couldn't go back. He couldn't open his heart to that kind of vulnerability ever again. Not even for Lilly.

He picked up the hammer again. He remembered that lost year when he'd created these statues to exorcise Emma and Kara forever. Just seeing the bronzes brought it all back. Slowly he slammed the hammer down hard, methodically nailing the lids over the statues, one by one.

It wasn't till Sando called that he realized he should never have let Lilly out of his sight.

Mike hardly had time to lock the warehouse and storm into his house before his phone rang.

"Sando here!" his overweight half brother panted. "What's this Lilly tells me about statues of the twins? And you said no show...."

Mike stared straight ahead. A freshly smashed snake lay in the road. The animal must have come out to sun in the spring warmth; Sara must have run over it.

Mike froze, his eyes on the mess.

Sando talked faster and faster.

"Sando! No—"

No wasn't in Sando's vocabulary.

Slam. Slam. Slam. Sando knocked the phone on something hard to get his attention.

"Kara's red-hot, pal, since she won that Oscar. Did you hear? She's supposed to marry our brother Raymond, your twin, any day. Can you believe that twisted relationship is ending in matrimony?"

Raymond and Kara, high-school lovers, reunited in Hollywood? His white twin? Now that was strange.

"Kara's a living legend! With a nude statue of her in your show, you'll be hot!"

"No show."

"It'll be great."

"Over my dead body."

"Hey, why didn't I think of that? You do it with both twins again. Get 'em mad. Get Ray mad. Mad enough to kill you. Then you vanish. Everybody will think one of them offed *you*.... I love it!"

"You're serious?"

"Kara's big-time, pal. We could get some play on the white twin bit."

Mike clenched the phone. Outside a faint breeze stirred a dirt devil around the snake's body. The reptile had awakened from hibernation and slithered out into spring sunlight to meet death.

It was a bad omen.

"Breathe a word about Lilly, and you and I are finished."

"Why don't you just let me do my job?"

Mike thought of the snake dance at Zuni.

"Michael, remember last year, New York? You owe me—"

"You bastard…"

"We'll do it at my gallery in Laguna Beach. Better chance Kara will show." Sando hung up.

Mike held the phone, frozen.

Twins. Good twin, bad twin. White twin, Navajo twin.

The birth of twins was an auspicious event in Pueblo culture. The part of Mike that was Navajo believed in the dual forces of good and evil. He remembered Kara and Emma. How they'd almost seemed like one.

Evil had to be contained, controlled.

For years he'd pushed his feelings for Emma deep inside him. For years he'd contained the deadly power that had stalked him when he'd stumbled away from the hogan, stalked him even to the Shaynes' ranch.

Stalked him still.

For years he'd been able to hide behind his marriage, in his studio, his art.

No more.

This land, and his daughter, had exposed him.

The spring sun was still warm and scented with lilac

and apricot blossoms, but last night ghosts had ridden the desert winds.

As if to remind Mike, a lone coyote began to yip in the faraway, sage-covered hills. A few of his buddies joined in.

Spring was that time between winter and summer, that time of awakening.

Mike hugged himself, shivering at the dangerous urgency in Lilly's question.

"Which one of the twins is my mother?"

15

Bumper-to-bumper traffic forced Mike out of his cab a block short of the gallery. He was late, very late.

Not that he gave a damn. He wanted nothing to do with these statues that told the story of two women he was determined to forget.

Kara's fans were screaming, their voices hoarse as if they'd been at it for hours.

"Kara! Kara!"

A chill swept through him. His ghosts felt dangerously close. On a shudder, he thrust a hand into his pocket, grabbed a stash of cash, and pressed it into the cabbie's sweaty palm. Lowering the wide brim of his black Stetson to conceal his face, he spun away from the cab and strode around the corner.

Limousines jammed the street. Glitzy celebrity groupies stood three-deep on the sidewalk outside the gallery. The street looked like a round-the-clock movie shoot, complete with lights, photographers, sound trucks and reporters.

Spotlights arced against black sky. Klieg lights blinded him. Rock music throbbed.

Sando. Mike's mouth curled downward as he elbowed

his way into the throng. That son-of-a-rattler had gone for broke.

Usually Mike enjoyed Laguna Beach. Once it had been a genuine art colony. It was a pretty town with fabulous homes perched on hillsides and canyons, with rugged cliffs erupting above a smashing surf. The main street was chock-full of art galleries, too.

Wishing he were a fly on the wall instead of the lead in tonight's star-studded cast, Mike held up his invitation and attempted to slide past a doorman. But Sando had alerted the doorman to look out for a rugged half-breed with long black hair, wearing old jeans and a battered Stetson.

The doorman waved at the band.

Drums stopped.

Female voices squealed.

"It's him! Greywolf!"

Mike stiffened when half a dozen pretty girls hurled themselves at him.

Tonight wasn't about him or about art. This farce was Sando's sleazy attempt to get media attention.

Mike's frigid gaze swept the sea of wealthy strangers beyond the pretty models hanging on to him. His glare got hotter when he recognized Lilly, Sando, Stuart, Z, Frances and Sara bunched together in a far corner like guilty conspirators.

Stuart's company was poised to take over Benedek Tech in L.A. this weekend—that was Stuart's excuse for putting in an appearance, for keeping tabs on the upstart sculptor. Frances and Z were here for Stuart. They'd flown Lilly out on the corporate jet. But why was Sara here?

When Mike's gaze narrowed on his daughter, she went paper-white. She tossed her head carelessly, causing her red curls to bounce and earrings to sparkle, which only made him more aware that her dark eyes brimmed with tears. When she took a step toward him, he almost softened.

Then, on a curt nod, he pivoted and strode to the bar. When she burst into tears, and Sando rushed to console her, Mike's heart slammed in slow, painful strokes. Swallowing a quick breath, he ordered a whiskey.

The bartender, a skinny blond guy with surfer hair and an in-your-face smile, held up a champagne flute. "Sorry."

With a frown Mike took the flute and drained it. He took another and drank it, too. When he reached for a third, the bartender quit smiling. So Mike poured himself another. After his fourth, he got a buzz and decided to slow down. Pulling out a book of matches, he raked one across the cover and watched it flare.

"There's no smoking," said the surfer.

"Who's smoking?"

Mike struck another match. He lit the whole book.

"Mister…"

Mike's mouth was dry and papery from the champagne. His mind was fuzzy. "Make my night. Throw me out—"

The smoke alarm screamed.

"Now you've done it."

The scent of lilacs floated to Mike in a wave that colored his night with way too many bittersweet memories.

Butterflies danced against cobalt blue. He remembered the warmth of long-lashed, dark eyes; he tasted the sweet eagerness of innocent lips. For a magic moment he recalled how love in that distant time had held such infinite possibilities of joy—

The smoke alarm stopped. Mike spun around, his cynical heart pulsing with idiotic expectancy.

Sara's gaze drilled him. Squeezed into green satin, her frizzy red hair was too big; her smile too brittle.

"Hi, favorite barbarian."

"What are you doing here?"

Sara took his empty champagne flute and twirled it, then sipped. "Is it true—what Lilly told the tabloids? How did you feel about Lilly telling all…?"

Violated as hell. Like he did now.

Lilly's tabloid story was the least of it. The little traitor had lured Mike off shopping and left his warehouse unlocked for Sando. Her I-want-my-mommy story had hit the stands the same afternoon. Mike had returned home to an empty warehouse with Sando's invitation to the show tacked to the huge open doors.

Furious, Mike had called Sando.

"Pal," Sando had begun, "when you reneged on New York, you signed a legal document."

"This is extortion. The bronzes are too personal."

"They have universal appeal. So do you. Be there, or I sue."

When Sara leaned closer, Mike began to sweat. "Lilly wants her mother, Mike."

"She's got me."

"As if you're there for her…for anybody. I should know. I lived in that vacuum we called our marriage—"

"As if you give a damn about our marriage—"

"The twins are back in your life with a vengeance. So am I. You took the best years of my life, Greywolf. You used me. You got famous. I got zip."

What are you talking about? "I married you. We had a life. You divorced *me*."

"And you loved *her*. Emma."

Mike felt on edge, raw—hunted. "When did you ever give a damn about love?"

Bleak, bitter pride flickered in Sara's eyes.

He made a fist.

She smiled. "You and your twins are my ticket to the big-time."

Shouts outside throbbed louder.

"Gotta go—*darling*."

"Damn you, Sara."

Sara hustled her camera to her shoulder and rushed out to see what the fuss was about.

Dimly, he heard people in the gallery making small talk as well as nonsensical commentary.

"Too sentimental," a man said of the statue in the foyer, which was of two identical little girls, their heads lifted.

"I came to see the nude," said a woman. "I loved the nude scene in *Betrayal*. The way he stepped through all that exploding glass and grabbed her—"

A sexier female voice whispered, "I'd rather sleep with the sculptor."

Mike moved deeper into the shadows. This wasn't an art opening. It was the final curtain of a melodrama. He had to get out of here. But no way could he leave.

The invitation had been fairly discreet—till its end. It read, "Sando Parsons Cordially Presents Mike Greywolf's 'Desert Daughters.' Early bronze nude of Kara Shayne included."

The tabloids hit harder. "Kara Shayne—Bares All"... "Navajo Lover Slept with Kara and her Twin"..."Kara's Love-Child Tells All"..."My Navajo Daddy Stole Me from My Movie-Star Mama."

A chill brushed up his spine, and he felt a devil behind him as he wandered out of the bar with a glass of champagne.

The sky was iridescent fire. The Golden Door, with its

wooden floors and soaring columns and flowing rock fountains accented with lavender orchids, was packed with the rich and the famous, with the pretenders and the curious gawkers—and with enough of the howling media to turn both groups on.

The parking lot out back was tented. Two bands competed. Outside, rock music pulsated, its drums pounding. Inside, violins whined. Catered hors d'oeuvres had been laid out on gold-clothed tables with lavish flair.

Sexy, redheaded waitresses swathed in gold lamé— Kara look-alikes—pranced through the crowd to the beat of the drums with heavily-laden trays of champagne and tender beef sandwiches. When the prettiest of these waitresses winked at him, Mike got rattled. His blush made her bolder. When her lashes lowered, he ran out of the room.

After that, when he saw a gold-clad waitress, he grew edgier. The night stretched—endless. How long could he endure being trapped in crowded boxy rooms with these statues that brought back that terrible time when love and desire and murderous jealousy had spiraled out of control?

The bronzes were *chindi*. He was doomed.

Mike saw Lilly flirting with the surfer bartender, and strode up to them. When he slammed into the bar, the surfer lowered his gaze, his voice dropping to a feeble whisper. Lilly flipped her hair nonchalantly.

The surfer drew a self-conscious breath. "Hey, maybe I'd better wash a few champagne flutes."

"Do that," agreed Mike.

Lilly stared sullenly ahead.

Mike started to say something, and stopped. After an awkward interval, he worked up his nerve.

"She isn't coming," he said, almost hating the flash of hurt in her eyes.

Her eyes narrowed. "Why'd you come over? Are you doing this to get even?"

He stared straight ahead.

"I—I had to...meet her. Uncle Sando said she'd come."

"He promised you that?"

Lilly wiggled Mike's champagne glass out of his large brown fingers and took a nervous sip. "Yeah."

He seized the slender stem from her so roughly that it splintered, spilling champagne.

Soaked, she ran to one of the mirrors behind a fountain. "My dress! I—I wanted to look so pretty...for her."

Lilly began to preen as excitedly as a parakeet with a new mirror. That's when Mike really noticed how her tight black mini exposed way too much of her breasts and shapely legs.

"If you don't stop all that twisting and turning, some vital part of your body is going to pop out of that skimpy black stuff."

"Ahimsa-silk," she said. "Made of silkworms that died naturally. Do you like it?"

"I just wish there was more of it."

"You bought it, remember?"

"Stop wiggling."

"You lectured and lectured me about those credit cards being yours. About how even if I sign the ticket, you—"

"Yes, yes." He nodded. *That* day, he thought glumly. The day she'd let Sando...

She beamed. "I was only trying to give you credit, silly."

Six diamonds adorned her ears. He'd never seen her wear so many rings on her fingers, either.

"Those jewels." His voice was weak. "Are they real?"

"I'm afraid so, Daddy. They were half price. I'm afraid

I simply couldn't resist charging them. I knew you'd want me to look my best tonight, in case Mother..."

Mother. Pressure, winding tight inside him. He balled his hand into a fist. "You don't have a mother." His voice was hoarse, tense.

"Kara's name is on my birth certificate."

"How'd you find that out?" Need he ask? She belonged to the nosiest species there was—she was a teenager. The minute he turned his back, she sifted through everything he had, took what she wanted, made a mess of what bored her.

"Maybe you wouldn't feel so pushed to the brink of ruin if my movie-star mama helped with my expenses." Her statement was careless. She licked her lips. "Champagne is so-o yummy. Uncle Stuart said to put in a slice of peach—" Lilly giggled. "It's so-o hot in here."

It wasn't hot. But she did *look* hot—in that dress—her eyes brilliant. *His* daughter.

"Why are you so flushed? Why is your speech slurred? Damn it, Lilly. Have you been drinking?"

Her eyes widened. "You were mean to me." She burst into giggles.

Stuart sauntered into the room, stopped short when he saw Mike and propped himself casually against a wall. His plastic surgeon, hair stylist, optician and tailor had sure done a number on him. The old Stuart with the large nose was gone. The new Stuart had the face of a cinema idol and the body to match. Contacts had replaced glasses. In place of his old surly expression was a constant smile.

Change of hair. Change of face. It was harder to switch what was inside. The pretty smile gave Mike the creeps.

Idly, Stuart plucked an orchid from a fountain and pinned it to his lapel. As CEO of one of the world's biggest computer companies, he was one of the richest men

in the country. He had everything he'd ever wanted and
more. Or did he? Did anybody?

Stuart waved to Lilly.

Lilly raised fluttering fingertips and blew him a kiss.
"I'd better go say hello."

"I asked you if you'd been drinking—"

She was long gone, having disappeared after Stuart.
When Mike gave chase, the pretty waitress in gold jumped
him. She smiled, her lengthy lashes dipping like sable
fans, her long neck was creamy and graceful. Her gold
sheath stopped many inches above her knees, the skimpy
skirt too snug on her thighs.

He blushed.

Emma.

The girl pressed herself against him. "Would you like
to take me home and get wild and sexy?"

His heart pumped. She stuck her hand in his pocket.

"I've got something for you," she whispered.

Warm fingers lingered, pressed intimate places, slipped
free. Her breasts swelled above gold as if she were dying
to shed that little scrap of gold and romp naked in his
bed.

No sooner had this fantasy taken shape in his mind than
she winked and vanished. He pulled a scrap of paper from
his pocket and memorized her phone number.

Then he saw Sando across the room, his short body
doubled over a cell phone. Pushy, bright-eyed, and
scrappy as a bantam cock, Sando beamed when he saw
Mike. Then he held up a fat stack of tabloids and flapped
them triumphantly.

Mike's gut tightened when the little man strutted toward him to show off the latest headlines.

"You've sure as hell done your best and your worst
tonight," Mike said.

"Thanks." Sando flashed his gutsiest smile, pushed his glasses higher and began to read. "Mike Greywolf slept with both Shayne twins. Well-placed Santa Fe sources claim the famous sisters were so alike, nobody could tell them apart, not even their Navajo lover."

"Give me those!"

Eyes aglow, Sando bounced back a step. "Who says these guys can't write?"

Mike grabbed the papers. Crumpling them up, he pitched them in the trash. "You're disgusting."

"You slept with them, pal." Sando's bright eyes rolled with lascivious envy. "There's not a guy here who wouldn't trade his balls to have your rotten luck." Sando snatched a paper out of the trash bin. "Listen to this. 'Words like *wild, bold* and *incredible* can't begin to describe the trio's sexcapades.'"

"Lies. Trash," Mike snapped.

"Whatever sells, pal."

"Sara said the same thing. I want to go home."

"Sara? She here?"

"I want to go home."

"When the show's over."

"You call this a show?"

"You should thank me."

Outside the screams got louder. *"Kara! Kara!"*

"She isn't *coming*. Why don't you give up?"

"In your dreams," Sando said. Then he spotted Sara in her green gown. "Sex-y! You care if I ask Sara out?"

"You're not her type."

"That was a yes-or-no question, pal."

"You always do whatever you want."

"That's my best trait."

"And your worst."

Sando leered at Sara. "Cool dress. Hot body."

Thirty minutes later the opulent gallery was jammed. Not that many serious buyers or collectors had braved the crowds. Not that Sando seemed to care once he'd cornered Sara.

Suddenly a stretch limo pulled up. When a veiled woman stuck a shapely leg out, the mob went wild. Reporters yelled questions. Flashbulbs popped. Fans stormed the thin line of uniformed police.

The rhythm of their hoarse chanting changed suddenly. *"KaRA! KaRA! KaRA!"*

Mike felt himself drawn to the door as if by an invisible magnet. His heart filled with dread when a tall, mysterious creature materialized in the foyer. The drums stopped. Eyes turned. Framed by twin waterfalls and swathed in frothy white, the glamorous lady tossed back her scarves.

Mike couldn't believe it.

She wasn't real.

But she was.

He would have known her anywhere. Her face had haunted him for as long as he could remember, although he would have denied it on his deathbed. The thin nose, those vivid, unsmiling, red lips, the high cheekbones.

She was quite old. Yet she was still beautiful.

Her glacial green eyes flickered over the gallery, settling on him.

Sando had sworn he wouldn't let her come.

"Indiana Parsons," an older gentleman in amber-tinted glasses gushed.

Her wild white hair stood out around her slim, crepey throat like an Elizabethan ruff.

When had her hair gone white? Why should it matter that she looked so thin, so...so vulnerable? Or even that she'd come?

The crowd gasped when she glided haughtily past

Mike. Neither by word nor deed did she acknowledge him. Not that she ever had.

When she reached the statue of Emma whirling with the butterflies, her thin, veined hand touched a single, bronze butterfly.

"Sweet." The word cut Mike like a blade. "Too sweet for an artist of Greywolf's caliber." Indiana laughed. "But it pleases some, I am sure. You were young. I'll buy it."

"It's not for sale," Mike said.

Indiana turned. "Everything has a price."

"Daddy!" Starstruck, Lilly ran to Indiana, who put her arms around her. "Don't be such a big silly, Daddy," Lilly said.

"I'm Indiana Parsons."

"The painter. Grandmother has some of your paintings. She took me to see more in your gallery. I just love them."

"You must sit for me." Mike felt a chill when Indiana patted Lilly. "You and I are going to be great friends."

Mike sucked in a breath and went to the back of the gallery. No way could he deal with this madness.

He had to get out of here. Fast.

He rushed through the crowded rooms till he came to the last. It was empty, except for the reclining statue and the flirtatious Kara-look-alike waitress. She'd set her tray of champagne flutes on the floor and was kneeling over the statue in a curious attitude of prayer.

The glare off the ocean was so dazzling that Mike could make out little more than the girl's silhouette. Still, her presence irritated him. He wanted to get past her without another awkward exchange.

A low red sun had the Pacific on fire. This copper ball

glazed multipaned windows and shot laser-bright shafts of sizzling orange into the room.

He took a long stride toward the door. When he reached the supine bronze with Kara's face and Emma's tears, the waitress looked up at him.

He stopped, his head pounding. One minute the kneeling girl touched a bronze tear with tender reverence. The next, her low, choked sob slammed Mike like a fist to his gut.

He reeled and then thrust the scrap of paper she'd given him at her. "I can't see you. Not tonight. Not any night. You remind me of someone I don't want to remember."

She froze. Silhouetted in red haze, her features were shadowy. Still, dark, terrified eyes burned a hole in his heart.

He sucked in a breath. "I said—"

"I heard."

That voice.

He shielded his eyes to see her better.

Slowly, the exquisite face backlighted by fire sharpened. He made out a sweep of tangled red curls, doe-soft, luminous, brown eyes, a slim curvy body.

Her face was world famous.

Kara.

Emma wasn't with her.

She'd come alone.

Of course. The twins were estranged.

16

"**K**ara!"

She started.

"Hello—movie star." Mike knew his harsh tone sliced like a rapier.

She squeezed her eyes shut, but the tears didn't stop.

"You're more beautiful off-screen than on."

She lowered her head, brushed her fingers across her damp cheeks. "Don't—"

"It's good to see you, too." His murmur was vicious.

"Would you stop." Her throaty voice held more torment than he believed possible for her to feel.

Sando's nasal baritone boomed from the next room. "Mother—"

"I have to go," Kara said.

He pushed her into a shadowy corner. "The hell you do. We have to talk…about Lilly."

She covered her lips with her shaking hand.

"Lilly thinks she needs her mother."

For a second Lilly strutted into view in her skimpy black dress.

"But she doesn't have a mother," Mike said, pushing

Kara deeper into the corner, so that Lilly wouldn't see her. "She has you."

Kara's skin paled to ivory. Her eyes were huge and stark with what looked like guilt. He couldn't believe her incredible concern.

"What kind of woman gives up her child—"

"You told me what kind when I handed her to you."

"Right," he muttered in contempt.

"What is life in its purest, rawest form?" Sando brayed in the other room. "What does man, woman, each of us…need to be happy? I think Greywolf, like all great artists, addresses that in these pieces. Mike's saying that what matters can't be seen, it can only be felt. But it can be felt by seeing these statues. Perception versus reality. He loved both these women. He was their lover. They were so much alike even he couldn't tell them apart. He still doesn't know which one—"

For a second Kara's eyes clung to Mike's. He didn't understand the lifetime of pain and guilt he saw in their depths. Then she sprang to her feet and raced for the door. Mike tore after her. When she grabbed the doorknob, he jammed his arm against the door so it wouldn't open.

"You haven't changed since that night when you carved out my soul," he said roughly. "You pretend to feel, to be easily hurt by something I say. All you are is a cheap actress with a pretty face who looks good on film, who took off her clothes and caused a sensation. You happen to look just like the woman I thought I loved. God damn you for looking so much like her, even now. You don't feel anything real, you just feed off those who do. Like Emma. And me. You deliberately came between us. Now you're tearing Lilly in two. You make me sick."

"You were just as guilty," she whispered.

Maybe. "What did you come here for—sex?"

"No."

"Of course not. Emma doesn't give a damn about me now, so neither do you. Why are you here, then?"

Kara's glamorous face changed, sweetened, softened—saddened. Tore his heart out.

"Lilly," she whispered. "I—I had to see her— No. I—I didn't say that."

"Stay away from her."

She went even whiter, as if his harsh words destroyed her.

He felt…*Emma.*

Why did he *feel* Emma?

He didn't give a damn about Emma.

But Kara's wounded eyes and pale skin startled him, made him feel her humanity, her vulnerability. Made him remember Emma.

Made him remember that wild dark night with Kara.

"Don't do that," he whispered. "Don't look…like *her.* How do you do that anyway—make your face look gentle and heartbroken, like Emma's—"

Kara moaned.

Emma. He forced himself to remember her betrayal. She hadn't believed him. She'd never trusted him. He never would've ended up with Kara if she had.

Kara stared at him in that way that touched him to the quick.

His flesh tingled as it had that night when she'd taught him that desire and hate could be one. He caught a ragged breath. Memories of Emma compelled him toward this woman he hated who shared her image. As they had that night—the night that had condemned him to hell. "Damn you."

Kara knew his weakness, how to *play* Emma. Pretend-

ing to care about Lilly. How to make him *feel* Emma.
Want Emma.

She'd done this before. Twice.

It wouldn't work tonight.

Shove her away. Run.

Mike meant to. Instead, he grabbed Kara, and the hands
that should've pushed instead yanked her against his
body.

Soft breasts, wide, flaring hips, long legs—all were
caught between his tough, muscular form and the cool
wooden planks of the door. He felt heat, electricity, all
the old wildness that had driven him to madness and ruin.
His heart hammered behind his eardrums.

Don't. Don't.

As before, he couldn't stop himself.

He ground her against the door. Sweet, lush, melting
heat flooded him, made him crazy with desire. He forgot
Lilly. He forgot everything except the woman in his arms
and the mad need to peel that little gold material strip of
nothing off her, hike her legs around his waist, and bury
himself inside her.

Emma's face! Emma's body! Why did she have to look
so much like Emma? How could that matter?

He touched her cheek, brushed her brow, traced a ten-
dril of her soft hair with the back of his hand…before he
remembered to hate her.

Kara squirmed to free herself.

That only got him hotter.

"You don't give a damn about Lilly," he said hoarsely.
"You never gave a damn about Emma. Well, you're going to feel something tonight before I'm through."

He rammed his pelvis against hers, thrusting, forcing
her to feel the raw, blatant power of his animal arousal.

Kara pushed at him, clawed at him.

Determined to control her, for once, he buried his face in the curve of her neck and shoulders. Oh, God. She smelled of lilacs. *Emma.*

He hated Emma. He did. Almost as much as he hated Kara.

He panted in furious, harsh gasps. His rough hands moved inside the golden fabric of her blouse and shredded her lace bra.

She quivered when his callused fingertips kneaded her nipples into taut beads. Together they stumbled backward into the wall.

Her soft flesh burned, even as she fought him.

His arms locked around her like iron bands. "Why'd you come here, movie star? To turn me on? Did you come to get more of what I gave you before?"

He felt her terror. Her hatred. Her lust.

And something else. Something quite extraordinary.

Her confusion and unwanted desire matched his own.

He wanted to hurt her, to violate her, to bruise her.

He wanted other things, too.

"Remember the nude scene in *Betrayal?*"

She gasped.

He reached inside her skirt, touching deeply with erotically skilled fingers, and found her soft and wet, steaming. His hand plunged inside.

She writhed, came, instantly—as if starved for him.

"Damn your soul to hell for being so damn fuckable," he whispered, but his breath was even rougher than hers. He wanted her.

Kara's face stared back at him with blank, bewildered pain. And passion. So much haunting passion, she broke his heart.

Never had Emma seemed so real. Her love and desire so hatefully dear. Or so utterly lost.

"You didn't win an Oscar for nothing. You're good. Too damn good."

He wound his free hand in her red curls and viciously yanked her head back. "Now it's my turn."

He brought his mouth down on hers.

Violate. Bruise. Destroy. Surrender to the dark.

He couldn't do any of those things without violating himself. And Emma.

Why the hell did he care?

He didn't.

He took a single taste of her and stopped, despising himself because he ached for more.

Emma. Kara. He had loved one and hated the other. Tonight his explosive feelings were all mixed-up.

This time she wouldn't win.

"Whore," he whispered, even as he savored her sexual response. His voice was strangely controlled. "Get out. Before we're both sorry."

"I already am," she said. "So very sorry, Mike."

She'd said that before, in her hotel suite, after she'd damned him to hell.

His hands fell away.

Strangely, hers did not.

Clinging, she kissed him with hesitant, soft lips. Her sad eyes drank him in; her velvet voice seduced. "I am sorry, Mike. I was right never to want to see you again."

Again, he remembered *that* night. Her hot tears wet his cheeks. Stole his heart. Enraged him. Inflamed him.

"Don't hate me," she pleaded, her dark eyes staring into his—holding them, and him, motionless.

He might have taken her then and there, but Lilly stepped into the room.

"Kara..." Lilly said softly. "Mother..."

"Dear God," Kara murmured. "Oh, Mike—what are we doing?"

Then Sara was there, video camera held high. "You wanted to know why I came, Mike? This is why!"

Another reporter's white flash blinded them.

Kara's arms fell away from Mike. For a second longer their gazes held. Then she looked at Lilly. "Dearest—"

"Get out!" Mike said.

Kara flung the door open and ran.

"No! No!" Lilly screamed. "Come back! Mother—"

A stillness descended over Mike. Kara was gone. Yet he felt reborn in some unfathomable way. New. Alive. And yet ancient and wise—lost.

Not like that night when she'd destroyed his heart and soul and cost him the woman he loved.

He felt like an abandoned child who'd found his way home.

It didn't matter that she was the wrong twin.

His soul had rushed to Kara Shayne.

As hers had rushed to him.

He closed the door Kara had opened, and leaned against it.

Lilly flung herself into his arms, her fists pounding his chest. The devastation in her young face matched the agony he felt.

He held her, whispering to her, stroking her hair.

Her head twisted against his shoulder, her tears streamed, her breath came in short gasps.

"Go get her, Daddy! Go get my mother and bring her back!"

"I can't."

She turned away.

"Lilly!"

She didn't answer. She just kept walking away from him.

He knew if he didn't go after Kara, he'd lose his daughter forever.

17

Thump. Thump.

Running shoes squishing heavily into soft sand.

Running made the music stop, so his thoughts could gel.

He had to do it.

Tonight.

Two's company. Three's a crowd.

A sensitive lover couldn't share his woman without feeling persecuted.

The bitch deserved to die.

A gust of wind sent garbage tumbling across the beach. A black trash bag spewed paper plates and paper cups.

The jogger pulled up the hood on his gray jogging suit and kicked at a cup. Squashing it, he used his heel to paw out a hole in the sand and bury it, the way he might a fresh corpse or a dog turd.

Malibu. What was so fucking great about Malibu?

She liked it here.

So what if the beach houses cost a bundle and had the Santa Monica Mountains behind them and the surf in front of them?

She thought she was such a big damn deal, too.

He'd been jogging on the beach for more than an hour, trying to pretend that he was part of the scene, that he liked beaches, sunsets, dogs and Frisbees.

Bullshit.

He wore the hood pulled up, not because he was cold, but so nobody could see more than his eyes, especially now that he was close to her house.

Who did she think she was? Showing herself to the whole world? Big tits and all. Forcing him to desire her? Turning on the music? Forcing him to kill her?

The beach was gritty and uneven beneath his running shoes. His left ankle had throbbed ever since he'd fallen in that hole a ways back and gotten wet sand in his socks and gritty bits of shell stuck between his toes.

When he killed her, all the bad feelings would be gone.

He would be free.

The music would stop.

He stared up at her house. Scaffolding, palms and cypress trees partially obscured his view. He frowned. The house, once of modern design, was now a monstrosity. Its three levels were stacked like shoe boxes in a narrow closet. Huge terraces and overhangs brought the outdoors indoors and provided views of the sea. But some stupid jerk had fiddled with its design. The new brown paint and artificial vigas were atrocious.

His gaze wandered over other houses, and he pretended an equal interest in the gorgeous white-walled, red-tiled mansion next door, with that rose garden spilling down the cliff.

He forced himself to concentrate on the target house, noting how every window on her lower floor was lit up, while only a single light glowed from the second story. Her garage and grounds, roof and palms were dark.

Hollywood actors were so snotty. A movie or two, and

nobodies—former waiters, truck drivers and high-school dropouts—thought they were royalty.

Slowly, carefully, he walked toward the weathered stairs that led up to her mansion and began to climb them, not furtively, but one at a time, with the bold, methodical assurance of someone who belonged here.

He even stopped, pretended to enjoy the view and check his wristwatch.

Then the music started, and he hurried again.

"Come to Daddy."

Run. Hide. Get away.
From Mike. From Lilly.

From that crazy fan who'd stalked her for years, whom she had to fear every time she went out.

Kara was racing for her limo, when Sara sprang after her from the gallery with her video camera still running.

The sky above Sara was redder than her frizzy hair. Beneath the row of tall palms, the alley where the limo was parked was so dark that Kara could make out only the vaguest outlines of her sleek, dark car.

A reporter's flash popped in her eyes. The glare blinded her. Kara put a hand up as Sara caught up to her, her video camera raised, its little red light on. "Did you come to see your love-child? Or your lover?"

"That's enough, bitch!" Raymond banged his car door against the brick wall with uncustomary violence. Jumping Sara, he lifted her onto her kicking tiptoes, letting her dangle while she struggled to breathe. A brief scuffle left Sara on the ground, panting. When she scrambled after her video camera, Raymond kicked it aside.

"You'll pay for that!" Sara yelled. "You'll both pay!"

Raymond wrapped Kara in his arms and hurried her into the limo. Doors slammed. Door locks snapped. Then the car shot out of the alley past the hordes of reporters and other cars.

"The border," Raymond said.

"No," Kara said. "Home. Malibu."

"But your fan... You have to get away. I want to marry you, protect you—"

"You can't."

"KaRA. KaRA. KaRA..." Her screaming fans stormed the police barriers.

"Careful, Hoke," Kara pleaded. "Don't hit them."

Honking their horns, cars and motorcycles gave chase behind them.

"Bastards. The last thing we need is another press parade." Raymond's silver-green eyes were bright. "They want to eat you alive!" At the sight of her stricken face, Raymond lowered his voice. "When we're married tonight...in Mexico—"

"No, no. Not tonight." Shading her eyes so she wouldn't be so aware of the headlights behind them, she sank gratefully against his wide shoulder. "Thanks...for getting me out of there. You didn't hurt Sara, did you?"

"No, but I wanted to."

When his overbright gaze lingered on her mouth, her throat, she flushed uneasily. Raymond hadn't wanted to come to the show. Much as he resented Sando, his legitimate brother, he absolutely despised Mike.

"I warned you about Greywolf, didn't I? About restarting destructive feelings. I know all about restarting—"

Mike. Seeing him, kissing him.... Shame washed over her that she still wanted him so much, that she'd willingly surrendered to him the instant he'd put his hands on her. She touched her raw lips and lowered her head guiltily. Had Mike left telltale marks? Hoping he hadn't, she stared at her lap.

Raymond was a shrink now. But not her shrink. Still, no matter how well she acted, he saw too much. She couldn't look at him. Not now, after Lilly...after Mike's kiss... She was flying to pieces inside.

She didn't trust him in his present mood.

She'd told herself she'd gone to the gallery because Lilly had poured her heart out to the tabloids. Now she knew that she'd gone to see Mike.

Burningly alive, as merciless as ever, he'd torn her heart out. As he'd done that night in Santa Fe, the last time he'd made love to her.

Would it ever be over? Would he and his motherless child always, always have this power over her? She couldn't, she *wouldn't* let herself feel...

She twisted her diamond engagement ring.

"I told you not to go," Raymond repeated. "Not to see him."

"I can't marry you, Ray."

"If my crude Navajo bastard of a brother made a pass at you, I'll kill him."

She went still.

"Why him? Why in the hell do you always throw yourself at him?"

She buried her face in her hands. "Nothing happened. I swear."

"Something sure as hell did."

Kara rubbed her temples. "Your mother was there."

"Damn her." There was real hate in his voice now.

"Lilly was there, too. She's so beautiful. I kept thinking about what she'd told that reporter—"

I want my mother.

"I kept remembering she came to Malibu..."

Which twin is my mother? I want my mother.

"And I wasn't there. In my whole life I've never been

there for anybody.'' Kara began to sob. ''Lilly is so much braver than I am.''

''Did you speak to her?''

''I—I wanted to—''

''And Mike?''

Hoke swerved and gunned the motor to get ahead of the vehicles in hot pursuit of them.

Kara shuddered, hating this part of her fame that never allowed her a single, personal moment. ''Oh, Raymond, I was selfish to involve you. My life's…complicated, unresolved. It was stupid of me to think I could marry anyone, especially you. But when you showed up again, I— I was so tired of being alone out here. Afraid. Hopeless. Lost… You were just there.''

''Like always,'' he said bitterly.

''It was timing, I suppose, more than rightness. I know this is going to end badly for you, and you don't deserve that—after all I've put you through.''

His face was grim. ''You're not alone. The whole world loves you. I love you. I've loved you…since high school.''

Behind them horns blared.

''You don't know me—not really. I'm not the same girl you knew and loved.''

His eyes blazed. ''You think I don't know that?''

Kara leaned away from him, pressing her hot forehead to the cool tinted glass. ''I feel pulled in two. You live a life with certain people. You think they'll always be there. And then, something happens and things go wrong… You find out nothing was like you thought. I'm not who you think. I don't deserve your love. I don't deserve…anybody's love.''

''You want to be his whore!'' Raymond caught himself. ''Sorry.''

But he wasn't sorry. He was furious.

"Forget him, Raymond. Forget *me*."

City lights swept by in a blur. Forbidden images from the past bombarded her.

You can run. But you can't hide.

Emma.

Lilly.

Kara.

Guilt. So much guilt. So many lies.

Even her relationship with Raymond was a lie. If she'd ever been attracted to him, it was because he'd reminded her so much of Mike.

She imagined a pair of twin little-girl faces, so alike in their bright youthful eagerness, sharing the same steamy, bathroom mirror every morning, sharing the same damp towel after their showers, racing to grab toothbrushes to see who could brush their teeth the fastest. Identical twin birthday cakes with the same number of glittering candles. Two eager little girls standing over their cakes like little princesses, sucking in great breaths of air, puffing out their cheeks, each racing to blow out her candles first. Secret words only they knew. Secret games they alone knew how to play.

Secret telepathic thoughts that had bound their souls so tightly that Kara still wasn't sure what was truly *other* and what was *self*.

Kara had always wanted to be Emma, and Emma had always wanted to be Kara. Especially after Mike had come into their lives.

They'd lost each other. Their bizarre estrangement was because of Mike—

Then Mike had had to be sacrificed. Lilly, too.

Brakes screeched. A hand stuck a camera out of the car speeding beside them. Lights flashed.

Fame held Kara a prisoner in this hellish, fairy-tale exile.

Early years shared with a twin who had effortlessly understood her had left Kara poorly prepared to form easy attachments to others, especially in Hollywood with its air kisses and shallow attachments.

"You're awfully quiet," Raymond said, his voice smoother, his jealousy contained.

"My fans don't know me. Sometimes I feel like I'm dying inside…of… I—I don't know what. The glamorous, passionate creature on the big screen they love isn't real."

"No star ever is. You're an actress. An illusion. A very good one."

She shivered. "Yes. But sometimes when your image doesn't match your reality, you feel crazy."

"Indeed."

His icy eyes saw too much. She ran a hand through her tangled curls.

Once, he had seemed safe, someone from the past who'd loved her. Suddenly she wished she knew more about how he really felt. She'd told him so much about herself—more than he'd ever told her. And yet she felt some great emotion seething beneath his smooth surface.

He deeply resented Mike. Until now, that was something she'd thought they shared.

She rarely went to parties, but strangely, she'd run into Raymond *at* a party. And it had felt nice to see someone she'd grown up with, someone who'd adored her.

Max, her director, had forced her to come to his bizarre, ultra-modern, '50s style, mountaintop mansion to promote a film. Max had introduced them in that house, with its outrageous curving glass walls, columns, and mosaic tubs and floors.

Not that they hadn't instantly recognized one another.

We'd like to send you two free books to introduce you to "The Best of the Best." Your two books have a combined cover price of over $11.00 or more in the U.S. and $13.00 or more in Canada, but they are yours free! We'll even send you a wonderful mystery gift. You can't lose!

Visit us at www.mirabooks.com

The Best of the Best™ — Here's How it Works:

Accepting your 2 free books and gift places you under no obligation to buy anything. You may keep the books and gift and return the shipping statement marked "cancel." If you do not cancel, about a month later we will send you 4 additional novels and bill you just $4.24 each in the U.S., or $4.74 each in Canada, plus 25¢ delivery per book and applicable taxes if any.* That's the complete price and — compared to cover prices of $5.50 or more each in the U.S. and $6.50 or more each in Canada — it's quite a bargain! You may cancel at any time, but if you choose to continue, every month we'll send you 4 more books, which you may either purchase at the discount price or return to us and cancel your subscription.

*Terms and prices subject to change without notice. Sales tax applicable in N.Y. Canadian residents will be charged applicable provincial taxes and GST.

If offer card is missing write to: The Best of the Best, 3010 Walden Ave., P.O. Box 1867, Buffalo, NY 14240-1867

BUSINESS REPLY MAIL
FIRST-CLASS MAIL   PERMIT NO. 717   BUFFALO, NY

POSTAGE WILL BE PAID BY ADDRESSEE

THE BEST OF THE BEST
3010 WALDEN AVE
PO BOX 1867
BUFFALO NY 14240-9952

NO POSTAGE
NECESSARY
IF MAILED
IN THE
UNITED STATES

After what they'd been to each other. It was probably amazing they hadn't run into one another sooner. She was the most famous of stars, and Raymond was the most famous of movie-star shrinks.

She'd tried to avoid him by taking a separate house tour to see Max's famous collection of lamps, but Max had seated them together at dinner. Even then, Kara had turned a cold shoulder to Raymond.

He'd leaned toward her, his gaze intense, his low tone intimate. "Don't be afraid. I forgive you for jilting me. I won't remind you of our past...or delve into your precious secrets that make you the most mysteriously, unknowable and desirable actress on earth."

"What?"

"I'm still your biggest fan. Remember all those nights on the mesa?"

"Please—"

"What will happen when the walls crumble, and your secrets are revealed, Miss Shayne?"

The atmosphere had grown dense, like air in a bottle when the lid is screwed on tightly. Choking, she'd struggled to stand, but he'd seized her limp hand underneath that Sansone II table, coaxing her back into her chair.

"Don't panic. I shouldn't have said that. I care about you. I always did. I even forgave you for throwing yourself at Mike Greywolf in high school when I was wild about you, didn't I?"

She hadn't reacted to that.

"You're eating yourself alive. You can't go on like this, you know."

Grateful, needy, she'd clung to that warm hand, to this man who'd loved her.

His kind smile that reminded her of Mike's had stolen some of her loneliness that night. "Maybe your secrets aren't so terrible,'' he'd said. "Everybody needs someone to talk to, someone they can trust, especially…out here."

His passions ran deeper than she'd suspected. He was the last person she should've trusted.

But she'd felt so bereft. "You must think actresses a temperamental, neurotic lot. Do you come to these parties seeking patients?''

He'd laughed. "Actually, I'm into houses. This one's quite famous. It's one of two that Zachariah Larson designed.''

"I—I didn't realize. You know he designed mine, too?''

"Really? Well, if you remodel, don't change anything.''

"But I want it to look like New Mexico."

"You'll regret it. It cost good old Max a fortune to renovate and yet stay true to the design. Honestly—I heard you were on the guest list. That's why I came tonight.''

"So…would you see me? As a patient?''

"Impossible. After what we were together. I'm still drawn to you in ways that might tempt me to unethical behavior. But I could recommend a colleague.'' He smiled. "I want to be your friend again."

"No.''

But he'd called. When she'd refused, he'd persisted, sending red roses, potted lavender, inviting her to concerts and operas.

She'd accepted an invitation to sail. Far from shore, with the blue swells of the Pacific surging beneath the heavy keel of his huge yacht, she'd felt safe enough to forget herself.

He'd asked her out again. She'd refused. He'd been patient, persistent, until she'd accepted again.

It became their custom to sail every Sunday. She would lie on the cushions and stare at the city and the desert mountains and feel safer than she ever felt on land.

Months passed before they really talked. Then they talked about everything—everything except Mike. In the end, Raymond's patience conquered her. He attacked, proposing marriage with his usual persistence—and wore her down.

Tonight, Mike had shown her she wasn't ready for marriage. Suddenly Raymond felt very wrong. Why was he so irrational about Mike? Suddenly it worried her that their romance had been all *his* idea.

"I will always be there for you, Kara. I've wanted you for years and years."

She twisted the platinum band he had given her, but it wouldn't come off.

"Don't make me beg, Kara."

"It's over."

"Not for me. I'll wait, give you the time you need—"

"I don't need time." How could she tell him he couldn't begin to compete with Mike?

Hoke braked when the electronic gates of her recently purchased mansion swung open. Three cars screamed to a halt as the limo sped inside the high brown walls of her oceanfront compound.

She got out quickly. When Raymond objected to her going in alone, she reminded him her maid, Marta, was there.

"But I thought her ex—"

"He's out of the picture."

She asked Hoke to drive Raymond home. Then she ran past huge pots of lavender and rustling palms; past the ornate gate to her courtyard with its terraced gardens, its granite fountains, and pool; up the curving stairs. In that last instant before she got the front doors open, her fearful gaze fell upon the massive bronze Howling Lioness in the corner of her cactus garden, where Marta had found Lilly.

Her only Greywolf.

Her lonely Greywolf.

Sometimes she went out into the garden just to be with the statue. She would imagine Mike creating it, his huge hands shaping the wet clay.

She flung herself inside. Leaning against her carved doors, she pulled out the remote to her security system and punched the code.

She had worked hard to buy this house and to renovate it. How eagerly she'd tiled the floors and put up mock wooden vigas. How eagerly she had the tall walls plastered by hand and repainted in earth tones. How happily she'd scattered all her priceless Navajo rugs everywhere. She hadn't yet decided what to do about the columns in her unfinished foyer. Nothing seemed to fit, and she was beginning to realize everything she'd done was a mistake.

She'd spent a fortune to recreate the home she'd run away from.

Fakes were always big mistakes.

One wall of her foyer was mirrored. In that glass she saw the reflection of a woman she did not recognize. Oh, the red hair, the slim figure were hers. But the eyes, the soul? Who did they belong to? Her twin's face seemed to stare back at her more often than her own did these days. Then she saw poor, motherless Lilly in that tight black dress.

The mistakes she'd made on her house didn't come close to matching the mess she'd made of her life.

The phone rang. She heard some sound upstairs, and called up to Marta. When Marta answered neither her nor the phone, Kara let her machine pick up.

Raymond spoke quietly, precisely, patiently. She put her hands over her ears.

The phone rang again. It was Raymond's custom to repeat the same message, especially when he knew she was home. She wandered down the gallery, passing through the breakfast room, through other unfinished rooms that flowed seamlessly, one into the other.

Lilly had looked too wild-eyed and sexy. Motherless...

Kara stopped, paralyzed. In seven years she had never felt so acutely alive nor alone. Never had this awful house seemed such a hollow monument.

Again, her phone rang. She opened a glass door and lifted her hot face to the damp, salty breeze. She thought of her long sails with Raymond. He had said they reminded him of their times on the mesa. What had she been thinking of? To lead him on?

Something rustled behind her cypress tree. Sensing something or someone in that darkness, and remembering her crazed fan's threats, she quickly shut the door and retreated to her cozy study, with its black lacquer screens and Chinese decor.

A shadow passed across a window shade. She caught her breath, telling herself it was just her imagination. Her security was the best.

Still, she avoided the tall windows that had a view of Mike's Howling Lioness, and sank down at her desk. A dog-eared Spanish language romance lay in a corner. Marta's probably. Poor Marta. In real life, she was as unlucky in love as was Kara.

Kara's gaze flicked over her locked desk drawers, up to the green, leather-bound volume Raymond had left open on her burled walnut desk. She wondered why he'd underlined that particular quotation by Pearl S. Buck.

"Every great mistake has a halfway moment, a split second when it can be recalled, perhaps remedied—"

He'd read that and then said, "If you've got the guts."

She began to shake. Mike. Nothing had prepared her for the shock of seeing him. Again, she saw his dark, chiseled features before he'd kissed her. She'd even forgotten Lilly in the wild sizzle of his kiss. He'd put his hands on her. What would have happened, had Lilly and Sara not interrupted them?

Kara forced herself to remember the reclining statue with its gleaming tears and the long-ago night that had made her determined never to see him again.

She'd hated him after that night. Now she wondered if he'd suffered, too. He looked so lonely. So lost. So much older.

Across the study, her Oscar gleamed on the mantel. The great Kara Shayne was a joke. Her life, not her movies, was her greatest role. No, that wasn't exactly true. She poured her pain into her films. For no reason, she picked up Raymond's book and hurled it at the ridiculous statue.

She missed, but the book's spine split open when it hit the lacquer wall. Twin halves ricocheted harmlessly into the fireplace, raining thin, gilt-edged pages onto her polished floor. When she flung herself down on the red couch, the cold cracked leather sent chills through her.

Scripts, some read, some not, were scattered beside the couch. She shivered. Unable to find work that compelled her. She was between projects. Everybody who was anybody in this town wanted her to do a film. She refused them all—except Max. Nor did she grant interviews.

But her silence only magnified her mystery, making her more famous. Movie critics said her face had an extraordinarily passive power to mirror emotions, especially painful ones that lay locked in the hearts of her audience.

The tabloids reprinted old shots of her famous nude scene, as well as sensational lies about her wild love life. The notorious psychic, Robin O'Hair, obsessed about her, endlessly analyzing her behavior and predicting her future.

Lies.

Why wouldn't they quit prying and just leave her alone?

Kara did one film per year. They were a catharsis for her personal suffering. Hating the applause and scandal generated by her fame and the celebrity media-machine, her success made her feel violated. She hated never being able to leave her house, never being able to shop or go to a movie unless she wore a wig and kept her face hidden.

Long ago she'd lived a different sort of life.

An ordinary life. She'd found pleasure in simple things.

There was no going back.

She had to forget Mike and Lilly.

But she couldn't forget.

She pulled an afghan over herself. She was tired. So tired.

She slept, as she often did at odd hours, and as always she dreamed....

She was lost and terrified in an ancient city of the dead carved from magically glowing, red rock. Her sister was somewhere ahead of her, floating through those one-room stone houses. Silently, oh, so silently, she wandered those abandoned plazas, kivas. She flew up ladders and cliffs as only dreamers do, exploring every upper terrace. Then she came to the cave that led to the hidden spring and that mound of bones and skulls. But her sister wasn't there. The earthen walls darkened and pressed close. Cats danced on the walls. The atmosphere grew eerie and so dense and stifling, she couldn't breathe.

Then her twin called her name. Too late, she realized that her twin was leading her down, down into a pool of hellish darkness.

When her own cries woke her, she felt a profound sensation of loss.

Feeling more exhausted than ever, she slowly sank back into that rich leather and dozed again.

Her fax rang and woke her. She sat up as a curl of slick paper spilled onto her sisal rug.

Fear swept her.

Some unseen danger felt very close. Spooked, she shredded the paper without reading it, pitching the pieces into a brass trash can, throwing in a lit match. Soon a gray plume floated above a hot golden blossom. Then the flower shriveled into a quivering red ball.

She lay down, more anxious than before.

Hours passed. The wind rose. She heard footsteps upstairs. No, they were outside. She called up to Marta.

A fist pounded her front door.

Worried, she decided she'd better go upstairs and find Marta.

Then her doorbell buzzed. How could anybody get over her wall without setting off her alarm?

She jerked up, fully awake, her heart racing. Grabbing the remote to her alarm system, she ran through the gallery. She stopped when she saw an eerie shadow dance in her foyer.

Then a huge dark hand hammered her heavy doors again.

A powerfully built man swayed unsteadily outside her front window. He was much too huge to be Hoke.

Fear shook the air out of her lungs. Then a hard, familiar, male voice wrapped her.

Mike's voice, slurring her name.

As he had that last night before he'd seized her and thrown her against the wall.

Sweat beaded her forehead. She remembered the famous nude scene in *Betrayal,* and her stomach felt hollow. She stabbed at the panic button.

"Kara." He rattled the doorknob. "Let me in. Before your damn bodyguard or maid sics the cops."

Mike.

He'd come back to her.

To her.

At last.

18

When the bitch threaded her fingers through the man's black hair, the jogger's face grew fearsome. The drums started and wouldn't stop.

She cupped her tits and began to dance.

Come to Mommy.

A jealousy-crazed, animal snarl tore from his throat. He couldn't take his eyes off her delicate face, her swollen mouth, or those perky tits—those tits that she was offering to another man.

His.

They were his.

If he couldn't suckle them, nobody could.

He would smash her flat, smash her till there was nothing recognizable left for any man to want.

Slowly, he examined the savage she lusted after.

Tall. Dark. Big. Muscular.

The jogger took a step toward them and then stopped.

He took a deep breath. Then another.

He had to calm down.

He had to regain his center.

He had to punish Mommy for being bad.

* * *

Kara stared at Mike wordlessly. His white T-shirt was stretched tightly across his broad chest and taut muscles. Faded denim molded his long, powerful legs. His black hair was unbound and hung like a black mane against his wide shoulders. His burning eyes were wild and stark—hate-filled.

"You're drunk," she whispered.

"Yes. Very. I called. Why didn't you answer the phone?" His expression was belligerent. Brown biceps bulged.

He was primitive, every bit as dangerous as the hero everybody had loved in *Betrayal.*

His fist punched her doorbell again.

The cold tiles scalded her bare feet like dry ice.

"Let me in."

"Hush. Go home."

His fierce black eyes stripped her—saw through to her soul. "It's too late—Emma."

Emma...

Pain knifed her. "Don't—"

"Emma."

Emma. Was he *pretending* to see Emma, to feel Emma? She hated him, because even to him, she and her twin were what they had almost believed themselves to be—twin halves of a single whole.

She wanted him for herself alone. That's what had caused such tragedy.

"Emma—"

"Stop it," she begged. "Just go—"

"Damn it, if you don't open it, I'll break it down."

Like in *Betrayal.*

He would. She knew he would.

Kara licked her lips.

"You kissed me like you wanted it," he said. "You

made me want it. Then you went home with my brother. Where the hell is he?''

"Gone."

"Let me in."

"I hate you," she said.

He opened his tanned, powerful hand and splayed coarse, lacerated fingers against the glass. "When did hate ever stop us?''

Her heart raced with unwanted memories. So did her body. In the movie, she'd placed her hands on the glass, too.

Punch the panic button. Punch it.

She swayed toward that broad, flexed hand, her own fingertips outstretched like a blind woman's, seeking the roughened, wounded shape of his big fingers. Carefully, yet hardly knowing what she did, she positioned each of her slim fingers against his wider, longer ones, her trembling fingertips slowly stretching their full length against that brown palm.

He fell heavily against the glass.

So did she, mashing her body against the same thin windowpane.

They say the imagination is the most powerful sexual stimulant.

Her hands, separated from his by that fragile, invisible barrier, her body there, too, pressing against his, like an unholy offering, open to him—

For an instant more he leaned into the glass, into her. Then he yanked his hand free, but the fiery passion in his eyes jolted her. He towered above her, virile and masculine, separated from her still only by that thin, transparent sheet.

"Open the door," he commanded roughly.

Her heart drummed, like the savage beat of some wild pagan tune.

"Don't do this, Mike."

"Maybe I can't stop myself."

Neither could she.

She raised her arms and continued to press the whole length of her hot body against the cool glass. She rolled, rubbed herself against the glass like a seductive cat, as she'd done in the film.

Mesmerized, his large, brown hands came back. This time when both his hands touched both of hers, she moaned. Then slowly he ran his fingers down the length of her slim arms, to caress the curve of her shoulders, touch her breasts. His hands didn't move away till her nipples hardened. Then he touched her waist, moving lower.

Even though the glass separated them, she knew just how hot and expert his touch would be. She wanted the heat of his big hands all over her. Arching her pelvis into that spot where his hand shaped glass, her loins melted like wax.

His green eyes shone with feral readiness. Flames of need spiraled inside her, engulfed her. He read her like a book he'd memorized by heart.

So what. She'd memorized him, too.

This was real. Just as their last night together had been real.

When he pulled himself away from the window, her pulse skittered like a rabbit's. He made a fist as though to break the glass with his bare knuckles.

Something inside her wanted to drive him mad with passion, so just as the actress had done in the film, she shook her head and laughed. Even when he knelt down and hefted one of her pots of lavender onto his shoulders, she couldn't stop laughing.

"Get back," he yelled, and then took two long strides toward her window.

Still laughing, she obeyed.

He hurled the pot. Glass shattered into billions of sparkles. Her alarm screamed.

There was no script for what happened next. They would have to improvise.

In a daze she watched dirt and ceramic explode on the red tiles. Then he sprang through her window, his fierce, dark eyes hot with unspeakable needs, his stance that of a conquering warrior as he stood before her, his long legs spread widely apart amidst glass shards, dirt and broken pottery.

There was a streak of blood on his face, another on his hands. Her laughter died.

"You're hurt," she whispered.

"A scratch. Nothing."

She backed against a column. His eyes swallowed her, devoured her, set her skin on fire. Her heart raced. Her throat was dry. He'd hurt her. Almost destroyed her. Yet she wanted him between her legs, inside her—again. She had never stopped wanting him, not one night or one day in the past seven years. And her long-lashed eyes said so.

Her alarm kept screaming. Tiny red lights above their heads flickered. Not that she cared. Consumed with desire, she was aware of nothing but him.

In three long steps he spanned the distance that separated them. He seized the remote. Frantically, she whispered the code. He punched it, and the alarm fell silent.

Her fingers skimmed the line of red on his cheek. "You're right. It's only a scratch. I—I'm glad."

He searched her eyes. The breath she expelled was softer than a sighing whisper.

"Sweetness…from you?" he demanded bitterly. "Don't try to pretend you've grown a heart." Then his mouth was on hers. Starved, his tongue plunged inside her lips, ravaging, and it was even more wonderful than she remembered.

"Your hair is wet," she whispered a long time later, her voice silken, drugged, yet more seductive. Kara's voice.

"I showered."

"You should've waited. I could've showered with you."

He laughed. "Later." His tongue came inside her again. "You taste like her. You look like her. She won't have me because of you, so maybe it's time I settled for this. You and I deserve each other." He ground his hips against hers until they were both breathless.

Emma. If they did it again, it would be the ultimate betrayal to herself, to her twin. It would be the biggest and the worst of all her sins and lies.

"Not like this. Not when you still believe all the lies."

"I know you're a liar, but sex is strange. Ever since the show, I can't stop thinking about you. I keep seeing your breasts squeezed tight in gold lamé. I have to have you. I don't give a damn about Raymond…or who you are…or what you've been. Chalk it up to madness."

Madness. Oh, God. She knew. She'd never felt so weak, so glorious, so high.

He wrapped his arms around her, pulled her closer, moved his forehead across hers. Reaching beneath her skirt, he touched her—deeply, inside. His fingers began to move. Shock waves rippled down her spine. Soon she'd be flying on top of the world.

Then, abruptly, he let her go and stepped back. She nearly wept when he leaned against one of her carved doors, his senses, his nerves, wired for sex. As hers were. Yet he didn't seize her, now that he could so easily have her.

He stared, not speaking, not moving, letting the sexual tension build.

His mouth curled. "You're so easy." His voice was thick. "You always were. I like that...tonight."

"You can insult me all you want to. But first—"

"Not so fast."

"There's something I have to tell you."

"Later." He groaned a rich curse that was both obscene and dangerous. "Come to me, Kara."

He would not say more; he would not beg.

He did not have to.

"Pretend to be Emma again."

She stared into the foyer mirror. She saw Emma, her face glistening with tears; but she saw Kara, bold and luminous and as sexual as a pagan goddess.

The sound of his voice lingered, throbbed inside her as it always had. She felt absolute, undiluted desire. She was his. She had always been his. Even though she hated him as much as he disliked her.

"Be Emma," he commanded hoarsely. "Tonight I want to pretend, too."

"Tonight...forever..." she promised in Emma's softer, sweeter voice. "Pretending—that's what I do best."

She'd do any sick thing he asked tonight. He had only to look at her with those insolent, hungry black eyes to communicate to her in that vital, complete way. Beneath the lies, between this man and herself, lay a profound truth.

She raised her hand and twisted a button at her throat.

He laughed when she revealed bare skin. "Get down on your knees. Crawl."

She sank to one knee. Her eyes filled with tears like a sinner's seeking his forgiveness. His eyes burned, incandescent, as if jets flamed inside them. His fists clenched reflexively.

Maybe she would have sunk to the other knee. Maybe she would have succumbed to a dozen more humiliating acts. Maybe...

Neither of them would ever know.

Suddenly, night turned to day. The yellow-white blast that rocked the foundation of her mansion hurled him outside and sent her sprawling across the floor toward her staircase. Bone and softer tissues slammed into a red-tile stair. A rib cracked.

When she looked up with huge wounded eyes and saw the entire upper story engulfed in an inferno, she screamed Mike's name.

Above her, windows burst like canons. Glass shattered. Waves of heat made the columns of her foyer billow. Warmth broiled her. A river of fire cascaded halfway down the stairs.

She had to get up, to get out.

The air was so hot and close, she couldn't breathe.

"Stay down," Mike yelled. "Crawl to me, Kara. Crawl!"

There was nothing sexual now in that demand.

In too much pain to move, she lay on the floor, motionless, unable to see him through the dense black smoke.

A beam crashed somewhere above her. Orange sparks rained down on her. The ceiling wouldn't hold much longer.

"Get up, Kara. Get up."

She barely heard him through the roaring flames.

She lifted her head. She made a feeble, low-throated cry of sheer terror.

"Mike—"

But *he* screamed Emma's name instead of hers.

And that made her want him more than anything else in the whole world. She always had and she always would.

She'd play her sister in bed and out of it for the rest of her life, if that's what he wanted.

There was a second blast.

Then everything went black.

19

Mike jerked awake to the piercing wail of sirens. Dry-eyed he stared at Kara's carved front doors, which lay toppled like a pair of dominoes against her jacaranda tree. His Howling Lioness was livid orange. Behind the statue, the mansion smoldered like a giant jack-o-lantern, sparks shooting out its doorway, black smoke belching from the windows, singeing the night with the stench of charred carpets and draperies.

Kara was in there.

Police and firemen wearing gloves and carrying big flashlights clambered over tangles of fat hoses. Massive floodlights lit the exterior walls of the mansion.

Dimly, as if he were in a glass bell at the bottom of the sea, Mike heard a man's rough shout.

"She's in there! Kara Shayne's still in there!"

Dear God. "Kara..." Mike's voice was raspy, uncontrolled. He had to get up. He had to save her. But when he tried to raise his head, he fell back weakly. A starless sky spun in a sea of flame. His eyes shut. He was only semiconscious.

On the edge of panic, crazy images bombarded him.

Bronze statues in coffin-like crates.

A girl in gold lamé, clinging, kissing him.

Kara in a teal-blue evening gown on the night of her premiere, stripping.

Lilly, pale and bereft, begging. *"Go get her, Daddy! Go get my mother and bring her back!"*

Kara. Emma. The statues. *Lilly.* Their images collided in the dark. Memories that had never quite made sense suddenly came together in a new pattern that did.

Lilly in the plaza. Then Emma there, her lashes damp, her cheeks radiant. He'd gone to Kara's suite after the premiere, demanding the truth about Lilly. She'd turned on the heat, peeled off that blue slip of a gown and seduced him. Afterward, she'd wept as if her heart was broken.

When she'd said the words, "Mike, Lilly's mine. I'm sorry," he'd felt dead inside, crushed. He'd wanted Emma to be her mother. He'd wanted Emma. Period. But what had he done? He'd had sex with her sister. Again.

He'd run from Kara, knowing that when he'd slept with her that second time, he'd lost Emma forever. Later, he'd made that statue with Kara's face and Emma's tears. He'd nailed it into that box, never wanting to see it again. Because he couldn't face what he'd done.

He remembered Kara leaning over that same statue last night, tracing those bronze tears with her fingertips, her own eyes wet and shining. She'd looked exactly like the statue.

Tears. So many tears.

Kara never wept.

She shook with rage. Her eyes turned gold. But she never wept.

Emma was the one who wept.

Emma!

How long had Emma been playing both twins? He remembered the way her eyes had sparkled when she'd first seen Lilly on the plaza.

Later, after the premiere, Kara had seduced him in her hotel room, and she'd wept afterward.

Mike, Lilly's mine. I'm sorry.

His rage had been too profound. He hadn't registered the depth of her genuine grief. Like a guilt-ridden thief, he'd run out of the hotel bedroom before she could say more. She'd run after him. He'd threatened her in front of her party guests. She'd pushed him over a dangerous edge. He'd tried not to remember that unforgettable night, because the woman in Kara's bedroom that night had taught him what he really was: a savage driven by his most basic instincts.

Only…only… That woman had sobbed as if her heart were breaking.

Kara never wept.

That woman had been so damn gorgeous that night, with her red hair falling to her shoulders, that tight, blue silk gown falling gently over her breasts and hips. Then she'd stripped. Set him on fire.

No wonder.

Emma.

Emma? Why had she pretended she was Kara that night?

Mike, Lilly's mine. I'm sorry.

She'd tried to tell him. He'd been too mad to listen, had hurt her so terribly that she'd run away.

Both twins had returned when he'd been accused of double murder.

Or had they?

They'd seemed so alike—more identical than ever. Emma—so changed, so sad. And Kara—all the bold bright light gone from her face, too.

Once they'd been inseparable.

After that, they'd never been seen together again.

Why? *What the hell was going on?*

And then tonight, Kara had—

Not Kara!

Emma.

God. Was Emma's body in that house? How could that be, if Emma and Kara were estranged?

He *knew* Emma had been in Kara's house. With a supreme effort of will, he forced his leaden eyelids open, forced himself to stand and run stumbling through clouds of ash toward the house.

He didn't stop. Not even when sparks stung his arms, his cheeks. Not even when choking smoke filled his lungs and men called him back. The inferno was so bright and hot, he had to shield his eyes to keep staggering forward.

"Get that idiotic bastard away from the house!"

"Emma!" Mike shouted into the howling flames. Heat consumed him, and he began to cough. Still, he plunged forward. *"Emma!"*

His shirt caught fire. He was inside the doorway when hard arms grabbed him, pulled him back, pounded his shoulders. Dazed, he realized they were smothering the flames. Still, he fought till two men tackled him, throwing him down, slapping the flames out.

Their heavy arms grasped him beneath the arms, and he was half carried, half dragged across bricks and dirt and broken glass.

A shard sliced through his jeans and gouged his thigh. Crying out, Mike grabbed his leg. Not that he cared—not when he was filled with a deep and all-consuming grief that left no room for anything else.

Emma was dying. Maybe dead.

"Hey, buddy? Sorry we had to hit you. You okay?"

Mike burst out laughing.

He *should* be dead; he had no right to be alive.

Not if *she* was dead.

He had to get a grip. "She's inside," Mike whispered, his voice scratchy, as the blood seeped against his fingers. "Get her out!"

"Nobody could live through that."

"You're wrong."

"What the hell do you mean?"

He began to sob. "I was in there."

"Hey! I saw you on TV. You made that famous nude statue of her that got her so pissed!"

"Just get her out!"

"What are you doing here?" one of the men asked.

"I'm an old friend of hers."

Get her out. His voice made no sound. His back began to ache. He shivered. The men's faces blurred. He saw only Emma.

Emma. He felt himself falling into blackness.

The next time Mike opened his eyes, a blitz of exploding camera flashes whitened the night.

Four heavyset cops were hoisting two black-zippered body bags from the smoking door onto stretchers.

Emma.

He saw her as a girl in that field of butterflies. Then she was in the barn, in his arms. He saw her crawling toward him, pretending to be Kara. Memory after memory bombarded him, all the memories that were so precious— and the one he'd fought so hard to forget. Emma playing Kara as she stripped off the blue silk gown.

Emma was dead.

For all practical purposes she'd been dead for years. Why did he feel such cold anger, such utter desolation?

"Who are they?" a reporter yelled.

"Kara Shayne and Ray Parsons."

No, Emma.

"Parsons?"

"Shrink to the stars. Her fat-cat fiancé."

"Anybody here see anything?" a short, beefy detective demanded. "Or anybody?"

Emma in bed with Raymond, after...

"That guy over there—the famous sculptor—"

A silent white flash exploded in Mike's head.

"—said he was inside."

Mike's chest hammered as he stared at the body bags. Emma dead.

He imagined her naked body pressed to Raymond's. God, his heart was breaking. And they were going to pin it on him.

Oh, shit. Oh, shit. He had blood on his jeans— Broken glass in his hair— He'd been inside—

"—swear he was over there a minute ago—"

Mike had already dragged himself to his feet and was limping into the shadows when he bumped into a mean-faced, short guy in a gray jogging suit.

"Watch where you're going—"

Mike stumbled, and a restraining hand planted itself squarely on his shoulder.

"Geraldo Chavez." A badge flashed. "Detective. L.A.P.D." Mike's burned shoulder muscles screamed in agony under the man's heavy hand. Chavez wore a wrinkled white T-shirt and dirty jeans.

"I understand you were the last person to see Miss Shayne alive. Mind if I ask you a few questions?"

Emma's tears.

Emma. Oh, God, please not Emma.

He couldn't face being accused of her murder now, any more than he could take it before. Flashbacks to his forbidden past seemed like a map of his future. Emma's haunted dark eyes. Emma's empty room, all her things gone. Kara vanished, too. Frances publicly accusing him of double murder. "Trouble stalks him. First his daddy. Now my girls."

The cops had believed Frances.

He'd felt so damn guilty about sleeping with Kara again. He'd been so damn scared about Emma, so heartbroken. The media had blown the story into a lead, bombarding the public with tawdry lies about all their sex lives. He'd been frantic about Emma.

But this was worse—because this time he knew she could never come back.

When she'd returned seven years ago, she'd made it clear she didn't give a damn for him anymore. He hadn't blamed her. He had thought Kara had told her about that night. In all these years he hadn't seen her or heard from her.

Until tonight.

She'd lied again. With words. But her eyes had told the truth.

At least she'd been alive.

Chavez was taller than average. He had a swarthy face with a broad nose, a thick chest and powerful shoulders. Even in rumpled jeans, he exuded authority. His cop's eyes burned through Mike like lasers.

No way could he tell a cop, especially this arrogant specimen, that the wrong twin was in the body bag. The press would go wild. They'd lynch him for sure.

Chavez took out a notebook. "What was Kara Shayne to you?"

"A friend."

Chavez flipped pages. "For how long?"

"We grew up together."

"You were close?"

"Yes and no."

"What were you doing here?"

"She came to my show."

Chavez barked out questions about the show, about the nude statue, jotting every single word down in that damn little notebook. "So she invited you over afterward—"

"Not exactly—"

"A front window was broken. The alarm went off a little after two. A potted plant was inside— Sir, could you explain that broken glass on your hands?"

Mike shrugged.

Chavez twirled his pen. The cop's black gaze nauseated him. Or was grieving for Emma what made him suddenly feel so sick?

"We'll need blood samples," Chavez said.

He was a detective. His job was to detect, to solve crimes, to nail felons. Chavez had the formidable resources of the state behind him.

"Just a few routine questions—downtown," Chavez continued.

Routine? When Emma, his darling Emma, Lilly's mother, was in that body bag instead of Kara?

Routine?

20

The jogger almost giggled when the body bags were loaded into the ambulance. He wished he could unzip her. He'd like to see what the fire had made of her.

Instead, he kept the hood of his jogging suit up and lurked in the shadows, watching the doors slam and the ambulance drive away, watching the Mexican cop grill the scowling half-breed.

He'd been sorry at first that the bastard got out alive. Scared as hell when the mean-looking half-breed nearly trampled him. Really scared when that heavyset cop with the eyes from hell appeared out of nowhere.

Then relieved when he saw the breed nailed.

With that cop riding the breed's ass, nobody would be looking for *him*.

People began to get in their cars, to drift away.

The fun was over.

She was gone.

He wanted to forget her.

Maybe he'd go to Mexico.

But the song she'd sung to and danced to right before she'd stripped for him and made love to him that last time began to play over and over in his head.

When he put his hands to his ears, it got louder.

Was it her ghost?

Or was she dead?

That's when he knew he had to see for sure that that was really her in the body bag.

If she was dead, the singing should've stopped.

Since it hadn't, he would cut out her tongue.

Chavez was bent over that damn little notebook, scribbling.

Mike gulped down a nasty swallow of stale coffee. "Is your ass made of steel plates, Chavez? Or do you feel as butt-bound as I do? This damn metal piece of crap you call a chair needs to be hauled to the dump."

"New chairs aren't in our budget."

"This damn interrogation room is worse than a jail cell. At least if you lock me up, I won't have to talk to you hour after hour."

"You don't have to talk." Chavez shifted his bulky weight. "But if you do, anything you say can be used against you."

Mike wearily combed his hands through his long black hair. "Damn. How many times—"

"You can have a lawyer, but you don't really need one."

Feebleminded with exhaustion, strung out with grief, the cop's slurred words seemed to run together. Mike glared. "How many times have you told me that? Fifty?"

Chavez punched his tape recorder off, leaned his chair back from the table and flipped through his scribblings. "I got you at the scene. You were the last person to see her alive. You and she were tight in the past, but there was this other sister, Emma."

Emma. Just her name wired him.

He thought of that naked witch against the wall, of that bright red head going down on him. He thought of her dead in that body bag.

"What's it like…I mean, sisters? Did you do 'em both at once? Is that why they were estranged?"

It makes you into a goddamn crazy man, that's what!

Mike leaned forward, hot rage surging through him.

"Shut up about her."

"She the favorite? That why Kara got mad?"

He almost felt her mouth at his groin. All these years he'd thought— He saw her young with butterflies in her hair.

"I said, shut up."

"Your show featured both twins?"

Mike inhaled sharply. *Get a grip.*

He nodded.

"So, maybe Kara comes to your show, sees statues of Emma, and gets jealous. So, she runs. Your kid thinks she's got a movie-star mother. You chase Kara home. Her front door is dead-bolted. The alarm is set. You break glass and get inside. House blows. She's dead. You're alive."

Mike's shoulders throbbed beneath thick bandages. "Tell me something we don't know."

"You tell me."

"I didn't hurt her."

"I've got motive. I've got—"

"You've got shit. I didn't do it."

"You're leaving something out."

"You ever sleep, Chavez? I'm dead."

"No, Kara's dead. And I'm wired. Twins? You gonna tell me what that's like— I mean two of 'em."

Two faces—one bold, one innocent—flashed in his mind's eye. He was in the loft, thinking himself in bed with Emma, only to look up and see her in the doorway, her face so radiant—and then so utterly, utterly crushed.

Mike stared at him, his face blank. "Why don't you go find the real killer?"

By dawn Mike felt glued to that metal chair and rum-dumb from the questioning. Just when he was absolutely sure he would never get out of there, a knock sounded on the door.

A blond cop stuck his freckled face inside. "Sorry, Chavez. The chief said to tell you there's a short fat guy screaming his head off outside. Asshole claims he's the carver's brother."

"I don't have a brother," Mike said.

"The chief says you can go home, but you gotta take the asshole with you."

"Whoa!"

"You wanna share a cell with him?"

When Mike stepped outside, Sando was bellowing through a bullhorn at the top of his lungs to reporters and TV satellite trucks. "They've gotta book him or release him."

Mike grabbed the bullhorn. "Shhh. They gave me five minutes—to shut you up and get you outta here." Mike put his arm around him and hustled him down the steps.

"A thank-you would be nice."

"In your dreams, *asshole*."

Sara burst out of the throng. "Hey, guys! I'm Mrs. Greywolf. Greywolf's ex-wife." She threw her arms around Mike's burned shoulders. "Darling…"

He shouted in pain.

She kissed him. Flashes exploded.

"I thought you two are supposed to be divorced," Sando said grumpily.

"Bingo," Mike said.

"So, you dating yet?" Sando asked Sara.

"You want to go out with me, short stuff?"

"Well?"

"Not in this lifetime."

Sando was unusually quiet in the car. "I don't like being alone much. You and Lilly got someplace to stay?"

Silence.

"Don't guess you'd want to stay at my oceanside villa? Laguna Beach?"

Bewildered that he actually did, Mike rubbed his temples. Maybe it was just that he didn't want to be alone with his thoughts about Emma. Whatever—he surprised them both.

"Thanks."

"Truce?" Sando said.

"That's pushing it."

Three days of intense media attention, convalescence, Sando's company, Lilly's stricken sulks, a battalion of Kara's fans camped on their doorstep, Sara's incessant phone calls, and his own grief had Mike too stir-crazy for words. By the fourth morning he couldn't even read the paper.

"Damn." He flipped a page so hard it tore. The bastards were running opinion polls on whether he'd torched Kara's mansion.

Emma. Dead. Murdered. They thought he'd killed Kara.

Emma, the mother of his child.

He'd been stunned by her, by her impact on him. Most of all he was staggered by his grief, by his helplessness.

All these years. If only he'd known.

For the rest of his life he'd remember the way she'd looked at the show, and then later at her house when she'd stood behind that window with the light coming behind her so he could see through her clothes.

He would never forget kissing her, holding her. Any more than he would forget how responsive she'd been. He would never forget the tenderness in her eyes when she'd looked at Lilly.

Someday… Someday, he'd have to find a way to tell his daughter the whole truth.

He should have gone looking for Emma years ago.

Damn Chavez for thinking he'd murdered Kara.

If only it was *just* Chavez. The sun was coming up. Sando's bright white, yellow and chrome kitchen jarred his senses at this early hour. When Lilly stumbled sleepily through swing doors, the boxy space felt even tighter than the interrogation room. Mike coughed. She was gray-faced, her dark eyes pools of pain.

He folded his newspaper and slammed it on the table. "Good morning."

Stonily ignoring him, she notched her nose higher. She got out a cereal box, a bowl, a carton of milk and a spoon.

"Couldn't sleep?" he asked.

She bit her lip and poured milk into her bowl. The hard surfaces magnified every sound, magnified her silence, too.

"I took a long walk on the beach," he said. "A couple of reporters spotted me. I barely beat them back—"

Lilly stared at him, lifting her carton, dribbling milk.

"Hey, your milk…"

She righted the carton. "How can you act so normal—"

"Finally. You speak."

Her wet eyes blazed. "H-how could you k-kill—"

"I didn't," he growled.

She lifted her spoon. "You were there."

"What does that prove?"

"Prove? I'm not Detective Chavez who has to prove—" Tears put a strained thickness into her voice.

"Lilly, listen. I damn near died."

"I—I wish you had. Oh, God, how I wish— I can't even go outside without people mobbing me and asking horrible questions about you." She pitched her spoon down. "How do you think that makes me feel?"

"How do you think it makes *me* feel?"

She shoved her chair back. "I can't believe I sent you over there."

"I didn't kill her."

"Mr. Chavez said you did, on TV."

"He's wrong."

She picked up her bowl.

"Where are you going?"

Lilly's face twisted. She splashed water in her bowl.

"How much longer do I have to stay here locked up with you?"

He got up and stared out the window. He heard every sound as she turned the water off and raced upstairs.

His daughter wasn't the only one who thought he was a murderer. Sara was feeding his life story to the press. The most negative stories were coming from Albuquerque. She personally saw to it that he was being vilified on national levels, too—on CNN, on every talk show, in every tabloid, in the evening news wrap-ups.

He suspected she was behind that unflattering shot— him being led into Parker Center, L.A.P.D headquarters— that had made the front pages of every leading California newspaper.

Reruns of Kara's old movies were being shown round the clock. After every one, Lilly grew more morbid.

Murder was in the air. Two bodies were decomposing

in the city morgue. Mike could feel an invisible noose tightening around his neck.

One minute he'd held Emma. The next, the house had exploded. He'd been outside when she'd screamed his name. He'd go to his grave with the memory of the fear in her voice. Just as he'd carry with him forever the passion in her eyes, in her kiss.

Last night he'd watched a late-night rerun of *Betrayal,* till he'd grown stiff and cold. Kara had been so incredibly beautiful. But seeing her in that nude scene hadn't aroused him at all. She'd been lovely, so lovely. But she wasn't Emma.

Where was Kara? What did she know about what happened? Had she had something to do with it? Had she deliberately set Emma up?

Even as his heart ached, a ribbon of doubts and new questions spun around him.

"When will you be available to give samples, Mr. Greywolf?"

Mike clenched the receiver. "Your lab people have called twice. I said, I don't know. I have to talk to my lawyer. He's coming over in a few minutes."

"Good. The sooner the better."

Pressure. Mike slammed the phone down.

Blood samples meant more public accusations, more media exposure.

The TV evening news blared. The sun looked like a fiery beach ball afloat on the distant horizon. The combination of noise and glare in Sando's living room, with its marvel of modern sculptures, merely darkened Mike's fierce mood.

He set his martini down and strode to the balcony. He slid the door open. A lone gull skimmed glimmering

waves. The narrow beach, the damp salty air, brought
back Malibu—and Emma. He saw her sister's house in
flames; he heard Emma's final scream. How long would
he see that image and hear that sound?

When the doorbell rang, he jumped. Then, welcoming
any distraction, he rushed to answer it, expecting his lawyer.

Shorter and stouter than Sando, Slim Price charged
across the threshold with the prickly arrogance of a nat-
ural-born fighter. Born poor, black and lethally ambitious,
he'd scrapped his way from a slum to the best Ivy League
school. After that, he'd quickly risen to the top of a tough
profession, made tougher by this tough city. Slim skidded
to a halt when he saw the DA pontificating on the nightly
news.

"Yes. We've got a suspect. Yes, we feel really good
about our progress."

"That the DA? Ha! Ha!" Large white teeth broke
through Slim's bushy gray beard. "I pay people to watch
these clowns, so you don't have to!"

Mike frowned when Slim switched the TV off. "You
got another martini?"

Slim didn't ask. He barked orders. Like a lot of short
guys who'd started at the bottom, he carried a hefty chip
on one shoulder and a bull-size ego on the other.

Mike mixed two more.

Slim heaved himself into Mike's favorite recliner, took
the glass and drank slowly, his eyes darting about the
room as he stroked his beard. "I feel sorrier for that blow-
hard than I do for you. They've got themselves a celebrity
murder. Kara's fans have gone berserko. The whole city
has, for that matter. But what's this crap about your mysterious, sexpot film queen being repackaged as Mother
Teresa?"

"The media smells blood—mine."

"The DA has to say he's about to solve the crime. Not to worry. You got me."

"What about the blood samples?"

"Chavez is after your ass. I'm all that stands between you and the slammer."

"Does innocence count for nothing?"

"You got it. If they can nail you—big macho sculptor—it'll boost their careers."

"I don't like being dependent on anybody."

"Fire me, then."

"And hire…who?"

"So, let the DA strut. Word is, he doesn't have much of a case. Give 'em the samples. When they test 'em, my experts'll be there. Now, I've got some real good news."

Slim slapped two airline tickets on the table. "Pack. Go home. Live your life. Carve rocks. Keep your mouth shut. Let me handle this."

"No way do I check out my brains—to you. I'm innocent."

"Presumed innocent…till proven guilty. Ha. Ha. In a court of law. But that nifty little legal concept won't take the heat off when you're on the street and strangers say you iced her."

"Tell me about it. My own daughter—"

Slim cut him off. "If you go to trial, I'll whip 'em. They're making mistakes galore. Hey, I caught your ex on the news last night. Sex-y. She datin' your short, fat brother, or what?"

Mike glared straight ahead.

"The things she says about you and those twins—"

Mike flipped the television back on. He didn't want to discuss Sara or Sando.

"Any chance of you setting me up with her?"

"Ask Sando." Mike stared at the set.

"Hey, that stuff's like a drug. It'll mess your mind."

"Then I'm an addict."

"With me it's women…and food. I've got three exes. Probably have three more before I'm done. If one of 'em doesn't kill me. Ha. Ha."

More of the same footage of those limp black slugs on gurneys being hauled out of Kara's mansion. Next followed clips of her fans stacking wreaths against the walls of her house. Then Slim's latest interview came on. Slim was joking with the reporters, having the time of his life.

"I wish my own lawyer wasn't enjoying the hell out of this."

"So, I like the spotlight. So, I like a good fight and all the strutting that goes before it. I'm your personal gladiator."

"I'm almost blown to bits," Mike muttered, "and a woman I've known all my life dies right in front of me. I want to know how. Why. Who. And fast! Do you understand?"

"I hired an investigator. He says anybody could've done it. Foxy, famous lady…living alone. Movie star with the power to get any movie she wants made in this town. And she's sitting on a dozen hot scripts. Fame and power like that, especially in L.A., attracts a lot of creeps. She's had a problem with a fan, too. Then there's her maid…. She's disappeared. Maybe she stole stuff, torched the house."

Mike didn't give a damn about her maid. He put his hands together, steepled his fingers, and held them up in an attitude of prayer. "I was this close to Kara when it happened. We should be sharing the same body bag."

"Then you're one lucky motherfucker."

Mike saw Emma's face, her tears. He heard her scream—*his name*.

"Lucky?" he whispered, his nerves so frayed he could barely control himself. "She's dead, and everybody on the planet thinks I killed her. Have you seen these?" Mike held up a stack of newspapers. He read a two-inch headline: "'Legend Kara Shayne and Fiancé Die in Malibu Fire. Navajo Lover There.'"

"Would you quit—"

Mike read anyway. "'Their nude bodies were discovered by firefighters in Miss Shayne's upstairs bedroom. The LAPD has issued a statement saying they suspect arson. The sole witness was Mike Greywolf, international sculptor and a former friend of Miss Shayne. So far there are no suspects. Obituaries on page C16.'"

Mike reread the article and the obituaries aloud.

He stopped in midsentence, struck dumb.

"Stop it!" Slim whispered.

Mike queasily pitched the paper down. He stared at the ocean for what felt like an eternity. *Upstairs.* The bodies had been found upstairs.

Mike held on tightly to his emotions. "You tell your investigator this story doesn't gel. Nude bodies—upstairs." He paused. He began to shake. "She was *this* close to me. How'd she get upstairs, strip, and hop in bed with another man? Somebody else died in that bed."

"She's dead. You're lucky to be alive." Slim drained his martini. "Wish I had time for a refill—"

"You're not listening!"

At the door, Slim saw the television trucks. "Hey, how do I look?"

What was the use trying to tell him anything?

"I asked you, how do I look?"

"Like you need a shave," Mike said.

Slim tweaked his beard. "Ha. Ha."

As soon as he left, Mike sank down in a chair. More than anything, he'd wanted Emma to be alive, but now that he believed she was, instead of relief or joy, rage filled the place in his heart that grief had occupied. *Where was she?* Why hadn't she come forward, when the whole world knew the cops were out to get him? Had she set him up on purpose? Why?

Then his rage softened. Maybe she was just scared.

He watched a repeat of the body bags being hauled out of Kara's mansion. Then there *he* was—panther dark, wild looking, his long black hair loose, his Navajo scowl lethal—holding Kara at his show.

Emma. She was white white. He was dark dark.

His skin had been artificially darkened.

Images. As an artist, Mike knew their power.

Mike swallowed. Her purity was a farce.

"Miss Shayne was planning to be married," the commentator said. "She and her fiancé drove to her former lover's show. Apparently, she was upset about a nude Greywolf had included of her to get publicity for his show. Miss Shayne and Mr. Greywolf quarreled. Miss Shayne ran away. He followed her home."

Bullshit. All they had was bullshit. And Emma knew it.

She was hiding somewhere. Was she scared? Was that why she was going to let them nail him for murder, if they could?

There was a clip of the nude statue, of a few lurid tabloid headlines along with a shot of Indiana. Then Kara—or rather, Emma—was struggling in Mike's arms again. Then she was running from him, while Lilly pleaded that he go after her.

Sara. Damn her hide. She'd taken that video.

Another closeup of Mike glowering.

Unnerved, Mike punched the remote.

Jimmy Rogers, the most notorious of talk-show hosts, was next. Jimmy was gray with pretend-grief as he led L.A.'s most flamboyant psychic, Robin O'Hair, to a plush red seat and introduced her to his wildly clapping audience.

"Jimmy! Jimmy!" they chanted.

Jimmy put a hand up to silence his voracious fans. He turned to Robin, who was visibly shaking with excitement. "Miss O'Hair, you've helped the L.A.P.D. solve several high-profile murder cases."

"Y-e-s, I have," she cooed in her famous, little-girl voice. "I'm always glad to help, Jimmy."

"You loved Miss Shayne—"

"She was a very special actress. Very special."

She was a liar to the core.

"Incomparable." Robin batted her long, mascara-coated eyelashes and stared quizzically into nothingness, as if she saw through misty veils to other dimensions.

"So, who killed our beloved Kara?"

With a puzzled frown, Robin waved a gaudy ring. She closed her eyes. After a long moment, she slowly opened them. "Kara isn't in that body bag. Mike Greywolf's being set up."

Audible gasps cracked through the audience like live-wire currents.

The air went out of Mike's lungs.

"What?"

"Our Kara ran away for love. She will never be found."

The crowd began to stomp and scream. "Jimmy! Jimmy! Jimmy!"

Then Robin lowered her voice. "If she is found, she's

in terrible danger. Somebody's after her. He won't rest till she's dead.''

Mike broke out in a cold sweat.

If Emma wasn't in the body bag, who was?

Who else knew the truth?

Where was Kara?

Emma?

Had they ever really been estranged?

Had they deliberately set him up?

Or did somebody else want them dead?

Or just want Emma dead?

Was she hiding? Terrified?

He had to find her.

Before it was too late.

Part III

INSEPARABLE

"The fault, dear Brutus,
is not in our stars,
But in ourselves...."
—William Shakespeare
Julius Caesar, I, ii, 134

21

A great ridge of black clouds stretched above a darkening, tropical sea. A green shadow passed over Emma's soul.

She ran, unseeing, past palms and low thatched beach huts. She had no idea that her bare feet were sinking deeply into pale wet sand as she ran heedlessly toward that warm, southern sea. She was in another time and another place—lost in a ghastly vision that she had long ago forgotten.

In her dream, Kara and Mike were fused together in a bar of moonlight, their bodies writhing on a narrow bed. Then that image receded, and her dream started over at an earlier time.

Again, Emma was an untried girl, hopelessly in love with Mike, who was forbidden to her, no matter how high he might climb, because of his race and culture. Guilty that she had forsaken her mother's teaching, remorseful that she had quarreled with him, and yet shyly aglow from their recent lovemaking, she was sneaking back to his bed.

With trembling fingers she lifted that rusty horseshoe out of the chain that secured the barn gate. Then, terrified of every sound, of her own feelings, yet thrilled, too, she tiptoed into the barn.

Shadowy saddles, blankets and bridles hung from pegs on the wall. The air was thick with the smells of hay and unmucked stalls. Their ears pricking forward, her mother's big, bright-eyed darlings watched her expectantly from their stalls.

Never one to be ignored, Rio whinnied. When she would have passed by him, he stuck his ebony head out to be rubbed. She went to him and touched the velvet muzzle, which he jerked back coyly when neither apple nor carrot was instantly forthcoming.

"My, my, aren't you spoiled. Greedy. Greedy." She laughed and blew him a kiss. "Eat your oats."

He snorted and pawed flirtatiously.

All the other horses whinnied and began to stomp, wanting her to notice them, too. They seemed oddly restless. When she climbed the stairs to Mike's loft bedroom, they set up a ruckus. Halfway up the stairs, a stall door slammed. She paused, listening, wondering if it had been blown open by the wind. Alarm trickled through her when she heard footsteps and then hooves slipping and sliding on concrete. One of the horses, maybe Rio, must've gotten out. She was about to go down, but Mike's deep voice and a woman's smothered laughter stopped her.

He had another woman with him.

As if hypnotized, she inched toward his door. Another stall door banged. More horses got loose.

When she pushed at Mike's door, his bed squeaked. The clamor of wild snorts and hooves died to nothing. There was only Mike and the squeaking box spring. Only the painful thunder of her own heart when she saw Kara's slim, voluptuous body joined to his in moonlight.

"Mike?" Emma whispered into that hushed stillness.

Blood rushed to her head, and she was too nauseated and dizzy to stand.

The two people she loved most.... Mike's big, rough hands were tangled in Kara's long red curls. He was whispering to Kara as he pulled her head down to his. Her twin's beautiful face held ecstasy.

Emma. Emma. Oh, God, Emma.

Why was he whispering *her* name?

Sickened, Emma turned her face to the wall. There had to be a mistake. She looked back, into Mike's eyes. Frozen in that split second of brooding calm before realizing the disaster that had overtaken her, she simply stared.

Nobody moved.

He said her name, *"Emma,"* and the low, sad way he said it rocked her like a body blow.

When she staggered against the door, he stood, white sheets spilling to the floor. Speared down the center by a dazzling shaft of moon-glow, his tall dark body seemed like some hideously profane statue carved of ebony and shadow. The half of his face she could see was deathly white and ravaged with pain. The other half was lost in blackness.

When he took a step toward her, Emma stumbled from his room.

"I loved you," she whispered.

"I love you," came his tight voice.

Emma laughed. And like a hysterical child bent on escaping a cruel tormentor, Emma had raced from them.

Emma. Oh, God, Emma.

Nothing had mattered but getting away from him. Somehow she'd made it out of that room, down the stairs that led to the horse stalls. She was so upset she hardly heard the horses screaming or the commotion of their hooves on the ground floor.

All of her mother's darlings were loose. Stall doors gaped open. In the darkness she made out the animals' huge shapes as they moved in circles, rearing. The more they ran, the more panicked and maddened they became, rearing and striking each other with their hooves.

Suddenly she was in the midst of them, running with them in crazed circles. Mike shouted to her. When she turned back, she spooked Rio. He charged, his hooves clanging and sliding on the slippery concrete floor.

She nearly made it past him, but her foot caught in the long loop of his reins. When she thought she was past him and picked up speed, his reins caught around her ankle and jerked his big black head down.

Terrified, snorting with fury, Rio yanked his head back and lost his footing. Horse and woman careened onto the concrete. When Rio scrambled to his feet, his reins coiled tightly around her ankle. He raced out of the barn, yanking her to the ground. The back of her head hit concrete, and the big horse dragged her into the melee of other stampeding horses.

None of them stepped on her. Just when she thought she'd be pulled to her death, the reins came loose, and she was miraculously free.

As Rio raced away, she got to her knees. Too dazed to stand quickly enough, something—maybe another horse—banged a stall door into her temple.

In her dream, Mike soundlessly cried her name, but she lay in the darkness, unable to breathe, unable to speak even when Mike lifted her in his arms. Mike had gone on holding her, his features wavering in the darkness, his face growing huge and almost ugly, before Emma shut her eyes and made him dissolve behind the thick screen of her lashes.

Still, she'd heard her mother scream at him that it was

his responsibility to see to the horses, that he was to go and never come back.

Kara stood briefly behind them. Her expression was detached.

Emma's dream passed over the next seven years to the warm sunny day on the plaza when she'd spotted Lilly with him. Lilly, her daughter. He was raising Lilly.

That's when she'd known she'd never stop loving him, no matter how much she wanted to.

A warm wave tickled her long, bare foot, and she screamed. Froth danced up her ankle and wet her skirt. Cool sand suckled her toes.

A second wave, more powerful than the first, burst against her and nearly knocked her off balance.

Suddenly Emma was shatteringly conscious. Tears pricked behind her eyes. She was breathing in and out so fast her chest hurt.

Black water. Wet sand. Salt air. The ocean.

Mike.

Why was she weeping for Mike? Why was she knee-deep in a dark ocean without the slightest idea how she'd gotten here?

She swallowed hard. Odd, how her throat burned. She tried to still the pounding in her chest. Some nightmare had driven her from her bed. Vague unsettling images of Kara in Mike's arms stayed with her.

What was she doing out here? How had she gotten here? She didn't remember anything she'd done this afternoon or evening.

Manuel's birthday party was the last thing she was sure she remembered. She saw little Manuel's shining face this morning, his huge brown eyes glued to the dark wedge of chocolate birthday cake she'd placed in front of him.

His luminous eyes had glanced at her, his smile widening when he saw her pink party hat.

And since that moment—nothing.

Palms rustled in the tropical sea air. She caught the odors of grease and Mexican chiles and frijoles being fried in one of those open-air seaside restaurants that were so popular with the American tourists.

A melodious Spanish voice crooned to a Spanish guitar. A woman's throaty laughter joined a man's.

Mexico. Isla Mujeres. She lived here. She'd lived here for seven years. And more before that. What was she doing on this beach—when the last thing she remembered was the birthday party?

Her dazed eyes focused on the dark ruin of The Presidente Hotel, on its own tiny island off the tip of Playa Norte. The hotel had been destroyed several years earlier in a hurricane.

Playa Norte. The familiar beach with its thatched umbrellas silvered by moonlight seemed eerily romantic. During the day, she came to write beside this aquamarine sea with its dazzling, sugar-white sand. She'd rent an umbrella or a hammock. Waiters would bring her food and drink as she scribbled. When she had a deadline, it was the only place on the island she could get away from the school, the clinic and the children to work.

But she was between books. Not writing. So, why had she dreamed of Kara and Mike? Why did she feel so jealous? So hurt?

She looked up at the waning moon. It was high in a black sky, which meant it was very late.

Manuel's birthday party had finished before noon.

She tried to remember what she'd done since, but there was only a fog. She saw a china frog falling in slow motion from a high shelf, smashing just as leisurely on *sal-*

tillo tiles, china bits and hard candies flying. She saw panthers leaping on some shadowy pink wall. Then she was behind the wheel of a sports car, driving too fast along a coastal freeway. L.A.

Mike's face swam in a sea of flame.

Mike's face bathed in moonlight. Kara in his arms. Green jealousy filling her heart.

Why? The images made no sense. She had no conscious memory of most of them.

The fog grew thicker. Her heart pounded painfully.

Breathing hard, she scrambled out of the water and stumbled toward a chaise longue on the beach. She fell back onto the cold, plastic slats, her head reeling. She closed her eyes and lay as still as possible, pressing her fingertips to her eyelids.

She'd had another blackout. It had been years since the last.

Blackouts meant she'd done something bad she couldn't face. Or at least that's what one doctor had said. The thought of another blackout upset her so much that she got up and ran. Only when a stitch in her side began to hurt, did she slow down and realize that she'd somehow injured herself. A few minutes later, when she limped more slowly past a lighted pier, she saw that a fishing boat had docked. Knives drawn, fishermen were heaving bloody carcasses of huge sharks onto the dock.

One of the rough-looking sailors called to her, *"Gringa!"*

Emma ducked down a narrow, dirt street crowded with centuries-old houses. Within minutes she was safely inside her patio gate, amidst a clump of bloodred hibiscus blossoms. Moonlight splashed the veranda, the potted palm, various statues, some of which were Greywolfs. She sped past the lemon tree by the tinkling fountain. A lush fern brushed her cheek as she opened the door of her bedroom.

Inside, she felt safer. Silver-framed pictures of dark-eyed children on her dresser glimmered in the moonlight. The sight of Manuel's plump brown face and sparkling black eyes were a special comfort to her.

Here, doing this work, she could almost forget…Kara.

Manuel had been so thin when she'd found him on the street in rags. She'd persuaded him to take her to the cardboard shack where he lived with his pregnant mother and three other children. Emma had convinced Isabela to enter Katherine's prenatal classes, and to let Manuel attend school. Slowly, she and Katherine had begun to educate and train Isabela, who could barely read or write. Later, when Isabela had died in childbirth, Manuel had become even more special to Emma, who knew how it felt to be alone.

How thrilled he'd been this morning when she and Katherine and all the children had surrounded him.

"Surprise!" twenty breathless voices had chirped in Spanish and English, as Emma had moved toward Manuel with a cake and glimmering candles.

Manuel had pointed at the cake. "What's this?"

"Your very own fiesta," Katherine said, setting down a platter of *ceviche de caracoles*—snails marinated in lime juice with chiles and cilantro.

He'd looked up at Emma shyly. "For me?"

"For you, *mi precioso*…to share."

When the children had begun to sing, his bright, hungry eyes never left Emma's face.

Ah, there were so many Manuels in Mexico. Yet he was unique, special. Her attachment ran too deep.

Emma's gaze flicked to Juanita's photo. The little girl loved school, now that she had books and pencils, now that her mother was well enough to take care of her brothers and sisters. Now that they had a real house. Juanita was as bright-eyed and gentle as...

For an instant, Emma remembered another baby girl. Another lifetime.

Atonement.

She saw Lilly—gorgeous in a black dress that was much too sophisticated for her.

Think. Focus. Remember.

The beach.

Kara.

Emma glided blankly into her bathroom and flicked on the light. When her ceiling fan began to hum, its slowly rotating blades stirred her chopped red bangs out of her dark eyes.

Chopped?

Her lip was cut, and her left eye was puffy.

Her hands flew to her shorn head. She touched her swollen lip, and it stung. Her fingernails—they were smudged and torn.

Where had she been? What had she done?

Kara.

Emma deliberately blurred her eyes, and saw Kara in the looking glass instead of herself. She felt a painful pull in her chest from that other half of her soul she'd tried to embrace and yet reject for the past seven years. Kara was sending her some kind of message.

Staring fixedly at herself, she focused till her own face came sharp and clear.

"Who are you today?" Trembling involuntarily, she caught her breath. "I want to be me. Me. For God's sake, just let me be me."

She raised her fists. Blood pounding in her arteries, she

backed away from the mirror till she slammed into the wall.

Then she saw it.

To the right of her reflection, bold swipes of greasy, red lipstick slashed her mirror.

Kara's name. Bloodred, in huge, crude, block letters.
KARA. KARA. KAR—

The lipstick had broken. Flecks of red dotted the white-tiled counter.

She began to perspire. Soon she was so wet that her cotton gown stuck to her skin like glue. She whirled and fled to her bedroom. Wildly, she switched on the fluorescent lights that buzzed as quirkily as her bathroom fan.

Her suitcase lay on her bed. Jeans and shirts had been tossed beside it.

She was running. Again.

The phone rang. When her mother's firm voice came on the machine, Emma sank to her bed on a shudder.

"Emma, I know you're listening. This is Sunday night, for God's sake. I've been trying to get you for three days."

Three days.

A silent alarm began to hum inside Emma.

"Pick up. Pick up, Emma. I can't face this without you. I don't know what's worse—the television vans, or Kara's fans camped at the ranch gate, or just not knowing what happened to her. I just got in from L.A. Stuart'll send his pilot to fetch you. And, oh, Emma—Greywolf was there, at Kara's house, when she died in that fire."

Sunday.
Kara dead.
Fire.

Greywolf there. At Kara's house.

She saw Mike's face in that sea of flame. Bronze statues

of herself and Kara flashed in her mind's eyes. For no reason at all, her fingertips touched her face, her lips.

Who was she underneath all the lies?

All she could remember was Manuel's birthday party... this morning... Thursday.... No, no.... She counted backwards on her fingertips. Not this morning. Thursday was three whole days ago.

Three whole days. The other times, she'd lost only hours...a day at most. When her therapist had told her they needed to work on why she had blackouts, she'd canceled her treatments.

Mike there. Panic filled Emma as she shoved her open suitcase and the clothes off her bed. Flippers and snorkels—all sizes—lay in a tangle beneath her jeans and dresses. Diminutive bathing suits hung in her bathroom, too.

She couldn't go home. This had nothing to do with her now. The children loved her, needed her. Especially Manuel.

Kara dead. Mike there.

The life she'd led for seven years was over.

Emma's hands shook as she picked up her suitcase and replaced it on the bed. She ripped clothes from the suitcase and tossed them back into the closet. She couldn't go home. She couldn't face him.

She was free.

But at what price?

Mike lived in New Mexico now. Lilly, too.

Emma's worried gaze darted to her bottom dresser drawer, where she kept the pictures she tried never to look at.

In her least favorite, Mike stood arrogantly over a deer, leaning on his rifle. She'd wept for hours over the deer. He had sworn he'd never shoot another.

Kara dead. Mike there.

Against her better judgment, Emma pulled the drawer out and lifted two photographs of Mike and herself that had been snapped in one of those little automatic booths. He'd drawn her onto his lap and kissed her while the camera did its business. He'd kept two shots and given her two.

"So you won't forget me," he'd whispered.

As if she could, much as she wanted to.

All these years. God, how she'd wanted to.

Kara had found the photographs, berated her for keeping them, made her feel like a betraying liar. Which she was.

Kara dead. Mike there.

Emma had torn the last picture out of a recent magazine. He stood in a museum sculpture garden, his hand resting on a magnificent bronze horse that had won an international prize. Even surrounded by admirers, he seemed so alone.

Kara dead. Mike there.

The thought of them together ate at Emma like poison. Emma had a vision of Kara's face, turning from her to Mike. Of Mike turning from her to Kara. He had come between them from the very first. The hurt and betrayal hadn't ended, even though years had passed. Would the pain ever stop? The only release she had was in her writing and in caring for the children.

Would the pain get worse, unbearable, if she knew... the whole truth?

She heard the violent thudding of her heart, the hoarse rasping of her every breath.

Emma pitched Mike's pictures back in the drawer. She picked up the snapshots of Lilly and tossed them into her suitcase.

Life had been simpler here.

Mike. He'd gone on with his life. He'd married that reporter, moved away, become famous in his own right. They'd raised Lilly together. They'd divorced.

He and Emma had gone terribly wrong long before his marriage. Again, she saw Kara and Mike entwined in moonlight.

Mike and Kara. Always, always Kara, seizing what was hers. Her toys, her friends. It had been all right...till Mike. Then Lilly.

Kara dead. Was Kara dead?

Emma buried her head in her lap and wept. Maybe that was why she didn't hear the front door, or Katherine's quick steps in the hall.

"May I come in?" Katherine said, cracking the door. "I've been out on a house call." She was silent for a moment. "Your mother phoned."

"I know." It hurt to speak. Her throat burned.

"She told me about Kara. I'm sorry." Despite her kindly smile, Katherine's narrow face was lined with exhaustion. "Where were you? Raquel said you'd come back. I looked...everywhere earlier."

Quickly Emma wiped her eyes and tried to smile.

Dear, stolid Katherine. Some people seemed perfectly programmed at birth. Had Katherine always known who she was, that she wanted to be a doctor? No matter how chaotic the clinic got, Katherine was always calm.

"I went for a walk," Emma said.

"Oh?" Katherine stared. "And...your hair?"

"I—I cut it."

"It was so pretty."

Once, long ago, Mike had wound a long red strand around his brown fingers as his warm lips seared her throat, and said he loved it, too.

Kara dead. Mike there.

Emma's hand fluttered to her bare neck. When she ran her fingertips through the soft shingled layers, an uneasy pang went through her. "It...it will be easier to keep."

"What's left." Then Katherine said, "Oh, well. It'll grow. How was your trip?"

"Trip?"

"To Puerto Vallarta—to write. Did you get a lot done?"

"Y-yes."

"How'd you hurt your lip...and eye?"

"I—I...I fell."

"And your voice?"

Suddenly she couldn't meet Katherine's steady gaze.

"What's really going on, Emma? Why—?"

"Nothing."

"Are you going home, like your mother wants?"

"I—I can't. I can't possibly."

That night when she tried to sleep, she twisted and turned, dreaming of Kara. They were quarreling again in that stone cell with the dancing panthers. Next, Emma was imprisoned by a wall of flame, and Mike was yelling her name.

She thrashed and turned till her mother called at dawn.

Breathless, Emma grabbed the phone on the first ring.

"You have to come home," Frances said. "I'm arranging a huge memorial service for your sister. Everybody will be here. The governor, heads of state..."

"Is this...really necessary?"

"Your sister was a world figure. You have to come home."

"But Mother—"

"What's the matter with your voice?"

"A sore throat. Nothing really."

"You're afraid…of *him,* aren't you? He's the reason you left and why you never come back."

Emma couldn't answer.

"You won't have to see him. I won't let him near you. Stuart understands how important this is, and will have a driver at the airport. By the way, I've offered a huge reward for information regarding your sister's killer."

Emma's eyes grew enormous. "Did you have to do that?"

"It would look strange if I didn't."

After her mother said goodbye, Emma got up listlessly to finish packing. When she looked under her bed to find the book she'd been reading, a wad of newspaper stuffed in a dark corner caused her pulse to skitter.

She stretched her arm under the bed, pulled it out, un-wadded it, and screamed. She muffled her next cry with her hand.

Charred red curls lay in the crinkled front page of the *L.A. Times.*

Blindly, she wadded newspaper and curls into a ball and shoved them back under her bed.

When she turned on her television to CNN, she saw two body bags being wheeled out of the blackened shell of her sister's house. As if in a trance, Emma sank to her bed and watched.

The next shots were of Mike, whose rugged, dark face grew blacker and more violent with every question.

"Did you kill Kara?"

He flushed. "What sane man would blow up a house when he's inside it?"

"Which twin did you love?"

"Neither."

His lawyer grabbed the microphone and finished the interview.

Emma turned off the television.

Knowing she had to face Kara's fans, her mother, Mike—*especially* Mike, who was a fierce, dark stranger now—brought a surge of blind unreasoning panic.

But she had no choice.

Later that morning, every child had to touch Emma's hair, which looked better after a shampoo and hot curlers. Each little black-haired, bright-eyed darling had to be hugged goodbye, too.

Emma was setting Juanita down when Manuel began tugging at her jeans.

"I love you, Miss," Juanita said.

"Hold me, too!" Manuel begged, beaming up at her.

Emma sank to her knees and hugged him close.

"Te adoro," he whispered shyly, patting her short, springy curls again.

Then they all had to pat her head again and giggle.

Emma picked Manuel up. She felt like crying over leaving them, especially over leaving Manuel. She didn't deserve his love, his trust.

"Oh, honey— Darlings— Manuel— *Mis queridos*—"

Others held up their arms. "Me! Me! Miss—me, over here!"

All the children jumped forward eagerly. They took each other's hands and formed a circle around her and Manuel. He put his arms around her neck and laid his black head on her shoulder. His trusting smile tore her heart out.

Somewhere a band of *mariachis* began to play. Mexico was poor, but it had so much soul—in its art, in its passionate music, most of all in the fiery black eyes of its precious children.

"This country," Emma whispered, staring up at Katherine through her tears. "This little boy. They saved my life."

"You saved lives, too," Katherine said.

"In Spanish, *Señorita Emma*," Manuel said quietly, "remember that you don't always have to say goodbye when you leave people you love. We can say, *Hasta luego*."

Till we meet again—

She thought of Lilly.

"I will never leave you, Manuel. We will meet again."

The fax machine rang and spit out a single white sheet. Emma grabbed it and began to shake.

"Que tienes, Señorita Emma?" What's wrong?

"I love you," she said to the children through her tears. She read the fax and instantly crumpled the page. "You be very be careful till I come back."

You're next.

The message burned in her brain. Her blackmailer knew the game she'd been playing. He had repeatedly threatened to expose her if she came home.

Kara dead. Mike there.

22

When Slim whizzed past a sign for LAX, the knot in Mike's stomach wound tighter. *Emma.* If she'd gotten out of the house, where in the world could she be?

They rounded a curve, and a snarl of satellite trucks, tripods, reporters and cameras brought traffic to a standstill.

Mike shoved his dark glasses higher up the bridge of his nose.

"Which airline?" Slim demanded, his tone eager as he eyed the rowdy crowd.

"Damn." Mike hunched lower. "Why don't the bastards pitch tents?"

Slim guffawed good-naturedly. "Ha. Ha."

From the back seat, a white-faced Lilly sullenly answered Slim's question about the airline.

Slim braked, and the photographers pounced, dozens of flashes going off in Mike's face.

Slim rolled down his window and beamed. "Afternoon, everybody."

His smile died when the newsmen rushed Mike's side of the car.

"Step on it," Mike ordered. "You can ham it up all you want—after I get Lilly out."

Slim shifted into neutral and jammed his foot on the accelerator. Reporters scattered like birds. Mike and Lilly shot out of the car, dashing through Kara's booing fans.

A voice panted in Mike's ear. A microphone was shoved against his mouth. "Is the DA right, Mr. Greywolf? Did you break into Miss Shayne's house? Will DNA prove your blood was on broken glass *inside* her house?"

"Mr. Greywolf, how can we tell our readers your side, if you won't talk?"

Lilly pleaded tearfully, "Leave him alone!"

Mike pulled her forward. "Keep moving."

There were long lines at security, but an officer immediately opened a new one. Mike emptied his change into a plastic cup and walked swiftly through. When a reporter tried to follow, an officer stopped him.

"Ticket, please—"

"I'm with *The Examiner*."

"Sorry."

Then they were safe behind a line of blue men and red cones.

"Mike! Lilly!" a familiar voice called.

Damn. Sara, running to catch them.

"You two on the six o'clock flight?"

Lilly ran to greet her. When Sara joined them, more flashes exploded. Sara whirled, clinging to Mike, preening.

Mike yanked his hand free of hers.

"Small world," Sara said.

"Too small," Mike agreed glumly.

"Can Sara sit with us?" Lilly asked.

"Lilly and I have a lot to catch up on," Sara said. "I've been trying to call."

"Sara works for a newspaper, Lilly."

"I can talk to who I want."

"Don't start on her, Sara—"

"If you'd talk to me yourself, I could tell people your side. Who better than your ex-wife?"

"Who worse?"

Mike had hoped the flight would be a recess from the media craziness. Not only was he trapped beside Sara for the duration, but even before they were airborne, nearby passengers began to ogle and whisper. A boy in braces thrust a notebook and pen at Mike.

Mike shook his head.

"Murderer."

Mike grabbed his wrist. "What did you say?"

"Let go, mister!"

Wide-eyed passengers stared. The bald man in front of him jabbed a button and a little bell rang.

"Sir," came the flight attendant's soft, professional voice from the aisle. "May I help you?"

Mike released the boy, ordered a drink and stared gloomily at the seat in front of him. Sara's incessant voice was a grating irritant.

Then Lilly asked him if she could go home with Sara for a night or two.

It was all happening—again. The world casting him out. Friends turning on him. Even his own daughter. Emma abandoning him.

Worse. *Two people were dead.*

Not Emma. He hoped his hunch was right. Please, not Emma.

Where was she?

How could he avoid more crowds? Where could he hide? Kara was known everywhere, adored everywhere. And all her fans thought he was her killer.

His boyhood fear came back, heavier and darker than ever. He did not try to fight it.

He was alone, an outcast, stumbling out of the blood-soaked hogan, into the desert. Nowhere to go. Only he wasn't alone.

Ghosts.

They'd stalked him from the hogan. From the rez. Into the white man's world. Where no matter how hard he'd tried or how high he'd climbed, he'd never belonged.

He'd felt them in the warehouse.

At the show.

At Kara's house.

They were with him now.

He had to find Emma.

"I'm not rolling over so you can fuck my company." Benedek lashed.

The hell you're not, Roger.

"I can see we need another meeting," Stuart said pleasantly but rage built inside him.

"I'll see you in court, you bastard." Benedek slammed the phone down.

Still furious, Stuart got his secretary on the line. His voice was smooth as glass. "That bunch that's doing the story on my new book get here yet?"

"Fella called. They're running late."

Stuart looked at the clock. It was 10:15. Ten a.m. sharp, the bastard had said.

Stuart's heart pumped. He wasn't just anybody. He was Stuart Shayne, fucking head of SKT, computer wizard of the fucking world.

His secretary wasn't finished. "Sir...your mother and some other people are out here—"

"My mother?"

Maybe she'd heard his new book was out. Maybe she wanted to see his offices. In all the years he'd been in business, never once had she dropped by. He'd invited her, and she'd turned him down. She would have made time for Emma, though. Emma was important.

"Tell her I'm in a meeting."

His mother's voice came on the phone. "It's urgent. I don't have all day."

Neither the fuck do I.

Fuming, Stuart swirled his chair, punched a button at his fingertips. Drapes swished across the long wall of glass behind his desk, and he leaned forward, watching the sprawling offices of his top hundred salespeople. They were young and hyper-excited. Every single one of them was glued to a phone or computer, fighting to keep SKT at the head of the pack. Business was booming. His personal fortune was nearing ten figures. He was a man with everything.

Too bad everything included some damn difficult problems.

But that was about to change.

His door opened, and Frances and Z hurried inside.

Stuart's huge office was built to impress. He dressed to impress, drove a car to impress, and had completely redesigned his face and reinvented himself to impress. He had a PR guy who had gotten him on the covers of almost every magazine in the country. Framed covers of his cinema-handsome face lined one wall. Image was everything.

The old Stuart was dead and buried. Or so he could delude himself, till his mother came around and treated him like nothing.

"Have you seen the book?" he asked. "The press is coming to do an interview."

"Really?" she said, sitting down, thumbing through her briefcase. "What's it about?"

"Me."

"Oh, my." She was barely listening.

He handed her a signed copy. "I wrote a personal inscription to you."

"Did you?" Barely glancing at it, she set it back on his desk. "That's nice. But I don't have a lot of time."

"Mr. Shayne," his secretary said over the intercom, "A Mr. Gregory and his photographer are here to do your interview."

"Z says I shouldn't think of money at a time like this," his mother began, "with Kara and her boyfriend in those awful black bags. But what better time? Her death has made my feelings crystal clear."

Stuart leaned forward.

"I want to do the right thing for both my children."

He smiled, his best movie-star smile. His mother was shuffling legal documents and didn't notice. Finally she looked up. "You're very rich. I couldn't give you anything you don't already have."

Your love.

You could give me your love.

Where the hell had that come from?

He waited.

"I've made a new will. I've decided to leave everything to Emma. She's just a writer—and a woman alone, which makes life much harder."

Her arrogant indifference made something explode in him, but he smiled politely.

"I wanted to inform you—as a formality."

"Of course. Thank you, Mother."

"You're all right with this, then? You won't contest my will?"

He laughed. "As you said, I have all the money in the world. And I love Emma every bit as much as you do. Who couldn't love Emma?"

"Then you're still sending your best driver to pick her up?"

"Of course."

She snapped her briefcase and got up. "Then that's everything."

When she'd gone, Stuart picked up his autographed book she'd left behind and dropped it in his wastebasket.

Her plane had been early. Emma felt as if she'd been waiting forever for Stuart's driver. Her stomach growled. She'd been too upset to eat airplane food. Now she was starving.

With its turquoise, beige and pink walls, the gates and shops of Albuquerque's international airport were prettier than most. Large windows offered expansive views and let in plenty of clear, bright light.

Emma, however, was downstairs, hiding in the deep gloom of the airport's lower level. Dozens of cars had already pulled up, collected passengers and sped away, leaving the street momentarily empty.

Anxiously she shielded her world-famous face with the hood of a soft, green cape. Just as she was trying to decide whether to run back inside to a vending machine, her gaze was riveted to a handsome couple in jeans and hiking boots standing beside her.

Lean and tanned, the boy was totally absorbed by the pretty redhead adjusting his collar. The girl smiled. He blushed. No sooner had they melted together and their lips met than a BMW pulled up, its driver waving frantically.

When the couple's kiss deepened, the BMW's horn blared.

Young love. The kiss went on and on. Finally, the horn stopped, and the driver smiled, waiting till the boy came up for air. When he did, he caught Emma and the driver watching them, and his dazed, lipsticky grin turned sheepish.

Emma flushed. Once she'd had what they had. Mike had been everything. Then Kara...

When another couple walked out laughing, a little redheaded girl between them, Emma backed blindly into the terminal. She had to get home, to her mother who would remind her such feelings weren't appropriate.

When she glanced at her watch, her hood fell to her shoulders. She still had enough time to rent a car and get home by dark. Just then a voice boomed behind her.

"For crying out loud, aren't—"

"Leave it alone, Bertie. We'll miss our shuttle."

Others stopped, too.

"It's her!"

"Short hair, but it's Kara—that actress that burned up."

Emma pulled her hood up.

"Kara!"

A wall of people crushed her. Hands yanked her hood down. Fingernails scratched her cheek.

"Why aren't you dead, girlie?"

A treasured bracelet Katherine had given her was torn from her wrist. Emma stepped back, stumbling on her suitcase. When she fell on top of it, they surrounded her. Hands thrust napkins, pens and airline tickets—to be signed.

"Please... I'm not who you think."

Emma stood up again.

"No, she's not!" declared a plump girl, hugging her baby to her chest. "She's the bad twin. The writer. She slept with Kara's lover—that Navajo sculptor. She hates Kara. They're estranged—"

The mob roared.

Alarmed by her mother's angry voice, the baby knotted her tiny fists and kicked at her blanket.

The crowd shoved, pushing the young mother down.

"The baby!" Emma said. "Be careful!"

When the crowd surged forward, the startled baby wailed. Then the crowd rushed Emma, and the mother was jostled from behind. "My baby!" She lost her grip on the child.

Dizzy with fear, Emma lunged for the baby, barely catching her.

Talcum powder. Emma had forgotten that clean, fresh, baby smell. And yet not forgotten it. Lilly's blankets had been this very same light shade of pink.

Memories of her precious little girl came sharply into focus. Lilly had had pale skin that had turned scarlet when she cried. She'd had soft red curls under her pink bonnet.

Emma quickly backed out of the crowd while she searched frantically for the mother.

Faces blurred. Clamoring voices dimmed.

Think. Focus. Remember.

The mob surrounded her. "Did your Greywolf, your Navajo lover, kill your sister?" someone yelled.

The baby shrieked. Strangling a sob, Emma clutched the child more tightly.

"Did Greywolf kill her?"

"Why don't you ask *me*," drawled a deep, contemptuous voice behind them.

Emma whirled, her eyes pleading. "Mike—"

He saw the wriggling pink blankets and understood.

"Get back!" he commanded, kneeling over the fallen mother. With strong, sure hands, he helped her to her feet. The crowd parted, and he led the shaken girl to Emma.

Her eyes on Mike, Emma froze. He looked tired, his dark face lined with strain.

"Murderer," a man accused.

The word brought a dark frown to Mike's ruthless features. He looked down at the child, then at Emma. When she blushed and lowered her gaze, his face turned to stone.

Wordlessly he lifted the baby from her and handed the pink bundle to its mother, who nodded weakly before scurrying to safety. Letting go of the little girl took Emma back to another place, to that shattering time.

Warm, callused fingers beneath her chin tilted her face to his. Mike's wide hat brim was pulled low, but his cold eyes, green and as dark and haunting as a moonless winter night, pierced straight to Emma's soul.

She'd fallen in love with him twice. Lost him twice. Never again.

But he was raising her child.

He couldn't know.

His hand fell away. Everything went quiet, the people surrounding them stilling in dreamlike flow. Colors muted. The baby's fitful cries faded.

There was only Mike, summer-brown from too much desert sun, his chiseled face etched with bitter experiences.

He'd always been able to see inside her, to understand her. Strange, how that very quality that had once drawn her was now what most terrified her. If he knew the truth—the whole truth—what would he do?

A crisp, long-sleeved white shirt and starched jeans hugged his lean, broad-shouldered frame. He wore a black Stetson, and badly battered, elk skin boots.

When the crowd surrounded them again, Mike let out a cowboy whoop, and stomped menacingly into their midst. They jumped back, all but a few scattering.

Mike seized Emma's elbow and propelled her to an out-of-the-way corner. "You gonna tell me what's really going on?"

That was the last thing, the *very* last thing she could do. Or so she thought. But on some level she trusted him more than she knew. Her face softened; her large, brown eyes misted. Nervously she licked her lips. "Mike, people are watching."

His hand clamped harder around her elbow. "Then, we'll just have to do something about that." His green eyes scanned their surroundings and fixed on a sign not far away. She followed his gaze.

"No." In a frightened whisper she spelled out the capital letters. *"W-O-M-E-N."*

His grip tightened. "Me no savage. Me can read," he muttered, hustling her past the crowd toward the ladies' room.

"You can't go in—there."

"Says who?"

"That sign! Unless you've had a sex-change operation—"

His dark head leaned closer to her bright one. "Just between me and you—I haven't."

Then he banged the door open, yanked her inside and said in a loud voice, "Man in the rest room."

Women screamed. Toilets flushed. Stall locks snapped. High heels clicked like computer keyboard keys as women scurried.

A woman pulled out a cell phone. "I'm calling security."

"Not with this." Mike grabbed her phone and dropped it into the trash can. "Out!"

When the door slammed, he shot the bolt.

"Alone, at last," he drawled huskily to Emma. He leaned closer. "*Estranged* my ass. Which one are you today?"

23

"What the hell is going on, Emma?"

She stared.

"Last time I saw you, you had long hair and you were crawling to me, playing your sister—*again*. Then Kara's house burst into flames. When I came to, I thought you'd died. It was you in Kara's suite that night in Santa Fe, wasn't it?"

She gasped.

"Why, Emma? For God's sake, why?"

When she realized his grief overrode his anger, tears sprang to her eyes. "I—I don't know what you're talking about—"

"Two people were carried out in body bags. I thought..." Mike's accented voice held anguish. "Damn it, how'd you get out? Do you have any idea what thinking you were dead did to me?"

When she tried to back away from him, his hand clamped around her wrist. "First you played Kara, then Emma."

He drew her closer. With his huge body, he trapped her against the door. He lifted a damp curl from her forehead. When his finger touched her face, her skin tingled. "You were good in both parts. But I like you better…when you're just *you*. Want to tell me why nobody's seen you and your sister together for seven years?"

Her breath stopped.

So did his.

She swallowed thickly.

"Tell me what's going on. I want to help you."

He wouldn't, if he knew.

Seconds ticked by. She was terrified. His eyes poured over her, their hot, seeking darkness like missiles heating every target they touched, first her eyes, next her lips, then her throat and white shoulders…her breasts.

"Two people are dead, Emma. I've got a cop breathing down my neck. The whole world thinks I killed your sister."

"I can't help you."

He sucked in a breath. "Can't you?" He moved in closer, slapping each hand, palm open, against the door beside her face, trapping her. His intimate eyes climbed her again. Then his voice cracked like a bullwhip. "How come nobody's seen you and your twin together for years? Answer that."

Her heart began to pound in her ears like a drum.

"How come?"

The cell phone in the garbage can began to ring.

"You were there…in *her* house," Mike whispered. "Did *you* kill her? If so—when? Where? Goddamn it, Emma! Why?"

Tears burned her eyes as Emma shook her head back and forth wildly.

"You're never seen with her. Not ever. How long have you been playing the movie star? Was it only that night? How long, Emma?" He brought a hard fingertip to her cut lip. "How did you hurt yourself?"

Even as her tongue flecked the bloody place on her lip, she cringed away from him, sweat beading her forehead.

Her shaking hands fumbled to unbolt the door.

"What about Lilly?" he persisted. "She needs her mother."

"She's *your* daughter."

"I've always claimed her. Why can't you? After all, she's yours, too."

Emma spun free and rapped on the door. But Mike pushed her back, effectively sealing her inside with him.

"You *are* her mother. So, what's Kara's name doing on her birth certificate?"

Emma drew a deep shuddering breath.

"You tried to tell me that night... That night in Santa Fe after the premiere. But I was too damn furious at you and at myself to listen. I thought you were Kara. I thought I'd slept with her again, for God's sake. I thought I was an animal. I couldn't listen to you, then. I was too damn afraid what might happen if I had. Emma, these are dangerous games you're playing. Two people are dead."

"Don't—"

"You owe me the truth."

Oh, God. The truth. He wanted the truth. She didn't know what to do or say. She was so confused. Her life was such a mess. She'd hurt other people. But she knew one thing—the truth could be worse than any lie. She was so sorry for what she'd done, but words couldn't undo it.

Somehow she had to get out of here, to run. But his body trapped her.

"Emma, the truth is our only chance. I don't care what you've done."

You would, if you knew.

She swallowed hard, choked back the tears.

"What if the truth…is more terrible than you can possibly imagine?"

"Emma. Trust me. For God's sake, whatever it is, you can tell me."

His pleading silence was so thick and palpable, her breath stopped. Her face softened for a single second. She almost believed him.

"Don't do that," he growled. "Not unless you mean it."

Helplessly she began to cry.

"Why did you come to my show? Why did you entice me to follow you?"

She wiped her tears away.

"Your sad eyes don't lie," he said. "When I look at you, I feel your pain…because it's my pain, too. I know who I'm with. I know that the night Kara's house burned, it was you I held. You kissed me. *You* made me want you. I remember the way you looked at Lilly in the plaza…at my show. You want to tell me everything."

She did.

A shaft of pure fear pierced her. She saw small hands moving fast as lightning, hurriedly stuffing bits of china into that dusty pile of brown cottonwood leaves. She saw feet finding footholds, climbing a tree. Up. Up into glorious, concealing green leaves. She saw a slim hand lifting the heavy lid of the cedar chest, helping her inside. She saw Kara and Mike wrapped in moonlight. Memories that she had blacked out…

Oh, God. Would she remember what happened to Kara? Would she remember what terrible thing she had done?

"Did you play Kara because you were trying to set me up for her murder?" he asked.

"Oh…. No. I—I would never deliberately hurt you."

His dark face relaxed. "Then trust me. Where were you when Kara died?"

Emma stared wildly. Again she stood soaking wet beside that yawning cave on the mesa.

She didn't know. For the life of her, she didn't know.

She had to get away from him before she blurted the whole awful story. What would he say if she told him that the night they'd had sex in Kara's hotel suite when she'd pretended to be Kara, what he'd said had made her realize the extent of Kara's lies? Kara had lied about the night in the barn. About Lilly, too. And Emma had been furious at her sister for costing her Mike and Lilly.

In a rage, the first real rage of her life, she'd deliberately driven to the ranch to have it out with Kara. But she must've had a blackout, because hours later she'd found herself on top of the mesa, and all she could remember was her rage. Blackouts always meant she'd done something awful that she should feel guilty about.

After deceiving Mike in Kara's suite, she couldn't go to him. How could she say, "I had to know if *you* were telling me the truth, or if she was?"

Too late, she'd learned what she'd wanted to know.

So, she'd run. It had been weeks before she'd found out that Kara had vanished that same night, and that because nobody knew where Emma was either, Mike had been accused of their double murder. So, she'd gone back and pretended to be Kara. Then she'd had to return as Emma, too.

Only not together. Never together again. So, she'd made everybody think they were estranged, and all the while she'd hoped that her fears were unfounded and that Kara would appear and resume her own life.

While she'd been home again, Emma had searched the desert, but the red rocks had told her nothing about her missing sister. So finally, in desperation, she'd returned to Kara's mansion by the sea. She'd played Kara to the hilt. And sometimes when she'd looked in Kara's mirror there, Kara really had seemed to stare back at her.

Emma had assumed both identities to save Mike. Not to hurt him.

"Where, Emma, where were you the night Kara's house burned?"

"Mexico," she whispered dully. "Puerto Vallarta."

"Prove it."

When she tried to wrench free again, he held on fast, his fingers digging into her skin.

"You're hurting me—"

"Were you with someone?"

"Yes," she lied. "I had a date."

"All night?"

She nodded.

"A man?"

"What else?"

"Describe him."

"Mike don't—"

"What's his name?"

"Javier," she lashed.

"What does he look like?"

She studied Mike's narrow aquiline nose, his thick, shiny-black hair.

"Tall. Dark."

"Like me?"

"N-no... He's nothing like you."

"So you still go...for my type?"

"No!"

"It's okay if you like tall and dark. I've accepted my hopeless weakness for impossible, live-wire redheads. Bad habits are hard to break."

Emma saw Kara. Then Sara, his wife. They were both redheads. The thought of him with other women made her feel queasy.

Suddenly it was all too much. The terrifying blackout, three lost days. The strange dreams. Kara's fake death. Coming home. Mike.

Emma pushed at his broad chest, but it was like trying to shove a wall of iron. "If you don't let me go, I'll scream—"

"Be my guest."

But when she opened her lips, he clamped his huge hand over her mouth. His other hand wound around her at the waist.

She struggled, biting his fingers, kicking, trying to scream. His lips were dangerously near hers when the door banged open and a uniformed officer stepped inside.

"That's him," said a woman. "He ran us all out of the ladies' room."

A flash went off. Another. A video camera purred.

Emma would've screamed if Mike hadn't closed his mouth over hers. A hot rush of desire, as unexpected as it was overpowering, washed her. Her scream died to a muted moan.

Instantly he let her go, but his deep voice breathed beside her ear. "The media's here. You win."

She was so upset she couldn't breathe. Thousands of tiny stars glimmered and swirled. Her ears buzzed. His dark face whirled. The clean taste of his mouth was the last thing she knew before the dizziness claimed her.

That same delicious taste was the first thing she knew when she regained consciousness.

Easy. Easy. Turn. Look. Smile.
No reason to panic.

Then where the hell was she?

His tall black-suited body carved its way through the tourists, the 9 mm Glock feeling heavy in his waistband.

Goddamn piece of shit-luck she wasn't in a body bag.

How the hell had her damn plane gotten in early? She hadn't come through security. She wasn't downstairs, either.

The airport was packed. Full of tourists tired of cloverleaf freeways and bustling big-city street corners. Full of kids in hiking gear with long hair and rings in their noses. Too many fat guys in blue jeans and big belt buckles and big sombreros.

He saw red hair and raced to catch up.

Too young. Too fat.

He was panting hard.

Easy. Easy. Look. Smile.

Couldn't be noticed or remembered.

Then he saw the TV cameras and gawkers. When he got closer, it didn't take long to figure out Emma was inside the VIP lounge.

So was that Navajo son of a bitch.

With the thrill of a hunter with his prey in his sights, the watcher patted the black rectangular bulge in his coat that concealed the 9 mm Glock, and smiled.

His smile was beautiful.

That's what made it so scary.

The VIP lounge was beige. So were the tables, chairs and sofa. Emma lay prostrate across the leather couch. Mike sat beside her, holding her limp hand. When she realized they were alone together, she felt too tired to be angry even at him.

Mike leaned close, softly ordering her to wake up and drink a glass of what looked like ice water. His deep voice was seductive and caressing. Through her eyelashes she caught glimpses of his bronze cheekbones and strong jaw. With a soft sigh, she turned her face into the rough hand that smoothed her brow.

"Say you're okay, Emma."

She lay quiet and still.

"I'm sorry if I was hard on you."

Gently Mike gathered Emma closer. She remembered how gently he'd lifted the baby from her arms.

"Wake up. Please." His low voice grew more urgent. His warm fingers feathered through her short curls.

She kept her eyes closed and held on to this little heartbeat of time when he acted as if she were precious to him. Slowly, she began to remember how vulnerable she was where he was concerned and that she couldn't let herself weaken. His very appeal was what made him dangerous.

Dear God. She had to get away from him.

Her lashes fluttered. "Where am I?"

"Drink this."

"How'd you get away from that cop?"

"You fainted. I told him you were upset about your sister and felt sick earlier. That I'd taken you in there for emergency purposes."

"And he believed—"

With a grin he handed her the glass. Without thinking, she swallowed the burning stuff and then choked.

Gin. Straight gin laced with a drop or two of water! It went halfway down her throat and then spewed back up.

She sat up, coughing. He patted his open hand hard against her shoulder blades.

"Stop it."

Even after her throat cleared, her sinuses still stung.

"Are you trying to kill me? You know I don't drink."

"You might have acquired bad habits in the seven years you've been away from my...beneficial influence."

"Not gin."

"Javier?"

"Who's...?"

He grinned. "Thought so." He raised the glass in a mock toast and gulped noisily as if celebrating.

She swung her feet off the couch. "I've got to go."

"Not so fast."

"I'm thoroughly tired of your company."

"You'll get used to me."

"Let me up."

"So you can faint again?"

"I'm not some helpless female in need of rescuing."

"You were in a house that blew up. You're scared to death of something or somebody."

"I'm—I'm just tired...and hungry—"

"I'll drive you wherever you want to go. I'll feed you. We have a lot to catch up on."

The thought of spending more time alone with him, of sitting across some candlelit table from him, unnerved her.

"No." But when she tried to stand again, she almost fell.

Quickly he put his arms around her slim waist. She was about to protest, when the room began to spin. She sank into him, almost glad he was there to catch her, until he seized his advantage, pressing her body against his. In the next instant he had them fused from chest to knee.

The rush of his heart was even faster than her own. He drew her close. His warm breath burned her cheek. His gaze intimately searched her face. "What's so terrible that you can't tell me?"

For one incredible moment, she thought she could tell

him everything—everything she knew...even what she feared.

She forced herself to remember finding Kara in the loft with him. Now Kara's house had exploded. He'd been there. She remembered his rage the night in Santa Fe after they'd made love in Kara's hotel room.

"I'm attracted to you, but I consider that a weakness. A weakness I'll fight till I die." She stared into his eyes until he forced his gaze away.

He seemed to come to his senses slowly, his eyes hardening as he deliberately reclaimed himself.

Slowly, his big, rough hands fell from her body. "Damn you to hell, Emma. Have it your way, then. You came on to me at Kara's house. Now you're cold as ice. I don't know why I still give a damn."

Spinning free, he strode swiftly out of the room.

The door slammed, and she was alone.

A heavy weakness descended upon her. She felt lost in some void as she ran shaking fingers through her cropped curls.

She had been afraid to see him. He stirred her and upset her too terribly. Her mother had promised Emma she wouldn't have to deal with him. She had to get home, away from him. As quickly as possible. Never, never again could she be alone with him.

But when she opened the door, pandemonium erupted.

An angry crowd had Mike pinned against a wall. When Emma's frantic gaze shot to him, his eyes warned her away.

Then Sara was there, and Mike lunged free, grabbing her.

"Leave her alone, Sara."

Sara writhed in his arms. "Which one of you killed Kara?"

Mike's face was fearsome.

"He did," Emma said. "He was there."

Mike's lips went white, his face still. Then his eyes blazed with hatred at this fresh public betrayal.

"So were you."

The crowd roared and then pushed Sara in an effort to get Mike, smashing Sara's camera to the ground.

Mike fell.

Sara had a final question. "Why haven't you and Kara ever been seen *together* in the past seven years?"

Emma ran.

The man in the black suit with the 9 mm Glock loped after her.

24

Emma wished she had nowhere to go, that she could just ride and ride. She wanted to run from Mike, from the past, from her mother. From Kara. Most of all, she wanted to run from herself.

But she knew it was time to stop running.

On one side of the highway, the sun was sinking into a vat of orange; on the other side the sky was iridescent purple. Ahead, lightning flickered on the horizon.

The big desert was stark and silent. Emma's nerves jumped when she looked down and saw her speedometer needle on 80.

Relax. She lifted her foot off the gas, but she couldn't still the shaking of her hands on the steering wheel.

Mike would follow her. She was sure he would. Why had she accused him?

She let her window down a bit, and a cool wind whipped her short curls. She didn't want to think about him. So she thought of home, of her mother's rambling, adobe mansion north of Santa Fe.

And always when she thought of home, she remembered when she'd left for the first time. She'd been seventeen, hardly recovered from her stay in the hospital after her accident in the barn. She'd wanted Mike in the hospital, but her mother had gotten very upset every time she'd asked her.

"Mother, I have to see him. Don't you understand, I can't bear the memories without at least finding out why. I want him to explain."

"Some facts speak for themselves. His do. Yours and your sister's do as well. I've never been more ashamed."

Frances had ordered Stuart to stand guard at her bedside, when she couldn't be there herself. Slowly she began to feel anger toward her family for treating her like a criminal for loving Mike.

Maybe *he* would have wanted her if *they* hadn't put up such powerful objections. Maybe he wouldn't have turned to Kara.

When Emma had come home, she hadn't found peace. Her mother's stern glances were a constant reproach. And everywhere she saw Mike. In the pastures, on the long porch of Auntie Z's ranch house, in the desert. She had only to smell the lilacs in blossom to think of him. But the memories that had once held happiness now held only pain. Her mother's house seemed dead and empty. So did the desert.

Under this pressure, Kara ran away to Hollywood. Stuart was curiously glum at her departure. Emma began to realize that if she didn't get away from her family, she'd be devoured by guilt. Their coldness was the last thing she needed when her own heart was breaking. But when she told her mother she was leaving, Frances saw this as the ultimate betrayal. Slowly, however, she had worn her mother down.

"But where, Emma, where will you go?"

"I don't know if that even matters."

By happy chance, Katherine, the daughter of a friend

of Auntie Z's, was a brand-new doctor working in Mexico
in a clinic for the poor. She was so kind, so sure, so
understanding of the entire situation that Z convinced
Frances to let Emma go to her.

On the day Emma departed, Frances had been too ill
to go to the airport. She'd stood in the doorway to wave
goodbye. White-faced, wasted, Frances's lips had twisted
into a semblance of a smile.

"You're too thin, Emma."

"So are you."

"You be careful."

"You, too."

"When will you come—"

"I don't know, Mother."

"But why—"

"Goodbye... Mother."

"You're never coming home," her mother whispered,
hugging her tightly.

As the car had sped away, Emma looked back. The
familiar soft grace of the adobe house beneath the soaring
blue mountains had made a picture that stabbed her with
pain. Piñon smoke had been rising from all the adobe
chimneys, floating like a gray cloud above the house. But
what had really saddened her was the stooped figure in
the thick, arched doorway.

You're never coming back.

Always when she remembered her mother, that stark
image standing there, looking so lost and forlorn, was
frozen in her mind.

Emma had almost told Stuart to take her back, but
oddly she'd been far more terrified of staying than of going. So, she'd watched till the house and the walls had
disappeared behind a red hill. And she'd lost not only
Mike, but Kara, her mother...her home.

Home. What would she find there now, after all these years? Would the memories of Kara still hurt, and those of Mike still tug as painfully at her heart? Would her strong, needy mother, who'd never understood why she'd left, still disapprove of her and demand total dominion over her again?

Every time her mother had come to Isla Mujeres since the premiere of *Betrayal,* she'd been fiercely judgmental, her questions and commands almost as frightening as Mike's questions now were.

Now Emma needed time to think about Mike. As always, he evoked both the wonderful and the terrible in her. He wasn't going to leave her alone. She didn't blame him.

Oh, for the happy childhood before he'd come into her life. Oh, for that time when love had been such a simple, joyous experience. She'd had her twin. Until Mike, they'd been inseparable.

Ever since the kiva, her family had told her not to trust him. Following her heart had proved disastrous. Somehow, no matter how he appealed to her and no matter how drawn she was to Lilly, for Lilly's sake and everyone else's, she had to keep her distance.

She still had secrets. She had made terrible choices and was caught in her own snare. The last thing she ever wanted to do was hurt Lilly.

Kara.

Emma stared at the desert. Where was Kara? Where had she been all these years? Emma thought of the faxes, the blackmailer's threats, his demands.

What did he know?

Who was he?

Who might he hurt next, to punish her?

She was afraid, and not just for herself.

She would not risk Lilly.

She could not turn to Mike.

A gaudy pink glow tinged the western mountaintops and shot streamers of pink fire across the wide, purple sky. The rapidly darkening moon-dead landscape was strange and beautiful, but it made her heart thud with foreboding. Always, always the desert brought a rush of her old feelings for *him*.

She'd had good reasons for running. Good reasons for hurting other people...even Lilly.

Good reasons for paying her blackmailer.

If only she could start over, make everything all right. But it was too late.

She would have to make her visit as short as possible.

Suddenly she topped a hill. Beneath her, the lights of Santa Fe spread across the foothills, twinkling in welcome like lost jewels beneath the darkening Sangre de Cristo Mountains. She saw Stuart's headquarters, SKT's immense cluster of low-rise, adobe buildings forming a large part of that glitter. She knew he had made enemies in his climb to the top, but she was proud of her brilliant brother, glad his business was booming.

The black sky toward Taos was whitening now. Bands of low, dark clouds hurtled out of the north and threw a curtain across the stars. Jagged slivers of brilliance arced across the sky. Thunder drummed. The cool gusts brought the smell of wet sage.

Rain.

A child of the desert, Emma always thrilled to rain. She didn't notice the headlights looming in her rearview mirror.

She flung her hand out as if to touch the electric storm's wildness. Fat raindrops struck her open palm. Then her rearview mirror filled with blinding white. The driver behind her was right on her tail.

She adjusted the mirror and took her foot off the brake, so the car accelerated downhill. It began to rain, really rain, and soon all was black wetness.

When she was north of Santa Fe, the rain was so thick she couldn't see. Where was she? Had she missed the turnoff?

Just as she rolled her window down to check, the truck behind her threw on its high beams.

She speeded up. So did he.

Then he rammed her, so hard she fishtailed. He hit her again, more violently than before. Her car careened into the left lane, and she narrowly missed an eighteen-wheeler. The big truck honked as it whizzed past her, ripping off her side-view mirror with a metallic *crunch*.

Panicking, she swerved back into her lane and then onto the first off-ramp.

The headlights stayed on top of her.

Shaking, she ground the accelerator to the floor. The rental car bounced onto a rutted road.

Her tire hit something, and she saw a yellow object rolling away from her rear bumper. Lightning spun a silver web across the inky sky. A yellow barrel tumbled off the narrow shoulder. A row of red cones set in a crooked line gleamed ahead of her.

She was lost on a road going nowhere—and now...construction. Just what she needed on a stormy night when a maniac was chasing her.

Huge slanting raindrops pelted her windshield. The road narrowed, curved over a hill. Her car jolted into ruts and chuckholes, sloshing muddy geysers over her windows.

High beams brightened. The maniac slammed her from

behind again. The impact sent her skidding, hydroplaning. Her wheels slung gravel and mud. Ahead, a wall of water rushed over a guardrail.

A low-water bridge was underwater.

She hit the brakes. Her tires slid in deep mud. Sliding, the car gathered speed and surged into the creek. A torrent of black water swamped her. Her engine sputtered and coughed, dying halfway across the bridge in the deepest part of the creek.

Almost immediately, the swift current rolling under her car, lifted wheels off concrete. Another wave whirled her against the flimsy guardrail. Once. Then again.

The rail splintered. Her right wheel fell off the bridge first. Emma held her breath as her car scooted forward, inch by inch, tipping slowly.

Emma screamed. Nose down, the car hovered a final second or two before plunging into the creek. Water streamed inside. Miraculously, the car still displaced enough water to float, and the raging creek swept her downstream. She was swirling around and around, yelling, pulling at the door handle, when a boulder loomed above a crashing wave. Before she could react or do the slightest thing, she was crunched onto the rocky island.

Airbags exploded. Pain knifed from her forehead to her neck. Icy water poured over the floorboards as she fell forward. Dark water oozed over her ankles, up her calves. Soon she was waist-deep.

Frantically, crying out for help, she pushed against her door, yanking the handle. A wall of water pinned the door shut. Waves pounded the car into the boulder and alternately tugged at it, trying to pry it loose and carry it downstream.

She banged against her window. Finally, she gasped in

exhaustion, her fingers splaying helplessly against the wet glass.

Teeth chattering, she was chest-deep in dark water. She began to shiver. Dimly, she was aware of high beams going out. A truck door opened. An interior light came on and went off.

A jagged sliver of lightning cut the sullen sky. A tall, black-suited figure with a handgun headed toward her. He picked his way slowly along the steep bank, as if he had all the time in the world. Then he slid down the slight rise and plunged into the water.

Her throat tightened.

Lightning turned the sky electric white. Then a massive reverberating roar beat back the night.

She stared straight at him as he stepped through the shallow part of the stream, wading as far out as he seemed to dare.

Almost casually, he lifted the gun and took aim.

The rain pelted her window. His image swam in the sparkling rivulets.

She swallowed.

Mike.

Rage. Panic. Icy water numbing her.

Lightning whitened his cruelly handsome features, then his face blurred in the smear of raindrops rushing down her window.

She put her hand up against the glass and squeezed her eyes shut. He squeezed the trigger.

A roar splintered glass.

Then blackness.

Dark clouds cloaked the Sangre de Cristo Mountains. A darker cloud hung over his soul.

Because of her.

Everybody thought she was so good.

They didn't know.

He knew.

She was screaming. He almost imagined he could hear her, even above the violent thunder of the creek.

He felt a terrible stillness inside himself.

He could still save her.

She looked toward him, pleading.

You wish.

He smiled.

Christ, the noise was awful. He put his hands over his ears. Lightning flickered like strobe lights, and during those flashes he saw the water climb higher against the car.

He wanted to see her face under water, the bubbles stop.

Like before.

Instead, he saw the distant gleam of headlights.

Shit.

It was raining hard.

Mike was nearly to his turnoff when lightning illuminated one of those little crosses that seemed to be everywhere on New Mexican highways. This one was tottering beneath the weight of plastic flowers.

A shadow flickered across Mike's carved features. He clenched the steering wheel more tightly. Somebody had died there. Somebody who'd been much loved. Mike was superstitious about such places. He thought of his grandfather. For no reason at all, the cross seemed a warning. *Emma.*

Where was Emma? He had to find her.

The screams. Follow the screams.

Where the hell had that come from? His heart raced. The silent voice had sounded like his grandfather's.

No. He couldn't let himself fall under the spell of his superstitious inclinations.

Then his pickup bumped onto the washboard road, and everything began to rattle. His eyes locked on the crooked line of red cones ahead. He was just susceptible because he felt tired and irritable, angry at himself for letting Emma get away at the airport.

Still, he sensed ghosts, the need to find her.

Not tonight, though, his logical mind said. She'd be safe enough with her mother for tonight. Tomorrow would have to do.

Follow the screams.

Again he felt a mysterious urgency.

Again he fought to calm down. Emma was alive. She was Lilly's mother. Seeing her in the airport, knowing she was alive, had made him come alive again, made him want her.

Then she'd called him a murderer. That's why he was in this strange mood.

Again he imagined Lilly on the plaza when she was seven, and that single moment when his life had almost come together again. Emma had stood there watching Lilly. Then she'd looked at him, her face soft, her eyes wet. She'd been so damn beautiful, he'd hurt.

She'd been even more beautiful today, with her bruised face and haunted eyes and short curls. If only he'd known, that night in Santa Fe when she'd run out of the hotel room after him, that she'd been Emma.

When she'd thrown herself against the window of his car, he wouldn't have driven away. He would have forgiven her anything. He could still remember how heartbroken she'd looked. Her pain had been as profound as his own.

He'd shaped her tears into clay.

Cast them in bronze.

But he hadn't seen.

Now he did. He knew that whatever it cost him, he had to find her and keep her safe.

What god-awful secret was she hiding?

Follow the screams.

One minute, rain rushed sloppily across Mike's windshield. The next, high beams blinded him.

He shielded his eyes. Who the hell could be racing toward him like a bat-out-of-hell from his own damn ranch at this late hour?

The murderous bastard was aiming straight for him.

The road curved and ran up a hill. The headlights vanished. Then they were back, whiter than ever.

The bastard was in Mike's lane, speeding right at him.

Follow the screams.

Mike swerved, rocketing his truck's huge mass into the other lane.

Ping. *Pong.* Red cones flew up into the air.

The gutsy bastard swerved, too. More red cones exploded.

A tingle of fear shot up Mike's spine. On a burst of adrenaline, he stomped harder on his own accelerator.

Mud sluiced up over his windshield. His windshield wipers slashed furiously. The killer lights loomed larger.

He had the eerie feeling that he was in a nightmare, that his speeding truck was standing still. The bastard was nearly on top of him. Mike was microseconds from death.

They say your life passes before your eyes before you die. Either it wasn't true, or he wasn't dying. All he saw was Emma. He saw her in the vision that had led him away from his grandfather's hogan. He saw her lying beneath him in the loft, her red hair spilling across his pillow, her brown eyes soft with desire and yet bright with pain.

He'd made promises he hadn't kept.

Then she was a girl-child, whirling around and around in a field of butterflies. He saw her swinging underneath the cottonwood. He saw her hiking up her skirts, wading through the shallows of the river near *La Golindrina,* hiding in the bushes, thinking he didn't know she was spying on him while he fished.

She'd haunted him even before the kiva. Then, as a child who'd followed him everywhere. Later, as the woman he'd loved and lost.

Next time it'll be better.

Follow the screams.

For an instant longer he felt suspended in that endless black moment—detached. Then he yanked the steering wheel to the right, spinning his truck sideways in the slippery mud. Out of control, his right tires fell over some edge, and he careened clumsily off road onto rocks.

Then he was flying.

Front wheels slammed rock. Mike was jerked forward against his belt, almost catapulted out of his seat. A tire blew. The rear of the truck rose. He was staring straight down at the road. Then he flipped and rolled. A window shattered. Mud and glass shot all over him through the empty frame.

Over and over he went till his truck lay in a ditch iced with thick mud. A suitcase banged open and rained clothes on his head.

When he came to, he was upside down, still buckled in, his head resting in a pillow of mud. His chest was buried with wet road maps, books, suitcases and garment bags. His radiator was hissing steam. Something electrical was on fire.

Sheets of water streamed through the broken window. Still, he lay there, listening to the ominous drumming of the rain on his truck. After he got his breath back, he undid his seat belt and wiped the mud off his face. He was suddenly glad Lilly was spending the night with Sara.

When he stood up, scrambling among the suitcases to find sure footing, his right ankle throbbed with pain. He leaned down and grabbed his hat off the ceiling. Then he opened the glove compartment and took out his Berreta and bullets. He jammed the gun into his waistband and the bullets into his pockets. Then he hoisted himself up and out.

For a moment he sat on top of the truck and let the rain soak him. When he finally dropped to the ground, he slid in the slick wet dirt and rocks, slamming down too hard on his bad ankle. Breathing fast from the bolt of pain, he scrambled to his feet again. After a while, the fiery pain dulled to an ache, and he tested the ankle to see if it would bear weight.

Lightning blazed. Thunder reverberated. A blast of cold wind hit him. Bad ankle or not, he was alive. Which meant he had to pull himself together—fast—just in case that roadhog came back to finish what he'd started.

The bridge couldn't be more than a mile. Mike didn't want to think about how much farther his house was. If it kept raining, it would take most of the night to get home. But if the bastard came back—

What if the maniac had been coming *from* his ranch house? In a panic, Mike wiped the cold mud off his face and hands and dove back into his truck.

Amazingly, his cell phone worked. But no sooner had

Mabel assured him all was fine, then it got too wet and died.

Damn. Why hadn't he told her where he was?

Follow the screams.

His grandfather's voice.

Then lightning arced down the length of the road that led to *La Golindrina*.

He saw a glowing figure at the end of that silver road in an electric halo of silver light. She had red hair and terrified brown eyes. She was screaming.

Follow the screams.

Bad ankle or not, he took off running.

Frances stared out her window at the black rain. It seemed to her she'd stood at that window for years, first waiting for *his* return, and then for Emma's.

Every gust of wind made Frances's nerves jump. Where was Emma? An elaborate supper had been waiting on the stove for more than an hour. Frances was too worried to drink or eat. Anxiety hadn't stopped Czarina. Frances frowned when she saw her plump sister munching the last potato skin.

"You've gobbled that entire plate of potato skins all by yourself."

"Somebody had to."

"And now you're working over all the assorted cheeses and crackers. The bottle of merlot is down to half."

"If you'd quit standing at the window like a sentinel of gloom and doom, maybe I wouldn't feel so depressed! I always eat when I'm worried."

"Emma's out there!"

"By the way, the skins were yummy."

"Her plane got in hours ago. Why doesn't she call?"

Czarina poured herself another glass of merlot. When Frances wasn't looking, she drained it in a single swallow.

"Stuart hasn't called, either."

Frances turned on the television. Her eyes narrowed on the screen. Sara Greywolf was the commentator. Behind her, a mob had Mike Greywolf pinned to a wall. Emma was big-eyed.

"He has her!" Frances hissed.

Czarina placidly smoothed cream cheese on a cracker. "Then we can relax. Why don't you have a glass—"

"Are you out of your mind? I'm calling the sheriff."

Follow the screams.

But the screams had stopped.

Rain dripped off Mike's Stetson as he peered ahead into the black wet. He was panting hard. The same otherworldly fear gripped him that had terrified him when he'd stood before his hogan.

"Damn—"

Blue lightning flashed against a sulky purple. The sudden brightness revealed dark water instead of his low-water bridge. A hundred yards downstream, a partially submerged car sat at a tippy angle against a wind-sculpted island of rock. All he could see of the car's occupant were five splayed fingers pressed flat against the window, as if in mute supplication.

Thunder boomed. Mike's face went blank. Hurriedly he pried several large rocks out of the mud before leaping into the black water and sloshing across the stream to the car.

The windows were darkly tinted. Still, he made out the shadowy outline of a woman slumped over the steering wheel. Something about those lifeless fingers spread helplessly against the dark glass tore at his heart.

He pulled at the door handles, but they wouldn't budge. Probably locked. He lifted one of his rocks and repeatedly smashed it against a back window.

"Goddamn cars! Built like tanks!"

He kept heaving his powerful, sculptor's arm again and again, each blow containing more force than the one before. He decided to use another rock, one with a sharper, thinner edge. His second blow shattered glass. He waited before gingerly slipping his fist through the fine webbing of diamond-like crystals.

He unlocked the back door, then the front. He was breathless and exhausted by the time he got them open.

"Oh, God. Emma." He brushed the glass off his hand into the creek before gently turning her head over to stare at her face. She was as still as death, her short red curls plastered to her skull and long neck. The water was up to her neck. A narrow cut sliced her forehead.

Odd, that she had chosen the road to *La Golindrina* instead of the one to her mother's.

He lifted her wrist and deftly fumbled under her soaked cuff. Relief flooded him when he felt her pulse beating strong and sure against his rough fingertip.

"Damn! Emma! Why'd you have to run from me?"

"Mike..." A bubble of water trickled out of her lower lip. Her ivory-white face was streaked with blood.

Quickly he scooped her into his arms and dragged her free of the car, wincing when she gave a little moan of agony. Despite her sodden clothes, she felt light as a feather.

Even in the middle of the surging creek, limping, his steps were sure and strong as he headed into the deepest part, toward the opposite bank. He knew she'd be suffering from exposure soon if he didn't get her out of her wet clothes. His house was too far.

Where, then? He thought of his hunting hogan in the foothills.

Her head lolled against his shoulder, falling back, as limp as a rag doll's. She wasn't unconscious, but she was too still. His own heart beat behind his eardrums. She could be in shock. Or worse.

"Emma," he whispered. "Can you hear me?"

Her eyelids flickered. She stared at him wordlessly.

No telling what he looked like with the rain dripping off his long hair, but he must have scared her as much as she was scaring him, because she squeezed her eyes tightly shut.

"I'm a little out-of-sorts that you prefer this sort of adventure to having dinner with me," he whispered.

Her huge dark eyes stared at him. She looked as young and as innocent as she had as a girl...as she'd been in his first vision of her...as she'd been when he'd loved her.

"Put your arms around me," he whispered gently. She didn't budge. "Emma, darling, can you hear me?"

"Don't—don't kill me," she whispered. "Please."

"What?"

"You...you were there." Her voice was low, throated, dying away with fear.

"So were you, damn it."

He was angry that always, always, no matter how he loved her, she never believed in him. Then his boot hit a loose stone wrong, and he stumbled on his bad ankle.

Her eyes widened. She regarded him in a dazed, frightened way that scared him more than the wild night, more than the torrential creek, more than the assailant who had run him off the road.

For the first time, Mike realized the murderous bastard couldn't have gotten to *La Golindrina*. Not if the bridge was out.

A dark thought came out of nowhere. Maybe the bastard had never intended to go to the ranch. Maybe he'd been after Emma.

Kara's house had gone up in flames. Two people had been carried out in body bags. Mike and Emma could've died there just as easily.

His hogan was a couple of miles across rough country, most of it uphill.

Mike stumbled forward into that rain-wet darkness, on his bad ankle, gripping Emma fiercely. Suddenly all that mattered was that he'd found her again, that they were both still alive.

No matter what happened, he wouldn't ever let her go.

25

Mike slid downhill on the loose slag. Downhill—that should have warned him of the danger. But he was too tired to think. Too tired to be bothered by the rivulets of water cascading off his hat brim, too tired to feel his aching arms and heavy legs. He only knew that he had to keep stumbling forward, one step at a time, blindly carrying Emma, if ever they were to reach the hogan.

Some part of him wished he knew where he was, how far they were from their destination, and how much longer he could go on before he dropped Emma and collapsed himself. But the wind-driven rain dulled his senses and blurred the stark red hills and mountains into fuzzy shapes he couldn't recognize.

Suddenly his bad foot stepped down on loose gravel and slid. When he pitched forward, over a steep ledge, Emma cried out. He held onto her as they tumbled off the sheer slope. A web of lightning arced across the sky, illuminating a boulder in their path right before he saw the shadowy ravine below. He lunged for the boulder, wrenching his arm when he hit. He stared down into the black hole, and fear coiled around his heart. Another six inches to the left, and he would have fallen fifty feet to his death.

Mentally he gave himself a hard shake. When he got up, his bad ankle hurt worse than ever.

His breathing came fast and harsh. He counted five heartbeats before he struggled to reclimb the hill. It was hard going. The craggy hill was steep and strewn with loose rocks. Emma was a small, slim woman, but her wet clothes made her heavier.

He had to save her. Rasping for breath, Mike gripped her against his chest. The ground under his boots constantly shifted. His bad ankle gave time and again. A rock rolled under his heel, and he slid backwards.

He stood still for a few seconds to catch his breath. His leg was swelling; his calf felt raw against his leather boot. How much farther could he walk on it? Was he lost? Had he missed the hogan altogether?

He thought of his grandfather telling him of their people, of their Long Walk. Many had died. But the strong had survived. His grandfather had tried to instill in him the traits of a warrior—courage, vision, compassion, and endurance.

Oblivious to their troubles, Emma hadn't opened her eyes since that one time after he'd gotten her out of the car. Nor had she made any sound other than that cry when he'd fallen. He knew she was alive because she was shivering convulsively.

The slanting rain beat against them, stronger and colder than ever. Water fell off his hat like a curtain, spilling in icy dribbles onto her still, ashen face. He had to get her inside, take off her wet clothes, get her dry and warm beneath blankets, before he fell down into some gulley and she died of exposure.

After nearly falling off that cliff, he didn't dare close

his eyes against the rain and walk blindly. So he gripped her thin frame tightly and kept walking, all the time staring into that liquid, murky darkness, searching for some familiar landmark. Finally, when he'd almost given up, a squatty shape near a fringe of dark trees popped up over the distant horizon. By then, he was barely moving, every leaden step dragging more heavily than the last.

When the low shape nestled in a grove of juniper at the foot of the mountain finally materialized into his octagonal hunting quarters, he was almost to it. A few minutes later he fell against the door, ready to weep. Then he jiggled the doorknob and found it locked.

Key. Woodpile. Under fifth log to the west.

His mind recaptured these necessary details one by one, sluggishly, the mental process costing him nearly as much as his physical exertions.

When he set Emma down beneath a summer shelter covered in grapevines that offered some scant protection against the rain, she whimpered, clinging to him. Her reluctance to let him go made him kiss her battered face. Her eyes opened briefly.

"Mike?"

"I've got to get the key."

When he trudged back for her and his hands went around her waist, she smiled. Her lashes fluttered, and he kissed her brow. Then he lifted her gently.

Carrying her through the low, narrow door, he strode inside and laid her carefully upon a low double bed.

The octagonal room was as dark as a cave. He lit a match and made his way to the black stove under the smoke-hole in the roof. The octagonal dwelling smelled musty despite the fresh odors of damp sage and wet earth. He was too damn tired to search for snakes or scorpions. It was enough that they had a roof.

Shivering, his teeth chattering, he struck another match and hurriedly lit his kerosene lamp. A fine layer of dust had settled over the rough tables and chairs. There was a well outside. He would have to wash the enamel coffee-pot, tin cups and bowls before they used them.

Later.

Pleased when he saw the stack of dry firewood and kindling beside the stove, he opened the black, cast-iron door and began to build a fire. When flames leapt inside the grate, he collapsed on the thin mattress beside Emma.

He lay there, one long arm flung across her waist, his ankle throbbing, his muscles aching. But even through her rain-soaked clothes, her body heat warmed him. He was glad he'd found her in time. Just being near her even like this was a profound comfort to him. More than anything, he wanted to crawl into bed beside her. To sleep. To wake up beside her. To have her near always.

It was too soon to hold such dreams.

Emma. Slowly he began to think more clearly. She could be in shock. When he got his breath and a bit of his strength back, he would have to tend her. Finally, he sat up and began undressing her, at first with expert efficiency—slipping pearly buttons through the satin loops of her blue cardigan, unsnapping the waistband of her denim skirt, then the zipper. Then his soldier-like attitude failed him.

The slight heat of her skin made him want to do more than undress her and cover her with blankets. He wanted to take her in his arms, hold her close.

She moaned, and he was reminded of how she would have fought him if she'd known what he was doing. When he pulled her skirt off, she trembled convulsively.

Mike's eyes roamed the slim contours of her shapely figure. When he got hot and hard, he cursed. What was

the matter with him? He was a sculptor. Naked bodies,
even hers, should be commonplace to him. She could be
in shock. He was damn near dead himself.

His hands shook as he tugged wet denim down shapely
thighs, over slender ankles. Forcing himself not to glance
at her body, he slid her sweater off her shoulders, turned
her over, undid her bra strap, slipped callused fingers beneath the elastic band of her sheer bikini panties.

As he pulled the panties down, he stared fixedly up at
the bare bulb screwed into a socket on the wall. Next, he
removed her bra. Still, he saw her. Every provocative detail. Ivory skin stretched like taut satin over her collar-
bone. The creamy swell of perfectly shaped breasts. Her
erect, darkly circled nipples. The natural indention of her
slim waist. The faint webbing of marks on her smooth
belly. Her dark mound of pubic hair mashed flat by tight
black lace. Curvaceous thighs. Her bony knees. Shapely
calves.

Everything.

He'd read something a famous writer who was going
blind had said about peripheral vision. "Don't discount
it. It's how we see the tiger in the grass."

The marks on her stomach hadn't been there before.
Lilly.

Mike's heart beat strangely. The stretch marks merely
confirmed what he already knew—that she was Lilly's
mother. Suddenly he wondered what she'd gone through.
She'd been so young. She'd had her baby alone, given
the child to Kara. Kara, whom she believed and trusted
more than she'd ever trusted him.

Mike went cold. Kara would've given Lilly to strangers. For years he'd hated Kara for that.

Mike sat beside Emma for a long time. The only sound

in the hogan came from his thudding heart and the rain falling on the roof.

He was too worried to be angry at her. He'd seen the love and the profound loss in her haunted eyes that day on the plaza. She loved Lilly. But she'd given up her child—their child.

Just like Indiana.

No. His Navajo heart knew Emma wasn't like that. There were good reasons. She would confide them when she saw she could trust him.

Emma was as white as paper, chilled in the damp air, her breath raspy.

Breathing hard himself, he drew the thick woolen blankets up to her chin. Forbidden memories of her had fed his male fantasies for years. She'd been so young and eager, and then he'd frightened her. For years he'd wanted to make that night up to her.

He limped to a cupboard and whipped out a towel. He came back to her, sat down beside her and began to gently dry her red curls. When he was done, he wound the towel around her head like a turban.

Firelight from the stove made shadows leap against the dark, cribbed walls. He felt so alone with her, as if they were the only man and woman in the universe. He remembered that first night they'd spent together in the kiva. She'd saved his life, created a bond that neither of them could break.

She'd nearly died in that fire.

Somebody had tried to kill her again tonight.

Somebody had tried to kill him both times, too.

Why?

He couldn't let anything happen to her.

He ran the tip of his fingers across her brow, smoothed

her soft hair. "Live, damn you," he ordered roughly. "Live."

She exhaled. Her inky lashes trembled.

Her wide, wild, hot eyes locked on his face.

Tentatively, she reached an icy hand toward his cheek, but it fell weakly before her fingertips could touch him. She fought to talk, but he couldn't hear her.

"You're safe."

"Mike—"

"I'm here."

Reaching for him, she whimpered when her hand fell again. He caught it in his own and raised her cold fingers to his dark cheek, pressing them against his warm wet skin.

Her crooked smile charmed him.

He dropped her hand, but he couldn't stop gazing at her. Suddenly he wanted nothing more than to strip off his clothes and get into bed with her. He wanted to crush her body into his, to lie with her, to hold her till she warmed.

"Damn."

Almost fiercely, he pressed the covers around her, not liking how they molded her body. "Live," he whispered against her cool temple. Then, cursing himself roundly, he limped over to the fire and tossed on more logs. Leaning over, he fanned the flames with a dusty magazine till they danced high and golden. Then he stripped off his own clothes.

He sat down on the rough chair and tugged off his boots, the right first, crying out when his ankle throbbed. She stirred, moaned.

After that he tried to undress more quietly, so as not to disturb her. But he heard every sound in the hogan, from the clatter of each leather boot slamming the log wall when he tossed them, to the scrape of his metal belt buckle as he unfastened it, to the whispery sound of his belt whisking through wet denim loops. When he was nude, she opened her eyes and stared. That got his attention. She watched him grab fresh clothes out of a drawer.

Darkly intense, her wide eyes drew him inside her, deeper than ever before. Her lashes fell, releasing him.

He blinked, shook himself. "Ah, Emma. What are you doing to me?"

Hurriedly he whipped on jeans and a shirt. When he was done, his ankle stung worse than ever. He dug a whiskey bottle out of his wooden chest. Two quick pulls burned all the way to his stomach. He killed the bottle, set it on the earthen floor and rolled it toward the door. Next he found a bottle of burgundy.

The more he drank, the more the dark cave-like room began to glow. By muted firelight, he watched Emma. Having her here, in these Navajo surroundings that felt so familiar, lit a warmth inside him that stole to every part of his body.

One side of her face was lit with golden light; the other softened by shadows. Her turban had fallen off. Her red curls gleamed against his pillow. She was sexy as hell.

He was on his third glass of wine when he saw a quarter in a blue enamel cup. He picked it up, said howdy to George Washington. He turned the coin over in his palm. Heads—or rather, good old George—he made a pallet on the dirt floor and slept alone. Tails, her bed.

He tossed the coin and lost. He tossed it again.

So much for good old George.

Mike tossed the coin back in its cup. When it clinked, her lashes flickered.

Mike took it as an invitation.

When he got into bed, she was on fire, burning from the inside out.

Her cheeks were flushed. Carefully he put his hands on her brow.

She was hot. So hot. Burning up with fever.

He ripped back the blankets.

"Oh, God—Emma."

26

Emma went from toasty warm to freezing cold. When her teeth began to chatter, she burrowed closer to the delicious source of warmth under the thick covers. A muscular arm came around her and pulled her closer. She felt warm lips nuzzling her hair, drifting down her neck. When she moaned, the kisses stopped.

Then she was hot again, and he threw the covers off. Later, deliriously, Emma's eyes drifted open. She squinted, trying to make sense of the odd, indistinct shapes in the shadowy room. The ceiling was dome-shaped; the octagonal room dark. Tiny square windows let in a feeble gray light.

Her temples pounded. She was lying on a low, hard bed and draped with scratchy Navajo blankets. Dying embers glowed in a black grate. Smoke was supposed to escape through a pipe that ran up through a hole in the center of the room. Nevertheless, the air inside was dense with smoke, and stiflingly hot.

She felt feverishly achy, weak—too weak to move. Even to lift her hand and rub her perspiring forehead left her groggily exhausted. Still, she regained consciousness bit by bit, rising gradually through thick, foggy layers to the surface, dimly becoming aware of her strange surroundings.

Aware of the man sleeping beside her.

Her head rested on his broad shoulder. His dark, muscular arm wrapped around her. She caught his scent along with that of damp sage and desert dust. Vaguely, she knew that he'd taken care of her through the night.

"Mike?"

"Go back to sleep," he murmured in a deep, reassuring tone, nuzzling her neck.

"My head hurts."

"You'll feel better in the morning."

"What am I doing here?"

"Later."

When she tried to move away, he pulled her back against his naked male chest, securing her bottom against his thighs.

"Sleep…you've got to be exhausted."

She probably should fight him, but she was too weak. Soon either his body heat or her fever lulled her senses. She closed her eyes.

When she woke next, her face was buried in the hollow of his throat. Her hand held a fistful of coarse, black hair. When she stirred, again he ordered her back to sleep.

Mike Greywolf. He was so overwhelmingly masculine. Usually that threatened her. But not now.

Of course, she knew she shouldn't be lying with him. But she felt small and afraid, and she needed his strength. She'd felt like this before when she'd gone into his arms in that other cave-like room. He'd held her then as he held her now—to keep her safe.

His eyes were shut, which made him seem less threatening. Sleep eased the lines beneath his eyes, and he looked almost as young as he had in the kiva when she'd formed that ridiculous attachment to him.

Then she was hot again, and the nightmares came back. She was under water in a car, her face pressed against glass, gasping for breath in an air bubble. A man pointed a gun at her face.

There was something so familiar about the man, but his face was a blur. Then Mike was there, dragging her out of the car, carrying her through a storm.

Then Mike was gone, and red walls darkened, pressed into her. Kara's face wavered in a black mirror.

Emma screamed.

A large hand gently shook her. "Wake up. You're having a bad dream."

She stared wildly.

"Emma! It's me! Mike! You're safe!"

Kara's face. Bubbles.

Emma screamed again and again. Her head thrashed desperately against her pillow. She was in that rental car, drowning, dying.

"Emma..."

She tried to open her eyes, but her lids felt like lead weights.

A cool rag bathed her face. A man's deep voice caressed her, soothed her.

The rain had stopped, but the clouds outside the hogan looked low and mean. Mike turned back to the bed. He didn't know what to do. All he knew was that he had to save her.

"Who are you? Who are you?" Emma screamed to some figment in her dream.

"Hush," Mike whispered. "It's okay. I'm here."

"Kara—"

"Sleep," he commanded.

She kept twisting and turning and repeating her twin's name. He wished the nightmares would stop. Her skin burned. But Mike kept a constant vigil. He was always there, easing the fear, giving her cool water to drink, bathing her feverish brow with a damp rag, squeezing the rag so the water would run into her hair, then brushing the wet curls out of her face. He changed the sweat-soaked sheets. He held her limp hand when she shivered. Every time she opened her eyes or screamed, he was there. Finally she began to shiver. He took her in his arms and held her.

She was burning up. But if he left her and tried to walk back to his house, anything could happen to her. She might wander out into the woods and get lost. Someone might come. Or she might simply die of dehydration. His ankle hurt so badly, he didn't know how long it would take him to walk home.

All through the next day and night he tended her. Holding her slim, limp body, he felt so helpless. The power in his own healthy body was of no use to her. She needed a doctor, medicine.

Mike couldn't stand seeing her so ill. He stalked toward the table and grabbed the bottle of burgundy. He almost hurled it. Instead he popped the cork out, and drank long and deeply.

She moaned.

He set the bottle down and went back to the bed. No longer did she thrash and cry out. She was so still and pale and limp, and her breathing seemed shallow.

Was she going to die?

He closed his hands over his black head. Pain swelled in his chest. He saw his father, spread-eagled in the dirt, his black eyes glazed. Flies everywhere, buzzing. He'd swatted at them wildly. It had seemed so important to kill the flies. He hadn't saved his family.

A hoarse sob broke from his throat. He'd waited so long to find her. He shut his eyes and didn't realize that tears slid down his cheeks. "Live, and I'll never let you down again," he whispered.

He didn't know he was crying until he felt her hesitant fingertips smooth against his cheeks.

When he opened his eyes, she was smiling. Tiny beads of cold sweat glistened on her brow.

Stiffly, he blinked back his tears and swiped his hands across his cheeks to dry them.

"Why did you cry?" she whispered.

His face darkened.

"Don't do that," she begged.

"What?"

"Don't shut me out."

He stared down at the floor. Then he felt her fingers tilting his chin. His gaze locked with hers. And he knew she saw what he was too weak to deny. And in her eyes he read the same emotion.

Its power swept them away. Time stood still. The years of hurt were as nothing. All that mattered was the truth that shone in her soft face.

He had always loved her. Kara and the past didn't matter. This moment was theirs. The future was theirs. Emma was his. Finally his.

"Forgive me," he said quietly.

She nodded. "Everything."

"Even Kara?"

She leaned forward and gently kissed him.

"I saw you in that car," he said. "You've been so sick. I—I didn't know what to do."

"You saved my life. In more ways than you'll ever know. I've been lost...till tonight...till you."

He could hardly believe her even when her hands came around his neck and clasped him tightly.

"A long time ago, you promised me something," she said almost shyly. "Do you remember? In the barn?"

"Yes." His voice was unsteady.

When she blushed tellingly, he buried his mouth in her hair. "I was so afraid I'd lost you forever."

"Me, too."

She asked for a drink of water and some toothpaste.

"Toothpaste?"

He laughed. Later he would tease her about that.

She wanted to make love.

"Later," he said, "when you're better."

"Then lie down beside me. Hold me."

Hours later, when she awakened to his dark gaze watching her, she smiled, and the first thing she said was, "Better."

"What?"

"You promised...when I was better."

That was all either of them said for a very long time. Tenderly he brushed his hand across her cool brow. She waited quietly, till his touch confirmed her report.

Then he reached for her blindly, and she opened her arms and pulled him on top of her. She lay looking up at him, her eyes on fire.

The humiliation he had felt that night in the barn when she'd run, was as sharp as ever. He had to go slowly, make it wonderful.

But her hands began to move. So did her body, and all the years of starvation had him hard as a brick in the space of a microsecond.

They didn't speak. They didn't kiss. They simply worshipped each other with their bodies. And the language of their bodies bound their souls.

"Emma," he protested warningly.

"Now," she whispered against his throat. "Please, Mike, love me now."

Then he was inside her. Only this time she was wet, ready.

They rose and fell together in that ancient and most primitive dance, and in that thrilling union, his world was no longer dark and silent, but wildly colored. His loneliness fell away. He was no longer in exile.

It was over immediately. But its fire had forged them. They lay together, their arms wrapped around each other, perspiring, smiling. Only then did he fasten his mouth on hers with fierce possessive ardor.

"Emma. Emma. Emma."

He drew back from her in wonder.

"Next time," he promised.

"Next time what?"

"I'll go slow."

She laughed. "Next time," she mused. "I can't wait... till next time."

There was the roar of whirling rotors outside.

"What is it?"

"A helicopter, flying low. If I know your mother, it's a search party looking for you. Do you want me to flag it down?"

"You're not wearing much. You might catch cold. I might have to nurse you," she said. "Besides, I'd rather make love."

He began to burn.

His harsh-featured face softened. Then the bed dipped under his weight. She put her mouth on his. Once more fierce passion swept him away on a hot dark tide. He was clinging, dying, spent too soon.

It was over in minutes. But not over at all. Because afterward he felt gentle and vulnerable, open in every part of his being, the way he hadn't since he'd been a boy— before the murders. He savored her sweetness, the sweetness she brought out in him.

It had never been like this for him before, with anyone. She was unique, precious.

"I couldn't stop," he whispered.

"I'm glad." Then she teased, "Next time."

She slid closer, and pleasure burst gloriously inside him. She felt his joy and curled against him. The way she draped her arms across his chest, and the way her breath burned his skin was poetry.

They fell asleep in each other's arms.

A pale streamer of sunlight woke Emma first. For a minute she didn't know where she was. Slowly, she became aware that beneath the Navajo blankets, she was naked. With a blush she realized she was wrapped not only in thick wool covers but in Mike Greywolf's hard arms.

What had she done? As her worried gaze wandered over the dark little octagonal room, hazy memories of his hard male body and the intimacies they'd shared flickered through her brain. She'd been totally, totally shameless. Thankfully, Mike was deeply asleep, so she was able to disentangle herself from his arms and ease herself to the other side of the bed.

Her mother would die if she knew.

Not wanting to wake him, she dressed quickly and tiptoed to the softness of the gray morning. Red rock. Green juniper. The air smelled fresh and pungent from pine and sage. Birds were singing. The wind rustled in the trees. Never had nature seemed more miraculously beautiful.

If she took Mike back into her life, what would her mother do? Stuart? Emma thought of the years she'd played both twins, the years when her life was a coil of lies...and fear.

Fear that Kara was dead, for if she was alive, where had she been all these years? Fear of whomever knew the truth and was blackmailing her.

Emma had hurt her family, especially her mother. But she'd hurt herself, too. All these years, she'd felt exiled. Everyone who'd mattered to her had seemed so far away. She'd thought she could never again feel any rightness about herself. And then last night...Mike.

She sank to the ground and buried her face in her hands. Sometime later a twig cracked nearby, and she was stunned when a huge cat slunk out of the juniper.

The mountain lion had a black face and black-ringed, almond eyes.

A good two hundred pounds, the cat's muscular body was sleek and tawny. The yard-long tail twitched while he studied her.

A mere twenty feet separated them—less than a pounce.

Mike... Her tongue was frozen.

She didn't dare take her eyes off the cat. All her life she'd been such a coward.

Now this.

This huge cat, this fantastic killing machine, his predatory attention focused solely on her, considering—and there was nothing she could do to escape him.

Suddenly it was as if a force outside herself wrapped around her, protected her with an invisible shield, and she was no longer afraid. With a courage far more powerful than her own, she stared into the cat's malevolent, golden eyes.

The tail stopped twitching. The cat had Kara's eyes, Emma thought....

He regarded her for a long moment. When Emma took a cautious step backward, toward the hogan, she couldn't believe it when the big lion melted into the juniper.

Breathless, Emma turned and saw Mike standing in the doorway of the hogan, his Beretta trained on the spot where the big cat had vanished.

"Mike."

She ran into his arms.

"I was brave—as brave as Kara," she whispered, awed.

"Braver."

"I wasn't afraid."

"You were wonderful."

The experience empowered her. She couldn't stop thinking about it or talking about it. Later, she thought that if she could face down a cat like that, she could do anything. She could certainly stand up to her mother and brother and find some way to make them accept her love for Mike.

She could stand up to anything—even the truth.

27

Flowering tendrils of yellow flame licked the starlit dark. Mike would've enjoyed the smell of rabbit sizzling on the spit if he hadn't been so aware of Emma sulking in his hogan. They'd eaten most of his stockpiled larder, so it had seemed sensible to him to take the Beretta into the woods and shoot whatever he could find.

But Emma wasn't much of a meat-eater, and she'd scowled at him and closed the door in his face when he'd stepped out of the juniper, holding two rabbits by the ears.

"Did you have to shoot two?" she'd asked.

"That's a baited question if ever I heard one." He'd taken out a knife and set about skinning the animals.

"You're a savage."

He'd ripped out the entrails and flung them toward the juniper. Appalled, she'd gasped.

"If you don't want to help, go inside."

"Gladly!" Then she'd done just that, slamming the door.

For a while after he'd built a fire, he'd enjoyed the peace and solitude. Now he missed her.

The meat smelled good. So did the sweet, astringent, smoking scent of the piñon fire filling wine-dark air. His ankle was beginning to mend. He felt alive, well. His thoughts drifted to what they'd done in bed together. He remembered her lying beneath him after they'd made love, her eyes shining. She'd felt so good. Nothing had ever felt so right or good as plunging inside her and holding her afterward. He wanted her out here, at his side. Now. He wanted her with him always.

For the first time since he'd been back in New Mexico, he felt home. For the first time since his father had died, he felt almost whole.

Because of her. He would always love this spot because they'd found each other again here.

Geography. Being here in these simple surroundings put him in touch with his Navajo culture, with who he really was, with his heart and soul. For a Navajo lives by his heart. The white culture had put him in the mainstream, brought him fame and fortune, but it was too intellectual, too stressful, and he'd lost his center.

Savage. Damn her for calling him that. In many ways her materialistic culture was far more brutal on the human soul than his.

He stared at the closed door, willing it to open. If she didn't come out, he was going to have to go inside, sling her over his shoulder and haul her out. He'd show her *savage.*

Suddenly the squeaky hinge on his door groaned, and Mike's black head jerked toward the dark opening to a slim figure wrapped in a Navajo blanket.

Emma.

The woolen draperies seemed to caress her body. Her beauty struck him like a blow. And he knew he had to sculpt her.

"You hungry?"

"Hungry enough...to eat two rabbits," she said.

In her soft dark eyes he read an apology. "Then you forgive me—"

"If you promise you won't kill things unless you have to."

"I never do."

They ate outside by the fire; then she snuggled next to him, her toes almost touching the blackened earth circling the flames. After supper he threw on more logs. Wrapped in blankets, they nestled close, under the stars, and began to talk as he and his grandfather used to talk before the fire. They had so much to tell each other. So many years to cover.

First he wanted to know about Lilly.

So she told him.

"You were gone when I was well enough to go home from the hospital," she began.

"Your mother blamed me—"

"I know."

"I went back to my people, hoping to find myself, I suppose."

Golden flames leapt toward the dark.

"And I went to Mexico. Auntie Z had a friend whose daughter was running a clinic on an island in Mexico. At first I helped in the clinic. Then I began to write, at first to get rid of the pain, and then it simply became a part of me. I started getting sick, all the time, throwing up...and Katherine said I was pregnant."

"Oh, Emma—"

"You wanted to know."

With his silence, he encouraged her to continue.

"Do you remember that blank spot on the wall in our portrait gallery in Mother's house where my father's portrait must've hung?"

"Your brother used to stand in front of that little name-plate."

"I was afraid I'd be like Father…and be *gone*. Erased. But I couldn't go home to Mother. She was so critical of you. Of me, too, so I called Kara."

Kara, he thought grimly. Always Kara. Never him.

"She was struggling to make it as an actress. All she'd done was a few bit parts, but she was living in a famous actor's great big beach house."

"I remember."

"She had lots of money."

"No doubt from her rich lover."

Emma didn't elaborate. "Kara told me things about you that almost made me hate you. She said you wanted us both…but in different ways. She said you drove us apart, and that that had broken her heart. She said you had seduced her."

"Damn it." Angrily he tossed another log on the fire, and a flurry of sparks shot into the blackness. "She lied."

"And I was too naive to see through her. Too unsure of myself…and you." There was a moment's silence before she went on.

Emma swallowed thickly. "I was pregnant. I didn't feel that I could tell you. I had no means of support. No education. No way to take care of Lilly. Kara had all this money. It was a difficult pregnancy. I was sick all the time. I trusted Kara to make the decisions. She promised to find a good home for the baby. She took care of me, of everything—"

"She sure as hell did. She would've given Lilly to strangers."

"Oh, Mike, I—I would've died if Kara hadn't taken such good care of me. I went to her doctor, under her name."

"She was probably using you—to trap that movie star."

"That's why Kara's name was on the birth certificate. But I was too sick too worry about that then."

"Again, she wanted to nail that movie star. The tabloids printed pictures of Kara leaving the hospital carrying Lilly, along with his picture. Everybody thought Lilly was his. His wife even filed for divorce. But blood tests don't lie. He sued the tabloids and went back to his wife. Kara landed a slot on a popular TV series. And I got Lilly."

"I didn't know any of that. But when I got better, I wanted Lilly. Only Kara told me she'd signed sealed adoption papers, and Lilly was gone forever to wonderful people."

"At least you know she lied about that."

"I couldn't forget Lilly. I celebrated every birthday. For years I looked into every baby carriage, watched every little girl around her age. I went back to Mexico and finished *Betrayal*. It was about us, Mike, and every bit as sad as our story. It was so personal, I couldn't send it out. But Kara read it and mailed it to a New York publisher. Nobody was more stunned than me when it was a huge success.

"Except for not having Lilly, my life was almost back on track. Then I went home for the movie premiere, and saw Lilly and you. I couldn't believe it. I loved you both so much. I wanted to be a part of your lives." Emma's face darkened. "And I was furious with Kara. She swore she'd done it all for me, that she could explain everything. We were supposed to talk that last night, after the premiere and her celebration party was over, but..."

"What happened?"

Emma bowed her head. "I—I don't know. That's what scares me more than anything. I woke up wet, halfway up the mesa. I was so angry you and I made love that night...when I pretended I was Kara. I was so angry at her after what you said in the hotel suite. I could have done anything—"

He felt a heavy weight slide over his heart as he remembered, too. "I know that feeling. What do you remember?"

"You and me...together in the hotel.... But first Kara seemed strange after the premiere. Upset. She said she had to be somewhere and asked me to pretend to be her, to play hostess at her party. Just for a little while. She slipped out the back way. Then you came."

"And I'd been drinking, to drown out my feelings for you. I couldn't quit thinking about you at the plaza. How you'd looked. I couldn't take my eyes off you during the premiere. Sando had told me you'd come to the gallery, that you'd wept over the busts of Lilly. I wanted to confront Kara with Lilly's birth certificate. To demand the truth. I heard about her party."

"But I was there, playing Kara."

"I was too blind drunk and enraged to see the difference."

"You kept shouting, so I suggested we talk in the bedroom."

Their eyes glazed. They grew silent and afraid, remembering. She didn't have to say another word.

The years spun backward to that night. To the noise of too many guests crammed into Kara's hotel suite.

He'd raged into Kara's bedroom at the Anasazi Inn, waving Lilly's birth certificate in her face, not giving a damn who saw, who heard.

"Which twin is her mother?" The woman he'd drunkenly believed to be Kara was standing in the darkness, deliberately hiding her face, he realized now. He hadn't noted that then.

Quietly, her hand shaking, her eyes misting, she'd said, "Mine."

He'd felt disbelief at first. But there was something in her face that told him she wasn't lying. And then he felt deep, profound hatred.

"Why is Emma so upset, then?"

"You know Emma." Her voice had been odd, off-handed. "She's stupid…sentimental."

Every muscle in his body had tightened with rage.

"Not like you—hard and cold."

"One could describe you in those terms."

"No more games." He lunged toward her, grabbed her by the arm. The smell of lilacs had made him dizzy.

"You know the truth, Mike. Do you think Emma would have signed her baby away—to you, to anybody?"

He'd felt all his dreams die. He let her go. "We could have been so happy, she and I. Except for you. Always you, there, between us. If you hadn't come to the barn that night…pretending…"

"Pretending?"

For a moment she'd looked oddly surprised. But she recovered.

"Don't play the innocent. You know as well as I do that I would never have touched you if I'd known who you were. It was like a snake had swallowed me. I felt defiled, sick. If only Emma hadn't come in right then. Hadn't seen—"

"You and your lies disgust me. I want to forget everything about that night," she'd said.

"Even your own daughter?"

She put her hand over her mouth.

"God, if only Emma were her mother. She'd want her.

She's not even Lilly's mother, and she wants her. I loved Emma. *Emma.* I still love her, damn you. But she won't have me. Because of you.''

"Tell her, not me," she said softly.

"What good would it do? She won't have me. Because of you. You've always been there, feeding her lies, telling her I want both of you.''

"Don't you?" Her voice had been so quiet.

The question enraged him so much that he grabbed her by the arms and yanked her to his body.

"Don't you?" she whispered in Emma's voice. "Tell me you don't want me now.''

When she touched him, he froze. Then the heat of her body burned through his skin. He saw the bed. She flicked a wall switch, and the room melted into darkness.

"Don't," he whispered, suppressing his desire.

She undid the diamond clasp that held her hair. When she kicked off her high heels, the scent of lilacs wafted on the air. She even smelled like Emma.

He should've known better than to strip her with his eyes. Because she did the same thing to him. By the time she undid her zipper, and the teal-blue gown pooled around her ankles, he was shaking.

"See," she taunted. "You do want both of us." Reaching toward him, she touched his face, traced the shape of his mouth with fingertips that stirred sensations so delicious he cursed.

The shudder of fierce denial that swept him turned into a hot rush of pleasure as she began undressing him. He was baffled by his feelings, but he let her pull him deeper and deeper into that velvet darkness, curling her hands around his neck.

He wanted her. No matter how terrible the price. God,

he wanted Kara more than he'd ever wanted anything or anyone—even Emma.

He had seized her and shoved her against the wall, his arms like iron around her. This time when she kissed him, his quick, raspy breathing told him he couldn't cry rape.

Pinning her, he groaned deep in his belly. His fingers splayed her thighs, opened her. In a single lunge, he pushed inside.

She made a broken sound, clutched at his waist and accepted him.

He held her by the hair, his teeth scraping her mouth, bruising the edge of her hairline. Velvet skin against his rougher hide, soft breasts brushed flat against the thick, muscular wall of his chest. Like a writhing animal, he pumped into her. Powerful thrusts that might have torn a less willing woman apart. But she was as ravenous as he, matching him stroke for stroke, clinging, arching, moaning, till he loosed lust and seed inside her depths. But it was sweet, too.

Intolerably so. The wrongness of what he'd done hit him like a blow. He hated her for seducing him into such an unholy act, hated himself even more.

Breathing hard, he pulled out. She just stood there, her arms flung out against the wall. She was wet all over, perspiration dripping from her face, her neck; her whole body gleaming.

Once wasn't enough for her. Nor for him, either. She pulled him back and wordlessly pushed him against the wall. She ran her mouth and tongue down the length of his brown torso, cupped his testicles. "No," he'd gasped when her mouth made that soft sucking sound right before she took him into her lips.

Instantly erect, as hot as a live coal, he felt powerful and solid. She slid her talented mouth back and forth. He grabbed her hair, shoved deeper, damn near completing the act then and there.

He'd pulled out in the last second, carried her to the bed, slung her down, shoved himself inside her and burst instantly. So had she. They lay together, heavy and sated, their limbs intertwined, sprawled across the bed, too exhausted to move.

He'd expected laughter from her, not tears.

When she reached for him, her lonely eyes glistening with unbearable emotion that touched him so deeply, he pushed her away. He was a savage. He hated himself and her too much to realize what her tears and newfound softness meant.

Hated Kara too much to see Emma.

"Don't touch me," he growled. "You got what you wanted. I fucked you, didn't I?"

She sobbed.

"You were right, and I was wrong. So, just shut up and leave me alone."

In Emma's voice she said, "I'm…I'm sorry. What I just did was maybe—no, *was* the worst thing I've ever done to anybody."

"Me, too. But there's no help for me now."

"Mike, Lilly's mine…. I'm sorry."

He got out of bed, tore his clothes off the floor and yanked them on. When he zipped his trousers, she got up and threw herself in his arms, tears streaming down her face. "I love you. I love you."

A chill shot through him that had nothing to do with the cool night air. He ran out. When she tried to follow, when she threw her arms around his waist, begging him to come back, he shoved her aside.

"Don't push," he whispered. "You should be happy. You wanted a savage. You got a savage. Tonight you proved I'm capable of anything. Don't tempt me—to murder."

The bedroom door was ajar. Alarmed, a cluster of her wide-eyed guests silently stared at her ravaged face and at his glowering countenance.

Still, she tried to stop him. "Mike, we have to talk."

He felt he was about to explode. "If you want it again, go fuck one of these other poor wretch's brains out."

He'd slammed the door.

When she chased him, he'd let the elevators shut on her. He heard her pounding the doors, crying in grief and frustration for him to come back.

He'd driven away, wanting to forget her, to forget their sex that night, knowing he would hate himself forever because he never would.

"Mike," Emma whispered across the firelit darkness, calling him back to the present, calling him back to her—as she had *that* night.

Her eyes flashed with an emotion as intensely gripping as what he'd felt for her on that long-ago night. Only there was tenderness beneath the fire.

"Mike, I'm sorry about that night. You'll never know how sorry."

"I do know. God, I know." His rough voice was unsteady. "That night was the best—and the worst—in my life. I believed Kara was you. All those years... I would've come looking for you if it hadn't been for that night. The relief I feel to know the truth is overwhelming."

The fragrance of lilacs, her scent, mingled with piñon. He felt thankful, despite their present danger, that he'd found her again.

When she smiled, he thought her lovely. Her smile alone erased years of frustration, anger and regret.

"Oh, Emma—"

Swiftly he pulled her into his arms.

At first his kisses were slow and gentle, but they soon sparked a fire that consumed them both. Afterward, he felt all the tenderness and love he'd lived so long without.

"Marry me," he whispered.

"I don't know." She hesitated. "There are still so many unanswered questions...problems."

"It wasn't a question. You're the mother of my child. If not marriage, where do you see this going?"

"What about the fire—those two people in the body bags? I've made a mess of my life. Mike, I'm being blackmailed."

"What?"

"It's way too soon to involve you or endanger Lilly."

"If you're being blackmailed, I sure as hell don't want you out of my sight. I keep seeing you in that car. I lay outside that burning house, thinking you were dead inside. How in the hell did you get out?"

"I don't know. Suddenly I was just back in Isla Mujeres. Oh, Mike— He even sent me a fax there. He told me not to come home—that if I did, someone would get hurt."

"You're marrying me—do you understand?"

"This is no way to start a—"

A helicopter roared out of the sky, pinging dust and grit against the tiny windows of the hogan. This time it landed in whorls of dirt. Reluctantly he let her go. She ran to the door, and opened it.

He got up slowly and followed her.

Will Gentry and his hulking deputy, their lips tight, their hands going to their leather holsters when they saw Mike behind her, strode toward the hogan.

The law.

White man's law.

Mike stood his ground. He swallowed hard and wiped his forehead with the back of his hand so Gentry and his sidekick wouldn't see he was perspiring.

Had Chavez sent them? Mike felt sick, but his harsh-featured face was a cold mask.

Gentry smiled. "You okay, Emma?"

"Why are you here?" she whispered.

"We found your car...his truck. You know Frances—"

Mike sucked in a breath. "I found her, brought her here...."

"For two days?" The deputy's gaze was hard.

Gentry concentrated on Emma.

"What he says is true," Emma confirmed.

"You about ready to go home, young lady?"

Emma nodded mutely, but as Gentry took her arm to lead her to the helicopter, a slim woman with frizzy red hair and a video camera hopped out of the helicopter.

"Mike," Sara said, when Will swept Emma toward the helicopter, "I have to talk to her."

"Not now."

"What happened in the hogan?"

"Mind your own damn business."

"She killed Kara, didn't she?"

He pushed past her and ran after Emma and Gentry.

Sara chased. "She killed her twin, and I'm going to prove it."

He hurled himself inside the black chopper. Engine noise drowned out Sara's barrage of questions. Still, Emma seemed tense and wary, more afraid of him now because of Sara.

The helicopter climbed rapidly, sweeping them higher and higher into the all-encompassing darkness. All too soon, they hovered over Frances's walled kingdom, and were setting down in her courtyard.

Their faces set, Frances and Stuart stood in the adobe doorway surrounded by a crowd dressed in black. Nearly a hundred cars were parked in the drive. But the real hordes were being kept at bay by roadblocks to prevent Kara's fans from overruning the Shayne compound.

Such crowds brought back memories of that other time he'd been accused of murder. Already Mike wished he and Emma were back at the hogan, that he didn't have to face Frances and her friends. What were they all doing here, anyway?

Then he remembered. Frances was planning a memorial service for Kara.

A single glance at the grim pair in black standing at the door told Mike they would do everything they could to shut him out of Emma's life.

When Emma jumped out of the helicopter and ran toward them, Stuart kept to the shadows. Mike caught a glimpse of Lilly at the window. When Emma saw her, Lilly let the curtain fall. It was Frances who ran to welcome Emma, braving the flying dust, wrapping her favorite daughter in her arms, squeezing hard, not letting her go.

Emma couldn't seem to tear her gaze from the window where Lilly had been standing.

"You're home." Frances's eyes almost shone—until she looked over Emma's shoulder and saw Mike striding toward them. Then tension deepened the lines of her thin face.

The forbidding adobe sprawl filled Mike with dread. Again he felt all the old lonelinesss he'd known after his family's murders, all the old uncertainty of knowing he would never fit into Frances Shayne's tight little world.

He kept walking.

He was here to stay.

"Are we too late for Kara's memorial?" Emma asked quietly.

"Will didn't tell you?" When Emma shook her head, Frances continued. "Chavez from L.A.P.D. wants Greywolf to call him."

Mike waited.

Frances's cold smile alarmed him.

"There've been some new developments."

Mike wanted to shake her, to make her spit it out.

"Kara's alive," she said finally.

"Kara…alive…" Emma went white. She gave a little wounded cry. Swaying, whispering Mike's name, she toppled forward.

He caught her easily. Lifting her into his arms, he stomped up the stairs into the adobe mansion.

Emma Shayne had come home.

So had Mike Greywolf.

28

The house was lit up like a carnival and just as noisy, until Mike shouldered his way inside with Emma. Then it grew as quiet as a funeral, its silence heavy and grim. After a while a few hushed murmurs began, then more strained grumblings.

What hit Mike next was his grandmother's rug under lights and thick glass. The Dontso figures shot him back like a bolt to that dark hogan, to that time he'd stood over his grandmother, awed by the miracle her gnarled fingers wrought out of strands of wool strung tight across a loom. The big rug, with the four Dontso figures and two corn plants and the Rainbow God, had taken her a year. It was the last piece she'd completed before her death.

From a window, Frances's cold gaze followed him, and he remembered that black night when she'd thrown him out. She'd stood at that same window and watched him go. As if seeking answers, he eyed the Rainbow God. But there was no bridge back to that time and world that was so far from Emma's. He was stuck with Frances, and she was stuck with him.

Do your worst, old woman. He strode through the door. He wanted Emma and Lilly; he wanted to be part of a real family. But marriage? Would Emma seriously consider marriage to him—a Navajo?

Well, he was here now. Deliberately he met Frances's gaze—and was stunned when she withered. Suddenly he wondered how much time she'd spent standing at that window, praying her little girl would come back.

Letting people go. Letting people back into one's life. Making a place in your heart for someone you could never want—because your child chooses that person for her mate. Life wasn't easy, not even for a powerful white woman. He caught himself. Frances Shayne was the last person he should feel sympathy for.

Not liking the drift of his thoughts, he tore his gaze from Frances. Six earrings twinkled across the room. *Lilly.* Huge eyes panicky, she rushed away toward the kitchen, leaving him to fend for himself in this white woman's madhouse that was jammed with too many overexuberant Shaynes. At least that's who Mike thought the rowdy bunch were, staring holes through him from the windows behind Frances.

Besides Shaynes, there were local Santa Fe royalty, Stuart's computer big shots, and movie people watching him in growing fascination. Only the little group that contained Indiana and Sando, Sara and Galbraith, several prestigious gallery owners, and members of the press, seemed absorbed in their own conversations.

Indiana.

His mother.

What the hell was she doing here? Deliberately he turned his back on her. Did she give a damn that he'd nearly been accused of murder again? That he'd damn near *been* murdered?

To hell with her. To hell with them all.

Angrily Mike carried Emma to a large beige sofa,

gently lowering her to the cushions. When he laid her head on the pillow, her lashes fluttered. Seeing so many strange faces made her tremble. Her breathing came in short gasps. Then her eyes glazed.

Or maybe what made her so anxious was that she caught the same loathsome snippits of hostile drivel he did.

"—just said the name Kara—"

"—boom…Emma faints—"

"He's the reason—"

"—*inseparable*—"

"The priest in the middle of Kara's memorial service—"

"Cop calls, says she's alive."

"Too bad Emma's here, and not Kara."

Emma shuddered deeply and closed her eyes, which made Mike scowl. When Sando came over, Mike was almost glad to see a friendly face—even Sando's.

"Can you believe it?" Sando clapped his hands. "Kara—alive?"

"That's the rumor."

"Her fans are something, aren't they? They've surrounded the ranch and overrun Santa Fe. Your sales are booming—especially since your truck and Emma's car were found, with you guys gone. But when Kara's red sports car turned up behind that hangar at LAX, the gallery went crazy. People are sure Kara will show up here."

"What have I done?" Emma whispered in a low, agonized tone.

"It gets better, pal. There were deep tire marks by Kara's car. Chavez says it looks like another driver left the scene in a hurry. The cops were sure of foul play, till Kara turned up in Rome."

"Rome?"

"In the fucking Colosseum. A fan chased her for blocks before she got away."

"Probably the girl wasn't Kara. She was probably some girl who thought the fan was a mugger."

"And you'll never guess who called."

Mike didn't even try.

"Ray. Mexico City. Saw CNN's coverage about Kara's house. At *F*-ing four o'clock in the morning, he calls. Tells me to tell Mother not to worry. Like she's up worrying at that hour, with her retrospective at the museum. He sounded pretty shook up, till I told him Kara was in Rome. Seems she jilted him again—just like she did in high school."

"And the bodies in Kara's house?"

"The maid—"

The phone rang. Z answered it and told Mike it was Chavez for him. Mike took the black cordless.

"Greywolf."

"'Bout time you turned up," Chavez said.

Mike waited.

"I got an ID on your charred corpses. Gotta suicide victim in East L.A. Character by the name of Emilio Sanchez. He left a note. Says he tossed the bomb into the upstairs window. Described the device to a tee. Seems he was the maid's ex. He's been stalking her for a year, ever since she took a lover. So Kara's maid and lover-boy are in the morgue—not your twin. Crazy son of a bitch came by the morgue, the day before he did himself, and tried to cut out her tongue. Bottom line, you're off the hook. Sorry about the chairs. I put in a complaint."

"You gave me a hard time, Chavez."

Chavez let that go. "Say, Gentry tell you the Albuquerque police picked up another guy after Kara by the name of Rolando Smith at the airport? Had a damn arsenal in his pickup. Fax machine, too. Miss Shayne will be real happy to know we got him. Says he's a big fan. Real nutcase—been after her for years. Said he didn't want to hurt her, just wanted to get close. The last lady he got hot for doesn't *have* a face."

Camera held high, Sara sashayed her way through the crowd toward Mike and Sando.

"Glad to hear you hooked up with...your favorite twin," Chavez said.

Mike hung up before he said something he'd regret.

Ignoring Sando, Sara tugged at Mike's sleeve. "Hey, you haven't answered my questions."

While Mike was distracted, Stuart wedged himself between Mike and Emma. "Little sister, glad you're safe."

"Oh, Stuart. Get me out of here."

"You got it."

Avoiding Mike and Sara, Emma smiled gratefully at her protective big brother.

"Just one question, before you go," Sara blurted. "Did you kill your twin—"

"Leave her alone or I'll have you thrown out," snapped Stuart.

Sara looked mad enough to spit nails. "Nobody talks to me—"

"Sando," Mike whispered, desperate. "Distract her—fast."

Sando grabbed Sara. "Hey, baby—" When she tried to push him away, he threw his arms around her and kissed her hard. They fell clumsily onto the sofa. Only when she quieted did he draw back, studying her flushed face for a sign as to how his burst of affection had affected her.

Her face was mottled, her frizzy head a bigger mess than usual.

"Sando!"

Before she could attack, he said, "Marry me!"

"Are you crazy?"

"I bought you a great big ring. Wanna see?"

She shook her head, but her eyes popped with real interest when he pulled out a small velvet box.

"You picked it out without me there—"

"Right after we did our...weekend. You swept me off my feet."

She opened the box and gasped at the huge diamond sparkling on black velvet. "Sando," she purred, and let him slip it on. "Mother is going to love this ring."

"I love you," he said.

When he threw his arms around her, she dropped her camera on the couch.

Love was strange. Mike, watching from a distance, couldn't believe it when they walked out, arm in arm, to enjoy a private moment under the stars.

No sooner were they gone than Mike wished them back. The crowd's hostile stares kept relentless tabs on him. He wanted to run. But he would endure anything—for Emma.

When the unpopular Galbraith joined him, the crowd got gloomier. Galbraith had the flu, so his hoarse, nasal voice was so soft Mike could barely hear him. He asked some question about excavating a high pool on the mesa. Said he had a permit.

"Sure," Mike agreed, not wanting to deal with this man or his ghoulish work of digging around in the towns of the dead. As quickly as he could get away, Mike headed toward the kitchen to find Lilly.

At first he couldn't see anything in the dark room. Then he made out a boy and a girl, their bodies glued together.

Lilly and a pink-haired punk. He was a chinless wimp

with a shaggy mohawk. Silver rings sprouted out of his face like a crop of pimples—above his eyebrows, three in his nose. And he had more of the damn things in his ears than Lilly did.

"Lilly!"

"Daddy." She wriggled loose. "I'm helping Leo."

Mike fixed Leo with a lethal stare. "Helping him to what?"

"Not helping him to—*helping,* you big silly. I'm sorry I acted like I thought…well, that you killed Kara. I'm so…so glad you're home."

"This is a funny way to show it."

She laughed.

Leo scowled. "You didn't tell me your father was a damn Indian. I don't dig Indians."

A thick wad of spit hit the floor near Mike's feet.

Mike sprang at the skinny creep, but the kid was out the door like a greased cat, the kitchen door slamming in Mike's face.

Footsteps running, pounding across the dark courtyard, the pink, half-peeled head vanished in the shadows.

Leo, the wimp, had bolted.

"Welcome home," Lilly said.

The pink bedroom was still a little girl's room. And yet, as always, it was their mother's room. Frances had chosen its contents and had insisted that they be arranged according to her desire. After all, she had a collector's eye.

Emma felt a shock of nostalgia when she stepped inside and saw their monogrammed silver brushes with their slanting *K*s and *E*s polished and set out, saw all her mother's exquisite dolls still lined up in their locked glass cases, saw the same silk bedspreads upon which they'd never been allowed to sit. Fresh lilacs and roses bloomed from several vases.

How she and Kara had detested the formality of this room, the oil paintings, the dolls.

She remembered her mother ripping off the posters of teenage rock stars they'd tacked to the walls—instructing them that they were Shaynes and should have better taste, since she'd taught them the value of beautiful things.

Untouchable things. The musty room even smelled dead.

Emma went over to the glass case. She'd been like one of her mother's dolls—locked up, protected...till Mike.

When she fiddled with the door to the case, it opened, and a blushing, blond shepherdess in pink satin fell out. When Emma knelt, she heard a quick footfall behind her.

"Emma," said her mother.

Emma tried to jam the doll back inside before her mother saw. But it was as if she were a nervous little girl again with clumsy fingers. When she dropped the little shepherdess, her mother rushed to take charge, kneeling quickly, her nimble hands deftly spreading the pink petticoats and setting the little creature in the precise spot where she looked best. Frances snapped and locked the case.

"It's best not to touch them, dear."

"I know—Mother." Her little girl's voice.

"It's good you're back. I will always be grateful to Kara—excuse me, dear, for mentioning her—for this little publicity stunt of hers."

"Two people died in that house—"

"A maid. Her lover," she said in that tone that meant they weren't important.

Emma paled. "Her name was Marta."

"And Kara, in her inimitable way, made the most of it."

"Mother—" A vision of Marta, poor dear sweet Marta, upstairs in that inferno, made Emma's throat constrict. Dear Marta, who'd been fighting to get away from her abusive husband. She'd almost made it. Almost. "Mother, please…"

"All right. I don't know why you brought them up." She took Emma's hand. "All that matters is that you're home. Home. Here with me." She patted Emma's hand. "I can't tell you how wonderful—"

"It wasn't a publicity stunt!" Emma persisted, a little surprised that she was standing up to her mother.

"Trust me. I know Kara better than you do. *You and she are estranged.* Don't defend her at this late date—"

"You always disliked her."

"Whatever do you mean?" Frances let Emma go. "She was my daughter. It's not my fault if she wanted to go to Hollywood or Rome and pay absolutely no attention to me."

"That's not why," Emma began weakly.

"How would you know?"

There was a long silence, during which Emma searched her own heart and decided what she had to do. "Mother, Kara's not in Rome."

"And how would you be knowing where your *estranged* sister is?"

"Sit down. What I'm about to say is…complicated— and…well, pretty incredible."

Her mother went still.

After a hesitant pause, Emma began. "I lied to you, Mother. To everybody. When Kara disappeared seven years ago, and I ran away, you accused Mike of murdering us."

Frances stiffened. "Under the circumstances, that was the natural conclusion."

A shudder passed through Emma. Then she sank to her knees, took her mother's hand, and told her everything about Lilly being hers, about Kara's disappearance, about coming back and taking Kara's place to save Mike. She left nothing out. But when she was done, it was her mother who stunned her.

Frances's thin face was very white. But she smiled gently. "I knew. All these years, I've known. And I've waited—all these years fearing the worst—I've waited for you to come home and tell me the truth."

"I—I thought maybe if I took her place, she'd return. But when she didn't, I began to fear the worst. Every year was more awful than the year before. Oh, Mother, I'll never forgive myself if I killed her."

"You didn't. You're not capable of murder."

"But I was so angry. I've never been so angry."

"Oh, Emma— Your sister...she wasn't quite right." Tears put a strange thickness in Frances's voice. "She took after Court...your father. But that's too long a tale for now."

Suddenly Emma was in her arms. "I'm so sorry, Mother."

"Oh, my dear, darling child."

They stared at one another, knew a moment of perfect clarity that brought forgiveness and a deeper understanding. Frances hugged Emma, petted her. "We mustn't tell another soul this story."

"I already have."

"Not Greywolf?" Frances eyed her with dread. "Oh, God. You're not still so deluded you think you're in love with him."

"I'm going to marry him, Mother." Frances was staring at her in confusion, so she rushed on. "I'll be right next door. At least *that* should make you happy."

Frances's aristocratic features grew colder. "You're protecting him, aren't you? You think he did it, don't you?"

"No." Emma's eyes pleaded. "Don't criticize him, Mother."

Frances looked away.

The old tensions that had driven them apart were back in their relationship, fiercer and more destructive than ever.

"Well, it's what I think. Look at the mess you've made. Don't you think it's time you listened to the voice of reason. I love you, Emma. I know what's best."

"Then why won't you ever talk about Daddy?"

"Oh, Emma...I will if that's what it takes to stop you from marrying this man."

Mike saw Emma come down the steps. So did everybody else. Her delicate features were swollen. She looked as if she'd been crying. Her mother tensed quietly when Emma's gaze settled on her, then swept quickly, almost defiantly, away.

Mike held his breath. Emma seemed to be looking for someone, her big, dark eyes searching every face.

He dared not hope. She seemed restless, anxious, more afraid than ever. Was she afraid of him?

What had her mother told her?

Damn Indian.

A wave of cold dislike washed over Mike. The punk's insult had cut, but it was no worse than what everybody else in this room thought, at least on some level.

Even his own mother.

But was that what *Emma* thought?

Emma.

She was all that mattered. His whole life seemed to hang in the balance while he waited. Then she saw him, and her astonished face lit up like a candle. When she smiled, it was as if all the lights in his universe whooshed on.

She gave a joyous little cry. Then she was rushing toward him, but no swifter than his long strides carried him toward her.

They met at the foot of the stairs a moment later, not speaking, just slowly reaching out for each other, each half expecting the other to disappear, not caring who saw, even her mother.

Her fingertips skimmed his face, his lips.

"Marry me," he said, kissing her hand gently. "Emma, tell them you'll marry me."

"What about Kara? What if I…"

"We'll find out what happened to her…together."

"And if we don't—"

"We'll love each other."

Their lips met. He wrapped her in his arms.

A flash went off. Sara, intuitively knowing something important was taking place, held her camera high and kept snapping.

"Mother. Everybody…" Emma began, when he let her go. She waited a moment till the conversation died. "Mike and I are getting married."

"Not in this house," snapped Frances.

An appalled gasp followed this statement. Then Indiana stepped forward. "Then they can have mine."

Mike's green gaze hardened.

The press went wild. More flashes exploded.

All he saw was his mother in the midst of that fiery dazzle, holding out her hand to him.

He hesitated for a long moment. Then he moved forward and took it, welcoming the love for him that glowed in her passionate green eyes.

"When you were a small boy, I loved the sky, the earth, the moon and your father," Indiana said softly. "And you most of all. You were everything. I used to take you out with me when I walked to the desert. We'd camp out. I'd paint. You would make things for me. Then one day I realized a big part of me belonged to another world."

Mike remembered every single glorious episode he'd shared with her. How she'd reveled in the moment, in his talent. Because of her, he was a sculptor. Every memory they'd shared had been precious. Only later had he taught himself to hate them. To hate her. To hate the weakness in him that had made it impossible to forget all the good times.

"I've always loved you, Mike. It was I who saw to your education. Not Frances. I know you thought she spent the money to get rid of you. I spent it to develop your talent. I've always believed in you."

It was too soon.

Mike made no response.

Kara.

The pain and the joy inside Emma was devouring her.

Emma was afraid as she tiptoed inside the dark adobe church and silently moved toward the glowing gold of the candles at the altar. There, she sank to her knees.

Tomorrow she was to marry Mike. Today, like so many pilgrims before her, she had stolen this precious moment to visit the Santuario de Chimayo. For the Santuario, which some called the Lourdes of the Americas, was believed to contain *tierra bendita,* blessed earth, with miraculous healing powers. In evidence of the church's many cures were row after row of abandoned braces and crutches, as well as photographs and testimonial letters in the adjacent rooms.

As Emma began to pray for forgiveness, she became aware of a figure in black, gliding out of the shadows.

Terrified, she whirled.

"Kara?" she asked in a hollow tone. Whoever or whatever it was made no answer. Then Indiana stepped out of the darkness.

"I often come here," she said.

"Why?"

"I don't know. Who knows the secrets of our hearts, the mysteries of our souls? That's our quest, our journey. This is a holy place. It can help with those questions."

"Then you believe in the power of this place to heal?"

"I believe in inspiration. In miracles. Even when I do not know what they mean. I paint, and often I don't know what I'm painting. I'm just compelled. As you are compelled to marry my son. To make a life. I'm glad, Emma. Make him happy. He's had so little happiness."

A group of tourists threw open the doors, and the little church was flooded with blinding white light. Emma blinked.

When she opened her eyes, Indiana had vanished, and she was alone.

Later, when she stepped out of the church into that brilliant light, she felt at peace for the first time in years. Had she been too quick to judge herself? As her mother was always too quick to judge Mike?

She stared up at the blue sky. She was going to marry Mike. Lilly would, at last, be hers. She didn't need her mother's approval. Or the world's. She had found her own peace deep within herself.

Everything was going to be all right.

29

Emma.

Her radiant beauty was gilded by moonlight.

His. Finally, she was all his.

Mike watched her, paying attention to every nuance, watching especially for those recurring characteristic expressions—that tender little look of fright, that wanton radiant, come-hither look. Her ever-changing smiles.

His studio was two stories high. A pot of water boiled on a wood-burning stove to keep the air moist and provide a place where he could wash his hands. Cutters and calipers hung within easy reach. Clay had been rolled out in soft workable strips, each about the size of a loaf of bread.

She stood on a model stand before the large north-facing window.

"Be still," Mike commanded softly.

Emma shook her head defiantly, her smile flirtatious, as the moonlight glittered in her hair and rippled across her breasts.

"Don't do that," he said, using one of his tools to strike a vertical line. "I can't concentrate."

"I want you," she purred.

There. That was the expression.

"Just a few more minutes, Emma."

"But this is our wedding night."

"Yes. And I'm on fire."

But he burned with a passion she couldn't fully understand. How could he explain how sculpting opened him to beauty, to her beauty, and to the deepest emotions of his heart—more than poetry or music? It had been so long since he'd really wanted to work. And now she was his glorious inspiration.

The passion had seized him when they'd said their vows. He rushed her through the reception; he hadn't been able to wait to begin this piece.

She stood above him, on that high pedestal, her body aglow, decorating the night, his studio, filling his soul with her sweet essence.

There it was again. He had to catch *that*.

Over her right shoulder, he'd draped Mabel's prophecy tapestry, the old woman's wedding gift that she'd hurried to finish before she and her weavers had caught a bus back to the rez to follow another of Mabel's visions. The blanket's stiff folds were simple and gorgeous, swirling around Emma's curves.

Only partially covered by the blanket, looking like a half-naked Navajo maiden, she both inspired him to sculpt her and roused him to lust. Combined, these twin desires spiraled into the most dazzlingly intense sexual, artistic experience of his life.

He worked in a frenzy. With aching fingers he dug into the wet clay, shaping it, furious in his hurry to capture his vision of her.

For a long moment he stared at Emma's nipples, which were large and dark. He went over to her, let his hands skim the surface of her stomach. With his thumbs he caressed the undersides of her breasts.

"Wh-what are you doing?"

His finger dipped into the delicate cup of her navel, and she gasped.

"Working," he replied with a smile.

The perfect female. His woman. His sexual goddess. *Emma.*

He cupped her buttocks and buried his lips in that swelling, triangular mound of satiny curls.

She gasped. Then her hands moved through his black hair.

With his lips, he tasted her. Then, panting hard, he broke free, rushed back to the armature and began sculpting without inhibition.

It had been so long since he'd found joy in his work. Tonight the glory of creating mingled with his love for her. He poured his entire spirit into this creation of her.

He went back to the woman and ran his wet hands all over her, again tantalized by that sweet, soft nest of red hair.

His pulse raced. He went back to the armature. He saw her watching, becoming as absorbed as he was in the miracle taking form. Lost in his creation, they were both stunned an hour later when Mike came out of his trance and quit.

Although unfinished, the statue promised to be magnificent, for it contained a part of his heart and soul. She had written of her love for him in her journal. He'd expressed what he felt without words, with his hands. He stood back, offering it to her.

"It's beautiful," she whispered.

"Not half as beautiful as you."

"You love me."

"I adore you, worship you—"

"So I see." She was walking around and around the

statue, the blanket trailing her. "If only Lilly loved me, too."

"Yes. Lilly," he growled. "All teenager and pure brat."

To their wedding, Lilly had worn black lipstick and black nail polish, and a floor-length black crepe costume set off by large combat boots.

"Give her time," he said wearily.

"She wants the movie star."

"Someday she'll realize how lucky she is."

He didn't bother to wash his hands, which were wet with mud. Instead he leaned into Emma and began rubbing them over the contours of her body, painting her with it, following the translucent whiteness of her skin the way he'd shaped the clay on the armature.

Wet clay.

Warm soft skin.

He had to taste her.

He ran a light fingertip down her belly. Then his big rough hands were all over her.

It was as if she were his statue come to life.

She tore open his pants and took his breath away with her mouth. Slowly, slowly, they sank down together onto the blanket. Then he was inside her, his body melting into hers as they flowed into one. His breathing roughened. He clasped her closer, closer, shuddering his release at the exact shattering moment he felt her answering spasms of delight.

Afterward, they lay in the dark for hours and stared up at the stars.

Married.

They were married. The dangers that had threatened them so long were over.

Not that their wedding, for all its sweet moments,

hadn't been tense. Benedek was fighting Stuart's takeover. Stuart's face was plastered all over the front pages, and the coverage wasn't flattering. His company's sales were down. Stuart's back was to the wall. At least, that was the reason he gave for being late and looking so sour.

Frances had been even tardier and grimmer, arriving well after the ceremony was over. Worst of all, Raymond had shown up and had stalked Emma with seething, gloom-ridden stares. Like everybody else, Raymond was obsessed with Kara's absence. He wanted to know where she was. Why she hadn't come. He'd scared Emma by asking her several times.

Only Indiana had been wonderful. She'd filled her house with a thousand white roses, all streaming with ivory ribbons. Mike had felt a reverence for the special occasion the minute she'd opened the door and welcomed him inside. He was glad she was a big part of his wedding day.

For a wedding present, she gave him a painting she'd done of him and her together on the desert when he'd been a small boy. But his mother's love had been her greatest gift. That, and the fact that she shared his joy in Emma.

As long as he lived, he'd never forget Emma's shining eyes when she'd said her vows, and he'd slipped her wedding ring onto her finger. That expression had transformed him, made him know that he was no longer alone.

But there was still Kara. Her shadow lay between them. Maybe it always would. Her supposed disappearance and failure to return were the reasons they weren't going on a honeymoon.

Maybe they would never know what had happened to her. But as long as they had each other, she would never come between them again. He and Emma would be together.

Lilly would come around.

They would be a family.

No force on earth could change that.

Then why did he feel so uneasy?

Emma. Kara.

Emma—married to that Navajo.

The watcher's heart twisted with rage as he stared through the tall north window of Greywolf's studio. Not that he could see much.

It was past midnight. Were they never going into the house? Finally, they got up and left, and he let himself in the back entrance of the studio.

The sweet beauty of Emma's wedding still revolted him. He kept seeing Emma on Mike's arm. That black-faced, filthy Navajo. Emma radiant and so in love.

She had pretended to love him, too. She still did.

But he knew what she was.

He couldn't bear it.

She didn't deserve a moment's happiness after what she'd done. But that wasn't why he had to do something about her.

The watcher had proof that her blackouts were fake. It was only a matter of time before she told what she knew. Every day since she'd come home, he'd felt the tension inside him building, building. Till he could stand it no longer.

One wall of the high-ceilinged studio was silver with moonlight. Against this wall loomed two eerie female torsos—one of bronze, one of marble. There was a male torso of Belgian black marble.

The opposite wall was black.

But what seized the sculptor's frenzied imagination was the way a single beam of moonlight lit the covered figure that stood on a pedestal in the center of the great room.

He ripped the cover off and gasped.

Anyone else might have worshipped the travesty as a thing of great beauty. Maybe once he would have, too.

It was stunning.

As the woman was.

Emma.

No one was more beautiful.

Nor more innocent.

Emma, the beloved.

The adored bride.

Her sweet beauty infuriated him. Pain burned in his broken heart, tearing soft tissue as if a chisel had ripped the organ in two. With difficulty, he stifled the silent soul-deep scream of agony that burst inside him.

No one was more treacherous than sweet Emma.

Not even that bitch Kara.

Emma deserved to die. He had warned her not to come back. Sooner or later she'd tell Greywolf. That was a risk the watcher couldn't take.

He stared at the statue with murderous intent. Inspired, the watcher's huge, powerful hands plunged into the clay and gouged out the slanting eyes. Again and again the watcher ripped at the figure, until its beauty was obscenely mangled.

Emma.

She was next.

Emma was afraid.

Mike was wrong. Nothing was right. Inexplicably, since their marriage, Kara had become Emma's constant imaginary companion. Maybe it was being home or finding happiness with Mike, but no matter what Emma did, Kara stalked her.

Once again the twins were inseparable. And as always, Mike, her husband now, was left out. Maybe, because of the distance between them, he put off completing the statue he'd started of her.

Even today, driving home from Santa Fe with Mike and Lilly on this dazzling afternoon when sunshine turned the desert into a stark fairyland, was no exception.

Mike's left hand was hooked around the steering wheel, his right possessively wrapped hers and pressed it against his warm denim thigh. But Emma barely knew he was there. She was somewhere else—with Kara.

Unseeing, she watched the dry red hills flying by. For once, Lilly's sour mood barely penetrated Emma's consciousness. What gripped her, what terrified her, was Kara's face swimming beneath a black pool, bubbles exploding from her fish-white lips.

Her twin seemed to be drowning, calling out to her one last telepathic message.

Emma gripped Mike's hand more tightly. Kara in a black pool? Why did that vision feel so real? And yet a warning, too? Feeling some unseen danger, Emma's dark eyes latched on to Mike's solid profile.

She'd had a similar scare yesterday, when she'd unpacked some old paintings and chanced across sketches he'd made of Kara and her. Plain as day, Kara popped into her imagination—Kara lifting the lid of the cedar box, scooping mothballs out, and laughingly beckoning Emma to climb inside. Trapped in that foul, suffocating dark, terrified out of her mind, Emma had heard Kara laugh. Emma had pounded at the lid for what seemed like hours.

No. Kara had sworn it was Emma's idea to crawl into the cedar chest.

Sensing Emma was troubled as she stared at the desert, Mike pulled her closer. "What's the matter?"

Emma felt a rising panic that he read her so easily. Kara was *her* problem, not his. "I'm fine," she said.

"Right," he growled, and let her go.

In the back seat, Lilly was a sullen figure in black crepe. She'd ignored them all day, as dramatically and rudely as possible. Every time Mike tried to talk to her, she mashed her headphones against her ears.

"This is a dumb trip," Lilly had said when Mike had driven by the plaza hoping to cheer Emma by showing her the spot where she'd first seen Lilly with Mike and dreamed they might all be together someday.

"Seen any more cute dresses?" he'd teased Lilly.

"I'm not in the mood to shop. I told you to let me stay home. It's boring to go places with you two."

"How would you know, the way you've been blasting your eardrums all afternoon?"

"Talk to your bride."

"That's not so easy, either," he'd said disconsolately, and Emma felt his worried stare.

Mike had forced Lilly to come with them because Leo kept calling, and Mike didn't trust her alone. Thus, Lilly had spent her day trying to make all of them as miserable as possible.

Behind them, her Walkman was louder than ever.

"Lilly!" Mike yelled over his shoulder. "Turn that off. Talk to us for a change."

"Okay! When's my real mother coming home?"

Will my daughter ever love me? Emma thought wearily, forgetting Kara for a moment.

"She's already home," Mike snapped, ripping the wheel hard to the right, swerving the sedan onto the shoulder.

Everybody in the car was stunned.

Then Lilly punched the back of his seat with her fist. "That's not true!"

"You asked. I answered."

Lilly turned on Emma. "I hate you!"

"Don't say things you'll be sorry for, young lady," Mike warned.

Lilly put on her headphones, hunched over and let the music blast her.

Emma swallowed. "Oh, Mike, why did you have to tell her this way?"

"Sorry. But I don't really see what difference it makes how she's told." He hesitated. "Emma, what's the matter? Dealing with you is almost as frustrating as dealing with Lilly."

"Sorry," was all she said.

Nobody spoke again till they drove through the ranch gates and saw Nigel Galbraith, Will Gentry, several deputies, an ambulance and a gathering crowd of press and family.

Laid out on a slab of marble in the amphitheater with the pink columns soaring to the sky was a human skull and a pitiful assortment of human bones. Half a dozen broad-shouldered, big-bellied uniforms were ringed around the debris.

For no reason at all, Emma saw that white face with the swirling strands of red hair, sinking deeper.

Nigel. He'd been excavating some pool.

Clear as day, Emma saw Kara, her eyes wide with fear, fall backward into...into...

Follow the bubbles.

Mike opened the car door for her. In the grip of her vision, she was filled with a deep lassitude and sense of impending doom as she got out and walked toward the little group of men, and the bones. Vaguely she was aware of Stuart and Raymond, her mother, all standing there, silent, like ghosts.

When she got closer, she saw the swatches of blue silk by the bones. The black crescent moons on blue silk were all too familiar.

Oh, my God.

Her dress. Kara had been wearing her dress.

Emma felt wetness on her cheeks. She looked up and wondered when it had begun to rain.

Kara.

She was back.

A week later, Will told Z about the coroner's report. The bones were no more than seven or eight years old. They belonged to a young woman about Emma's size. Her teeth were perfect, so there wouldn't be dental records. He added that bodies were found in the desert all the time. Almost never were they identified.

Mike was afraid. Gradually, hour by hour, day by day, he was losing Emma, and with her all his dreams of happiness.

To Kara.

Like before.

Only this was worse. Emma couldn't let go of Kara. While she cleaned house or unpacked boxes, she silently tormented herself with questions. Had she pushed her twin?

"We don't even know the bones are hers!" Mike had yelled.

"I remember her stumbling down that cliff, falling, and those bubbles...all those bubbles."

"Don't."

"I was wet so I must have jumped in. Maybe I waited too long. The water was so black, so much colder and scarier than that airless cedar chest. I couldn't breathe. I tried to dive, but the pool was so deep. And I got tired so fast."

"You don't even know for sure any of this happened."

"Am I going crazy, then? Or did I kill her, Mike?"

"Damn," he muttered in a clipped, low tone. "As if those are the only two possibilities."

"I can't bear to think that I—"

"Then, damn it, don't—"

"If you ask me, if it did happen—if you did it, I mean, accidentally—she got what she deserved," he said another time.

After that she stopped talking to him.

He was losing her. She couldn't let it go. She couldn't love herself, so she couldn't let him love her. Once again her heart became a guarded, secretive place, all its doors sealed tightly against him. Against Lilly, too. Every day, their marriage got darker.

Sometimes he walked out into the desert and let the emptiness remind him of the bleakness his life would hold without her. He had to find a way to help her.

But she grew thinner, paler and more withdrawn. In the evenings when they sat together or did anything together, she never spoke to him unless he forced her. When they made love, she wasn't really there.

They went through the motions of being married. Her things were shipped from Mexico. All her Greywolfs were set up in the amphitheater. He turned a spare bedroom into an office where she could write. But little by little, they drifted further apart, her grief and guilt devouring her, devouring their love, too.

Kara.

Her ghost lay between them.

He cursed this invisible witch who sucked Emma's life-blood and tore out his heart.

Emma began to climb the cliffs up to the mesa, as Kara had once done. He hated knowing that she stared broodingly into that black pool and willed it to reveal its dark truths.

Superstitious about death and all places related to death, he did not follow her there. But he railed against her morbid excursions every chance he got. His anger just drove her further away—she'd sneak up to the pool without telling him. So he quit yelling, but burned inside with anger and frustration when he knew she'd gone.

It was a long, lonely climb, and a dangerous one. He wished she'd take a dog or a companion, but she violently opposed him on that, too.

And always she returned sadder and paler.

Once, their love had seemed to hold such infinite possibilities of joy. Now it held only morbid quiet and grief. There was no place in her heart for him or Lilly.

That made him angry, and he had a harder and harder time keeping a tight rein on his temper. They fought. She retreated. Nothing he tried worked.

Kara. Like an invisible witch, she cast a dark spell, possessing Emma far more powerfully in death than she ever had in life.

His marriage was doomed.

Confess.
Tell Will you were there. That you killed her.

When Emma thought such thoughts, she would look at the bronzed, handsome man she'd married or the redheaded teenager with earrings and headphones, and know she couldn't.

Not yet.

She'd spent too many lost years without them. She was making Mike miserable, but she wasn't ready to let him go.

One afternoon, when Lilly was at school and Emma was putting clean clothes away in Lilly's drawers, the telephone began to ring. Emma picked up without thinking.

"Why did you kill me?" slurred a dark voice that reminded her of Kara.

"Who is this?"

"You won't get away with it! You shouldn't have married Mike."

"Who—?"

Laughter.

"You know who. We used to be inseparable. Till you murdered me."

Kara's laughter.

Then the phone went dead.

Emma stood as still as stone for a breathless eternity. Then, shaking, she flew out of the house. She had to find Mike.

He was in his largest studio, working on a big piece of marble that was going to be a waterfall made of four wild horses. It was a big commission. Too important to interrupt. Especially since he'd been blocked till their marriage.

Stripped to the waist, his raven black hair tumbling over his brow, he was cutting raw granite with a pneumatic hammer. Rivulets of sweat poured off his muscular chest. He was handsome, his lean, hard body so gorgeous that it stopped her breath. He stayed out here long hours—to avoid her. To avoid her grief. To avoid more quarrels.

She was driving him away with her guilt and sorrow. Life was so unfair. She'd found him after all these years.

They could've been so happy...

Except for Kara.

She shut the door and didn't bother him.

30

The sun was sinking fast, splashing bloodred color on the tall rock faces, but all Emma saw was the stark white face shivering on the ripples of the black pool, its opaque, empty eyes staring up at her.

"Kara, what happened to you?" Emma whispered.

A chill wind moaned.

Then a stone dropped into the pool and the face dematerialized. Why did Emma hear rattling sounds, the beating of drums, the clacking of turtle shells? Was it the music of the ancient ones? Was Mike right to be afraid of this place of the dead? "Too many dead spirits up there," he always said.

Murderer, rang an unearthly voice.

Emma felt a rush of air, a coldness behind her. Her breath stilled. Her heart accelerated.

A footstep crunched gravel behind her. Little rocks rolled under a man's black boot heel, cascading down the talus slope in a miniature avalanche, a reminder to Emma of her tenuous position on the steep cliff.

The pond became a wobbly sheet of black glass. When she looked again, a second face gleamed beside hers from the pool.

"Spooky as hell up here," he said.

She gasped in horror. The countenance rippling on that black surface revived a bewildering memory. Again, she was trapped in her rental car in that rushing creek, her hand pushing against the window as the icy water rose above her breasts. He'd stood on the bank, his face swimming in the black rain that dripped down the glass.

Only she'd forgotten till now that he'd been there.

"Mike!" She began to back away from him, but she stopped when her foot hit the edge. "Mike—"

A bitter memory assaulted her.

This man had been at the pool when Kara died.

He was going to kill her.

"Mike!" she screamed, but they were too high on the mesa for anybody to hear her.

And then she heard the rattles and jingles of dancers. Shadows swept the crumbling stone walls. The music and shapes seemed to be coming from the kiva where she and Mike had first found each other.

Spirits. Did she hear the ancient ones because death was near?

"Damn."

Unsure, Mike strode around and around the huge piece of pink granite. Then suddenly, inspiration struck. He strode to a table and looked at his bridge saw.

The blades were dull. He'd have to change them before he could do anything. But when he rustled in the cardboard boxes where they usually were, he couldn't find any new blades.

Then he remembered putting them in his smaller studio next door, the one where he'd made love to Emma on their wedding night.

He'd almost forgotten how happy they'd been together that one night. He hadn't been back in the room since.

Emma.

He wanted her. The more he feared losing her, the more he loved her. That's why he'd avoided the other studio where they'd spent their wedding night. That's why he worked nearly all the time. Work kept him occupied, kept him from going mad with worry.

His smaller studio was dark and silent. When Mike stepped farther inside, he stumbled over two decapitated statues that lay sprawled on the floor. He picked himself up. For an instant he was back in the hogan, seeing bodies.

"Christ!" Rage filled him. Everything in his studio had been destroyed. His charcoal life sketches that were usually tacked to the walls were confetti on the concrete floor. Some maniac had overturned all the pots of water and smashed all his plaster casts. His electric tools had been dumped in a sink full of water.

The armature that had held the figure he'd sculpted of Emma lay broken in four pieces. But her sculpture had suffered the worst damage.

Emma's eyes had been gouged out, her breasts amputated.

He heard a low-throated growl of fury, and was stunned when he realized he'd made that savage sound.

Who? Who could have done this?

Hurt and vengeful thoughts raced chaotically. He picked up part of the nose and caressed it. He heard the wind outside.

Follow the screams.

He had to forget his pain and grief over the statue. Forget his fear for Emma.

Think. Concentrate.

He remembered her coming into the studio a while ago.

She'd looked so sad and frightened. He hadn't wanted to get in a fight. So he hadn't looked up or even smiled.

Why the hell hadn't he stopped working?

He picked up the rest of her statue's broken head. Who had done this?

Where was Emma?

He threw the broken head down, smashing it into more bits. He felt cold with fear as he tore out of the studio at a dead run.

Follow the screams.

His big feet thundering across red-packed dirt, stomping into the house. He banged the screen, opening and slamming more doors, repeatedly screaming her name.

"*Emma!*"

But she didn't answer.

The windows in their bedroom were open. Peaceful sounds from the outside floated in. Cicadas thrummed in the cottonwoods. Birds sang.

He stared out the windows up at the mesa.

Follow the screams.

Suddenly he saw a vision of her stricken face glimmering in a dark pool.

Grabbing his rifle, stuffing bullets into the pockets of his jeans, he tore out of the house and ran all the way to Frances's barn.

Bart snorted when Mike threw on the bridle. Without bothering to saddle the temperamental stallion, he leaped onto the broad black back. Bart reared wildly.

Then Mike whispered in Navajo into his big black ear.

Bart shot out of the barn. Mike hunkered low, his legs wrapped around the flying horse, hands gripping mane and reins.

Horse and man galloped away like the wind.

Follow the screams.

* * *

Lilly was in a state of shock when she saw Emma running toward the mesa.

"Emma! Mother! I made you a present!"

Emma kept running.

Clutching the present, Lilly took off after her.

She'd carved a little cat out of wood in her art class, a cub to go with the Howling Lioness her father had given her.

Guilt-stricken, Lilly kept running.

She hadn't liked being deliberately cold to Emma. It was just that she'd been overwhelmed by Kara's murder, by Emma's return, by Kara running off to Europe and not once calling home.

She'd bragged so often to the kids at school about Kara being her mother. So, when her dad married Emma instead and the kids had teased her, she'd lashed out at Emma. She'd wanted to make her as unhappy as she was.

Emma had been so nice to her at first. And what had Lilly done? She'd been mean and hateful.

It was all her fault that Emma was so unhappy and that her father stayed in his studio nearly all day and night. All her fault that Emma had quit coming into her room to try to talk.

Sara had gotten quiet and sad like that, too—before the divorce.

Lilly didn't want Emma to go!

She wanted Emma to smile that smile that lit up her whole face, the way she had when Daddy carried her into Grandmother's house. That day Lilly had pretended not to see.

Mother. Emma was her mother. She knew that now.

Lilly was through the juniper now and panting hard. She didn't want to climb so high on the mesa, but she

had to find Emma. No! She had to find Mother. She had
to tell her how sorry she was.

Then Emma's cry rent the stillness.

Lilly stopped, paralyzed, unable to move, as her mother
screamed. Over and over again.

New terrors instead of old shuddered through Emma.
The rattles and jingles from the nearby kiva had stopped.
"Stuart," she whispered, backing away from him in
heart-numbing panic. "You were here, too, with Kara that
night."

"I knew you remembered."

"But I didn't—"

He pulled a square, black automatic out of his waistband. "No more games, sweet Emma."

"Stuart! You're my brother—"

"Too bad, sweet Emma."

"Did you kill Kara?"

"No— Her death was a mistake. But that doesn't matter. If you tell the truth, I'm ruined."

"I'm sure we can talk this out."

"Talk? We already have."

"When?"

"You called me a while ago, pretending you were her.
You've been blackmailing me for seven damn years!"

"No!"

"Just like she blackmailed me before!"

"Why would she?"

"Like you don't know. Because I was in the barn when
you climbed down those stairs that night. She was always
watching me, tattling on me. Ever since we were kids.
Only *that* night, I thought you were her. I knocked you
down, nearly killed you. She saw."

"But why?" Emma asked.

"I was furious because she'd stolen and cashed a huge check Mother had given me to start my first business. She wanted to go to Hollywood. I found out and followed her to the barn. When I saw her slink into Greywolf's bedroom, I got crazier. By the time you came down, I was seething. When I heard you on the stairs, I opened Rio's stall door, hit him. I let out the others, too. But it was you—*you* not her. I slammed Rio's door into your head, not hers."

"You tried to kill her."

"No. I just wanted my money and to scare her. But Mother was wild when you were so hurt. Every time I asked Kara for the money back, she threatened to tell Mother I'd hurt you. I knew if she did, Mother wouldn't ever help me again. But that wasn't the end of it. When Kara went to Hollywood she acquired expensive habits. She wanted more, always more."

"And you paid."

"My business took off so fast. I had a name to protect. But when she came back for the premiere, I decided to put a stop to her game, once and for all. She was a movie star. She could pay her own way. She told me to meet her here, that all she wanted was one final payment." He paused. "You know how she loved it up here. Thought she was queen of the universe. That night she bragged that she was a movie star, and I was still a computer nerd. She got me madder than ever."

"So, you killed her?"

"That's the irony. I got angry. I sprang at her. She fell sideways and slipped. She must've hit her head on a rock beside the pool. I froze and sort of stood there, watching her sink, watching her bubbles. Then you came and dove into that icy pool again and again, till you were shivering and exhausted and hysterical. You begged me to try when you were too tired to move. But I knew she had to ·be dead. So I left you and walked down the mesa.''

''Oh, Stuart.''

''When they found you the next day with that bullshit story about another blackout, I fell for it.''

He went on. ''Then you ran away—and came back as both twins. You shouldn't have started blackmailing me, Emma.''

''I didn't—''

''You shouldn't have called and pretended to be her, either.''

''Stuart, I didn't do any of those things.''

''The voice on the phone was the same. I'm through talking. No way am I paying you five million bucks.''

''But I—''

''It's your turn to die.''

He aimed straight at her heart.

''I didn't blackmail you, I swear. Somebody's blackmailing me. Somebody called me, too. She said she was Kara. Said I'd pay for killing her—''

''You're good. Too damn good!'' Tears were running down his handsome face. His gun hand wobbled. ''Shut your eyes,'' he whispered.

''No!''

''Now jump like she did. If you don't jump, I swear I'll push you off that cliff.''

When he moved menacingly toward her, he set off another miniature avalanche. Off balance, waving his outstretched arms, he slid toward her.

Emma screamed.

Follow the screams.

Mike was squatting on his haunches, his rifle propped on a boulder to steady it. Squinting, he pressed an eye to his scope. Framed in that circular glare, split by cross-hairs, Mike captured two figures high on the mesa. When the man lunged, Emma screamed, and the echoes re-sounded in the dark canyon, resounded in Mike's own dark heart.

He scanned the sheer face of the cliff. Even on Bart, he'd never get up there in time. He was afraid to shoot. Afraid he'd hit Emma. Again he experienced the wild panic he'd felt in that other long-ago canyon when he'd heard the screams, when he'd stumbled blindly down.

There was no way he could save her.

Suddenly he felt a chill; his body began to tingle. He was Navajo, and the ancient beliefs and wisdom of his people possessed him. He flung himself to the earth and piled rocks like a child. And all the time he did this, he was imagining his life without her, the long empty years ahead, worse than the empty ones before. He sank to his knees, and as dirt sifted through his brown fingers he sang a prayer in Navajo to Mother Earth. And whispered an-other in English to her God.

Then he screamed for his mighty grandfather's spirit.

Every prayer, whatever the language or religion, was the same.

"Save her."

"One more tiny step backward, Emma," Stuart urged in that soft, maniacal tone. "It won't hurt."

Beneath her heel, loose rocks rolled, more and more of them, skittering down that unstable slope. Soon she would fall, too.

Emma's life flashed before her. She remembered the fierce light in Mike's eyes when she'd stripped out of the blue gown, his softer expression when he'd married her. She remembered the fire, crawling out the front door,

Mike on the ground unconscious as she ran to her garage and drove away. Then Kara was telling her to steal peppermints from the frog cookie jar. Kara was coaxing her to climb up to the mesa so Stuart would follow them.

More rocks were sliding under her feet. She was sure she would fall to her death—

Suddenly a slanting sunbeam lit up a petroglyph on a nearby boulder that she'd never seen before. It was a panther like the panthers in the nearby kiva, like the panther that had slunk out of the juniper. Again she felt the animal's feral power, those glowing, predatory eyes fastened on her face.

Something had protected her that evening, something outside herself. Strangely, she felt that same force again, rising from deep inside herself. The petroglyph put there by some ancient hand was her salvation. Or was it her love for Mike protecting her. Or Kara's spirit? Or her own fierce will to live and love? Or was it all those things that emboldened her and made her wise and courageous? Or was it really something mythical and more powerful than she could possibly imagine? She heard the faint rattling sound from the kiva.

Suddenly she was fearless.

"Stuart, for God's sake," she whispered calmly. "Listen to me. You're my big brother. I love you—no matter what you've done or why... Whoever's blackmailing you is blackmailing me, too."

The sweetness in her voice only made Stuart crazier. He stumbled forward like a blind man on a rampage. "Don't play the saint with me," he sobbed, rocks raining down the cliffs under his feet. "It's your turn to die."

"No, it's yours, you bastard," said Raymond's voice from behind a ruined wall near the kiva.

Stuart whirled, pulled the trigger. There was a sharp

crack, but his hand shook so badly that the bullet hit stone.

A brilliant blue light flamed from the *Sipapu*. At the center of the light was a slim girl with flaming red hair. Ankle bells jingled. Then the light darkened around the girl and a gray shrieking cloud swirled upward out of the *Sipapu*.

"Kara!" Stuart screamed.

"Bats," Emma murmured, unafraid of them.

The bats whirled, darting higher and higher. The rattles and jingles stopped abruptly. Stuart stumbled backwards, taking one fatal step too many to escape this apparent supernatural vision. Then his body was falling and falling and falling.

His feet hit the pool. His head cracked on stone. He was already dead when his body slipped into the water, his clothes ballooning, holding him up for a few seconds till water saturated the cloth. Then he sank. There were bubbles. Then nothing.

Raymond had Lilly by the throat.

"Lilly! Raymond!" Emma whispered in horror.

"Is the damn bastard dead?" Raymond demanded.

"I think so," Emma said, her voice thick. "It was you," she whispered. "All those years…blackmailing me, terrifying me nearly out of my mind, saying you knew I killed her. Blackmailing him, too. You had that woman call me today. Scare me nearly out of my wits."

"Yes."

"But why?"

"I loved Kara—maybe even more than you did. We didn't have the kind of love you know about, but there are all kinds of ways for a man and woman to come together. Our path was violent and dark. Nobody could satisfy in me what she could. She was my one obsession. I wasn't hers. But she'd use me from time to time, like a drug. I was her lover in Hollywood long before you stole her identity. She lured me to Santa Fe for the premiere. I was supposed to meet her out here the night she died. She'd seduced me with some fantasy of making wild, pagan love, the way the ancient ones had. It'd be like doing it in a church, she said. Only she never showed up. When I couldn't find her, I was terrified. I saw you and Stuart come down from the mesa. I knew from the looks on your faces that one or both of you must've killed her, and I vowed revenge. Then you ran away—and came back as her. I had to know what happened. Who killed her. I thought you'd break, but you didn't.''

''So that's why you dated me in L.A.''

''You were so damn tight with your secret.''

''Because I couldn't remember.''

He laughed bitterly. ''Well, it's all over now. You and I are no longer in our self-ordained purgatory. Stuart died, the same way she did. He scared himself to death and fell…just like he scared her to death. I didn't lift a finger. He shot at me. The human mind is the most powerful weapon of all. It's scary as hell. Kara knew that, too.''

He turned to go.

''You can't just leave. You killed Stuart.''

''He shot at me. He killed himself. Who are you to tell me I can't leave? The world's full of places to hide. You and Stuart taught me that. A nose job, a new hair color, a change of identity.'' He began to laugh. ''Maybe I'll even join Kara in Rome.''

''But you can't just—just walk off—''

''Watch me.''

When he turned to go, Emma flung herself at him. ''You've got to tell everybody what happened.''

''You tell them for me.'' He pushed her aside.

Lilly, who'd been quiet up to then, came to life. "You hit my mother," she screamed, and leapt at him like a protective lioness. Caught off balance, Raymond staggered. When she kept coming, he slammed a fist viciously into her jaw, and she slumped in a heap at his feet.

"Lilly!" Emma screamed, throwing herself on top of her daughter to shield her from more blows.

Raymond stepped over them and was gone.

When Lilly came to, she was on the ground beside the boulder with the super-cool petroglyph of a panther. Both her mother and father knelt beside her, relief flooding their overjoyed faces. She opened her mouth, closed it, just to make sure her jaw still worked.

"You still got all your teeth?" Mike asked anxiously.

"Sure, you big silly." She would've smiled, but it hurt too much.

Emma was cupping Lilly's face, her head in her lap, smoothing her hair from her brow.

Mother. She had a mother. At last.

"Mother..." The magical word trailed off, the sound more precious than a jewel. "I—I made this for you," Lilly said shyly. "At school today. I was bringing it to you, only the man...who looked so much like Daddy... Raymond...grabbed me."

"Why, it's beautiful—the most beautiful cat in the whole world," Emma said.

"Careful, I might get jealous," Mike teased softly.

"I made it because I think the cat is your totem," Lilly said to Emma.

"I think you're right," Mike said.

"Where's Uncle Stuart?"

"He fell. He had a bad accident, remember?" Emma said.

"Was he going to shoot you? Your own brother?"

Emma hesitated. "He was all mixed up...about a lot of things."

"But I liked him."

Emma patted her hand. "I'm glad. He liked you, too. Always remember that, no matter what anybody tells you."

"Would you do me a favor?" Lilly asked weakly, for her jaw was beginning to ache.

"Anything, my darling."

"Don't go away. Don't ever go away again."

"I won't, my darling. We're a family. And families are forever."

They held hands as they went back to the house to call the authorities.

The healing would take years, but they were on the right path this time.

The late-afternoon sunshine on the plaza felt magical even from inside the trendy jewelry shop. Mike's stomach rumbled. He was hungry. Lilly was bent over a case of inlaid Navajo bracelets, her gaze glued to the colorful turquoise and coral masterpieces. She had four on each arm. Emma had instantly chosen hers, but she was so patient that she never said a single word to encourage Lilly to hurry.

Mike turned his back on the window and joined them at the counter. "Make up your mind, Lilly," Mike whispered. "I'm starving."

Slowly, Lilly lifted her gaze from the display case.

"Which one do you want?" he asked. To a male, it seemed a simple, logical question.

"All of them."

"Naturally," he said dryly.

"Do I have to choose, Daddy?"

He nodded.

"Then I want one like Mother's. So we can be twins."

Mother and daughter tilted their bright red heads toward him, their smiles identical.

It was twilight and the slanting sunlight blazed down on the emerald grass and the two stone crosses. In the distance a sprinkler was going, diamond drops splashing both trees and grass. Birds were twittering, cicadas humming. Mike could hear the creek in the distance, and somewhere there were wind chimes.

On such a day, with the woman he loved at his side, and his teenage daughter down to two earrings, a man should feel content just to be alive.

The afternoon was way too beautiful for a funeral—two funerals, really. Images of death or horror didn't seem to go with sunshine and birdsong. Yet they did. His Navajo wisdom told him that was so.

Frances, Z, Mike, Emma, Lilly and Indiana had assembled in secret before those two stone crosses that stood side by side for double burials. In one coffin lay the bones Nigel had found on the mesa, and two golden necklaces—one with an *E*, the other with a *K*. In the other, Stuart rested.

Emma knelt and laid pink roses beneath both crosses. When she got up, Mike put his arms around her, while Frances and Lilly watched sadly.

"I've been thinking," Frances said a long while later.

"Oh, no," said Z.

"Sad as this is, we have so much to be thankful for. Emma's home and safe. With her daughter and her husband."

"Her mother, too," said Mike.

Frances's eyes warmed more and more often when they fastened on Mike these days. "I've been wrong…about a lot of things. What happened is my fault."

"You can't blame yourself," said Z.

"I can if I choose to, and I do. I loved, really loved, only one of my children. Kara and Stuart both reminded me of Court, their father. I rejected them because he rejected me. I'm sorry. But I can't undo what I did. I can only try to learn…to open my heart—even when it isn't easy. Just because one husband cheats, doesn't mean they all will." Her kindly, somber gaze continued to study Mike thoughtfully.

Mike didn't smile. The situation was too sad, too permanent for that. But the tension that had always been between them had eased.

A broad green, cottonwood leaf fluttered down to earth, and then a second fell, raining down on the graves like the two tears that glistened on Emma's cheeks.

Carefully, Emma picked up each leaf and placed them with the pink roses. When she looked up, she saw new affection between Mike and her mother, and her eyes shone. She got up slowly, her expression brightening. Mike took her hand.

He squeezed her fingers, caught her close. The desperation with which he held her was all too obvious. It wasn't going to be easy to forget how close he'd come to losing her.

Holding his hand, Emma linked her arm around her mother's waist. As she drew Frances close, Emma began to cry.

Mike captured her face with his fingertips. "No more tears, my love," he whispered.

"I love you," she said.

* * *

The studio was dark, save for the moon. Again Emma stood in its white light on the model stand, a soft contentment wrapping her like the Navajo blanket.

Mike had left the armature. He was walking around and around the model stand in long silent strides, staring up at her, devouring her with his eyes. "I've got to do it again."

"Maybe you can't," she teased, still a little saddened at the destruction of the first statue.

"You don't think so, huh?"

"I think you're good—maybe the finest sculptor that ever lived."

"That's not what I'm talking about it, and you know it."

"What are you talking about, Michael Greywolf?"

"Sex. Wild, unadulterated sex."

"You're supposed to be making a new statue."

"Later." Suddenly he caught her to him. "I love you. I could die, I'm so happy."

"Do you really mean that? Or are you just saying that to have sex?"

"What do you think?"

"Thinking is the last thing on my agenda tonight," she purred. She dropped the blanket to the floor and dazzled him with her beauty.

"Show-off." He gazed up at her breasts. "You're so damn gorgeous."

She jumped down from the model stand and placed her hands on the waistband of his jeans. "If I'm gonna be naked, so are you." She knelt and unzipped him, and with no inhibition, she smothered her face against his groin, her lips and tongue tasting his sex until he couldn't stand it anymore.

He groaned and eased out of his jeans. Dropping to the

blanket, he pulled her down beside him. Her head lay in the crook of his arm, her short curls gleaming against the soft wool. Her smile—that smile that was only for him—held that special radiance that lit a fire deep within him. The urge to sculpt her in that seductive pose rose within him.

Then she touched him, and that other urge was stronger.

When his searching lips trembled teasingly above hers, Emma gasped, her heart thundering, just the way his was.

When she whispered his name, he was already inside her.

"I love you," he said.

"Forever," she murmured.

And that time he finally kept his promise and made it last and last. Afterward, it was an eternity before he let her go.

The studio was dark, but he didn't want light. It was enough to hold her, to be together, to know she'd always be his.

"You know what we need to do," he said finally.

"What?"

"Go on a honeymoon."

"I thought you'd never ask," she said.

"You sound like you have somewhere special in mind."

"Do you like beaches?"

"Oh, yes." He waited.

"There's a little boy in Mexico...Manuel. He has shiny black eyes and ink-black hair, as black as yours. He lives on an island. He told me not to tell him goodbye. To always say, *"Hasta luego."*

"Till we meet again," Mike translated.

"I made him a promise that I was coming back—"

"As you came back to me, my love," Mike said softly. "We must keep your promise."

"There's a beach, too."

"I'd rather stay in the hotel room…and make a baby—when you're not with Manuel."

"Oh, Michael, can we?"

"It's up to you, of course."

"Oh, let's not wait for Mexico. Let's try now."

"The sooner the better, my love." His merry eyes made her feel blissfully happy and completely cherished as he drew her still closer.

"I'm not ever going to let you out of my sight," she whispered.

"If we're not careful, people will start saying we're inseparable."

She laughed. "Aren't we?"

Then he kissed her, and he didn't stop there. They were going to make a baby. Lots of babies.

He had promises to keep.

A disk.
A simple disk
that named names.

JASMINE CRESSWELL

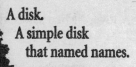

THE INHERITANCE

That was Isabella Joubert's inheritance
from her father—a man she loved but
could not trust. To right his wrongs, she
is determined to turn the incriminating
list over to the authorities.

But danger is stalking her. Someone
wants the disk even more than
Isabella. And she is forced to turn to
Sandro Marchese, the man she'd left
years earlier. But no matter where
the disk lands, Isabella fears
Sandro is doomed. For his name
is on the list.

"Cresswell's women-in-jeopardy
plots are tightly woven with no
loose ends." —*Publishers Weekly*

*Available the first week of January 2000,
wherever paperbacks are sold!*